Book one

Spells and Secrets

That Damned Witch

A Note from the Author

Please note the "That Damned Witch" duet is a modern-day fantasy tale, set in Scotland with dark romance undertones and a splash of horror.

The story includes representations of some of the interrogation methods used within the witch trials. Therefore, please be warned that it touches on some potentially sensitive subjects, including execution, torture and death.

Adult language, including profanity, is frequently used.

Please read responsibly.

For the witches.

PROLOGUE

<u>Hazel</u>

The nightclub is a mass of writhing bodies under the strobing lights and for a moment it feels like I'm trapped in some Hellish dimension of flesh and hedonism. Pain shoots through my abdomen again and I wince against the discomfort. It's usually bad, but tonight? Tonight, it's the worst it's ever been.

"Are you sure you don't want me to come with you?" Esme shouts into my ear, trying to combat against the loud bass of the Uni bar's speakers. It's Fresher's week, and even though it's my second year, we go to every one of the themed nights, and, despite my blistered feet, ruined sleep pattern and the worst period pains ever, the show must go on. My housemates and I have the reputation of being *the* party girls on campus, although tonight it's impossible to get into the spirit. Mother Nature has come to collect, and my PMS is being a B.I.T.C.H.

Esme leans back, her pretty face flush and her dyed pink hair is plastered down her forehead from dancing with Dahlia on the podium. We're not technically supposed to, but Karl, the DJ, has a soft spot for us. He's been making moon eyes at me all night, and whilst ordinarily I'd consider it, tonight all I want is my bed and the tub of triple chocolate ice cream stashed in our freezer.

Esme's glazed eyes clear for a second, and her face twists into sympathy, "Did the spell not help?"

An hour of chanting, shoving herbs under our noses and enough painkillers to take down your average Mundane, and none of it has even scratched the surface. Spells and Paracetamol seem to have done the trick for Ez and Dahls, but that could just be the two for one Sambuca and Tequila shots they've been pounding back. I try to

1

keep up, but after the fourth shot of cheap, sickly-sweet alcohol, the cramps are not dulling. All I want is a duvet, dairy and Disney. All at the same time.

Dahls stops dancing and drapes herself over me. "What's wrong, Haze?"

"Just not feeling it," I give her a pained smile. It's both a blessing and a curse having your roommates syncing up with your cycle. "Have a lemon drop in my honour!"

"No," Dahlia whines, her glossy lips twist into a downward line of disappointment. "You can't leave!"

"Dahls," I wince as another cramp twists in my abdomen. "I need to go home before I collapse on the dancefloor, which I don't think has been cleaned since our Fresher's night! I want to go back to the flat, watch 'Hocus Pocus', eat my weight in chocolate and curl up in a foetal position."

"Hocus Pocus?" She scoffs, "you're such a cliche!"

"And you're such a witch," I say as wink at her playfully, before blowing her a kiss, "bitch!"

"I'm going!" I wrap my arms around both of them, ignoring the pain up my spine and the way my womb feels like I've just been drop-kicked. "Try not to miss me too much!"

"You're not walking, are you?" Esme gives me a look of concern. "It's half an hour to get back to the flat!"

"It's a fifteen-minute walk back to halls, Ez," I correct her before giving her a peck on the cheek. "Besides, you need to look after Finn. The poor guy is going to end up on the floor if he doesn't pace himself!"

Esme looks back at her boyfriend. Finn is handsome, sweet and practically perfect in every single way, apart from being a complete lightweight. Also, his terrible attempt at dancing nearly gives one poor girl whiplash as she ducks just in time to avoid her face meeting one of Finn's very enthusiastic elbows. Correction, that's two things Finn sucks at: dancing and drinking. Thank Goddess he's hot.

Dahlia looks behind us at Finn who's now slow dancing with Ian, one of the guy's in the flat below us. Both of them are completely wasted.

"Seriously, Ez," Dahls manages to look judgemental, even though she's practically falling over six-inch heels. "I hope he fucks better than he dances!"

"Ewwww!" Esme lets out an embarrassed giggle. "Don't be gross!"

"And on that horrifying image, I'm going," I turn on my heel.

2

"Be good!"

"Never!" Dahlia shouts over the music.

"Promise you'll text me when you get back?" Esme calls after me.

"Promise, promise!" I shout back, before my friends are swallowed up by the drunken crowds.

I have to suppress a shudder as sticky flesh grinds and gyrates against me. I regret my choice of the black pleather minidress for the night. I'd naively thought wearing something sexy might improve my mood, but after two hours of faking fun, all it's done is make me want my purple penguin pyjamas all the more. Goddess, being a woman sucks sometimes!

"Hey sexy," a drunken fresher with beer breath and a suspiciously stained rugby shirt grabs possessively at my waist. "Can I buy you a drink?"

"Thanks, but," I peel his sweaty hands from my hips, "no thanks."

"Oh, come on," he demands. "Just one teeny, tiny drink."

"And I already said," I give him a sickly-sweet smile, lacing my tone with venomous warning. "No thank you."

"Come on," he grabs hold of my wrist and starts pulling me towards the bar. "Just one shot."

"Listen pisshead," I snarl at him and wrench my arm out of the creep's grasp. I am really, seriously, not in the fucking mood. Another cramp twists in my stomach. "I'm tired, cranky and currently haemorrhaging out a 'Shining' level amount of blood, so unless you fancy getting your head bitten off or dealing with my period all over your penis, I'd suggest you move the fuck along. Although, I have heard sex is fantastic for menstrual cramps-"

He looks horrified, "don't be disgusting!"

"Aw, now I'm sad," I pout, feigning disappointment. "Don't you want to be my human tampon?"

He flinches and lurches back like I've just struck him. Drunky gives me one more look of revulsion before he staggers off towards the bar and I'm sure I hear him mumble, "Crazy bitch."

Smug at my one small step for feminism, I return on my quest to leave the land of the inebriated and uncoordinated.

Another stab from my uterus and I clutch my bag to my stomach like a poor man's hot water bottle.

"Just let me get home," I whisper to my body, when my vision blurs from another wave of agony. The cramps are definitely getting worse. "Once we're back in the flat, you can be the biggest bitch on

3

the planet."

I push open the heavy club doors with one hand, whilst the other grips my abdomen. Don't throw up, people will think you're drunk, not because you're doing your own one-woman performance of 'Carrie'.

"Hey there, beautiful," Karl is leaning against the club's wall, puffing on an e-cig and looking every bit the hipster bad boy, right down to the kohl rimmed eyes and deliberately distressed leather jacket.

"Hey Karl," I try to keep my tone breezy, despite the very real fear that one good sneeze and my guts will drop out of my ass. "I've gotta head home, but let's catch up soon?"

He kicks off from the wall, swaggering towards me as smoke trails behind him, like every single girl at Uni does. He's the sexiest guy on campus and the bastard knows it. But I can't deny the rush it gives me seeing the way he watches me whenever I walk into a room.

"Listen," he stops in front of me to trace a hand over my bare shoulder and involuntarily I respond to his touch. Sparks shoot up and down my body like I've just been struck by lightning.

"I'm done for the night, so if you want, we could grab a drink back inside?" His thumb traces small circles across my collarbone and everywhere his fingertips linger he leaves behind desire and goosebumps. "Or we could go somewhere else?" His hand moves to my hair, gently weaving his fingertips through my strawberry blonde waves which brush against my neck. His touch is confident, self-assured and every bit that of a guy who knows he can get any woman he wants. His lips curve teasingly on his next question, "Or maybe back to yours?"

Wanton desire washes through me, and sure my uterus is trying to perform its very own fire sale; everything must go! But for some reason Karl, his royal hotness, is the only one being allowed to go against the tide, so to speak.

"I-I can't," I chew on my lower lip, and his grey eyes track the movement, like a wolf stalking his prey. "Believe me, I really, really want to but," I suck in a breath and curse my menstrual cycle once more, "I can't."

His hand moves upward so that his thumb rests on my lower lip, prying it free from my nervous chewing, his touch lingers on my mouth, caressing its curves as gentle as the softest kiss, and again feral lust washes through me. I desperately wish he'd replace his fingers with his lips. His mouth. His kiss.

Why of all nights is this the night he finally makes a move?

4

When I have a womb that's on the war path and I already have a geyser in between my thighs, and not in a fun way.

Before I can stop myself, I gently catch his thumb in between my teeth, softly biting, before pulling the digit into my mouth, sucking at the tip gently. His eyes darken as the metal transforms to liquid steel. We both know I'm playing a dangerous game, but only I know I'm not going to follow through on anything tonight.

His breathing hitches as I place a kiss on the tip of his thumb, before giving him a flirtatious smile, "Raincheck?"

"Fuck, Hazel," he laces his voice with the promises of dark deeds, and I wish I could explore. "Don't do this to me."

"Just think," I take a step back, willing my legs to refrain from shaking, either from pain or from desire. "It'll be worth the wait."

He gives me a pained look, filled with yearning, before he yields with a small, resigned nod. Karl knows not to beg, hell, he doesn't need to. All he needs to do is flash that smile of his and he can have any girl he fancies. And knowing my luck he probably will; he'll think I'm turning him down indefinitely. Even though it's just because I don't want my first time with him to be when I'm on shark week.

I try to keep my smile playful, even as another cramp twists through my gut and I subtly shove my bag into my stomach to stop from doubling over.

"Can I walk you home?" he asks, and I hear the note of hopefulness in it. Definitely a bad idea, if he walks me home, he'll come into the flat for a drink and then that'll lead to a bloody catastrophe. Literally.

I take a step back, despite my body wanting to lean into him, willing myself not to fall on my ass. That's the last thing I need to happen tonight.

"I'll be fine." My vision turns to stars when agony surges through my body. I will not have Karl's impression of me tainted by me curling into a ball from period cramps. "It's a really short walk."

I turn, heading in the direction of the flat, cursing my body, bad timing and Mother Nature for ruining a night with Karl. Fuck you menstrual cycle and your bloody timetable.

I'm still cursing my womanhood when I narrowly miss breaking my ankle on a stupid pothole as a herd of fresher lads almost barrel into me. Apparently, they are entitled to the whole of the pavement!

"Well, excuse me for existing!" I shout at them as they descend the sloping cobbled streets with their drunken bellows and stumbles.

The temptation to follow them is snuffed out when my abdomen twists again. Painful blood loss quickly squashing blood lust. I know I promised Dahlia and Esme the ice cream was for sharing, but desperate times call for desperate measures, I'm eating that entire tub.

I pause my lurching ascent when I reach the fork in my journey. Option one is to follow the well-lit, longer route (which adds an extra ten minutes to an already agonising walk) or take the shorter route through the already-creepy-in-daylight park. Mother Nature makes the decision for me when she gives me another sucker punch and I begin staggering down the darkened path through the eerily quiet park.

The drunken hoots of students dims as I'm swallowed into deathly silence. I've never noticed the park's streetlights are spaced out so far apart, and in between each meagre light there is an ocean of blackness. There are just seven streetlights interspersed across the expanse of lawn and overgrown hedges, and the final light winks at me by the exit, a solitary and distant lighthouse cresting the horizon. I hasten my pace between each beam of light, calmed by the false sense of security they afford, but every time I step into the inky shadows dread settles deeper in my stomach.

I hear the snap of a twig from a few yards away and I freeze like a deer sniffing a hunter on the breeze.

"Hello?" I whisper into the darkness.

Only silence answers me, but there's a nagging feeling that whilst the park may be quiet, I may not be alone. I'm frozen in place, and it takes all my willpower to force my legs to move.

"Stop being paranoid," I murmur quietly to myself. "There's no one there, it's just your imagination." I quicken my pace, when the shadows swallow me once more. "And even if there is anyone there, it'll just be some harmless pisshead."

There's another crack of branches that echo through the silence, and I swear this time they sound closer.

I quicken my pace, cursing past me for wearing stilettos rather than something remotely sensible. But then again, they wouldn't have gone with the outfit.

I hear footsteps from a few metres away and they are unnervingly close.

"Fuck," I whisper to myself. Stop panicking and just keep walking, don't turn around and just act normal; this was a very, very, extremely stupid, short cut.

Another cramp twists, but for the first time in the entire night I'm able to ignore it, all I can focus on is the footsteps behind me.

I've got two more lights to pass and then I'm out of this bloody park, just two more lights and then I'll be back home in the flat.

A silhouette steps out from behind one of the hedges, directly in front of me and moves with deathly precision to block my path. As my footsteps falter, a strong hand from behind me covers my mouth to stop my scream.

The hand smothers my face and locks me in place as the other figure moves forward and it tightens when the figure in front of me produces a very large, and very sharp knife.

I try to kick and flail against my attacker, but it does nothing except cause them to strengthen their hold. I'm trapped in a cage of muscled flesh and heat. But I keep fighting, trying to break away, even as the dagger is plunged into my chest, directly into my frantically beating heart.

Eight Years Later

Chapter One

<u>Esme</u>

My night has been a disaster.

But I knew it was going to be.

I'd known the minute I'd agreed to a drink with another random guy off another random dating app.

He'd been all prim, cable-knit prudishness, and well, I'm not.

I'd sat through two hours of painfully stilted conversation and awkward silences, imagining all the ways I'd like to magically improve the evening. I'd almost performed a glamour on him, just to make him seem at least a little more appealing. A little stubble, a sexy twinkle in his eyes, a little danger… maybe just an iota of sex appeal. Anything to help make the date more bearable.

But every time I felt that familiar prickle of my Magick tingling under my skin I stamped it down, remembering Mum's warning about being reckless.

"With great power comes great responsibility," Mum would always say when I was younger; it was years later I found out she stole that from 'Spiderman'. "The more you let your power sparkle and shine, the brighter it will burn out. And the more likely you'll be noticed by *them*."

By them, she meant the hunters. Witch hunters who sniff out my kind like bloodhounds. For as long as there have been witches, there have been those who hide in the shadows, trying to control, or in some cases, kill us, if they get the chance.

Hazel, my housemate, my friend, and a strong-ass Wiccan, had been one of those witches. Her power burned so bright they dazzled. Everywhere she went she was noticed by men, women, Magical or Mundane. Everyone saw her. And that had cost her. It had cost me. Her death was one of my biggest life lessons.

So, I'd been boring and sensible, kind of. I settled for drinking my body weight in Strawberry Daiquiris in the vain attempt to make the night more fun. It hadn't worked. Instead, I'd been stuck sitting opposite Mr Boring. The cherry on the top of the shit sundae was him telling me that I shouldn't drink so much in the week. I'd practically chewed off my own tongue to avoid telling him he shouldn't be so straight-laced. Who the hell spends their dates talking about tax brackets and fishing trips? I could have sat there telling him stuff that would have made his tiny little Mundane head implode.

But I'd behaved, just like Mum wants. Wanted. My chest twists when I use past tense. Again. Being a witch comes with a whole other set of rules, first and foremost to not disclose to a Mundane, a human, that you're a witch. If you do, you have to trust them implicitly that they won't betray that confidence.

Mum's voice echoes in my head again: "A witch should never be reckless, always conscientious and to remember that whatever we put into the universe, we'd get it back. Threefold."

I look up at the night sky, the stars barely visible behind the cloud filled night. Only the moon can be seen, as effervescent as a starlet on a red carpet as she shines down on me. She's a beacon, guiding me back to my cosy flat away from the nightmare that had been my date and the cruelty of the world outside.

My flatmate Dahlia and my kitten Ink are going to be waiting eagerly for me to regale them with stories of my latest hot mess of an evening.

I dodge around another cracked paving slab in my well-worn pink Converse trainers.

I look up again. A new moon cycle is beginning, fresh and bright, brimming with possibilities. I huff out an exasperated breath.

My life is always about new beginnings. The bigger problem is trying to reach the end of anything. Hell, even a mid-way point would be something! Swirling from one adventure to the next and never putting down roots. Because roots mean responsibilities, and I'm not the settling down type.

A chill wind rushes through the winding city streets, and I wrap my arms around myself for warmth. Despite it being early June, it's still cold. But then again, this city is always full of surprises. Edinburgh is permanently braced for chilly weather. This city is in love with the winter. Like an infatuated teenager, Edinburgh is always eagerly awaiting the return of frosty temperatures and drizzle. Another gust blows through the sloping streets with its biting embrace. The temperature is like my dating life: Cold, unyielding… and never-sodding-ending.

But there has to be an end, I remind myself. I'm working on a deadline after all!

Old Town is eerily quiet for a Saturday night, hardly anyone is out. The only sounds come from inside the clubs and bars. The orange glow from the windows beckons to me and a small smile teases at my lips when I hear the drunken, cackling laughter from their raucous patrons. So much life and laughter, not like the outside. With me. I pull my purple jacket tighter around me, whilst trying to dodge the precarious cobblestones.

I shudder from another unwanted kiss of the frosty wind at the nape of my neck. I pull my hair free from the messy bun that I'd meticulously styled before my date. My pastel pink hair tumbles onto my shoulders, cocooning me in a rose gold halo. Another decision my dad disapproves of.

Over the years I've lost count of how many times I've heard the phrase "such a disappointment, Esmerelda," muttered under his breath. The top three are dropping out of Uni; never holding a job down longer than six months; my disastrous excuse for a love life.

I pop a piece of strawberry bubble-gum into my mouth and hopscotch across three particularly vicious cobble stones. Ahead of me I see a loving couple who look like a perfect picture of a storybook romance. His protective arm encircles her gallantly, whilst she looks up at him adoringly as they wait for the traffic lights to change. They look so sweet they give me a toothache, and I have the biggest sweet tooth in Scotland!

That's what has wound me up so much about tonight's date… he's just so…. Vanilla. Which is weird, because I usually love vanilla. But not as a personality. I don't want to have sex with someone whose main characteristic is that they blend into the background. Bleurgh! I'd imagine he'd be done in two minutes, all the lights off and he'd probably shake my hand when he finishes. Harry. The trainee accountant. With his cream jumper and mousey brown hair, he could have blended into the beige wallpaper if I hadn't been trying (and I really did try!) to talk to him despite the yawning chasm of awkwardness. Unsurprisingly, there was no spark. Nothing. Zilch. Just like all the other disastrous dates I've been on over the last few years.

I haven't felt anything remotely spark-like since Finn. The guy who used to send my pulse into overdrive, having me smiling so brightly my face would ache and make my toes curl in the best way.

A car whooshes past me at breakneck speed, startling me so much I have to pause at the curb to collect myself.

Goddess knows where he needs to go in such a hurry. Last call at the kebab house, perhaps?!

Once I manage to stop my heart from beating at a frenetic pace, I skip up the sloping street, the tall buildings close in around me, hugging me tightly the higher I ascend. As I round the corner, I'm greeted by the familiar coral glow of the cheery pumpkin lantern above "Thunder, Lightning or in Rain".

Mum's shop. Technically, now my shop, apart from that pesky 51% that Dad's hanging onto like a barnacle at the bottom of a ship.

She'd left it to me in her will. Now it's my mission to prove to Dad that I can settle down, just enough, so that I can be the sole owner of Mum's inheritance to me. Just so long as he believes I'm capable of doing at least one thing right. One hoop for me to jump through, I have to get married, or at least engaged, before I'm thirty.

Someone really needs to introduce Dad to feminism. He's clearly missed the memo.

I pause outside the shop, admiring the dusky rose window display that Dahlia and I carefully crafted. Pink quartz tarot cards, fuchsia runes and pastel candles, all strategically placed to entice either curious Mundanes or aspiring Witches into the little Wiccan shop.

Sure, witchcraft has a reputation for being all dark and moody, but that's why I want to change people's opinions. If you're going to master the dark arts, what's wrong with them being a little pink and sparkly?

I stroke a hand lovingly across the pale blush of the windowsill before continuing my uphill excursion.

My phone vibrates in my jacket; pulling it out, I see a message from Dahlia.

"So how was the date? Should I make myself scarce? X"

I giggle at my roommate's text before hitting reply, *"If you do that, who's going to console me over my shit show of a love life?! X"*

A second later another message pings back, *"I'll get the ice cream out and pour us some wine! X"*

"Screw the wine glasses! Just give me the bloody bottle and a straw! X"

I pocket my phone, as I meander up the last remaining yards to our ramshackle little flat at the top of the hill.

Like most things worth anything in my life, I'd inherited the flat. An estranged aunt gifted it to me on my 21st birthday, and whilst I hadn't really planned to settle down in the city I was born in, it seems to have happened anyway.

I pull my keys from my bag and dodge around the humongous violet hydrangea that takes over the entryway.

Trying, and failing, to be as silent as possible, I clamber down the spiral staircase to my modest two bed flat. I tiptoe to avoid the wrath of my next-door neighbour, Iris the Formidable. The angry old widow with a blue rinse, a vicious walking stick and bad case of the Mondays!

I quickly, and quietly, open the door and am immediately greeted by Ink, my six-month-old kitten, who launches himself at my leg with all his claws out, and sticks to me like a fly trapped in superglue.

He looks up at me and meows loudly. I nudge the door closed with my foot, hoping Ink's wails won't stir Iris.

"Hello to you too!" I extract the kitten from my black jeans, bringing him to my chin and nuzzling him softly. "I missed you as well, my sweet boy!"

I'd painted the hallway in a mixture of periwinkle and buttery yellow stripes, so it feels like you're walking into a happy space. I duck to avoid banging into the various crystals and charms hanging from the ceiling that are placed at entryways to dispel any negativity from crossing the threshold.

My home is my safe space, and I'll be damned if I let any of the world's chaos and cruelty cross my checkerboard floor!

I walk into the lilac open plan kitchen and living room, Dahlia is perching on one of the cornflower blue kitchen units, trying to pull down two of the biggest wine glasses we have on the top shelf.

"I'm pulling out the big guns," she says by way of explanation. "I got the feeling you needed a glass of wine as big as your head!"

I chuckle, plonking down into the squishy fuchsia sofa, "Are you suggesting I have a big head?!"

She grabs a hold of the jade green wine glasses, which I'd forgotten I even owned, that are as big as fish bowls! "No! Your head is in proportion with the rest of your body!"

"Ok, so, you're calling me giantess! Lovely! Thanks for that!"

I look down at my long limbs: there's no denying I've never been diminutive. At five foot ten, I always take up space, either through my imposing height or simply by just being me... I'm not made to sit in the background! But then again, neither is Dahlia. She's the opposite of me in many ways; I strive to embody as much sparkle and sunshine as possible, but Dahlia? She's all the darkness and mysterious allure you'd expect from a tarot reading witch. Her silky onyx locks swing around her and she's covered from head to toe in black rune tattoos. But that's why we're flatmates, workmates and friends; we compliment each other as naturally as night and day.

"So," Dahlia fills up the glasses to a dangerously high level with dark red wine. "How bad was it?"

"He's a trainee accountant. His hobbies are fishing and crosswords. His favourite musician is Bruce Springsteen-"

"Oh Goddess!" She places one of the glasses in front of me, managing to miraculously not splosh any over the coffee table. "So, I take it no second date then?"

"Not unless I need a hand balancing the shop's books or want to spend a lifetime chewing my own arm off for entertainment!" I sigh, slumping deeper into the squishy purple sofa. "I know I'm expecting a lot... and I know he's a Mundane, but does he have to be so...."

"Boring?"

"Aye. That."

"It's still so weird your dad is so dead-set on you getting married before you're thirty-"

I take a large gulp of wine. "It was in my mum's will. It's a bit hard to argue with her when she's dead."

Dahlia nods. "Fair point. But it's still such an odd request. It's so old-fashioned!"

"I guess she thought that if I could settle down with a Mundane, then maybe I could handle the lofty responsibilities of retail management!"

"But why a Mundane?" Dahlia's face scrunches. "They are just so dull!"

"You're such a snob!" I tickle under Ink's chin, and he purrs loudly. "Remember Finn? He was a Mundane and he was lovely!"

"Aye, he was, but then you know," Dahlia sips from her glass, silence lingering between us.

"He died," I finish her sentence, trying to ignore the sting of loss in my chest. I nuzzle my face deeper into Ink's black fur, listening to his loud purrs of contentment, and trying to hide my flinching expression at the memory of Finn.

Dahlia reaches across the table, patting my knee softly. "Sorry-"

"Don't be," I attempt to sound casual, trying to ignore how the memories of him still hurt. "It was over seven years ago."

"But... you did love him."

"I did. But he's not here anymore." I release my grip on Ink to take another swig of wine, the taste suddenly bitter, "and I have a deadline to hit."

Dahlia leans back in her chair, pretending to push imaginary glasses up her nose, her imitation of my dad is eerily accurate, "I've told you before, Esmerelda, you must be married by your thirtieth birthday or-"

"Or I'll take control of the shop and sell it!" I grumble, Dad's threat is practically burned into my mind. "It's insane!"

"Not to mention out-dated!"

"Anti-feminist!"

"Patriarchal bullshit!"

Dahlia laughs, "It's still so funny that he's trying to get you to conform, I mean, it's you!" She waves a hand up and down my appearance.

She's not wrong: I'm not the best example of what passes for a traditional little Mrs. With my blush pink hair, ripped skinny jeans, pink bustier top and the floral tattoos covering half of my body. My appearance is more suited to working in a rock club than baking pies and doing school runs.

I shudder inwardly at the thought of parent teacher evenings and helping toilet training a pudgy faced toddler.

"I've got until April next year. I need to find a guy who's willing to get engaged to me," I shrug, trying to ignore bubbling anxiety. "That's plenty of time!" My voice goes up with each word, ending on a slightly hysterical sounding squeak.

Dahlia smirks, "Well, when you say it like that it sounds so easy!"

I tickle Ink's tummy, earning me a swipe from the feisty little beasty!

She reaches for her cards on the coffee table. "Want me to do a reading for you now? I can find out if Prince Charming is just around the corner?"

I shake my head and chug the remainder of my wine, "Not tonight, I need to recharge." I stand, still holding Ink. "Thank you though."

Tonight's worn me out. Both from the failed date and the looming deadlines set by my imposing father. I just want to curl up into bed and start fresh again tomorrow. Hopefully, I can shift this grey cloud of a mood by then.

Dahlia settles back into the sofa and flicks on the TV, "I'll give you a freebie tomorrow at the shop if it's quiet-"

I laugh as I leave the room, "Oh, you flirt!"

I pad down the hallway to my bedroom. Our rooms are opposite each other in the narrow hallway with the big turquoise bathroom dead ahead, the large clawfoot beckoning to me.

Flicking the light on in my room, I gently place Ink on my rose embroidered bedspread and make my way over to my full-length mirror. My room isn't massive, but I've managed to conjure enough storage space to hold all my clothes inside my modest closet. If I'd been Mundane, I'd probably have to sleep in a sea of skirts and dresses!

I quickly undress and shove on my Disney princess sleep set. At 29 years old I know I should have outgrown this by now, but dammit, I don't want to. Life is already filled with enough doom and gloom, what's wrong with a little silliness every now and then?

I sit down at my dresser, which is cluttered with every type of lotion and beauty potion I could either buy or brew. Tiny, jewelled containers sit alongside shop-bought beauty products.

I look down at the shell covered frame. "Why'd you have to ask me to do this Mum?" I sigh, picking up the picture. "Why did you have to leave me alone to deal with Dad?"

Past versions of Mum and I grin up at me from the photo. My six-year-old self gives the camera a beaming, gappy grin. The smile of someone who doesn't even know how to spell responsibilities. I gently stroke the image of Mum, frozen in time. Always smiling. Always perfect. She cuddles the bite size version of me with such pride and adoration. I'd give anything to feel that safe again. My attention is always drawn to her, her beauty and aura shine bright even in the grainy old picture. A soft, warm golden hue radiates off her. Mum had been the most powerful witch in one of the most prolific coven's in Scotland when I was little; her powers were awe-inspiring and so wide-ranging, but she always said that at her core she was a green witch.

She'd passed her love of flowers and plants to me. I didn't have half her gifts; the magic of flowers is the only thing I excel at. My excuse for my limited skills is apathy but it's more than that; I just don't want to be compared to Mum, especially when I know all I'd end up doing is coming up short. But bewitching and nurturing flowers and plants? That I can do!

As soon as we'd moved into the flat, I'd conjured flowers for every room, much to Dahlia's disdain… but she did eventually warm to the Chocolate Cosmos I enchanted around her mirror. Flowers and chocolate are the way to any girl's heart!

The night jasmine around my iron bed frame begins to bloom,

releasing their heady, sweet perfume. They remind me of the late summer nights when Mum would take me into the garden and teach me to draw the buds from the soil. She had been the embodiment of summer with her sun kissed skin, golden honey locks and the way her caramel eyes would warm you from a single glance.

I look up at my own reflection, noting the stark differences between us. My mother's eyes, soft and wide, like a doe's. Whereas mine are the palest sea green and tilt upward slightly, like a mischievous Siamese cat. Rather than the pretty gentle cupid's bow lips of my mother, my mouth is always turned upward in a hidden smile. Concealing a secret that even I don't know.

I try to squash down the memory of Mum's death. Of being stood in a rainy, grey cemetery. It had been a tragic accident, one that Dad had shouldered the brunt of before he told me. There had been no suspects arrested. No closure. It was a hit-and-run. He'd tried to remain stoic, but I saw the way his throat bobbed as he spoke, and he couldn't hide his dry, red-rimmed eyes. He never showed emotion. Despite how much I tried to bridge the gap between us, it was an impossible space over which to forge anything remotely close. Mum had been the warmth and the heart of our little family. The sun that everything grew around.

Mum and I differed dramatically in appearance and in temperament. If my mother was summer: warm and inviting; then I'm spring: bursting with frenetic energy. But the energy helps. It stops me from dwelling on the shadows and sadness that always lurk in the corners of my mind.

Except tonight. Tonight, I need to wallow, at least for a little while. I need to remember. To feel the ache of grief.

I climb into bed and Ink launches at my toes as I wriggle them under the covers. I retrieve the shoebox from under my bed. I know I shouldn't pander to nostalgia, but I can't help it. The whole night I've just thought about him and now I just want to reminisce. At least for a little while.

My memory box is bruised and beaten, reflecting how I really am inside. I push aside the lilac leather grimoire my mother had written in for conjuring. She'd gifted it to me when I was twelve and had heavily caveated that it wasn't a true grimoire. A collection of her abstract comments, rough incantations with pressed flowers laced between each scrap of notes. She had said it was good practice for me to learn to preserve the texts of sister witches and to understand the importance of grimoires. It's mainly nonsensical spells, but I couldn't bear to throw them away. Every time my fingers would trace

16

Mum's writing, I'd feel a pang at how much of an impression she'd left on the world. Not just in her coven, but in every person who met her.

My attention snags on the collection of photos in the box. Pictures of Finn. Pictures of us. Whilst we'd only dated for ten months, I'd known in my bones that Finn and I were two sides of the same coin: Fun-loving, reckless and carefree. He'd moved up from London and had quickly acclimated to Edinburgh nightlife. I'd seen him at every Fresher night and then one night, we finally spoke and that was it. Stars aligned. Fate entwined us like vines in an inescapable choke hold. I knew he was mine and I was his. My fingers shake as I grip the black and white strip of photo booth images. We'd taken them on my 21st birthday. Finn and I had snuck out of lectures and gone to an arcade. We spiked our slushies with vodka and played video games until our hands cramped. He'd said we needed a souvenir from the day, so we squished together in that tiny little booth. It was so small I had to sit on his lap so we could both fit. He'd brushed the hair from my face and kissed me so sweetly. Our first kiss. I felt so giddy I could have sworn I'd journeyed to the Astral Plane!

Another photo, one from my old polaroid camera, we are laid in bed. Finn had taken it of us. Flushed and happy. So young and so in love. Taken just before Mum had died, before I started to see the world for what it could be capable of.

After Mum, Finn had been my rock. Staying with me through those months of grief and helping me ignore the crippling ache inside. Until he was taken from me too.

The birthday card Finn had written for my 21st birthday peaks out from beneath the photos. A picture of a puppy chasing a butterfly. He'd said that that the card had reminded him of me, always running after the next adventure. He even came up with a secret nickname for me which he'd call when we were alone, or whisper into my ear whenever we were in the throes of passion; "Pupperfly". It was stupid. Childish. Adorable. So us.

Once we finished Uni, we were going to go on our own adventures. Chase our own butterflies and go travelling. China, America, Australia and New Zealand. We were going to see the world together.

I drop the card in the box as the tears escape from my eyes before I can stop them. I tuck the box back under my bed and turn off the bedside light.

I fall asleep cuddling Ink and thinking of the love I'd lost and wonder if some part of me died that night with Finn.

No matter how much sparkle and glitter I put over it… my heart is still just as broken as that night seven years ago.

Chapter Two

Sleep evades me all night, and by 6am, I decide that lying in bed moping isn't going to help me. I need to distract myself. So here I am, unlocking the shop at an alarmingly early hour.

A smile teases at the corner of my mouth, and my mood immediately brightens as the bells above the door chime and jingle. The familiar scent of cinnamon incense and cedar candles greets me as I step inside. Every one of the tall shelves is crammed with books and Wiccan paraphernalia, interspersed with rose and peony garlands that I bewitched to bloom when someone enters the shop. I can't count how many times Mundanes would gasp with wonder, asking how I managed to create such a cleverly convincing trick!

I move to the till, turning on the fairy lights; they twinkle to life and sparkle across the ceiling, creating an artificial sky of stars which orbit the antique French chandelier in the centre.

I lovingly trace my fingers along the shelves as I make my way to the back of the shop to the little staffroom and turn on the kettle. There's barely room for the tiny circular table and natty old wooden chairs. The room is painted sunshine yellow and every one of the surfaces is covered with tea caddies, overstuffed biscuit tins and large bell jars filled with weird and wonderful dried herbs and ingredients for both brewing Magick or hot drinks. Everything about the shop reminds me of Mum. When I was little, I'd always helped her, even when I was barely tall enough to reach the till! I'd loved to watch my mother talk to customers, seeing even the most cantankerous patrons bewitched by her. Nobody was immune to her charm and beauty. She was sunshine and could warm even the coldest hearts. Mum was the real Magick. Not the candles, crystals or

19

the books she sold. Just her.

I pluck a rhubarb and nettle tea bag from one of the tin tea jars and pop it into my daisy painted teacup.

I'm foregoing coffee this morning; the last thing my brain needs is more fuel!

I hear the tinkle of the chimes from the front door and check my watch. Strange. I'm not expecting Dahlia yet, she'd said she had a shift at the bar this morning and wasn't coming in until one.

I poke my head around the corner to peer into the shop and see the familiar copper curls of my old Uni friend, Zoe. We'd become fast friends when, at a drunken fresher's night, we'd both accidentally let slip that we were witches. Neither of us were particularly powerful, still fledglings, but we'd shared a love of nature, particularly flowers and plants.

She'd gone on to get a degree in botany, meanwhile I'd dropped out and had followed one of my half-arsed career aspirations of being a florist. That career change had lasted less than two months. I love flowers too much to watch them die. I wish I had realised that before I was booked for that wedding and had to give them back the deposit.

Zoe is busy scouring the shelves. Completely engrossed in her hunt, she hunches over one that contains spell books.

"Morning Zo!" I give her a gentle tap on the shoulder, and she shoots upright like I've just dunked her in an ice bath.

My smile dims when I see her expression. Her pretty, round face is pinched, and her eyes are wide with fear and rimmed with the dark circles of someone who hasn't had a good night's sleep in weeks.

I place my hand on her shoulder. "What's wrong?"

Her lower lip wobbles, a small shudder coursing through her. "Zo?"

Two fat tears roll down her ashen cheeks, "I'm sorry, I know it's early... I... I..."

I take hold of her hand and pull her over to the darkened corner of the shop, Dahlia's reading area, where two burgundy armchairs sit around the little mahogany table perched between them. I park Zoe in the seat nearest the wall, facing away from the window. A small white rose on the shelf next to her begins to bloom.

"Stay put," I command, making my way back to the boiled kettle. "Let me get you a tea, I'll be back in one second."

I make quick work of brewing Zoe a honey and chamomile concoction. Hopefully the calming brew will soothe her.

20

"Th-Thank you," she gratefully takes the teacup, still shivering, despite the warmth of the sun pouring in through the large bay windows.

"Zoe, what's wrong?"

"I think I'm being followed."

My brow furrows, as dread causes my stomach to drop like a boulder into a Loch, "By who?"

She takes a sip of the tea, another shudder courses through her. "Last week I thought someone was following me home and then yesterday," she sucks in a shaky breath. "I came home, and my flat door was unlocked. It felt weird. Like someone had been in there."

I can't stop my brain from thinking about the word I dread to say out loud. Hunter. Could it be a hunter? It's been years since we had an attack. Maybe it was just a stalker. Although 'just a stalker' seems to be putting it mildly.

I lean forward. "Have you made sure your wards and protection charms are still working?"

She falters, her cheeks flushing, "I-I don't use them."

"What do you mean you don't use them?!"

"I kind of just thought they were," she looks embarrassed, "erm, bullshit."

I pinch the bridge of my nose. Goddess, give me strength!

"No, what's bullshit is you not having wards, Zoe!" I try to keep my tone gentle, but I can't hide the disappointment in my voice. "You need to protect yourself!"

The blush deepens on her cheeks, "I never knew how to do them."

"Dahlia and I will help you," I try to sound like I'm not chastising her, the last thing she needs is to feel worse. "You always know you can ask me for help."

"I don't think Dahlia will," she looks uncertain, "she doesn't really like me."

"Of course she does."

That's utter bollocks, but she doesn't need to know that. Dahlia disliked Zoe all the way through Uni, she called her a priss and a hidden Witch. Someone who prefers to hide who she is rather than face the judgement of other people. But then again, Dahlia has her own issues with that; it wasn't fair she'd laid so much of her anger at Zoe's feet.

Zoe still looks uncertain, fiddling with the cup in her hand. "If you're sure she won't mind?"

"She'll help if she thinks you're in trouble," I pat her knee

21

comfortingly. "I'll check if she's free tonight and we'll both come round and triple our efforts on the wards. Three witches are better than one, after all!"

The white rose next to her blooms and transforms to a pretty, crimson hue, matching Zoe's cheeks.

She chews her lip. "I don't think I can really be classed as a witch anymore. I don't do spells. I don't follow any of the practices."

"You're still a witch," I say kindly. "Even if you don't believe it."

She sighs, her shoulders dropping. Relief spreads through her limbs.

"In the meantime," I stand and make my way to the herbs. "Take this."

I hand her the small bundle, wrapped in a lilac ribbon.

She takes hold of it, sniffs and crinkles her nose. "What is it?"

It takes all my willpower not to roll my eyes, Goddess she really is out of the loop. "It's sage and some other protective herbs. When you get home burn this and move from room to room to dispel anything malignant. Then Dahlia and I will come round and help cleanse and ward, ok?"

She stands, still a little shaken, but definitely less like she's about to shit herself from fear.

I pull her into a hug. "Don't worry, us witches have to stick together!"

She gives me a small nod before heading out the door, and as she passes the shop window, she's practically running up the high street. So much for me putting her mind at ease.

I stare at the window for a minute, remembering the last time I felt this worried for a friend. The morning after we'd been out for fresher's and Hazel's room was empty and her bed untouched. We didn't know what had happened until the police knocked on the door later that morning.

Nope! Not today! We're only allowed one pity party a week and I'm not about to start another one when I'm still dehydrated from crying last night!

I mentally shove all the unwanted memories into a metaphorical box and bury it. When in doubt, distract! Nothing stops your brain from wandering down dark paths like something that needs doing.

As soon as I think that a flustered woman with a pushchair and a screaming toddler comes tumbling into the shop asking for a natural sleep remedy for herself.

The next couple of hours are uneventful. Trickles of customers steadily stream through my little shop, including one very loud group of American tourists hunting for nick-nacks, who purchase some of the Goddess Hecate candles. I also spend a good twenty minutes with a woman claiming she's looking for ingredients for a love spell, but the herbs she buys are definitely for more of a passionate affair than a long-lasting relationship. She nods vehemently that that is what she wants and says it's been so long since she felt the flutter of desire, she's worried she's actually forgotten what it feels like.

You and me both, I think absently before giving the thought a swift kick out of my brain.

At 11am the door jingles and my customer service smile turns genuine as my mum's old friend Agnes enters. Agnes is my surrogate aunt, she was part of Mum's coven and had always taken care of me during Solstice celebrations, particularly when Mum's focus was occupied in coordinating the festivities. Even after the coven had disbanded, Agnes has always taken care of me.

Whilst she's roughly the same age my Mum would have been, Agnes always seems older and a lot more eccentric. With her sharp tongue, and an even sharper mind that she hides under her flamboyant outfits. She always dresses eclectically, and whenever I ask her about it, she just shrugs and says, "This is who I felt like being today!"

And today is no different, despite the summer sun, she's wearing a voluminous black trapeze dress, frothing with tulle skirts, huge bell sleeves that are covered in embroidered sunflowers, neon yellow trainers and matching beret. She looks like a bumblebee or a yellow ladybird.

The garlands in the shop notice and proceed to switch their shades from pretty pinks to violent yellow.

I shoot one of the roses a warning look before returning attention to Agnes, "Good morning!"

She fumbles with her yellow parasol, trapped in the doorway by the umbrella that refuses to fold. Once she manages to wrestle it into submission, she gives me a bright smile. "Morning Esme dear, how are you?"

"Good thanks, want a cuppa?"

She shakes her head, before halting, "Actually I will, if I can have some of that lemon cake you have in the back, please?"

I chuckle, I always forget Agnes likes to play this game. If there's tea, she'll only have one if there's a plate of biscuits or a slice of cake in the offer as well.

23

"Have a seat," I wave a hand towards Dahlia's table, "I'll be back in a second."

I give Agnes a generous slice of the lemon cake as well as a giant mug of Breakfast tea.

She smacks her lips appreciatively before tucking in. "I will always say Esme dear you're my favourite of all my Coven nieces!"

I laugh, "that's only because I ply you with cake!"

She chuckles heartily, her ruddy cheeks turning a darker shade. "Not true! It's because you are as much sunshine and sweetness as your dear mother! She would be so proud of you, the way you're running the shop so well-"

My smile falters a second, the shop. Not my shop. A small pang in my chest reminds me that the shop isn't entirely mine. Not yet anyway.

Agnes continues, oblivious that what she says is a grim reminder of how Dad still holds the strings. "I came by as I needed to talk to you about something. Something quite unsavoury I'm afraid."

I hear the jingle behind me as a customer comes in and begins browsing the candle section.

She lowers her voice, "I'd heard from one of the covens in Glasgow there's been another murder. One of their fledgling witches, pretty little thing... oh what was her name? Celeste something... anyway. I just wanted to let you know."

My smile completely evaporates.

Another witch murder.

It's no wonder so many of the covens have disbanded and most witches practise alone in the shadows. After Mum died, the coven she and Agnes were part of, had gone their separate ways. They'd decided it was safer to be solitary. But that comes with its own risks: alone means you have no strength to pull from and no sisters to guide you. If you did manage to find a coven you were also a target; gatherings and solstice celebrations are prime targets for hunters. The history books say witch-hunting stopped centuries ago. I was all too aware that it hadn't. Not by a long shot.

Agnes notices my change in mood, putting the plate down and leaning towards me. "Oh! Don't worry dear, I just wanted to let you know. I know it's grisly business, but I have to check in on you." Her large eyes fill with concern. "I must make sure you're safe. I promised your dear mother-"

"I know, don't worry though, I'm being careful. I promise. I always wear my tiger's eye, burn sage regularly and Dahlia and I do fresh wards every week."

She winks at me. "And that's why you're my favourite! I don't have to remind you to do the basic safety measures!" She takes a big gulp of her tea, "Honestly, some of the other girls... you'd have to check they had their heads screwed on half the time."

I raise an eyebrow, "Just how many girls are you having to look after?"

She waves offhandedly, "I wouldn't be doing my duties by the coven if I didn't look after you all."

I frown, "But Mum's coven disbanded years ago?"

"True," she pauses for a moment. "But just because it disbanded doesn't mean the ties aren't still there. Some bonds are too strong to break!"

She stands up, brushing crumbs off her luminescent outfit. "Anyhow, I'd best be off! I just wanted to stop by and check how you were doing!"

The doorbell jingles cheerfully despite the bad news Agnes has bestowed on me.

All bad things come in threes. So far that's two; Zoe, Agnes... What's next?

I make my way over to the confused looking Mundane man, who's trying to decide which candle to buy. I steer him away from accidentally buying a virility candle for his daughter in law as a birthday present!

My phone vibrates on the counter, and it takes all my courage to answer my dad's call. Even his ringtone is ominous.

I pick up the phone and try to sound breezy and not like my mood just plummeted to the floor.

"Hey Dad, how's it going?"

"Hello Esmerelda," his voice is clipped and devoid of any paternal affection. "How are you?"

Why does he always have to full name me? I always feel like I'm in trouble when he calls me that. Actually, scrap that, I always feel like I'm in trouble when he calls me, period. Also, don't make out like you care Dad. I know you're only calling for one thing!

"Good thanks, busy day today! Lots of customers and I even-"

"The reason for the call is I wanted to find out how you're getting on with the, erm," he flounders. "Well, your birthday is coming up soon."

"Dad," I grind my teeth. "It's not for another nine months."

"That as may be," his tone is all business. "But it takes time to date, find a suitor and-"

25

"Please stop, Dad!" My father trying to relate to me about my dating life, or lack thereof, is the worst kind of torture.

"Do you remember Mark?" he continues, ignoring the pained groan I make. "The young man you used to play with when you were younger. Well, he was visiting a few weeks ago and I mentioned that you are unattached."

"Oh, Dad," embarrassment floods my cheeks. "You didn't, did you?"

"He's young, friendly," Dad sounds as uncomfortable about this topic of conversation as I do, "and normal."

'Normal' is his code word for a Mundane. Dad has now reached the level of desperation he's willing to palm me off on my childhood friends.

"Look, Dad, I've got to go. A customer just came in."

"Esmerelda," his tone is serious, and I can practically see him pushing his glasses up his nose in exasperation. "Also, it's coming up to your mum's anniversary."

I pinch the bridge of my nose. Like I could forget that. It's practically burned into my memory. That day when I'd come home from classes to see Dad sat at the kitchen table with Agnes. Their expressions alone were enough to tell me something was wrong.

"I know," I answer, barely audible.

I hear shuffling at the end of the line. "Can I expect you to pop round?" His voice returns to its usual curt and clipped tone. No emotion. Just like always.

"I'll be there."

Our macabre little tradition: I'd go round to Dad's, sit in silence with him and we'd have lunch, before making our way to visit Mum, tidying her grave, clearing away weeds to plant fresh flowers. My hatred of picked flowers was the same as Mum's: we hated to watch them die. So, every year I'd plant new flowers on her grave. She had loved flowers, plants and bees. She loved every living thing, so it made sense for her final resting place to be somewhere nature would bloom.

"Good."

Silence sits between us until finally I can't take it anymore.

I clear my throat awkwardly. "I'll talk to you soon! Byeeee!" I quickly hang up and throw my phone away from me like it's a poisonous snake.

Why did I answer? I knew it would just be a reminder of the looming marital deadline! I used to love birthdays, now I dread them!

The rest of the morning I help customers who are either

26

browsing or hunting for specific items. It's a steady trickle of trade which keeps my mind occupied and it's just what I need!

At 1pm Dahlia whirls in, still wearing her apron from the bar and covered in beer and cocktail stains.

"Seems a little early for happy hour?" I arch an eyebrow at her as she walks past the till, heading to the backroom. "Didn't you get time to change?"

"Bottomless breakfast hen party! Apparently, brunch is too late for some people!" She sighs as she walks towards the back room, "I just need one second!"

She stops, turning to look at me with narrowed eyes. "Your dad called you."

"He felt the need to remind me about Mum's anniversary," I slump against the counter. "Oh, and Dad decided to tell my childhood friend that I'm still single."

"I mean, he can't be any worse than those awful dates you've been on!"

I shoot her a warning glare. "Go get changed before I put a hex on you!"

When she returns, she's dressed wearing a sleek black maxi dress, her hair freshly straightened and the smell of smoky musk trailing behind her.

I nod approvingly. "Nice."

She casts a look at me. "You want me to change yours too?"

I baulk, looking down at my pink tank top, lilac denim mini skirt and trusty pink Converse. "There's nothing wrong with what I'm wearing!"

"If you say so!" She sashays over to her table. "Why are there crumbs all over my reading chair?!"

"Agnes was here."

"Oh, that explains it," she begins batting at the cushion covers. "Also, my lemon cake is now nothing more than a sliver!"

"She said there'd been another murder. Another fledgling. In Glasgow."

No point sugar coating it. I might as well tell Dahlia. She's no stranger to the darkness lurking in the corners of the world.

She stops brushing the chair, turning to look at me with concern in her eyes. "Like Hazel?"

I grimace. "I didn't really want to ask for details. But it sounds similar. Another coven witch."

"Oh Goddess," Dahlia collapses into the seat, she pales in worry. "Are you ok?"

I move to the shelves, feeling the need to keep my hands busy by rearranging the crystals. "Why wouldn't I be?"

I can still feel her watching me. Her green eyes are like lasers burning a hole into the side of my head, digging to get to the truth my mind is desperately trying to squash down.

I turn after plastering a smile on my face. "I'm fine."

She looks doubtful. "You don't look fine."

"I'm fine," I say firmly. "I told Agnes that we're fine. That we're doing all the right things to keep us safe."

"Damn right we are, we're not rookie fledglings who can't even do a simple ward," she stops. "Why are you looking at me like that?"

"How would you feel about coming with me to help do some protection spells for Zoe?"

She groans, flopping back in the chair. "Oh, for fucks sake, Ez! Do we have to?"

"She doesn't have anyone to help her, and she doesn't know how to do it."

"Of course she doesn't!" Dahlia returns to dusting off the crumbs from her table, "She's bloody useless!"

"Come on Dahls," I pout, putting on my sweetest smile, "for me?"

She throws one of the pillows from the armchair at me. "Now it's your turn to get me wine!"

Chapter Three

<u>Esme</u>

We arrive at Zoe's flat just after seven. The sky is a burnished orange, an early sunset for summer that casts a pretty glow across the crimson red door to her flat.

"She owes me big time!" Dahlia grumbles as she presses the doorbell, hoisting the large satchel higher up her shoulder.

I frown at her. "Hey, she's our friend!"

"Not *my* friend," she mutters.

"She needs our help."

Dahlia throws her head back and groans theatrically. Such a drama queen!

"Besides," I wave the two large tote bags at her, "I prepped everything! All you need to do is help me do the wards and then we can all drink wine, relax-"

She turns to glare at me. "I thought the wine was just for me!"

"You cannot drink three bottles of rose all by yourself!"

"I might need to if I'm going to have to cope with-"

Just before she can finish her rant, the door opens a crack, and Zoe greets us with the same twitchy expression from earlier.

Guess the tea didn't help that much after all?

She quickly settles her face into a polite smile and opens the door wider for us to come in.

"Thank you for coming," she chews on her lower lip again.

Dahlia pushes past her, letting herself in. "Thank Esme, I'm here for the booze! Speaking of, where are your wine glasses?"

Zoe closes the door and ushers us into a clinical looking kitchen. Her flat is the exact opposite of ours, all white walls and minimalist furniture. I'm terrified I'm going to spill something! Maybe I should have bought vodka instead?

Zoe follows along behind Dahlia. "Oh, well, I don't really drink, so I don't have any wine gla-"

Dahlia whirls on her, her annoyance palpable. "You've got to be kidding me!"

I sigh, giving Zoe an apologetic smile. "Zo, do you have mugs we can use instead please?"

Zoe gives a small nod, making her way to the cupboard above the kettle and pulling out two coffee mugs, which are all, unsurprisingly, pristine white.

"See?" I shoot Dahlia a warning glare, who gives me a pointed look. "Panic over!"

I start emptying out the totes and Dahlia snatches up one of the bottles. She proceeds to fill the cups and shoves one at Zoe. "You're drinking with us."

Not a question. Apparently if Dahlia's going to get wankered she's taking everyone down with her!

Zoe shuffles uncomfortably, holding the overly full mug. "But I don't really drink?"

"You do tonight! Trust me," Dahlia smiles mischievously. "You're going to need it!"

I don't like the way that smile feels like it's aimed at me. Anytime she looks like that trouble ensues! I start pulling out my pre-prepared tinctures.

"What's that?" Zoe asks, looking dubious.

I smile brightly at her. "Home protection oil! I already had a batch made, so I just syphoned some for you."

"It's dried mint, cloves, frankincense, myrrh and almond oil," Dahlia explains, before taking a huge gulp from her mug.

I nod reassuringly at Zoe. "We need to sprinkle a little bit by all of your doors and windows. It will help prevent any negativity coming into your flat. Don't worry Zo, Dahls is an expert at setting up wards."

Zoe points at the collection of crystals which I've already hooked up on long threads. "What are those for?"

Dahlia can't stop her mouth from hanging open, unable to hide her shock. I, at least, try to keep my face neutral. I knew Zoe had tried to avoid all things witch-orientated, but I hadn't realised she was this clueless.

I clear my throat, trying to hide the surprise in my voice. "We need to hang these by your front door; they'll help ward off negative influences from outside forces."

Zoe frowns, but decides not to question me, after all she came to me for help. So that's exactly what I'm going to do.

"Dahlia, can you and Zo do the protection oil?" I look between

30

the two witches who are both wearing the same look of alarm, like I've just told them to douse themselves in petrol and run with matches. "I'll start hanging these in the hallway."

Before either of them can argue, I grab the crystals and make my way to the front door.

I string up the crystals and place them in the corners around the doorway. Onyx for blocking negative energy, tiger's eye and smoky quartz for protection, black tourmaline to fight negative energy and rose quartz to… well, it just looks pretty.

"Which one's your bedroom, Zo?" I ask, clutching my bundle of remaining crystals. All the rooms are so sterile, I'll be half surprised if she's got a bed. You wouldn't want to ruin the stark and sparse design decor with something useful after all! I tell myself off. I think Dahlia's rubbing off on me.

She points down the hall, a frown furrowing her pretty face. "Why?"

"You need these for where you sleep," I give her another reassuring smile, "they'll help."

She gives me a slight nod, "Down the corridor, on your left," before turning to continue helping Dahlia.

I make my way into another blindingly white room. At least I don't need to clean them; half the job is already done! On her bedside cabinet I place the two remaining crystals. Amethyst to help soothe stress and rainbow fluorite to calm overactive minds. They look so lonely on the empty tabletop. It's so sterile I'm paranoid I'm going to accidentally spread glitter or leave a shred of colour in here!

I'm just about to leave the room, when I barrel into Dahlia and Zoe, who are making their way into the bedroom.

I stop Zoe at the door frame and hold out the final crystal to her, a beautiful hematite necklace I'd borrowed from the shop, perfect to help the wearer feel centred and balanced.

"Oh! I can't wear this," Zoe looks at the necklace like I've just asked her to wear a peacock as a hat.

"You bloody well will!" Dahlia orders.

She accepts defeat. Dahlia is not someone to mess with when it comes to protection. She shrugs, accepting the necklace and puts it on.

"What's next?" Zoe asks, once she finishes coating the last windowsill.

"Now, we get to have a little fun," Dahlia smiles brightly.

"Why don't I like the sound of that?" Zoe asks, her apprehensive expression trebles in intensity.

"Are you sure this is a good idea?" Zoe slurs as she rests her hands on the planchet. Despite saying she's not much of a drinker, she's been keeping up with Dahlia the entire night!

Dahlia takes another swig from her mug. We've demolished two of the bottles and she has that sleepy smile on her face she gets when she's pissed.

"Oh lighten up Zo!" She sighs, "It'ssss just a bit of fun. I ssswear I'll even burn sage once we finish soooo you don't have to worry about a thing!"

This is Dahlia's way of offering an olive branch, trying to tempt Zoe to embrace her inner witch. Why she thought a Ouija board is the way to go about this I have no idea. I suppose it beats trying to get Zoe to do a rune reading or scrying… baby steps, and all that.

Dahlia clears her throat, trying to summon that same alluring aura she uses when customers come in asking for her to do readings.

She chuckles when she sees Zoe fidget nervously. "Honestly Zoe, you need to relaaax! Go with the flow!"

I smile apologetically at Zoe. "Trust me, it's easier if you just indulge her!"

Dahlia ignores me, putting two fingers on the planchet, next to mine and Zoe's. "We call out to the beyond, can anyone hear us?"

Nothing. But then again, I'm not surprised. What kind of spirit would want to come talk to three drunk women?!

Dahlia raises her voice to an obnoxiously loud volume. "Yoohoo!"

"Be respectful!" I whisper at her. "You know they get annoyed if you talk to them like that!"

"It's because they are always such divas," Dahlia sways in her seat. "Oi! Dead fucks! We want to talk to you!"

I shoot her another glare, which is softened and blurry by the three massive mugs of wine I've drunk. "Dahlia!"

"What?!" She hiccups, "I'm trying to commune with the beyond-"

"By pissing them off?"

"They're dead! They're always pissed off!" She giggles. "Is anyone thereeee?"

Zoe looks between us nervously. "Maybe we should stop?"

Just as she suggests this the planchette moves to 'Yes'.

"See! Sometimes you just need to show them who's boss!" Dahlia beams triumphantly, "Is there someone over there who wishes to speak to someone here?"

The planchette remains still on yes.

I sigh, "They are already talking to us, which means there's someone there, who strangely enough, wants to talk to us."

"Fair point." She continues, "What's your name?"

The planchette moves down, trailing the letters across the board.

F. I. N. N.

I glare at Dahlia. "That's not funny, Dahls."

She looks up at me, she looks as stunned as I am. "I didn't do that-"

I huff out an exasperated breath. I'm already tired of this game. It was a stupid idea to do this. Especially when we're drunk.

"Either you're lying or whoever the fuck is on the end of this board is!" I retort.

"Guys," Zoe murmurs quietly, "I don't like this."

"I swear, I didn't move it," Dahlia says, she seems to be sobering with every passing second. "Honestly Ez, I'd never do that."

"Ok fine," I huff. "If this really is Finn... what's the nickname you used to call me?"

The planchette begins to move again.

P. U. P. P. E. R.-

I move my hand away from the planchet. "This is bullshit." I stand up, nearly knocking my wine all over the spotless tabletop. "Also, this really isn't funny!"

Zoe and Dahlia stay rooted, keeping their hands on the wooden disc.

"You're not supposed to break the circle," Dahlia looks up at me apologetically, her expression pleading.

"Screw the circle!" I snap down at the pair of witches.

"Why are you shouting at me?" Zoe looks like she's on the verge of tears. So much for a fun evening of bonding.

"I'm not shouting at you!" I snap at Zoe and try to focus on my blurry roommate. "I'm shouting at her!" I point a wobbly hand at Dahlia.

"I told you," Dahlia says slowly. "It isn't me. I swear to the Goddess! I'm. Not. Doing. It!"

I gather up the remaining tinctures and begin stuffing them in my bag, trying to fight the sting in my eyes.

"I'm not in the mood." I shove the remaining bottle in my bag, hoping I've screwed the top on tight enough. "I'm going home."

Dahlia makes a move to stand but keeps her hand on the planchette. I don't know what to believe, either Dahls is screwing with me in the cruellest joke, or there's some bored spirit who's lashing out because she was giving them shit… or…. I halt my train of thought. Nope. Not touching that.

"You need to say goodbye to whatever shithead is at the end of that thing!" I pull on my jacket. "Also, make sure you burn the damn sage before you leave!"

I turn to Zoe, trying to stop my voice sounding as hysterical as I feel, "Zo, let me know if you need anything else. Make sure to re-do the oil again in seven days. Whatever you do, do not take that necklace off!"

She nods at me mutely, her hands remaining on the Ouija board.

I throw the totes over my shoulder, not even looking at Dahls. I don't want to see what her expression will tell me; either she's bullshitting me… or she's really got no idea what's going on. And it could have been… No, I'm not even going to entertain it! There's no way…

I stalk out into the night, the heat from the day drying my clammy skin.

That sodding planchette. It had started spelling out his nickname for me. No one else knew about that. It was our secret. His strange little habit, but it was him. It was us. And I've never told anyone. Not even Dahlia. So how the hell did it know?

I kick at the ground, annoyed that I'm even contemplating the possibility that it could be him.

"It's bullshit," I mutter to myself. "Even if it was actually a spirit, there's no guarantee it was him."

But the nickname. That damned nickname.

"Ok fine," I grumble. "If you won't shut up, I'll drown you out!"

I shove my headphones on and start blasting Garbage from my phone. Can't follow these annoying thoughts if Shirley is in my ears!

I mentally sing along all the way home, deliberately ignoring the irony of listening to "I think I'm paranoid" on repeat for the twenty-minute walk back to the flat.

When I unlock the door, I'm surprised Ink isn't running, meowing loudly to greet me with that little demanding strut I love so much.

"Ink?" I call down the darkened hallway. "Where are you my sweet boy?"

I kick my trainers off at the doorway and make my way

through the narrow corridor, the crystals jingling as I disturb the air with my movement. It's unnervingly quiet.

"Inky boy?" I call again, trying to keep my voice high and jovial, despite a sense of mounting dread that something's wrong.

When I enter my room, I stop dead at the doorway. But it's not Ink playing on my bed, batting playfully at one of the jasmine flowers that makes me freeze, but my mirror. Fogged by condensation, I see my secret nickname written in the steam and as it evaporates so does any of my doubt that it was Finn. Because after that message dissipates another appears, which makes my knees buckle; "*I miss you so much. I can come back.*"

I walk further into my room, and I discover my memory box is now on my bed. And most definitely not where I last saw it, which was *under* my bed, not nestled amongst the blankets and duvets next to a playful black kitten.

"Okey dokey, just what my evening needs: a poltergeist who has a problem with privacy…" I cautiously walk over to the box to return it to its rightful home when I notice my mother's grimoire has been opened and a random selection of her torn paper notes have been laid out on the bed.

I pick up the wax paper and with shaky fingers I pull it up to the moonlight, 'A spell for summoning and conjuring those who have passed beyond the veil.' Under this note are incantations scribbled in Latin, an illustration of a star, candles at each point and what looks to be a trinket in the centre.

I look around the room. "Mum?" I ask, barely above a whisper.

Nothing. Just the silence of the flat.

"F-Finn?" I ask and I feel the lightest breeze against my neck. I can't help but squeak in alarm when I feel the featherweight touch of ghostly fingers along my collarbone and the faintest whisper in my ear. But I hear it.

As clear as if he was right beside me, I hear the whisper of a word, caught somewhere between the living and the dead.

"Pupperfly."

Chapter Four

Esme

The next morning the atmosphere in the shop is strained. Not only because Dahlia is hanging out of her ass with one of the world's worst hangovers, but because we still haven't spoken since I stormed out of Zoe's flat last night.

Even as we're getting ready to leave this morning, we don't speak, we navigate around each other like two feral cats, unsure how the other is going to react, and both of us are likely to start hissing and swiping at the other with our claws if they get too close.

I'm trying, and failing, to avoid thinking about the message on the mirror. If it had really been Finn. And he could come back. Why would he want to? I thought the afterlife was supposed to be all milk and honey… or in my case Netflix and Prosecco. I've always avoided looking into what actually happens to souls when they pass… call it blissful ignorance. Or stubbornness. I passed my threshold for grief and trauma seven years ago. I don't need to know what's on the other side, the time to find out will come soon enough.

I head to the back room, ignoring Dahlia, who is passive aggressively shuffling her tarot cards in the corner. Bugger yesterday's virtue of forgoing caffeine, I'm off the wagon, I'm going to brew a coffee the size of a swimming pool!

"Can I have one too?" Dahlia asks behind me. Her voice is uncharacteristically meek.

I snatch her 'Witch please!' mug out of the cupboard and begrudgingly place it beside mine.

She remains a safe distance away from me by lingering in the doorway. "Can we talk about last night yet? Please?"

I turn, finally getting a chance to really see how rough she looks. She leans against the doorframe, on the verge of collapsing or puking, or maybe both?

"Do you need to sit down?" I try to keep the smugness out of

36

my voice at seeing her self-inflicted condition exacting my vengeance for me. The most I managed was giving her a withering glare when she took too long unlocking the shop.

She shakes her head, making her look extremely green around the gills. "I'm good." She takes a tentative step towards me. "I feel awful, and not just because of the hangover. I'm so sorry and I wanted to make it up to you, so I made you something, well, I tried to."

She holds a tangled bundle of vines, thorns and miniscule buds. "It's supposed to be a necklace, but they got all sad, and didn't bloom properly."

I take the plant from her, and it trembles nervously in my hand. "Yellow roses?"

She gives a small nod.

Flowers all have meanings and yellow roses have one key message. Friendship. She's tried to enchant flowers for me as an apology.

A blush creeps up her cheeks. Creating a strange mixture of colours as it spreads across her grey-green pallor. "I'm not particularly green-thumbed."

"They're perfect, they just need a little love and time to grow," I stroke the delicate velvety soft petals. "Don't you baby?"

The flowers quiver under my touch. I dread to think what threats Dahlia has been shouting at them whilst she enchanted it! Poor thing! I stroke the plant again, and it begins to unfurl, winding tentatively around my fingers.

"Pretty little thing, aren't you?" I coo as I stroke a leaf that curls around my index. "Thank you," I look back up at Dahlia. "I love them!"

She smiles, looking relieved. "I'm just glad I didn't kill it!"

I trace a finger along a tiny bud that opens under my touch. "It's just shy," I smile down at the yellow petals. "Aren't you?"

"I really don't know how you do it," Dahlia's voice fills with awe. "That's the most complex green Magick I can manage, and I barely kept it alive! And within thirty seconds of you holding it, you've got it sprouting flowers!"

"Dahls, it's about the only thing I can do," I look back down at the plant as more buds begin to appear. It's amazing she managed to enchant a rose to grow, Dahls tends to turn most of them into compost. This peace offering wasn't easy for her to do. "I really appreciate it. Thank you."

My annoyance at her evaporates as quickly as summer rain

and I pour coffee into the two giant mugs.

"Now it's my turn to apologise to you," I hand her a coffee, filling mine with the adequate amount of sugar cubes, before walking to the front of the shop. She shuffles along behind me, groaning like an extra from 'The Walking Dead'.

I feel a twinge of guilt at taking such satisfaction in her hangover. Her aura is severely dampened by a night of wine.

Witches aren't really supposed to drink to excess, bad things can happen. It's always been frowned upon, and for good reason. I heard a story from the nineties where the employee of a kebab shop was turned into a toad after denying a drunk witch's request for fifty deep fried mars bars. She was nowhere near powerful enough to be casting transmogrification spells and had to get her very angry coven to step in and fix things. Ever since then the elders have told their fledglings to lay off the booze.

"I shouldn't have snapped at you like I did," I take a sip of coffee. "It was wrong of me to think you'd do something like that."

She grimaces, "I get why you might wonder if it was me doing it."

"Well, wonder went out the window the minute I got home."

She raises her eyebrow, signalling me to continue.

"It was Finn," I take another gulp of coffee, hating the tremble in my hand. "Or at least I think it was."

She nearly drops her mug in shock. "What?"

"He delivered his message," I take another gulp. "He says he can come back."

"What do you mean 'come back'?"

I shrug. The spell ingredients Mum had written onto a scrap of paper from her grimoire is practically burning a hole in my back pocket. "Your guess is as good as mine. But for some reason he thought this might come in handy," I fish out the paper and Dahlia unfolds it, a frown deepening on her face as she processes the contents of the note. "I found it lying on my pillow this morning."

She gives me another concerned look, before reading the paper, her frown deepening when she looks up at me again. "These are ingredients for a spell."

I nod, taking another swig of coffee, nearly draining the mug in less than five minutes. My new personal best.

"What's the spell?" her jaw gives a small tic.

"Er," I clear my throat. "Bringing someone back from the dead, I think."

Silence falls between us and if Dahls wasn't in hangover hell,

38

I'm certain I'd be on the brunt of a tirade about messing with things way beyond my level.

But instead, her eyes flicker with intrigue. "You're not seriously considering it," her mouth twitches, "are you?"

"Considering and deciding are two very different things," I splutter, nearly choking instead of swallowing my drink. "I've never dealt with that side of the arts. My summoning goes as far as this," I signal to my inner garden encircling the shop's shelves. "Besides, I'm not sure that's something I really want to mess with."

Dahlia wave's Mum's note. "Where did this come from?"

"I'm not sure, but," I hold out my hand and Dahlia places the frail paper back into my palm; she watches me as I carefully fold it back up and place it back in my pocket. "That's Mum's handwriting."

She nods slowly, her face turning thoughtful. "I could do some reading?"

"Honestly Dahls, I don't think it's a good idea," apprehension knots in my stomach. "Isn't it a little out of our league to summon someone from the spirit realm?"

"I think we're improving!" she baulks, before wincing at her own volume.

I raise an eyebrow. "Did you forget that you yelled 'Oi! Dead Fucks!' at the spirits last night?"

"It worked though, didn't it?!"

"Kinda?"

"You had a message from the beyond, your ex-boyfriend spoke to you! I'd class that as a success!"

"Not judging by the state of you today, Dahls," I grimace. "You're barely standing!"

"That's the wine," she heads back over to her table, shuffling her Tarot. "Not the Ouija."

I raise an eyebrow. "Maybe the spirits gave you a hangover?"

She places the cards down on the table, along with her head. "Trust me, this is all my own fault. I'll be fine in a few hours, once I feel, and look, less like death!"

"I'd recommend not looking at mirrors until then," my mouth tugs into a cheeky grin. "No offence."

She lifts her head up, trying to fix me with the kind of glare that would make most people shrink away in fear, but it comes up short. Right now, she looks as threatening as an angry gerbil.

Just as I'm about to say this, my phone lights up on the counter.

Oh crap, I'd forgotten that I'd arranged another date tonight!

I look down at the notification from the dating app on my screen of the guy's smiling face. He looks sweet on paper: Greg, 29, barman and no mention of Bruce Springsteen on his profile. But he's just not him. Not Finn.

And after last night I feel like I'm betraying him by even going out for drinks with this guy. That's how much of a hold he had on me. Has on me. My feelings for him hadn't died when he did. Hell, if anything it'd made them stronger. I didn't want to settle down with just any Mundane. I didn't really want to settle down at all, and if I did, the only person I could even consider doing that with would be Finn.

It's stupid, reckless and it probably won't work but…

"Dahls?"

"Hm?" Her voice is muffled from being squished onto the table.

"Do you think you'll have recovered by tonight for us to try a spell?" I make my way to the bookshelves, trying, and failing, to sound casual.

She lifts her head, and despite looking like death warmed up, I see the curiosity sparkle in her features. "Why?"

"Well," my fingers trace over the paper in my pocket. What's wrong with trying? If I don't try, I'll never know. "Maybe we could…"

Dahls arches an eyebrow, "Could what?"

I head to the back of the shop, passing the staffroom, towards the small stockroom. The tiny little box room is where I keep all of the artefacts and books that aren't suitable for your average Mundane to stumble upon.

Flicking on the light, I begin scouring the cluttered space, halting when I reach the 'Advanced Spell work and Dark Magick' items and start pulling books off the shelves.

Dahlia lets out another pained groan as she enters.

I turn, holding one of the dark, leather-bound tomes titled, 'Necromancy, Demonology and the Dark Arts.'

I wave the book in front of her, and I see her excitement as I say, "To try and get Finn back?"

After combing through the shelves, we find the summoning spell ingredients Mum had listed. Patchouli to connect with the spirit; Mandrake, Mugwort and Aconite to strengthen the summoning. This spell calls for a lot of strength. Three plants worth! Which I suppose isn't surprising, I'm just glad there's nothing on there about blood or sacrifices!

The knot of nerves in my stomach reminds me that this spell

40

is a long shot, but I have to try.

Once we gather the supplies, we close the shop early and head back to the flat.

We shove the sofa and coffee table to the side of the room, pulling up the turquoise rug to expose the mahogany herringbone floor.

I make my way to the kitchen cupboards, pull out a large jar of salt and start drawing out a circle in the middle of the floor. After I finish pouring the salt, Dahlia begins drawing a pentagram in the centre with hot pink chalk. I place tall lilac and lavender candles at the end of each of the five points. I then sprinkle the dried leaves and petals that I borrowed from the shop.

The ivy that encircles the windowsills begins to grow over the windowpanes, darkening the room and the atmosphere becomes ominous and spooky.

"Are you sure about this?" She brushes chalk dust off her hands onto her denim clad thighs.

"Nope," I give her a grim smile as I pull the note from my pocket. "Not even a little bit. But I have to try."

She nods with determination in her eyes. "Ok. We need an offering. Something personal to you and Finn."

I go to my bedroom, finding Ink sunbathing in a stream of sunlight from my window. I pull the shoebox from under my bed, retrieving the polaroid photo he'd taken.

I return to the pentagram, avoiding Dahlia's attention, as I place the photo in the centre of the star. "This'll work."

She grabs a box of matches to light the candles and I open the book to the grimoire for the summoning spell.

I look over at Dahlia as she lights the last candle. "Ready?"

"Nope, but," Dahls now looks as nervous as I feel, before squaring her shoulders with determination. "Fuck it."

My thoughts exactly. I'm not half as powerful as Mum. But I have to try. For Finn. For me.

"Okey dokey! Here goes nothing," I clear my throat, trying to sound more confident than I feel. "Repeat after me."

She nods again.

I read aloud the words written in loopy handwriting. "Oramus vos mortuos custodes,"

We beseech you guards of the dead,

"Oblationem nostram et gratiam nostram suscipe,"

Accept our offering and our gratitude,

"Patitur velum ad stillabunt,"

41

Allow the veil to drop,
"Da iter amori nostro perdito ut ad nos redire,"
Grant passage to our lost love so that they may return to us,
"Transeant."
Let them pass.

As we say the last words, complete stillness and silence eclipses the flat. Nothing other than the crackle of the candle wicks.

I wasn't really sure what I'd expected. Maybe smoke, or some kind of something, or... well, anything really. The well of uncertainty in my chest deepens further.

Dahlia seems to have the same thought as me. "Did it work?"

I scour the room, looking for any sign that the summoning has worked, "Buggered if I know..."

We both nearly jump out of our skin as Dahlia's phone rings from the coffee table. It's obnoxiously loud.

She groans when she sees who's calling her, giving a small sigh, before answering, "Hey Bri."

Bri, the manager of 'Poison', the bar Dahlia works part time at, a rock club and cocktail bar in the darkest part of Old Town. She's no doubt calling to ask her for last minute cover because one of the other bartenders has bailed. Again.

She looks over at me, whilst still listening on the end of the phone. "I-I don't know if I can tonight, Bri-"

I wave a hand at her to stop her saying no. "Don't miss a shift because of me!"

She holds the phone away from her ear, "Are you sure?"

"Completely," I attempt to give her a reassuring smile, trying to ignore my broken heart, like shattered crystal. The spell hasn't worked. Just like everything I try to do. "Just go. Honestly, it's fine."

She's still watching me, and it takes all of my willpower to keep the benign grin plastered on my face. She puts the phone back to her ear, "I can do tonight. I'll be over in about an hour." She hangs up, narrowing her eyes at me, "Are you really sure?"

"Stop asking me that!" I move away, trying to dodge her scrutiny. I kneel to blow out the candles and keep my attention locked on my task, masking the disappointment in my voice. "Sure, I'm gutted it didn't work. It was a long shot though."

I head to the sink and grab a cloth to begin scrubbing at the chalk outline, anything to distract me from the siren blaring one word in my head. Failure. "Honestly, I am fine. Go to work."

"And what are you going to do?" Her tone laces with scepticism.

42

"I'm going to clean this up, have a bath and drink a glass of wine." I wring out the cloth, smiling brightly and hoping sadness isn't screaming from my face. "Probably not in that order though."

She still looks conflicted about leaving, and when I see pity in her expression, I can't stop a surge of annoyance. I don't need people to feel sorry for me. Pity does nothing. It's as useful as a chocolate teapot!

"I'm alright, Dahls," I clear my throat, ignoring the lump in it. "Don't worry."

She loiters for a couple more seconds, until she realises that her sympathy is just pissing me off. But my annoyance isn't at her, it's at myself; for thinking that I might be able to do something other than enchant plants and flowers. I scrub harder at the chalk markings on the floor.

She lingers by the door. "Call me if you need me."

"To grab more wine?" I cut in. I twist the sponge tighter in my fist.

She gives me a cursory laugh, before walking to the door and I grip the sides of the sink as I hear it close.

I shut my eyes, trying to stamp down the shame at my naivety. It was stupid to think it would've worked. I was barely above a Fledgling when it came to summoning.

"Stop," I tell myself quietly. Mentally shoving the sadness and disappointment back down into the corners, along with the other shadows of grief and anger.

When I open my eyes, I notice that the ivy moved away from the bay windows and dusk is now settling across the skyline. I look down at the summoning spell and it takes all my self-restraint to avoid ripping it up into tiny pieces. I'm certain the spell works, it's just that I'm not powerful enough to do it. I wasn't her. I'm not Mum.

I toss the sponge down at the pentagram, stomping my way over to the fridge to pour myself a large glass of red.

Actually, screw using a glass, I can't be bothered with washing dishes, I'm going full feral!

I unscrew the bottle cap and take a large swig, walking back across the living room and absentmindedly kicking the edge of the salt ring.

I scowl down at the mess of candles, herbs, chalk and salt. "I'll deal with you later."

Heading to the bathroom, I turn on the taps of the bath, causing the moonflowers around the tub to recoil and flinch out of the way of the scorching fog.

43

"Sorry, I need a hot bath to boil the memory of tonight out of my head." I take another swig. "Actually, the last twenty four hours," another gulp. "Or maybe the last seven years!"

I drop a pink glitter bath bomb into the water, which immediately begins fizzing and foaming. As steam fills the bathroom I shed my clothes, staring down at the summoning spell peeking out of my pocket.

I don't know how I'd messed it up. I'd followed the spell to the letter and still...

It hadn't worked.

The room fills with so much steam, I can barely see the door. I set up the speakers on the side of the sink, connect them to my phone and begin blasting Alanis at full volume before sinking into the tub.

Mum loved 'Jagged Little Pill', she'd play it on repeat when I was little. So much so, that I was the only five-year-old in my Reception Class to know all of the lyrics to 'Hand in My Pocket'.

I wonder how she'd have reacted to me attempting to do a summoning spell. Would she have been proud that I'd tried to step out of my self-imposed apathy? Or would she have been disappointed that I'd failed, like I did with most things I tried to do?

Would she even be happy that I was still practising?

Or was the request in her will for me to marry a Mundane her way of telling me to abandon being a witch?

I swallow another large gulp of wine before shoving my head under the water. When I emerge, I see my skin is coated in tiny flecks of rose gold glitter. I lift my hands in front of my face, watching the sparkles twinkle in the dwindling daylight that bleeds from the skylight above.

I take another sip from the bottle, feeling drowsy, not only from the alcohol I've drunk on an empty stomach, but from the eventful, and ultimately disheartening, afternoon. I allow sleep to wash over me for a second. Just for a moment.

I jolt upright in the tub. I'd only meant to close my eyes for a couple of minutes, but the hot water is now tepid at best, and the music has stopped. The moonflowers seem to have recovered from the hellfire sauna I'd inflicted on them and are now back to their normal position around the bath.

I look at the nearly empty bottle... Well, that explains it, I'd gotten drunk. I could have drowned! But at least I didn't get sad and drunk; that's a win in my books!

44

I haul myself out of the cold water, my limbs feeling heavy after weightlessly floating for too long.

How long had I been asleep for? Just as I get one foot out of the bath, I hear a loud bang at the door.

Three more follow. They're so loud it sounds like they are trying to break the damn thing down! The noise startles me so much, I practically fall out of the tub, my knees slamming painfully into the sink as I try to regain my balance.

Why the bloody hell didn't I put the bathmat down? Dumb ass!

I regain my footing, grabbing my phone to check the time: midnight. I'd been in the tub for over three hours. How had I not woken up?

Another loud bang comes from the front door.

The knock is insistent, demanding.

The fucker isn't just going to go away!

"Twat!" I huff out a breath. I grab hold of my dressing gown that hangs from the radiator and wrap it around me.

I waddle out of the bathroom, leaving glitter and water in my wake.

I'm going to rip whoever that is a new asshole for banging on the door like the world's about to fucking end in the middle of the night!

I flick on the hallway light and throw the door open, my wet hair swinging like strawberry shoelaces in front of my face.

All the air escapes my lungs as I look at the person who's been pounding on my door.

He's taller than I remembered.

I manage to get enough oxygen to stammer. "H-How?"

Finn steps forward, a small smile on his face, "Hey Pupperfly."

Chapter Five

Esme

I stare open-mouthed at Finn. He looks the same: effortlessly handsome with his golden blonde hair, warm smile and those bright blue eyes. Wearing that grey t-shirt, I used to steal all the time when I slept at his, his favourite jeans and blue converse. The clothes he'd worn that night. The night he died.

So, I guess my dreams of him have evolved into full-blown hallucinations!

My knees buckle and his warm smile falters as he lunges to catch me before I collapse on the ground. We're in a weird crouching position, him partially scooping me into his lap. I clutch at his biceps, he's warm, strong… I pinch his arm.

"Ow!" He murmurs into my hair.

"Sorry!"

Ok, maybe not a hallucination, maybe I'm still dreaming? I could still be in the bath…

I pinch my own arm.

I dig my nails into my flesh. Pain.

Ok, guess I'm not dreaming either!

He chuckles as he pulls me up to stand, amazingly my legs don't falter again from the shock. "Is this your new way of saying hello?"

I pull back from him, looking up at his features. That teasing smile back on his face. The smile I'd fallen in love with so many years ago.

"H-how are you here?" I stammer, stepping back from him.

"I'm kind of fuzzy on the how," he shrugs, looking charmingly clueless. "I know why though: Because you wanted me to come back.

So here I am."

"But you're dead?" I say dumbfounded. How the hell is this possible? He can't be here. He's supposed to be in the ground, dead and decaying… not standing here looking just as gorgeous as he always had.

"Do I look dead?" He steps closer to me, brushing a hand through my wet hair. "Do I feel dead?"

"Well," I scramble back further, banging into the crystals which dangle along the walls. "No. But you are! Finn, how the hell are you standing here?"

He smiles again, his hands trail from my hair to wrap around my waist.

Maybe I have gone crazy. I've finally snapped after all the years of trying to hide from grief and it's finally taken my sanity. I suppose there are worse ways to go.

He nuzzles into my neck, his familiarity and affection is playing havoc on both my hormones and mental stability. "I got a message that I needed to come back. So, I did. They let me cross over."

"Cross over?" I parrot back at him, looking into those sky-blue eyes. "Was it the summoning spell?"

Not possible. I'm not powerful enough to have done that. Maybe because Dahlia and I did it, but even still, we aren't a coven. Did we really have enough power to help someone cross over? Could we? Could I?

He pulls back from me to give me a small nod. "It seemed to do the trick-"

A hysterical-sounding laugh escapes me. This is madness. Or some cruel trick of my mind.

I feel my legs start to wobble again and I'm grateful that his arms are still around me.

"I-I-I," my knees begin to shake again. "I need to sit down."

He practically carries me into the living room, my whole body won't stop shaking. I've gone into shock. Or I've gone insane. Or both, they aren't mutually exclusive.

He gently places me on the sofa that is still shoved over to the side of the room by the window. I scoot away from him as soon as he places me on the settee.

He looks over to the pentagram, the salt which has been kicked carelessly across the floorboards. He moves to the centre of the star, picking up the photo in the centre, my offering for the summoning.

He smiles at the picture, "You kept it."

My cheeks flush with the memories of us together entwined, so happy and in love. "Of course I did."

He turns his face back to me; concern pinches his handsome features. "You need tea."

He makes his way over to the kitchen counter, flips on the kettle, opens the cupboard and retrieves my favourite pearlescent pink teacup and matching saucer.

How the hell does he know where everything is? Or which cup is mine? This must be a dream. Maybe I didn't pinch myself hard enough.

I give my leg a sharp squeeze and yelp.

He finishes making the tea, walking back over and hands me the saucer. "If you keep doing that, you're going to be covered in bruises, Pupperfly."

"Sorry," I take the tea, my hands shaking violently. "It's just a lot to process..."

I take a sip. It's sweet. Five sugars. The way I always take it. He remembered.

"I understand," he sits down next to me. Close, but not touching.

"So," I place the cup on the coffee table, aware of the trembling in my hands, "you're not a ghost?"

He smiles softly, "I think we established that with the whole me being able to touch you."

"But you're dead," I furrow my brow. "So... a zombie?"

He chuckles again, and I remember how adorable those dimples were. Are. I guess past tense is a little redundant whilst I indulge in this incredibly vivid dream.

"I don't think so," he smiles, causing my heart to flutter. "But if I get the urge to start eating brains, I'll let you know!"

My own laugh bubbles from my chest. Way more high-pitched than normal. The flutters I'd felt in my heart kick into overdrive, and I feel hysteria taking over. Not real. This can't be real.

"This- this can't be happening!" I splutter, standing too fast and kicking the coffee table, which almost knocks the teacup from the surface. Panic is firmly taking the wheel and she's not letting go.

Finn becomes blurry, my eyes start to dip in and out of focus as my vision starts to dim.

So not only am I going batshit, but I'm also now about to pass out. I feel the faintness take over as my legs give out, and before imaginary Finn can reach me, my body slams to the ground. It hits the

48

wood floor with such force that my vision explodes into stars. I hear the loud smack of my head hitting the floor. But I don't really feel it. Not really. Just distant awareness that the numbing darkness is swallowing me whole.

I suppose a dreamless sleep is better than dealing with whatever warped fantasy my brain is creating whilst I'm unconscious?

But the figment moves to me. I'm dimly aware of being cradled and carefully carried. My head lolls against his broad, imaginary chest.

Kudos to my memory, the details are spot on, I can feel the heat from his skin and feel the definition of every muscle…

I'm being gently placed into a bed. The smell of blooming night jasmine. My room. The covers pull up over me.

"Don't worry," a voice says quietly. Strangely close, but also so far away. A hand strokes my hair. "I'll take care of you. Everything is going to be ok."

I feel the weight of the bed shift as the dream version of Finn moves away and unconsciousness moves closer.

Chapter Six

Nox

My vision comes into focus slowly. It always takes a few moments to adjust, that's to be expected.

The other senses swiftly follow. It's the same feeling every time, even in a different body. Possession's always a bitch, but this time we're playing by different rules. My rules.

Slipping into a new skin always feels strange, like wearing someone else's shoes. But my essence floods the human's body, stretching as languorously as a sunbathing cat. I fill the form from head to toe. This puny mortal doesn't even put up a fight, not that it would be much of a brawl. I mould into every muscle and nerve, shoving his consciousness into the back of his mind.

I clench his (now my) fingers, watching the veins in the forearms rise up against the corded muscle.

He's strong. That's good. That means he'll last long enough for what I need to do.

I sneer disdainfully at his scuffed and scruffy trainers. These need to be thrown into the fiery pits of Hell.

Moonlight makes its way across the room, and even in the dim light, I can take in the chaos. Magazines, books, clothes and general shit are scattered across every surface. I peer towards the kitchen area, and it's even worse. Fuck. Lip-stick smudged cups and empty bottles are piled high on the counter units along with a mountain of dirty dishes.

I've seen trolls with better cleanliness. Even the fucking floor looks like a demented toddler's been drawing on them. I peer closer, I half expected it to be a hopscotch grid, but no, it's a messily drawn pentagram surrounded by a scattered salt circle. A smile creeps across my lips.

I stand, stretching out the tall body, he's almost as tall as me,

50

and I bet he's a smug bastard about it. I'm certain I'm more handsome though. At least, I am when I can manifest my true body.

I trace my hand over the back of the sofa and walk around this den of squalor. I halt when I catch sight of movement in the corner of the room. Just a reflection.

I move towards the mirror. His limbs are stiff and slow from sleeping on the sofa.

I ruffle his blonde hair. He's handsome, in the way a golden retriever is. Wholesome. Innocent. A guy whose worst sin was cheating on a maths test in college. Which ironically it is, I checked his file before being ushered out the back exit. My being here is not strictly HR approved. And by not approved, I mean I'm forbidden from being here, but that's why it makes it even more satisfying.

I give my reflection a wink. Sure, he's not me. Not by a long stretch. But then again, how could he be? He lacks my charm, my alluring darkness that women gravitate to like moths to flames. He also doesn't have my bone structure, my colouring… but he does have my eyes. I don't imagine many mortals have amber whisky eyes. Strange. Possessions don't usually entail this change. Hopefully they won't be too different from his.

This body will do for now. Nowadays possession is seen as gauche, but this could work out nicely.

In fact, I peer closer at my new handsome face, this is the perfect disguise for a wolf in sheep's clothing. Because that's exactly what I am. A wild animal that's been tied up for too long. But now, I'm free.

I turn away from the mirror and wander down a narrow hallway. I am greeted by three doors. The one straight ahead of me is open, I move closer and see large puddles of water all over the floor of a nauseatingly turquoise bathroom. I lurch back from the visual assault of the room. Why humans feel the need to vomit colour all over everything I'll never know.

My home is monochrome and minimalist. This place is a fucking headache. I push open the door to the right, relieved to find this one is much more aligned to my colour palette. An empty bedroom, dark damask wallpaper hangs around a large four poster bed with black satin sheets and pillows. Sandalwood perfume lingers in the air but it's then that I'm hit with the overriding stench of Magick that permeates the atmosphere.

How did I only just notice? I blame what passes for a sense of smell on this poor excuse of a mortal, mine is at least twenty times more powerful. But now that I do smell it, it's overpowering, I have to brace myself as I step in further. Plants and charms drape the walls, and as I look over to the bedside table, I notice the runes, crystals and tarot cards: a witch's altar.

I smile darkly.

"Your kind still hasn't changed." I pick up a large slab of onyx, weighing it in my hand, enjoying the feel of something solid and sharp. "Witches and your bloody trinkets. You're such hoarders."

I freeze as I hear a small moan behind me, coming from the room opposite, hanging open like a question waiting to be answered. I toss the rock onto the black bed sheets before prowling towards the sound.

Stealthily I approach the threshold and push the door ajar.

Even in the meagre moonlight the obnoxious tirade of colours skull-fucks me so hard a wave of nausea passes over me. The entire room is bubble-gum pink. The walls, the bedding, the chandelier. Even the unconscious form in the bed has pink hair and her scent is as sickeningly sweet as everything in here! I've stepped into my own personal version of Hell. The irony is not lost on me as I enter the room and wince.

The only dark thing in here is the tiny fluffy orb, which comes bounding over to me from across the bed.

"Hello little imp," I say quietly to the kitten. I like cats, but not kittens. They are all claws and no class.

Speaking of no class…

Another whimper comes from under the duvet, and I prowl to the side of the bed facing the large window where moonlight pools across the sleeping witch.

It caresses her features and I carefully brush the pastel hair away from her face, making sure she doesn't stir. Her features are eerily elfin. Unnervingly long lashes flutter on high cheekbones, a full, teasing mouth and a nose upturned with impish defiance. Her face is befitting of a Fae, and as I tuck her hair behind her ear, I'm surprised to see her ears don't tip in points. Her lips part as another whimper escapes, her expression contorts into a frown. Her closed eyes are pinched shut and her lips turned downward. I edge closer, when I see the beads of sweat crowding her forehead above a huge purple bruise. I have to breathe in through my mouth to save my sense of smell, she reeks of spells and sugar. I shake my head, trying to clear the strange, intoxicating perfume emanating from her. I feel an unexpected pull tugging at my chest, which both infuriates and intrigues me. It's just because I'm smelling something other than fire and brimstone, I reason.

52

Another whimper comes from under the duvet as the nightmare clouds her mind. Maybe she's having to cope with living in a world that doesn't look like fucking Pepto Bismol? Her frown deepens and I stare down, transfixed. She is beautiful, despite her nauseating colour preference. In a brattish way. It's difficult to place her age, but by the state of her room I'd guess around eight.

The enchanted weeds around her bed shrink away from me as I glare at them. I move away from the witchling, walking to her dresser and notice more trinkets and tinctures. Witches are incapable of keeping a single surface tidy.

Witches and clutter: two things I absolutely despise.

Another wail from behind me, louder this time, followed by a wild thrash as she throws the covers off. She rolls to her other side. Her dressing gown falls open, my attention is drawn to the milky flesh of her thighs and her pert round ass which is now on full display.

I instinctively move forward, to do what? I have no fucking idea. To leer, to caress, to admire? It irritates me. I'm not supposed to feel like this, she's everything I hate. Witches are like children playing with toys that they don't understand. Selfish and small minded. And this one is no different. Juvenile, stupid and useless. She probably can't even spell a word without sounding out the letters first.

My feet remain firmly planted, and my eyes remain locked on the dreaming girl. "I don't have time for this."

I finally regain control of this body's limbs, take one more lingering look and leave the witchling to her nightmares.

I return to the shitshow of a living room and spot a picture in the middle of the chalk-drawn star. A polaroid of the body I'm inhabiting cuddling up with Pinky Pie. In bed. Interesting. So, the witch and him were together… explains the reaction this damned body had to her. Death has a way of forcing celibacy on a person, hardly a surprise that he would react to even the tiniest scrap of feminine flesh.

"Sorry pal", I think. But I'm not going to sit in the backseat whilst he gets his rocks off.

I spot a set of the keys on the coffee table and snatch them up. Finally, something useful...

Speaking of things to do. I need a drink. A real one. These witch bitches probably only drink diabetes in a glass.

I head out, closing the door as quietly as possible, and climb the spiral stairs to the front door. I step into the summer night, savouring the scents and sounds of the street. After so many years this city still conjures the same feelings. I shove my hands into my pockets and begin sauntering down the hill, reacquainting myself with the gentle hum of the city whilst its inhabitants sleep soundly.

I find a pub, and as I venture in, I hope my powers of persuasion aren't too rusty after being cooped up below for so many years. Not to mention the limitations of this body. Useless mortals. So damn fragile. Turns out golden boy has no cash and I'd completely forgotten I'd need it here.

Fuck, I really am out of practice.

I manage to beguile the barman, and he hands me a bottle of Glenfiddich. Before he has time to question his actions I make a swift exit.

I pull off the top of the bottle taking a hearty swig as I continue strolling.

Nothing compares to the warming burn of whisky. Although I'd never admit that back home… they'd crucify me.

I meander across the city, taking large gulps of the scotch as I go. I note how the streets and buildings have changed so much in my time away. But below the facades I see it, the bones of the city.

Centuries of banishment but I can still hear its heartbeat.

Feel it.

I can still feel her.

I continue until I arrive at the foot of the Royal Mile, where I halt. I know what it leads to. Nothing but painful memories. But even as I think it, as I will this stupid mortal body to stop, I begin my ascent. The pull to the castle. I can't fight it. No matter how much I try.

Passing the tourist traps, pubs, bars, coffee shops, even a quant wiccan shop. On and on. Until I see it. The looming presence of the towering turrets. The place where she'd taken her last breath. Screaming in pain as they'd burned her on a pyre of their own self-righteousness and fear.

That day Culum had returned to Hell with the news of what he'd seen at the castle. I'd broken his jaw and three of his ribs.

A black rage had engulfed me, and I had beaten my friend to a bloody pulp. And I hadn't cared. All I'd wanted was to eviscerate every single damned soul who had just stood there. Stood there watching as one of the purest spirits who'd ever lived was tortured to death.

They had to pay.

Every single one of them.

I'd made each one of them suffer the moment that they'd arrived in hell. The confusion on their faces when they realised where

54

they were. They thought their destination of the land of the pious was preordained. Stupid, arrogant fucks. Once they'd finished their orientation into their new afterlives I'd snatched them away. I inflicted my own judgement. My own righteous retribution, and as I stripped their skin from their bodies I'd smiled serenely. I did it hundreds of times and whilst they continued to scream, I would tie them to stakes and set them aflame.

Repeatedly.

But soon enough, their cries of anguish brought me little comfort.

All I wanted was her.

To be reunited with her.

But I'd scoured the cities of Hell and never found her. There was no way she would have been sent above to those self-righteous pariahs, but if she was neither above nor below there was only one possible place she could be- somewhere, somehow, her soul was still on Earth. I still couldn't believe my luck that I'd been conjured to the same place I'd lost Sarah all those centuries ago. Now all I need to do is find her.

I sneer up at the castle, wishing I could rip apart the bricks as easily as I'd torn limbs from the witch hunters' bodies.

The only thing I hate more than witches- the bastards who'd hunted and tortured them.

But both have stolen from me.

The witches took my freedom, banishing me from ever being able to walk the Earth again and the hunters took my Sarah.

But now, with this handy loophole, I've been able to find a way back. Flying under the radar of the curse, I can finally try and find that grimoire. Then I can get back the two things that matter most to me: Sarah and my body.

Culum had spent years looking for both the grimoire and any trace of her but if you want a job done properly you have to do it yourself.

I turn on my heel and begin walking down the hill.

This body, my body, sways and staggers. He's a fucking lightweight.

Whilst his limbs are as useless as overcooked noodles, my mind remains sober and razor sharp as I work to coordinate these clumsy appendages.

Maybe I shouldn't have drunk the whole bottle.

Fuck it, I'm celebrating.

I catch sight of my reflection in a shop window. I grimace at the scruffy t-shirt, trainers and jeans.

If I'm going to be inhabiting this mortal, I need to change a few things.

I continue until I see a shop to my liking. It's closed, but not to me.

I unlock and open the door and begin scanning the rails. Cashmere jumpers, crisp cotton shirts. I thumb through the racks, knowing exactly what I want. Culum always teases me for my penchant for fine tailoring, but I believe clothes make the demon, or as is now the case, the man.

I find a suit jacket I'd happily have worn back in Hell, but I can't wear them here; not without raising questions, and for now, I have to remain as under the radar as possible.

I sigh as I move away from the suits. Casual attire it is, then.

I pull out a pair of black heavy woollen trousers and a thin cashmere jumper from the shelves. I thumb the fabric: Luxurious but basic.

I take several pairs and find some black boots and a soft leather jacket to finish the ensemble.

After I undress, I am tempted to set the discarded clothing aflame, but decide better of it.

I look over at the floor to ceiling mirror. This guy dresses like a slob but at least he has the discipline to look after his body. Toned and muscled, in much better shape than I'd have been prepared to settle for.

My mind slips into a state of calm. My skin sings with relief, now free from the rough, scratchy fabric of whatever bargain bin scraps I'd been forced to awaken in.

I appraise my appearance, pleased with the result.

Not entirely what I'd choose to wear but a damn sight better than before.

I grab a bag from behind the counter and pack up some black t-shirts and trousers which I would be wearing for my stay.

If I must play the doting role of the no longer deceased boyfriend to the pink-haired harlot, I'm at least going to do it in better clothes.

Chapter Seven

Esme

I'm never drinking again.

I roll over as a pained groan escapes me.

Can you die from a hangover?

I've never been so drunk that I've hallucinated before- this is a whole new level of reckless stupidity for me. My mouth's dry and my head feels like… I reach up and touch my forehead.

What the hell?

So, I did fall over. Wonderful. I'm going to have a giant bruise. At least I can probably glamour over it.

Ink bounds up to me, his adorable little face presses into mine.

I try to bat him away, but he just thinks that means it's playtime. "Not now, baby. Mummy's dying!"

He meows loudly again in my face. Demanding little tinker.

"Alright, fine!" I throw the covers off me and stagger to the kitchen. My limbs feel like they are filled with lead… or pickled in wine.

I look down at the chalk and salt all over the floor. "Oh, good! I forgot about you."

My failed attempt at summoning- my only reward? The most vivid dream I've ever had in my entire life.

Stupid subconscious.

Stupid summoning spell.

I try to frown, but all it does is make my forehead scream in agony.

I feed Ink who begins to purr loudly as he eats. I flip on the kettle, but I immediately turn it off as the sound of boiling water is too loud for my delicate ears.

Maybe a nice hot shower will help ease my aching head?

I make my way to the bathroom but stop dead when I hear water running.

I check my watch... 6am... There's no way Dahlia is awake yet. Not if she finished late last night. She's not a morning person even when she does get a full eight hours.

I lean closer and I can definitely hear the shower running. I tiptoe back to the kitchen and grab a knife from the cutlery drawer.

No need to panic, it's probably just Dahlia. But if it is some stranger using our shower... Well, that's what the knife is for!

I push the door open, and I'm greeted by a wall of steam. I really need to get the fan sorted in here... I can't see a bloody thing.

"Dahls?" I call into the fog.

No response.

"Look," I try to sound more authoritative than I feel. "I don't know who you are, or why you're using my shower, but you've got exactly thirty seconds-"

The shower curtain pulls back, and I'm greeted by the sight of a very wet and very naked Finn.

"Or you'll join me?" he responds, his dimples blooming on his gorgeous face.

Ok, so not an hallucination. So that spell had actually worked. He is actually here. Oh fuck, it worked!

I drop the knife I'm clutching and nearly fall back out of the room. His cheeky smile drops as he rushes to stop me from tumbling over.

"I don't remember you being so prone to fainting," he says, his hands are all slippy and wet as he grips me.

It's true.

It's all true.

He's here.

How the hell has this happened?

I can barely summon a teacake, let alone a spirit from the beyond!

"I-I-I-" my vision fogs and as my head becomes lightheaded again. Oh, this is bloody terrific! I'm going to pass out again! I fight against the faintness and my vision comes back into focus as I gasp, "How?"

Finn peers at me earnestly. "We talked about this last night, don't you remember?"

"I kind of thought it was a dream."

He smiles at me. "Aw, that's so sweet!"

"No, I mean, it's just a little hard to believe!"

"I know babe, but I'm really here!" He gives my arms a small stroke. "I'm really real."

I slowly nod. "You're really real."

"Yep."

I look down, he's just as mouth-watering as I remember. "You're also naked."

His dimples return. "Also, yep."

I manage to look up at his face, which takes all my willpower. "Why are you naked?"

His eyes twinkle with amusement. "Kind of pointless to have a shower with clothes on."

Fair point. He's not wrong there.

"I was going to wake you to see if you wanted to join me," he smirks. "But then I saw that bruise, and thought it was best to let you get some sleep."

That's Finn all over. Kind. Sweet. Caring. Sexy as fuck…

I can't remember the last time I'd felt desire like this but turns out the sight of Finn lathered in shower gel was all I needed to awaken it.

I feel my cheeks flush.

"Erm well," I try to stand, but accidentally slip on the puddle he's making on the floor. Speaking of puddles! "I-I would, but erm, it's a bit soon."

Also, the whole him possibly being a zombie with a penchant for brains is just barely keeping my hormones in check. Very barely.

"Soon?" He pulls me closer to him and I can feel, and see, how much he missed me. "I used to have to sleep at yours because you demanded we had sex every night-"

"That was seven years ago!" I splutter. "I just need some time. You understand, right?"

I give him a quick peck on the cheek, and he immediately brightens. "That's ok right?"

He nods, a small smile on his face. "Take as long as you need," he runs a hand through his soggy hair, still lathered with shampoo. "I'm not going anywhere."

I stroke his jaw, still in a state of complete disbelief as he lifts me to my feet.

I don't know how I've managed this.

But somehow, I've got the love of my life back from the dead.

The fire in his expression grows again. "You need to let me finish my shower before…"

I lean into him, threading my fingers through his hair. "Before?"

He smiles down at me. "I carry you into the shower and show you how much I missed you."

"Oh."

"Yeah," His grin grows, along with something else which is taking all my willpower not to look down at. "Oh."

I pry my hands out of his, trying to keep my eyes locked on his face. Don'tlookdowndon'tlookdown-

I back away, accidentally slamming my shoulder into the doorframe. "I-I'll go make coffee!"

His smile remains on his face. "Mind the door, Pupperfly."

I rub at my now injured shoulder as I reverse out of the bathroom, another bruise. I'll add it to the collection.

I go back to the boiling kettle and brew up two coffees. Finn and I used to take our coffee the same way- cream and five sugars.

I place one of the cups on the coffee table whilst I cradle the other one in my hands. I don't know how I did it. But I did! I'd brought him back.

I stare at the floor, fixed on the pink chalk.

I hear the jingle of keys in the door and Dahlia walks in. Despite the shift from hell, she still looks gorgeous. As usual. She freezes in the doorway when she catches sight of me.

"What happened to you?" She makes her way over to me, her eyes fixed on my forehead.

"I fainted last night."

"Oh Goddess!" She sits down next to me, placing a comforting hand on my leg. "Are you ok? What happened?"

"Erm-"

She looks towards the bathroom. "Is the shower on?"

"Erm-"

I take a sip of coffee. Maybe caffeine will help me remember how to form sentences.

She leans forward to grab the mug on the side, taking a sip she makes a face of disgust. "Ez, I know you like your coffee sweet, but you don't have to make *all* coffee sweet!"

Just as she's talking, the bathroom door swings open, and Finn wanders out. He has a towel wrapped around his waist; a relief and a disappointment to me.

Dahlia springs up and drops the coffee on the floor. "What the fuck?!"

He quirks an eyebrow, pointing at the mug Dahls dropped in

her alarm. "Was that my coffee?"

Dahlia looks like she's on the verge of jumping out the window.

"Erm…." I flounder, holding out my mug. "Do you want mine?"

He shakes his head. "Nah, don't worry babe, I'll make one."

He looks at Dahlia, who looks like it's her turn to faint. "You want another one, Dahls?"

She stands frozen with her eyes wide with fear.

"Can you make her one, please?" I ask.

He smiles warmly at me. "Sure thing, babe."

He turns and makes his way to the kettle, and I have to stop myself from swooning when I see his tanned and muscled back.

Sure, he may be a corpse but he's still sexy as hell.

Dahlia grips my arm tightly; she whispers at me as though she's afraid Finn will overhear. "What. The. Fuck?!"

I clear my throat, "I know-"

"How is he back?!"

"The summoning spell worked like a charm," I offer weakly. "I guess?"

"You guess?!" Her fingers dig into my arm, creating another bruise. "The guy has been dead for seven years and he's walking around, talking and looking-"

"Hot as fuck?" I blurt.

Despite the terror in her face, I see her mouth twitch in a ghost of a smile. "Ez. Focus. For fuck's sake!"

"Sorry! Sorry!" I take a gulp of coffee.

I'd blame my dry spell… but Finn always had this effect on me. Even after seven years, he is still capable of sending my hormones into hyperdrive. When we were at Uni together, we barely left my bedroom!

I pull my brain back to the present, looking over at Finn as he busies himself making coffee. "He's fuzzy on the details about how he managed to cross over, but he came back because of the summoning."

He looks over his shoulder at me and smiles again.

I beam over at him. "He came back for me."

Dahlia's grip is so tight that my arm has gone past tingling to numb. "Can you let go of my arm please? I already have enough bruises!"

As she lets go the sensation in my fingers begins to return.

She sits back down on the other end of the sofa. "I mean it's weird," she keeps watching Finn. "But it is pretty badass…."

I suppose it is badass. In a 'I nearly had a heart attack from shock' kind of way.

Finn returns holding two steaming mugs. He hands one to Dahlia and sits down next to me. He smells like my cinnamon shower gel... definitely not like rotting flesh.

"Are you talking about me?" He gives me a cheeky grin.

"Can't really blame us," Dahlia must look as shocked as I did last night. "It's not every day that guys pop back from the dead after seven years!"

"It really doesn't feel like seven years to me," he says thoughtfully.

"How long does it feel to you?" I ask.

He smirks at my accidental innuendo.

"Timewise." I clarify and feel my face heat again.

He frowns slightly, looking down at the floor, like he's struggling to find the words. "Time moves differently there. It feels like it's only been a couple of days," his attention returns to me, "but it could also have been centuries. It's hard to explain."

Dahlia leans forward, her face earnest. "What was it like?"

Finn looks hesitant. "I'm not exactly sure-"

"Oh, come on!" Dahlia whines.

"No, seriously, I remember things happened, I remember feelings, but it's all kind of hazy, and I think it's fading, like waking from a dream." Finn's tone is uncharacteristically grave.

Dahlia looks sceptical. "Really? You aren't holding back?"

Finn looks uncomfortable and remains silent.

"At least we know for certain there's an afterlife!" I say brightly, trying to break the weird tension. "That's a good thing!'

"True," Dahlia gives me a wink. "Plus, now we can bring people back!"

"I think it may have been more luck than design." I look over at Finn, who seems preoccupied with staring at a beam of light on the floor. "I'm not even entirely certain how we managed it..."

Dahlia frowns. "Maybe it's more of a push and pull," she says slowly, carefully choosing her words. "You asked for someone you loved to be returned to you."

That would make sense that it can only work for people I care about. Not just some random stranger.

I quirk an eyebrow remembering that Finn is sitting in only a towel. "Do you maybe want to put some clothes on?"

A smile teases at the corner of his mouth. "This may be a first: Ez wants me to put clothes on!"

He's not wrong. I'd spent most of the time at Uni ripping them off of him, but I was aware that this conversation was already bizarre enough without the practically naked, resurrected guy sitting next to me. It's very distracting.

"Goddess, give me strength!" Dahlia cringes and takes a sip of her coffee.

I roll my eyes at her.

Finn gives me a playful nudge before sauntering off down the hall again. "I'll remove the temptation..."

I can't stop the laugh from escaping, which earns me a glare from Dahlia.

"Stop looking at him like that!" she warns.

I feign innocence, plastering a benign expression on my face. "Like what?"

"He's seven years younger than you now! He's still technically twenty-one!"

"So am I!" I laugh. "At least mentally!"

Dad's favourite words he uses to describe me, 'Immature', 'Reckless' and my personal favourite 'Irresponsible.' Although after last night, he might not be entirely wrong.

"I remember how you two were in Uni," she sounds resigned. "But can you just take it slow? I mean, we don't technically know if he's ok."

"Didn't you just say we are badasses for doing that spell?"

"We are," she agrees weakly. "But we don't know if he's… safe."

Finn walks back into the room. "Don't worry Dahls. I told Ez, if I get the urge to eat brains. She'll be the first to know."

Dahlia laughs, but it sounds bleak.

An image flashes in my mind of Finn and me in the throes of passion when he suddenly gets a hankering for my cranium. Talk about a mood killer.

I take in Finn's outfit: he has new clothes. Expensive clothes. Whilst they are still casual, there's no mistaking their quality. Also, they're all black. I've never seen him in black- it's usually navy or grey. The fit is tight, and the fabric hugs every single one of his muscles.

My mouth waters.

He looks gorgeous.

I give my brain a shake, trying to demist the fog of lust which is clouding my thoughts.

"You look…. good." My gaze is verging on a leer. "Where and

63

when did you get those?"

He shrugs. "Don't know, I woke up and I was wearing these and had a whole bag of shirts, trousers, boots and a new jacket."

"You woke up wearing a completely different outfit next to a bag full of expensive clothes?" Dahlia looks at him sceptically.

He makes his way over to the mirror, pulling a black leather jacket from the bag, which looks like it's worth more than everything in my entire wardrobe combined.

"And that doesn't seem odd to you?" She asks, her eyebrow is so arched it looks like she's drawn it that way.

"I mean this whole thing is a little unusual right?" I reply, trying to ignore my own worry that he's blacking out and doing shopping sprees. "What's a random bag of clothes in comparison to a dead guy walking about?"

I snap my mouth shut when I notice Finn's face. He looks offended.

"Sorry," I grimace.

Ok, so he doesn't like being called dead. Noted. Not sure what else I'm meant to call him.

"Would you prefer I say re-alived?" I offer.

He gives me a small nod, looking less like a puppy I just kicked.

"I wouldn't," Dahlia says. "It's a made-up word."

"All words are made up!" I reason.

I'm too tired and too hungover for 'Grammar with Dahlia' this morning.

I look back over at Finn, who is still pulling out clothes from the bag. How is he still finding more? Is it a Mary Poppins bag? Or did he learn to do summoning too?

I keep watching Finn. "Maybe we should do a bit of digging into that spell?"

Dahlia looks at me like I've got a head injury. Which I do have, so that tracks. "You think?!"

I could have sworn I'd read through it thoroughly before we did the spell, but I can't deny that Finn's mysteriously acquired wardrobe is bothering me. And you know, the whole possibility of him eating people. Usually when I black out the only thing, I had to show for it was an empty wallet and an angry liver!

I stand, my head feels like it's trying to split in two. "Ok, we'll go to the shop. Do some research on the spell and-"

"Do you want to maybe get dressed first?" Dahlia asks.

I look down at my dressing gown.

64

I nod. "Probably a good idea. Just give me five minutes."

"Might want to glamour those bruises as well?" she prompts.

"Are you going to be ok if I leave you with Finn?" I ask.

She moves to the kitchen, picking up the same knife that I'd brandished an hour ago. Great minds and all that.

Ok, not exactly what I had in mind.

"Please don't kill my boyfriend," I plead as I start moving to my bedroom, stopping only for a moment to admire Finn, who is still unpacking and assessing his new clothes.

"I won't kill him," she smiles sweetly, "because he's already dead."

I glare at her, "Don't say that word in front of him!"

I head to my room, hoping I can get ready quickly so that Dahlia doesn't have too much time to consider what to do with the knife.

As I see my reflection I realise 'quickly' isn't going to be an option. At least I look as shit as I feel. Not sure how that's a good thing, but at least they match.

I make my way to my bedside table and pull out my moonstone and clear quartz. I calm my breathing and place the crystals on my chest. I take in another deep breath and feel the crystals' strength ebb into my skin.

After a few moments, I can feel their healing power flow through me, and I use their essence to soothe my headache. I place the crystals on my forehead over the bruise and my head begins to lighten from the hangover. The pain from the injury begins to subside.

A minute or so passes and when I open my eyes I feel almost as good as new.

There's still a lingering soreness in my head, but to my relief the bruise and my attempt to give myself alcohol poisoning have all but disappeared.

Ink gives me a small meow of approval from my bed.

I lean forward; my eyes are bright, my skin glows and the bruise is now the lightest shade of lilac, which I can easily cover with concealer. Even my hair is brighter.

I peer into my reflection. "Not too shabby!"

I pull out a pink and white striped summer dress from my wardrobe and quickly shed my dressing gown, put on the garment and zip up the back. The dress swings prettily just a few inches above my knees.

I give my hair a quick brush, before pulling it into a messy, high bun and tease out a few of the loose tendrils so they frame my face. I add a quick flick of eyeliner and apply a ruby red gloss to my lips.

I smile at the mirror, surprisingly pleased with the result. I normally don't manage to summon enough Magick to be able to make a spot go away! This is damn near miraculous considering how much of a state I was in when I woke up!

I give Ink a playful tickle as I pass by him and make my way back into the living room. Hopefully, Dahlia has settled, and isn't still poised for action with that knife! No such luck.

She perches on the edge of the sofa, holding the blade and watching Finn like a hawk.

Finn has finally stopped unpacking. He's managed to find the TV remote and is now flicking through the various streaming channels.

"Oh cool! Netflix is still going!" he proclaims as I hear the familiar 'Dun Duuun!' of the loading screen.

Dahlia looks at me appraisingly with surprise. "Wow, didn't expect that level of glow up!"

Finn turns to me and that heat in his eyes seems to grow a little brighter. I feel a smile and a blush creep across my face.

"Seems to be a little more effective than when I've tried in the past," I give a small twirl.

Finn stands and pulls me into his arms, his hands grip my waist almost possessively. He pulls me in so close I can feel every single inch of him again and my mouth immediately waters.

Dahlia clears her throat pointedly. "Am I going to need to throw cold water on you two?"

The smirk on Finn's face suggests that's a possibility.

"Babe," I smile sweetly up at him. "We need to go to the shop…"

Dahlia stomps over to us, trying to be as matronly as possible; the knife she's still holding might be a bit overkill. Literally.

She scowls up at Finn. "Yes, and by we, I mean Ez and me. Finn, you're staying here."

He pulls me closer to him. I can't help but let out a giggle when I feel just how much he wants me.

"Can't I go as well?" He ignores Dahlia and looks down at me, with those big puppy dog eyes of his which have always made me melt.

"Stop doing the eye thing!" Dahlia snaps. "Ez, we're going now!"

She grabs hold of my arm and starts tugging me out of Finn's grasp.

I give him an apologetic smile. "We'll be back soon, Ok, babe? Meanwhile, you stay here. Watch TV and don't leave. Please."

The last thing I need is someone to spot a guy coming and going out of our flat. Or even worse, recognising him.

I've got to do something about that...

"How long will you be gone?" he asks, a lost look on his face.

"No more than a few hours," I say as Dahlia continues to drag me towards the door. "I'll pick you up food on the way back."

He brightens at the promise of that, the boy loved his food. Loves. He loves his food.

It is going to take a while to get used to saying that.

Dahlia slams the door before I get the chance to say bye to him and I stand sulking in the stairwell for a moment.

"Oh, come on," she grimaces. "I remember how long it took you two to say goodbye before. We haven't got the time for your lengthy declarations of love to-"

"Ssh! Don't say his name out here!"

She quirks an eyebrow. "Because the stairs are the biggest bunch of gossips?"

"Just...." I look around. "Just let's be careful."

She huffs out a breath of exasperation as we begin climbing the stairs. "I'd forgotten what you two are like together," she grimaces. "It's nauseating. I'm going to need to soundproof my bedroom." She looks over at me, "Or maybe I could just do yours!"

I smile at her as we begin walking down the cobbled streets, "I thought your advice was not to do anything with him?"

"Only until we know he's not going to start craving human flesh," she links her arm through mine. "Once he has the all clear, by all means go for it. You need to get it out of your system. It's been years since I've seen you look anywhere near that interested in a guy!"

Seven years precisely. No one made me feel the way Finn does.

"Thanks Dahls, I appreciate you taking such an interest in my sex life!"

"Well for the past few years there's been no sex life! It's nice to know that it's not dead at least!"

We continue walking down the street. "Going to keep making dead jokes huh?"

She grins. "Only until they stop being funny."

I glare at her, and her smile widens. "I should clarify; funny to me!"

"Just don't say that kinda shit in front of Finn."

"Fine, fine! I'll try not to piss off the potential zombie," Dahlia halts, her smirk evaporating. "Actually, that's pretty sound advice."

Chapter Eight

The witches finally leave. Whilst they were dithering, this poor guy's dick was on the verge of an explosion.

Possessions are incredibly subjective, it's possible to be a passenger in the back of a mortal's mind. Or one can dip in and out, taking control as and when it suits. But full possession is always cautioned against as the flesh will corrupt quicker.

I keep my mind peaceful and still, ignoring the glittering, chaotic whirlwind as the women buzz around me. I must remain calm. Even as I feel time slipping through my fingers like sand. It won't be long until my absence back home is noticed.

I feel a slight push from the mortal's consciousness. A petulant, sulking shove and I quickly squash it down.

Turns out human bodies don't like being rented by demons and I need to keep him alive as long as I can.

"You can watch 'Spongebob Squarepants' soon," I mutter to him, picking up the picture from the floor. I walk back over to the mirror holding it up against my reflection. I look exactly like the skin suit. All but the eyes. His are as clear and bright as the summer sky, but mine? Mine have the fire and the hue of long aged whisky. I fish into the shopping bag, pulling out a pair of Ray-Bans to mask them.

"There," I give my reflection a smile. "Problem solved."

I feel the mortal's annoyance crackle in the back of my mind.

"Oh, come on, pal," I groan. "I know it's not an ideal solution, but we have to make the best of it. Besides, your brain is blood deprived, and your dick needs a break!" I absent-mindedly gather the cups and turn on the kitchen tap.

I'm actually doing this idiot a favour and trying to keep him

69

alive; the pink haired cock tease is determined to give him a libido induced aneurysm! I'm riding shotgun on this guy's second shot at puberty!

I glare down at the flagpole in my trousers, resisting the urge to punch his manhood. I keep my hands busy, scrubbing at the food-crusted plates and bowls.

If he can't get control of his body, I fucking well will.

I roll my neck, attempting to ease the tension and frustration that courses through every muscle and through both of our minds.

I've got to get a message to Culum. I need someone to cover for me. My banishment was as much the higher powers of Hell as it was the coven's desire.

I feel a surge of achievement when I make quick work of the dishes. Cleanliness reigns supreme on the drying rack within a few short minutes. One small island of order in the ocean of chaos. I pluck a large butcher's knife from the soapy water and head to the bathroom, wincing again at the colour of the walls.

I quickly fill the tub with lukewarm water and use the knife to make a small slice across my palm. I squeeze out nine drops of blood into it.

Something rubs against my ankles, and I see the small, black bundle of fluff from last night. I give him a nudge away with my leg. I'm not in the mood to play cat sitter whilst I make a call.

"I summon thee, Crepusculum Praestigiator, Twilight Trickster, Scourge of Hell, Jester of the Damned."

Culum appears in the water, a look of confusion on his face. With his shaved head and skater clothes, he could pass for a young delinquent mortal. I still argue I'm the best-looking demon in Hell, but Culum gives me a run for my money with his boyish charm and perpetual smirk.

At least I outrank him, so however much he hates it, I'll always win in our pointless competition.

He arches an eyebrow. "Who the fuck are you?"

I can't stop the humour creeping into my voice; it'd be so easy to screw with him, but I really don't have the time. I've no idea how long the witchlings will be out for.

"Technically I'm your boss," I click my tongue disapprovingly. "A bit of respect goes a long way, Culum."

Culum's face edges closer to the surface of the water. "Nox?"

I smile, removing the sunglasses and giving him a wink. "The one and only."

"What the hell are you doing in that meat puppet? I thought

70

you couldn't make it up there anymore?"

"Let's just say, the opportunity presented itself and it was too good to pass up."

"So, you've found a way to get to Earth?" He blinks in disbelief.

"I found a loophole," I correct him, giving the kitten another gentle nudge away with my foot. "You know me and rules don't get along."

"And," he sighs. "Let me guess, whilst you're playing stowaway you want me to cover for your ass?"

"Well since you offer so nicely…"

"For fuck's sake!" he grumbles.

"What was that?" I let the fire erupt from my eyes, allowing molten heat to flow freely.

Culum quickly shuts his mouth. "Nothing."

"That's what I thought," I allow my gaze to cool; the last thing I need is to burn holes in this mortal's retinas. "Just keep them distracted. If they ask where I am, just say I'm staying away from the whole social scene."

"-Still pining away for that mortal witch?"

I let the silence hang.

He continues, "You're still trying to find her, aren't you?"

"Well, she's not down there." The kitten at my feet lets out a yowling meow. "There's only so many places she can be."

He nods slowly. "I guess so."

"It's not just something I can switch off."

Some bonds are too strong to break. It may have been centuries, but I can still remember her smile. Her laugh. Her strength. Somewhere on this shitty little mortal coil she's being hidden away.

"How do you think you'll find her?" Culum asks, dragging me back to the present.

The kitten winds around my ankles, purring loudly. This stupid animal has zero self-preservation.

"I need to find that grimoire," I answer.

Culum looks doubtful. "The one that coven used? It's centuries old, there's no way it'll have been preserved."

"It's bound in demon skin," I counter, "blessed by the devil and the dark sisters themselves. Even if the whole world burned, that book would be fine. It's just hidden. Luckily, I'm persistent."

Culum gives me a look of begrudging respect. "That's an understatement. Is there anything I can do?"

"Do some digging. Quietly. I know you've asked before but

71

ask again. Someone down there must know where those damned witches hid that grimoire. I don't believe for a second that in the entirety of Hell no one knows anything."

Culum's smile turns sinister. "Maybe they just haven't been asked nicely enough?"

I return his grin. Culum's technique for questioning is even more brutal than mine.

"Meet me in two nights at our local," I say, dragging his twisted little mind back to the matter at hand. "Do you think you can manage that?"

He gives me a nod, all business. "On it."

"Just remember," I point into the water. "Not a soul, living or demon, can find out I'm up here or-"

"Or there'll be hell to pay?"

I smile, but my grin has lost all humour. "Exactly."

Chapter Nine

Esme

"Found anything?" Dahlia calls from her corner of the shop.

"Nope," I groan from the other side. I'm nestled between mystical charms and dark spells, propping my back up against the shelves.

As soon as we'd unlocked the shop (before promptly locking it back up again), I'd stationed myself in this corner and the flowers have been blooming next to me ever since; they seem to have learnt some new colour coordination's and they're showing off: pretty cornflower blue ebbing into a vibrant fuchsia. They don't do anything by halves!

I have checked every single spell book on summoning and have definitely read through all of them. Twice.

My knees crack as I stand; that's what I get for sitting cross-legged for three hours. "Maybe we didn't do anything wrong?"

I walk over to Dahlia who is sitting with her own pile of books. She looks up at me, her eyes blurry and bloodshot from scouring tiny fonts and handwritten texts.

"Maybe you're right, but I really think we should keep checking?" She closes a book, arching an eyebrow. "How do you account for him losing time?"

"I have gone through every one of our books on summoning, and as far as I can see we did everything correctly," I shrug. "And the losing time? Well, we all do that. That's not specific to Finn! How often have we sat and binged an entire series and forgot to go for a pee break?"

"But what about-"

I shove the books I'd been reading back into the shelves with a little too much force. "Can I not just be happy that our spell worked?" I turn to face her, not hiding the wobble in my voice. "Can I not just be happy to have him back?"

I don't want rationality. I just want to feel something other than grief and sadness. Just for a little while.

She stops whatever rationale is about to come out. I've won the argument by playing the emotional turmoil card.

"I've missed him for seven years, Dahls," I say. "Can I not just be happy he's here?"

She gives me a small nod.

I smile at her gratefully. "Thank you."

"OK so, in the interest of being supportive," she sighs. "How about I open the shop and you head home?"

I quirk an eyebrow. "Dahls, are you actually encouraging me to have a love life?"

"Or any kind of life really!"

"Hey!" I snap. "I have a life!"

"Oh sure," she rolls her eyes. "By the way, work and Tinder dates don't class as a life. At least not a happy one!"

I look down at my watch, it's just past 1pm and we've missed out on four hours of trade. Although the idea of leaving Finn alone in the flat is starting to make me twitchy.

"Are you sure you wouldn't mind?" I ask.

She pulls a face, "I'm pretty sure I can handle it! I had to deal with an entire bar of drunk students last night!"

I quickly return my final book to the shelf and before she can change her mind, I skip to the door to flip the sign to 'Open'.

"Thanks," I say. "I owe you one!"

"I'll add it to the list!"

As I exit, I almost barrel into a young woman with auburn hair in an old-fashioned outfit. I don't get a chance to see her face as she's practically running up the sloping cobblestones.

She's probably a guide for one of the historical tours around the city and I guess she's late. I bet she's the type that takes their job a little too seriously. Just as I'm about to call out to her, she's swallowed up by the crowd. It's so quick. If I wasn't so distracted I'd be sure she had just disappeared.

I give my head a shake. I've got bigger things to worry about. Like an unsupervised, undead boyfriend in my flat, who might accidentally set the place on fire!

I power walk up the hill, before halting at one of the pharmacies.

If Finn is going to be able to go out and have a normal life, he's going to need a disguise. The last thing I'd want to happen is for someone to recognise him and pass out from shock. Like I did last night.

I make my way in and stop when I reach the hair dyes, quickly snatching up one of the semi-permanent brunette shades.

Sure, I love him blonde, but it won't do us any favours when it comes to him walking about in public!

I practically throw myself into the flat as I unlock my front door.

"Hello?" I call out, making my way down the hall. "Finn?"

It's eerily quiet. Oh Goddess, what if the spell was only temporary? What if it's already worn off? He can't have gone, he only just got here!

I make my way to the living room, and as I cross the threshold I'm snatched up and pressed against the door. I instantly forget about the carrier bag in my hand, and it drops to the ground.

Finn picks me up easily, like he always did. His hands greedily grip my ass and the backs of my thighs.

"I missed you babe," he nuzzles close to my neck. His hair tickles me as he peppers my throat with kisses.

"Is that so?" I say breathlessly.

"Also," he traces his lips up to my jaw, "I realised you've not given me something yet-"

I arch an eyebrow. "What's that?"

He moves his face away from my neck to give me a cheeky grin. "A welcome home kiss."

I feel my own smile broaden. His eyes smoulder with desire. "Is that all you want?"

I roll my hips in his hands and hook my legs around his waist. He groans, repositioning his grasp to carry me into my bedroom.

I can't stop a giggle escaping. "How'd you know this is my room?"

"Pupperfly," he places me gently on my rose print bedspread. "No one loves pink as much as you do!"

I lie on my back, gazing up at him, breathless as he begins crawling up the bed, trailing kisses across my bare legs.

His mouth continues its ascent up to my left knee. "Dahlia could never cope with this amount of pastel..."

He traces his fingers up my legs, my thighs, subtly pulling my dress up higher and higher. My core tightens as I look down at his gaze, his chiselled face completely focused on mine.

He pauses, awaiting my reaction.

I clear my throat, finding my voice. "Don't you want a welcome home kiss?"

He smiles at me, and again, I can't believe he's here. He's too perfect to be real.

Moving up the bed, he leans over me, and I remember all the times we'd spent our days and nights wrapped up in each other.

He rests one arm above my head, gently stroking my hair, the other cups my cheek so tenderly he makes my heart hitch. "Yes please."

Our control is on the verge of breaking, but he remains as considerate as he always was; he never needed to push, but he always knew when to take it slow.

He strokes my bottom lip with his thumb. "Is this ok?"

I nod, unable to find the words. He places a soft tentative kiss on my mouth but as the seconds slip by, I feel him gently pry my lips open wider with his thumb. His hand moves from my lip to my neck, gently holding me in place, as his mouth continues to explore mine.

This welcome home kiss has quickly moved from sweet, to passionate, to borderline pornographic. He gently nips at my bottom lip, which causes me to retaliate by grabbing hold of his and sucking it into my mouth.

He groans, and all my good intentions about taking it slow disappear. His kisses always make me lose myself: intoxicating and all consuming. My legs wrap around his waist again and my dress rises past my hips. The hand at my neck makes its way down past my waist and he shifts to make room for his hand.

I feel the gentlest trace of his fingers on my inner thigh, and I break away from the kiss. Flashes of 'Night of the Living Dead' play in my mind.

"Maybe we," I say breathlessly, "take it just a little slower?"

I hate myself a little for saying this, but I remember what Dahlia said. Maybe it was sensible to tread carefully? Damn Dahlia and her logic! Damn my stupid survival instinct! In some ways I'm pleasantly surprised, I wasn't even sure I had one.

Finn pauses, and with what looks like great effort, he eases himself off me and lays down by my side. I instantly miss the weight of him.

He looks over at me. "If that's what you want."

No, it's not what I want! But now I'm worrying that you'll rip my skull open and feast on my head with the same level of feral hunger I have for late night ramen!

Finn's arms linger around me, he traces small circles on the underside of my knee.

Before my brain has a chance to short-circuit, and before I tell my newfound survival instinct to 'fuck off', I blurt, "I got you something."

"If it's not you naked and spread out like a banquet for me, I'm not interested." Another image of Finn devouring me, and not in a good way, creeps through my mind.

He bites on his bottom lip before smiling apologetically. "Sorry."

I place a small kiss in the corner of his mouth. "That would definitely be stretching the meaning of a welcome home kiss!"

Before he leans over me again, and I lose whatever remains of my self-control, I wriggle out of his grasp.

"I wanted to make sure you could go out and, you know, live," I skip to the living room and collect the carrier bag. "But there may be some people who might think you look familiar…" I flounder.

"To someone who passed away seven years ago?"

I nod. "Exactly. So," I pull out the cardboard box and fling it onto the bed next to him. "I thought changing your hair colour may help."

He picks up the box, arching an eyebrow in amusement. "So, you'd rather my hair was 'dark chocolate'?"

I sit down at the edge of the bed, a nice safe distance. "I wouldn't. Personally, I love you blonde. But," I place a hand on his, "I thought you might want to go out and explore. Live a bit. So, you don't feel cooped up in here."

He continues to look sceptically at the box. Like I've just given him a weird and slightly insulting gift.

I make a move to stand, feeling self-conscious. "Forget it. It was a stupid idea-"

"No," Finn stops me, grabbing hold of my hand to keep me next to him. "It's possibly the second sweetest thing you've ever done for me."

Heat floods my cheeks. "What's the first?"

He smiles at me. "Bringing me back to life of course."

He twines his fingers through mine as he leads me into the bathroom, and I pull out the instructions and gloves.

I point at his expensive looking shirt. "You might want to take that off?"

A smile tugs at the corner of his mouth. "Is dying my hair just a cheap excuse for you to get me to take my top off?"

"I think there are less messy ways to do that!"

He obliges, revealing an expanse of tanned skin and a toned torso, before sitting at the edge of the bath. I drape a towel around his shoulders, wishing it were my legs.

Bad brain. Bad, bad brain. Also, speaking of brains? Remember zombies? I mentally scream at myself.

I quickly brew up the hair dye mixture and begin massaging the dark brown concoction into his golden locks.

He moans appreciatively. "You're good at this."

I laugh. "You just like me playing with your hair!"

"Can you blame me?" His tone is so earnestly sweet. "I've missed you so much, Pupperfly."

I continue to work it in, the dark dye eclipsing the blonde.

When I finish coating every strand, I move over to the sink and set a timer on my phone for twenty-five minutes. I lean my back against the mirror.

"So do I just sit here," he smiles, "whilst you admire my naked body?"

"Half naked." I correct. "I saw a fair share of your body earlier."

I also remember my clumsy attempt to flee, the slight pain in my shoulder a persistent reminder of its collision with the doorframe.

Mischief twinkles in his eyes, "As good as you remember?"

"Better," I answer, before I can stop myself.

A beat of heated silence simmers between us.

"So," he leans his hands behind him across the rim of the tub and I have to look away as his muscles flex, "is it wrong to hope that you're still single?"

I laugh. "Very much so."

"No one special?"

"No one like you."

"What have you been doing for the last seven years?"

"Aside from missing you?" It's meant to sound light-hearted, but the weight of truth grounds my words. "After you… and mum… were gone. I dropped out of Uni. I just didn't see the point in it anymore. I'd mainly gone just to make Mum happy and without her there, or you to keep me going… I no longer saw the point in it. Mum left me as the co-owner of her shop and Dad has the other half. With a caveat that I will inherit it all as long as I'm married by the time I'm 30-"

Finn arches a brow. "That's the weirdest retail management

requirement I've ever heard!"

"My mum put in her will," I rest my head against the wall, "that if I'm not married, or at least engaged, the shop goes to Dad," I fidget, "and if he owns it fully. He'll sell it-"

"He can't do that, surely?" Disbelief on his face. "He knows how much that shop meant to you guys."

"He can, and he will," I sigh, the thought of the shop being sold and gutted into some tourist trap makes my heart twist. "He says it's too painful for him to run it..." Dad's excuse feels even more unbelievable as I say it aloud.

"So that's why you brought me back?" His voice is serious, but I see how his eyes twinkle. "Because you need a fiancée?"

"You're more than that," I fidget as my shyness blooms. "You're the only person I could ever see a future with."

He looks at me sadly, "I'm so sorry I went out that night. If I hadn't... things would have been so different."

Another beat of silence. I still remember it vividly. Although the sting of that memory is now sweetened with his return.

I clear my throat, "I suppose if it hadn't happened at least we wouldn't look like a cougar and her toy boy!" I tease. We don't look that different in age at all. If anything, with his newly acquired wardrobe, he looks older.

I'm uncomfortable about his apology for that night. There's no denying how different my life would have been.

"I have to keep the shop," I say to remind myself more than him. "I have to do right by Mum." I hate how much resignation there is in my tone. "She did so much for me. I have to keep a part of her alive. Even if to some people it's just bricks and mortar."

It wasn't just a shop. It never was. It holds a piece of Mum's soul, and I must protect it. I'm not sure Dad will follow through with his threat, but I can't risk it.

"So," he rolls his shoulders, "this is a relationship of convenience?"

"Nothing about summoning you was convenient!" I trace my trainer across the checker floor tile. "Although, I didn't have to sacrifice a goat. So, I suppose that's a good thing!"

"That's my girl," his face blooms with pride. "Always finding the positive."

His girl. A flutter skips in my chest as he says that. I haven't been anyone's girl in... years.

"Plus," I kick at the ground, "it helps that I still fancy the absolute arse off of you!"

"Is that so?" His grin widens as he stands, walking towards me and resting his hands on either side of my face.

"I know you asked me to take it slow," his breath warms my skin, "but I just want to remind you that every cell in my body is screaming at me to touch you…"

His hand strokes my hair, pushing it back off my shoulders to expose my neck. "Kiss you," he leans down, his mouth hovers over my throat and my heart speeds to a frenzied rhythm as he places a tender kiss on my neck. "Lick you," his tongue traces up to my ear lobe.

My resolve is faltering.

"Bite you," he gently nibbles on my ear lobe and causes my breath to hitch.

Resolve crumbling…

His lip brushes against my skin as he whispers, "Fuck you."

As if on command all the moisture in my body pools between my legs.

He still turns me on so much I can barely think straight.

I clench my thighs, naively hoping it'll ease the tingling, but all it does is make me feel even more heady with lust. My self-control and self-preservation are hanging by a thread.

Just as I'm about to reach for him, the alarm on my phone goes off.

"We need to rinse the dye out," I say throatily, "or else it'll burn your scalp." I can't decide if my phone saved me or if I want to flush it down the toilet.

He gives me a small nod before kneeling over the side of the bath, waiting for me to rinse the colour from his newly darkened mane.

I test the water, making sure the temperature isn't too hot before wetting Finn's head. He moans as I massage his scalp, I hold the showerhead over him until the water runs clear.

I give his hair a gentle tug, before kneeling behind him and turning the faucet off. My front is flush against his back muscles. I trace my hand down his naked chest and bring it lower to…

Stop. A voice in my head orders, my hands freezing at the command.

"What's wrong?" Finn's voice is bubbling with anticipation as my hand hovers near his belt.

Don't tell him anything. The voice in my head demands.

The voice is strange. Not my normal internal monologue but one filled with authority.

My hand continues to float suspended in midair.

I give my head a shake, trying to clear the presence of this new voice but as I move to trace my hand against Finn's torso the voice shouts louder.

I told you to stop!

I flinch back, like the voice has just struck me and tumble back onto the tiled floor.

"Are you alright, Pupperfly?" He turns and gathers me up in his arms.

That's what I'd like to know! What the hell is going on?

Just before I can say anything, my phone blares a loud insistent ring.

Dahlia's name flashes up on the screen. "Dahls? What's wrong?"

"Ez," her voice is hushed and ominous. "Whatever you do, don't freak out and don't say anything weird."

I keep my face neutral, giving Finn a small apologetic smile as I stagger to my feet and lurch out of the bathroom whilst I rub my freshly bruised ass.

"Ok," I say quietly. "What's up?"

"When Finn came back," I hear rustling in the background. "Did he mention anything about seeing anyone or doing anything?"

"No?" I look behind me, checking that he's not followed me into the living room. "Between the concussion and the shock, I didn't really think to ask him about his whereabouts after I passed out."

"Fuck," she curses down the line.

"Why?" I flick the kettle on, hoping the sound will mask some of the conversation.

"Because Agnes just came in and told me there was another murder last night," I hear the panic in her voice. "Another witch. And it was bad. Like, really, really, bad," I hear her take in a shaky inhale. "Just outside Old Town and you know with the whole possibility of Finn being a zombie-"

I grimace at the word, thankful that I can hear Finn rustling around in my bedroom.

I look behind me to double check, before saying, "do you think he might have-"

"Ssh!" she hushes me. "Don't say anything. But I think it could have been… Finn."

"Why do you say that?"

"Because," I hear more clattering in the background of the call, a customer loudly chattering near Dahlia, "the heart and the brain

81

were ripped out."

"Fuck," I clutch the sink. Black spots burst in my vision.

"My thoughts exactly," she says grimly.

Now it's my turn to watch Finn like a hawk, attempting to look casual, whilst I clutch the same butcher knife behind my back. Weirdly this is the most the knife has ever been used. Well, except for the time when I got trapped inside the flat and had to jimmy the lock. That was an expensive repair, plus Iris the Formidable was not happy.

Finn wanders in, that adorable smile plastered over his face. He can't be a killer, he's too gentle and kind.

Who up until yesterday was dead, the new voice in my head deadpans. *Who also has blackouts.*

I give Finn a benign smile, as I barrel past him and sprint to the bathroom and lock the door.

"Ok," I stare at my reflection, my eyes wide with alarm. "So, are you a new voice in my imagination or, the more likely option, am I finally going crazy?"

Silence reigns supreme in my head.

"Oi," I lean in closer. "Whatever, or whoever the fuck you are, you need to knock it off! Finn is the sweetest guy and there's absolutely no way he'd kill someone."

"Babe?" Finn calls through the door.

I jump and accidentally head-butt my already bruised forehead into the mirror, "Fuck!" If his dastardly plan is to kill me with a series of mild contusions, it's working.

"Pupperfly," the bathroom door handle jiggles. "Is everything alright in there?"

"Fine!" I call back, my voice is unusually high. "Everything's fine!"

Just you know, you might be some cannibalistic zombie. But other than that, everything is peachy! I need Dahlia to come home. Right now. Also, where's my knife? Fuck, I think I left it on the sofa with my survival instinct.

"Can you, erm," think faster, think faster! "Can you, erm, get me erm, er, er-" lie faster! Lie faster!

"Oh babe," he calls through the door, as if suddenly understanding something. Which would be great. If I know what it is. "Is it that time of the month?"

"Er," fuck, why can't I think of a convincing excuse? I look at my reflection, but she's no fucking help. "Sure?"

"Don't worry," his voice is full of concern and care. Nothing cannibalistic. "I'll be back soon."

I hear him move away from the door and relief washes through me. I pinch the bridge of my nose, a tension headache blossoming in my skull.

"Wait," registering what he said. "Back soon?"

I throw the bathroom door open, just in time to hear the front door click closed.

"Double fuck!" I bolt across the hallway, in hot pursuit but Ink seems to decide this is a game and he wants to play, he darts under my feet and to stop me from squishing him, I collide with the kitchen unit, knocking myself off balance and landing in a broken heap.

I'm back on the floor. Again. "Make that triple fuck."

Ink bounds over, nuzzles my face, gives a loud purr and then scratches me.

"It's a good thing you're cute," I grumble, lifting myself to sit, my hip screaming at me from where it met the very sharp edge of the counter. I'm certain that by this point, even my insides are bruised.

The front door unlocks, and Dahlia comes whirling in, anxiety is screaming through her pores. She halts in the doorway looking at me sitting on the floor.

"Where's Finn?" She looks around the room.

"He went out," I wheeze as I lurch upwards, just about managing to get vertical again.

"What do you mean he went out?" Dahlia's eyes look like they might shoot across the room.

"He thought I needed supplies," I rub at my hip as I limp towards the medicine cabinet in the kitchen. I need a bucket of painkillers and a mountain of quartz.

"Supplies for what?" her voice, full of alarm, follows behind me, "for trapping a potentially dangerous killer? Also," she halts, "why are you limping?"

"My hip and the counter finally decided to say, 'fuck it' and smash," I throw two tablets in my mouth and shove my head under the tap, trying to avoid my hair getting caught in the drying rack, which is weirdly full of clean dishes. Sure, he might be a killer, but at least he's tidy!

She shakes her head, "I don't understand a single thing you just said."

I groan, looking skyward, or I guess, ceilingward. "Finn went to get me period supplies, because he's sweet and thoughtful and-"

"You're on your period?" Dahlia's eyebrows shoot up. "I thought we weren't on for another week."

"Dahls," I pinch the bridge of my nose again, "that is not the thing to focus on right now!"

"You're right," she glares. "It's the potential murderer who's now wandering the streets!"

"He'll be back in a few minutes," I counter. "He'll just be getting me the usual." And by usual, I mean a jumbo pack of sanitary towels, a huge bar of Galaxy and hopefully a vat of double chocolate ice cream.

"Do you really think it wasn't him?" Her voice barely above a whisper.

"I don't know, Dahls," I look around the kitchen. The sides have been wiped down and are now sparkling in the afternoon sunlight. "All I know is the Finn I know would never hurt a fly!"

She asks the question that I'm trying to smother in my brain, just as I hear the front door unlock. "But how do we know that he really is the Finn that you knew?"

"Easy peasy," I lean in, as my injured hip screams at me. "I'll spy on him."

Chapter Ten

<u>Nox</u>

This is the problem with backseat possession; I must be here all the fucking time.

Normally I can have some downtime- return to Hell, relax and generally take a more laissez-faire approach.

But that's completely out the window. I can't very well be popping back and forth without raising suspicion. It's better for me to stay away completely.

I'm trying to keep myself occupied and out of the mortal's thoughts. I occupy myself by reminiscing about the past, but inevitably that leads me back to the grimoire, and the frustrating mystery of where the witches hid it. I wonder about my body, the one I'd manifest when I was able to walk the streets, before I was a fucking fugitive. I miss that body. Granted this one isn't bad, except it's like living inside a hormonal teenager.

And now, here I am, laden with carrier bags full of feminine care products, wine, dairy and overly processed confectionery.

I kick the door open, finding the witches huddled together, freezing like frightened rabbits when I walk in.

"What's going on?" I keep my tone jovial as I drop the bags on the counter. The pink haired harlot offers me a half-hearted smile that doesn't meet her eyes. She leans up for me to plant a chaste kiss on her cheek, whilst I hold my breath. Her scent makes me consider fashioning a makeshift anti-nausea device by shoving tampons up my nose.

"I fell into the counter," she offers, her face frozen, her eyes as big as saucers.

"Dare I ask how?" I shove the tub of ice cream into the

freezer.

A tense silence hangs in the air.

"Oh, you know, Ez," Dahlia offers, her tone strained. "She's so clumsy!"

"She's not wrong!" The pink haired witch bursts into a forced, strange high-pitched laugh. She pauses, a perplexed expression crossing her features. "Why are you wearing sunglasses inside?"

"Headache," I answer quickly. Both witches look at me with suspicion. "You know, maybe it's an after effect of being dead."

Dahlia looks like she's about to say something, but the pink haired witch gives her a strange look that I do not like.

"Or," I finish unpacking the bags, "I'm just tired," I fake yawn. "Maybe I should take a nap."

They both stare after me as I walk down the hallway towards the bedroom. Their stares drill into my back. As I enter the pink room of nightmares, it feels like my excuse may end up being legitimate. Thank Lucifer I still have sunglasses on. I collapse face first on the bed. At least when I shut my eyes there's the reprieve of blissful darkness.

The meat puppet's consciousness wriggles in the back of my mind. Childish petulance roils in my brain.

"Alright," I groan into the bedspread, "if I give you two hours to watch cartoons, have a wank, whatever... will you be quiet?"

Agreement blooms in the back of my thoughts as the mortal's consciousness pushes forward and I recede into the shadows.

I hear a gentle rap come from the door and I'm dimly aware of the witchling sitting beside him.

"Finn?" She leans in, touching his head.

"Yeah babe?" He lifts his head from the mattress, the sunglasses askew.

"Erm, maybe if you take the sunglasses off," she sits on the edge of the bed. She fidgets and seems nervous. Twitchy. "To help with the headache?"

He sits up, immediately bright sunlight floods the shadows I'm sitting in, as he pulls the sunglasses off.

"Headache?" he asks, his voice full of confusion.

Her brow furrows. "You said you had a headache?"

"Oh, yeah," he clears his throat. Fuck he lies almost as bad as she does. "It's definitely feeling a lot better now."

She chews on her lower lip, shuffling on the bed. "That's, erm, good."

He places a hand on her knee, and she looks down at it

86

warily. "How are you?"

"Me?" She continues to stare down. "Oh erm," she coughs. "Oh, you know, cramps and stuff."

Is this how all mortals normally converse?

He moves his hand to stroke down her back and her spine straightens in alarm. Interesting.

"I'm sorry, babe," he traces small circles through her dress. Oblivious to her nervousness. "Do you want to come lie down and rest? It might help?"

She chews her lip again, before giving her head a small shake, and her face brightens with a saccharine sweet smile. "That sounds really nice."

He pulls them both under the duvet and she lets out a squeal of surprise. He nuzzles up behind her, inhaling the scent of her hair and I must fight the urge to gag. Both from his affection and her closeness. She's too sweet. Nauseatingly sweet. We're going to end up with tooth decay if we keep breathing this in!

I try to force his body to edge away, but all that does is make him hold her tighter.

I use his peripheral vision to glance at the clock on her bedside and swear internally that I have another hour and a half of this bullshit to endure.

She turns, her eyes searching his face.

"Finn?" Her voice barely above a whisper.

"Yes, babe?"

Her long eyelashes flutter against her cheeks, she chews her lip again. "It doesn't matter." She snuggles into his chest and lets out a small, contented sigh. The top of her head nestles under his jaw.

I squirm at the closeness and wish I could return to hell for a reprieve, relive the tortures I'd inflicted on the clergy who'd tortured Sarah as a distraction or by doing my taxes. Even paperwork would be more appealing than this.

But now? Now for some reason it's impossible. I'm stuck in this weird state of awareness where I can see everything this mortal is doing, feel everything he touches, sense his emotions and smell everything he breathes in. The scent of vanilla, sugared oats and Magick floods my brain- making it impossible to think straight, and no matter how much I try to ignore it, it keeps ensnaring me. Bewitching me like a siren's call. Demons are not meant to spend too much time with witches, much like possessions, they can have disastrous effects on my kind when overexposed... I know the former well enough from experience.

The late afternoon sunlight dapples through the room and the witchling pulls back slightly from under my, no wait not mine, *his* neck to find the nook in his shoulder. She nestles down deeper before letting out a small snore.

Her mouth is slightly open and her eyelids flicker delicately against her high cheekbones. She's so close I notice the light dusting of freckles across her cheek and nose.

I look at the clock and see an hour has passed.

Screw this, I say mentally. *You've had an hour and I'm bored.*

I shove his consciousness out the way and reclaim control of his body. I try to pull my arm free, but she begins to stir.

How am I meant to get her off me without her waking up? I feel something resembling smugness tickle at the corner of my mind, and he flashes a memory up of him and the witchling cuddling like this for hours.

"Well, that's adorable," I whisper sardonically. "But some of us don't want to spend their whole existence curled up asleep in duvets!"

Amusement and another image flashes, only this one is of the two of them performing some very flexible bedroom acrobatics. I look down at the gap between us and see once again the evidence of his attraction to the harlot.

"It's a good job you died," I grumble, "or she never would have got anything done!"

He doesn't seem to think that's funny. The Finnster is no fun.

A small frown puckers on her forehead and she begins to mumble in her sleep.

I catch a few words, "Stop… Don't… Grimoire."

I stop breathing, waiting for her to say more. She stills again and the frown lines on her face smooth.

I can't just lie here. The longer I wait, the more likely the brat will wake up. I try to move again and successfully extricate myself from her snare.

I sit up and breathe a sigh of relief, looking down at my crotch with disdain. How does this guy not feel permanently faint?

I feel the whisper of a caress from a hand that traces up my spine which is quickly joined by the press of warm soft flesh against my back.

"I swear I only shut my eyes for a second," the sleepy voice behind me yawns.

Oh shit, it's awake.

I sit completely still, mentally willing Finn forward, but for some reason now is the one time he doesn't want to take the reins.

I keep facing away from her, quietly searching around for the sunglasses he'd discarded. If she sees my eyes all that will do is provoke questions and she's already suspicious enough as it is.

I feel the mattress move and the witchling attempts to wind herself around me and sit on my lap, but before she can plant her ass on me, I lurch forward and pluck the glasses from the ground. I shove them on my face and turn, she's flopped sideways, her hair mussed from sleep and her dress rumpled from being unceremoniously tossed aside by me.

"Babe?" She leans up to sit, her face scrunched in concern. "What's going on?"

I stand upright from my crouching position. I keep my distance and attempt to look nonchalant.

"Nothing," I answer, keeping my tone light and casual. I shift uncomfortably as she continues to study me. Away. I need to get away from her. I need to scrub the memory of her sweet scent and her softly curved body draped over mine.

She moves to me, placing a hand over my clenched fist. I back away, her touch is a strange jolt of electricity on my skin. I play off my reaction by brushing my fingers through my hair.

"What were you dreaming about?" I busy myself by tidying the bed and tuck the sheets back into place and fluff the pillows.

Maybe if I catch her off-guard, she'll tell me why she mentioned the grimoire in her dreams. I turn to look at her, trying to keep a safe distance away.

"Just weird dreams." She stretches out languorously and reaches her arms up behind her, the vines and flowers on her headboard seem to trail over her fingers.

She yawns before continuing, "I never usually remember them," she gives me a curious look. "Why are you making the bed?"

I place one of the sequin embellished pillows down at the front of the bedding I've just put in order. Just because it looks like a five-year-old decorated it, doesn't mean it needs to be messy.

"I just wanted to make it tidy," I pull the duvet tight to eliminate the wrinkles.

She crawls across the bed towards me, ruining my progress and causing the pillows to fall to the ground. "Since when?"

I huff, retrieving the pillows. "Since when what?"

She lets out a surprised gasp of breath. "Since when did you care about things being neat?"

Fuck. I didn't think about the possibility that he was as much of a slob as she is.

"I just want to make it nice," I offer. "You brought me back, so I want to make sure I'm earning my keep."

"You're not a servant, Finn," her mouth twitches and amusement dances across her face. "You're my..." her voice trails off and I see that apprehension flicker across her face.

Something is going on inside that pink sparkly head. She's suspicious of me.

Tension hangs between us, and I busy myself again by putting the pillows back into position. "I just want to be useful."

"Finn," she reaches for me again and I flinch away. Whatever that strange spark was when she touched me before I don't want a repeat of it.

I head towards the door. "I'm going to make a drink; do you want one?"

She stares after me, sitting cross legged with a confused expression on her face. "Er, yes please. Tea?"

I give her a nod and smile. "One tea. Coming right up."

I give my hair an exasperated tug.

How was I meant to know he lived in squalor when he was last alive? I thought most beings had a modicum of pride in their living quarters. Also, what's so wrong with me making the bed? This feels like sexism.

I flip on the kettle, fishing out two mugs from the cupboards and huffing out an exasperated sigh. I need to check if there's something, anything, in this pigsty which might point me in the direction of the grimoire. Although finding anything in this mess is going to be enough of a challenge.

"Fucking mortals," I grumble. "What's wrong with a little order and cleanliness?"

Irritation prickles under my skin at not getting a straight answer about her dream. It felt like I was close to snatching a clue from her subconscious, but the useless little creature had instead become fixated on my desire to make the bed. It does seem odd that she's begun having nightmares since the boy's return. Could it somehow have loosened something in her subconscious mind?

I hear shuffling behind me and am overwhelmed by the perfume of vanilla and Magick.

She wraps her arms around my waist. "Are you ok babe?"

The kettle finishes boiling, and I extricate myself from her embrace. "I'm fine."

I head to the fridge, grab the milk, add it to one of the mugs and hand the brew to her.

She looks down at the mug with a puzzled expression on her face.

"What?" I begin cutting up a lemon and add a slice to the remaining mug.

She sniffs the mug and wrinkles her nose. "There's no sugar in this."

My eyebrows shoot up. "Do you want sugar?"

Her mouth drops open in shock like I've just admitted to drowning kittens for fun. I grab the sugar pot from the side and plonk one of the cubes into her mug.

Her eyebrows rise even higher, understanding, I add another one in. That same look remains on her face. I add another.

"Did you forget how I take my tea?" she asks apprehensively.

"No of course not," I put the tub down and take a sip from my own mug. The lemon lightens the bitter taste of the tea leaves.

"Are you drinking tea without milk or sugar in it?" She looks aghast.

"I forgot to add it in," I shrug, shoving two lumps of sugar into my mug and lifting it to my face. I try to hide the grimace as I take a sip of the sickly-sweet concoction.

The witch watches me with suspicion, her almond eyes studiously tracking my movements. I didn't realise my whole plan would unravel over a cup of fucking tea.

"You're being weird," she takes another sip and heads to the sofa. "First there's the whole tidying and cleaning thing," she points to the rack of drying dishes. "Then for some reason, you decide to change the way you take your tea."

"I forgot to put it in," I sit down in the armchair opposite her. "Simple mistake."

"And you didn't put milk in," she takes another sip. "And you added lemon. Which, by the way, you never used to do. You used to hate lemon."

Bugger, I forgot about the milk and the lemon.

"I decided to cut out dairy," I offer weakly. "I've heard about the negative effect farming is having on the environment-"

"Since when?" she splutters. "You've been dead!"

"I read the mortal news," I shrug again, which is starting to feel very much like a nervous tic. "We get the internet in the afterlife," I lie. We don't.

"You once told me you hated lemon," she counters. "You

91

threw up when I made you a hot toddy."

"That may have been more so because a hot toddy is generally disgusting," I answer. She probably put glitter, candy floss or some other kind of revolting shit in it.

She points at me, "Then there's the whole sunglasses in the house thing."

"I'm just tired," I groan, scrubbing a hand along my jaw as I try to stamp down the irritation bubbling inside me. This woman is fucking relentless. You'd think she'd be happy her boyfriend was back, not constantly looking for something to be wrong? I mean there is something wrong, but still, I didn't expect her to be this astute. At least not this soon.

She fiddles with the mug in her hand as her leg bounces nervously. "Last night, when you came back... did you... did you do anything else besides come here?"

My eyebrows knit together. "No, why?"

"Erm," her leg bounces again. "No reason."

"Esme," I sip my tea, then grimace. I forgot about the sugar. Fuck. I put the mug down on the table. "Why are you asking that?"

"Erm, well, Dahlia called and..." she nearly drops the mug. "Wait. Did you just call me Esme?"

"Aye, that is your name," I say slowly. "It is customary to call someone by their name."

She jumps up staring down at me with alarm. "Ok, that's two more things! You said 'Aye', you never say Aye! Also, you never, ever, ever call me Esme!"

I grimace. Fuck. She's a lot more observant than I gave her credit for. Serves me right, just because she looks like an overgrown five-year-old doesn't mean she has the brain of one.

"I forgot?" I offer, picking up the tea and taking another swallow to diffuse the tension. I forget about the sugar again and fail to hide my grimace this time.

She gives me a small nod, but I see the wariness in her face as she continues to sip her drink. It would seem a lot more threatening if the mug wasn't in the shape of a unicorn.

The rest of the afternoon eases into a slightly less frosty silence as the hours pass by, and by 6pm, the witchling seems to have forgotten about her suspicion and is curling up next to me on the sofa watching some animated shit on TV.

The front door unlocks and the dark-haired witch staggers in, her face full of alarm.

"Hey Dahls," Esme leans over to glance at her roommate who looks flustered and panic-ridden. "How was the shop?"

"The shop?" She lingers in the doorway. Her eyes dart between both of us. "Oh erm, yeah! The shop is fine!"

I look at the pair of them, both have strange looks of alarm, and their voices are high pitched and anxious.

I pause the film, where the talking rat is dancing around in a restaurant. "What's going on with you two? Why are you being odd?"

The pink haired witchling narrows her eyes at me. "Seems like there's a lot of it going about."

"Wait," Dahlia moves forward. "Did you not tell him?"

"Tell me what?" I grind my teeth. These two are as subtle as a sledgehammer.

"Should we tell him?" Esme lets out a shaky breath. "Can't we just-"

"Look, Ez," her friend leans forward and places a hand on her knee. "I get that you just want everything to be ok. And you want to be happy that he's back and everything is fine, but..." the last part of her sentence dies as I see two fat tears rolling down the cheeks of the Disney loving girl next to me.

"I just wanted to be happy for a little while," her voice comes out meek and broken. Like all the glitter and pink, she douses herself in is camouflage. I tilt my head, giving her an assessing look.

"I get that," her friend gives her knee a light squeeze. "But burying your head in the sand isn't going to solve anything."

"Solve what?" I feel the muscle in my jaw tense. "Can you two please tell me what the fuck is going on?"

The brunette witch fixes me with a glare. "There's been a murder."

"Right?" I'm struggling to figure out what business that is of ours, particularly mine. They both look aghast, and I remember: murder's a bad thing, and fix my face into a look of concern. "I mean, oh no, that's terrible!"

They share a look before the brunette continues, "It was a witch."

"Oh no!" I shuffle in my seat, getting irritated by their scrutiny. "How awful! Why would a witch kill somebody?" As if that wasn't obvious.

Dahlia splutters, "No, the witch was the victim!"

"Oh, that makes more sense!"

"Sense?" Dahlia looks at me with suspicion. "What are you talking about?"

I clear my throat and shove the sunglasses up the bridge of my nose. "Why are you both looking at me like that?"

"Because her brain and heart were, erm," Esme fiddles nervously with her necklace. "Well, they were gone."

"And you know, we just had someone come back from the dead who could potentially be interested in eating them?"

A laugh escapes my throat before I have a chance to temper it.

"It's not funny!" Esme baulks.

"You think I ate a witch's brain and heart?" I double over in hysterics. This is fucking priceless.

"Why are you laughing?" Dahlia shuffles back in her seat as if preparing to bolt for the door.

"Because it's funny," I manage to wheeze out in between my laugh. "Why would I want to eat a witch?"

"Well, you know, we were thinking you might be a zombie," Esme's cheeks are almost the same colour as her hair.

"Because I forgot how to take my tea and I have light sensitivity?" I arch an eyebrow and the crimson in her cheeks deepens.

"Maybe a vampire then?" Dahlia shrugs. "Vampires don't like light."

Esme pinches the bridge of her nose. "Finn is not a vampire."

"I'm also not a killer," I reason. At least not in this body.

"Ok, so, say we believe you," Dahlia's eyebrow arches. "Say it wasn't you, who was it then?"

"Oh! Oh!" Esme squeaks next to me, "Remember what Agnes said? About the other witch getting murdered in Glasgow?"

"Ez, I think they were slightly different. For one, this girl last night was ripped apart-"

"The killer might be experimenting," I interject. "Finding what works best for him to get the thrill."

Esme points at me, her eyes sparkling brightly. "That makes sense!"

"Oh sure, take his side," she slumps back in her seat. "Sure, it makes way more sense that there's a killer out there targeting witches than a flesh-eating zombie on the rampage-" she halts. "Actually yeah, that does sound more logical."

We finish watching the strange rat movie and then they decide to shove on another film. This next one has singing and dancing. Lots of singing and dancing. And it's set in a high school? I

94

make a mental note that this may be a new torture method when I get back to work.

An hour or so later the pair of them are huddled into the sofa, covered in blankets fast asleep and snoring softly. Thank. Fuck. Finally.

Dahlia's news about the murder has piqued my interest and despite telling myself I would keep a low profile, there's nothing to stop me doing a little bit of research, especially if it's got to do with witches. I might find something useful.

I carefully extricate myself from Esme's limbs and pluck the flat keys from the coffee table. Once I step into the night, I suck in a greedy breath. The scent of lingering summer evening sun, petrol and sweat are a welcome relief for my nostrils.

I stalk down the cobblestones and shove my hands into my pockets. I need to focus, but it's hard to do that when my skin is covered in her, and even through the smells of the city, I keep catching the scent of sugar and Magick. She's infested this body.

Dahlia had mentioned the murder had taken place in Old Town, so I head in that direction, my lengthy stride making fast work of the journey. I almost crash into an old lady and give her an apologetic smile which she tuts and mutters something about the "youth of today." I bite my tongue, I am considerably older than her, I am older than humankind.

I round the corner of the crowded buildings and meet police tape with several police officers behind it.

One of the constables' strides towards me, his chest puffed up in self-importance. "Apologies, sir but you'll need to find another route. This street is closed off."

I remove my sunglasses and fix him with my stare.

He halts, and his mouth hangs open as he falls quickly into a trance. I've still got it.

"What happened?" I ask, peering deeply into his mud brown eyes and stamping down any resistance he has to my control.

"A murder."

"Of?"

"A young girl, she had her head bashed open on the pavement, part of her brain looks to have been removed and her chest was ripped open."

"Hmmm," A knot of dread twists in my stomach. "Any suspects?"

"We have several. There was also a witness, a woman who

knew the victim, a strange woman. We don't think her statement will help much. She said she saw someone fleeing the scene."

"What's her name?"

"Agnes. Agnes Buckthorn."

Interesting. Agnes was the name that Dahlia had said earlier. So that's two murders this woman has knowledge of.

I point at his notebook. "Write down the address for Ms Buckthorn, officer."

He gives another jagged nod, before scribbling the address and handing it to me.

Chapter Eleven

Esme

As soon as Finn slams the door shut, I immediately let out the breath I've been holding in. Something's wrong. I don't know exactly what, but something definitely is. I can feel it.

I quickly give Dahlia a shake, who has a rather unbecoming streak of drool leaking from the corner of her mouth.

"Fmurmurh?"

"Dahls!" I give her another shake and narrowly miss an elbow to the face. Man, she really hates being woken up.

"What?" She grumbles, pulling the blanket back over her.

"I'm going to go follow Finn," I grab my keys and phone. "You stay here and call me if he comes back."

"Ok fine," she mutters from under the fabric. "Wait, what?" She throws the duvet off.

I pull on my jacket. "I'm going to go follow Finn and see where he goes."

"I thought you believed him?" she asks.

"I did," I clear my throat. "I do. But you know. It's still weird that he loses time and keeps wandering off."

"So, you're going to follow a potentially dangerous person around the city in the middle of the night!" She stands, nearly toppling over in the nest of blankets. "Are you insane?"

My cheeks heat. "No, but I don't know what else I can do!"

She untangles her legs and clambers across the sofa. "If you're going to do that, you need to take more than just your phone!"

She offers me the butcher's knife.

"I'm not taking that!" I splutter as I head for the front door. "Knowing my luck, I'll fall over and accidentally stab myself!"

"Good point," she discards the knife and rummages in her

bag and pulls out a small vial. "Take this. It's powdered Vervain. I'm not sure what it'll do against a zombie-"

"Not a zombie," I correct her.

"Or whatever the fuck he is!" She huffs out an exasperated breath. "Even if it won't knock him out, it might at least slow him down!"

I take hold of the small vial. "What are you doing walking around with this?"

She shrugs. "Sometimes there's creeps at the bar who don't take no for an answer."

"So, you drug them!"

"I leave them in safe, well-lit places," she counters. "Which is a damn sight more respectful than they are to me!"

"We're going to talk about this when I get back," I shout from the hallway.

"Yay," she drawls. "Can't wait. Be safe, don't get killed."

"Thanks, you too!" I call as I slam the door shut, bolt out of the apartment and try to figure out where Finn's gone.

"Ok," I huff out a breath. "If I were a supernatural zombie, but not a zombie, where would I go?"

I scan up and down the street and see a flash of movement under a streetlight a few hundred yards away and take off after it like a demented bloodhound.

After a few minutes of following the silhouette, in the least stealthy way imaginable, I catch sight of the figure heading into a pub. His back is to me, and I can't really tell who it is.

If it is Finn, there's nothing wrong with him going to the pub. He used to go to them all the time.

Did he used to eat brains too? The voice in my head deadpans.

"Oh good," I groan as I head into the pub. "You're back."

I stand on my tiptoes looking around, scanning for someone vaguely Finn-shaped.

A gaggle of old men who are huddling around a table by the doorway all giving me varying glares of lechery and suspicion. Lucky me.

"Good evening gentlemen," I smile brightly and head for the bar.

"What can I get you?" asks the disgruntled barkeep, who looks like he'd rather be anywhere else than here.

"Errrrr," I stall, looking around the room. The door in the back opens and a young handsome guy dressed in all black saunters out.

98

Bollocks. Not Finn. Right height and build, but he has a walking stick. I know it's dark but how did I not spot that?!

Ok, so it turns out I suck at stalking. I'll add it to the list of things I'm bad at. Shitsticks and fuckwaffles. So, where the hell did he go?

The barman is looking at me like I've gone bonkers, and the look only amplifies when I give him a sheepish grin and step backwards. "Never mind! I'm not thirsty after all!"

I edge outside and try to ignore the rising embarrassment.

That went well, the voice in my head quips.

"Ok, how is that helpful?" I snap as I march back up to the flat with my tail firmly between my legs.

"Did you find Finn?" Dahls calls from the living room.

"No," I groan as I kick off my Converse and stagger in the direction of my bedroom. "I lost him."

"I don't think he's in there," she shouts as I close the door.

It's a long shot but maybe, maybe I might have enough power in me to figure out what the hell is going on. Maybe it'll be handy that Finn is out so I can try out this spell.

Or he's out killing again, whilst you sit on your arse and do nothing, says the voice.

"Again," I grumble as I gather supplies. "Not helpful. If you haven't got anything nice to say, don't say anything at all!"

Did you just quote 'Bambi', the voice drips with disdain.

"It wasn't Bambi, it was Thumper. Also, you're still not helping!" I growl, whilst carrying armfuls of supplies over to my bed. I tip the crystals onto the bedspread, disturbing Ink from his sleep. He lets out a disgruntled meow.

Ok, confidence! I'm centred. I am one with the universe. I am a strong, capable witch who can do everything… ok … Ok?

Are you asking me to weigh in on this? The voice asks.

"You. Be. Quiet." I suck in a calming breath. "Guide me Goddess," my hand lingers over the crystals, "I beseech thee to show me the truth."

I sit on the edge of my bed, crossing my legs beneath me. Ink purrs as he snakes his lithe form around me. I ignore him. Focusing on my limbs. My breath. The steady rhythm of my heart.

"Guide me, Goddess," my hands fall like weights to my sides and my head falls back. "Also, if you could reassure me that I did the spell right and Finn isn't a zombie, that'd be great!"

I look up and realise my jasmine has wound itself around my

99

chandelier, blooming amongst the light bulbs.

I breathe in and out, my breaths growing deeper and slower every second that passes. "Show me." Inhale. Exhale. "The. Truth."

My vision darkens and I'm being swallowed by the shadowy waters of time. I realise, dully, that I fall back onto the mattress, but I can't feel it. I can't feel anything.

I close my eyes and when I open them again, I am back in my dream.

A swirl of bodies and fire. A circle of women dancing naked around a huge pyre. Heat warms the air, not only from the flames, but from the ground which has been baked rough and hard by the rays of the sun. Summer flowers adorn their heads like crowns. A celebration. A solstice.

"They're all here for you," a male voice whispers into my ear.

His voice is like liquid honey pooling across stone. Sweet but jagged. Silken yet deadly. That of the finest dagger, encrusted in jewels, but with a blade so sharp it could pierce flesh like warmed butter.

I shake my head, my crown of antlers and flora is heavy, my neck can barely support it.

"No," I reach down, my hand stroking the ruby red leather of the bound book. It emits an aura of breathtaking power. "They are here because of this."

I jolt upright, sucking breath like I'd just been submerged in the deepest ocean.

What the hell was that? So much for me asking vague questions. All I wanted to know is Finn ok and instead I have some weird hallucination.

I flop back down letting out a groan full of disappointment and confusion.

I grasp at my comforter and my fingers grip it like it's a life raft. That's never happened to me before.

Sure, I've had fleeting images, passing Déjà vu's, but never ever full-blown visions.

It was like I was there. I could practically smell the wood as it crackled and burned on the pit and the summer flowers that adorned my head. What's happening to me?

Ever since I've brought Finn back, my power has stopped feeling like something I own, but like something that is owning me. Swallowing me whole.

Maybe it isn't Finn that has come back wrong, but that something has changed in me. Maybe I'm wrong?

Ink bounds up to me and meows loudly. I check my watch, it's past eleven. I've been in a trance for over two hours!

I untangle my legs, feeling wobbly and weak. Ink bounds off the bed and meows again.

"I'm coming, sweet boy," I say, my entire body shaking. Maybe I need something to eat?

I try walking but have to hold onto the door frame before I attempt to move again. I close my eyes and count to ten, willing the dizziness to dissipate.

I hear the jingle of keys in the front door, maybe Dahls is going to work, or Finn is home. Maybe. Hopefully.

"Dahlia?" I call out, hating how weak my voice sounds.

Finn walks in, carrying three massive pizza boxes. "What's wrong?"

My vision blurs and my knees buckle. "F-Finn?"

He quickly puts the tower of leaning pizza onto the kitchen side before making his way over to me. He places a cooling hand on me. "You're burning up."

I feel sweat trickling down my back. "I-I had a vision."

His brow furrows as he focuses on my face. "What?"

I lean down, placing my hands in front of me and the feel of the wood grounds me a little. "A vision."

"We need to get you into bed," Finn gently lifts me and carries me back into my room, placing me softly on the mattress. "I'll get you some water."

"Finn?" I call out, my voice a plea. I hate how much of me just wants everything to be ok.

He pokes his head around the doorway. "Yep?"

"Can I have some pizza please?"

He gives me the sweetest smile. "Sure thing, babe. Although, I think pineapple, olive and pickle pizza might make you feel worse!"

I lie back down, looking up at the flowers blooming around my head. He's definitely Finn. My sweet, reliable and loving boyfriend. No need to worry about him. I just need to worry about my brain being broken.

I eat four slices of pizza, as well as swiping the pickles off the rest, before hunkering back down under the blankets. Finn cuddles up next to me in bed. He sets up my laptop to watch 'Hocus Pocus' from under my duvet. I feel a twinge of sadness remembering how Hazel would always watch it when she was hormonal.

"Feeling any better?" he asks, brushing crumbs off my cheek. "You've got a little more colour."

I nod, swallowing down another pickle. "Thank you. I think my blood sugar might have gone down or maybe the summoning spell is still affecting me."

"I was so worried when I came in," he pulls me into an embrace that calms my mind. There's no way he could be hurting people. No way. "You started talking about a vision, what was it about?"

I frown at the laptop, the images still swimming in front of me, "A summer solstice. But not like one I'd ever been to when I was little… I was in the body of the High Witch. A-And there was this voice, this guy… his voice was so familiar. Then I looked down and saw this red book on my lap. It felt like it was mine."

Finn stills and I swear he stops breathing.

"It probably doesn't mean anything," I flounder. He's going to think he's been brought back to life by a crazy person!

"You're probably just over-tired," he strokes the top of my head. "You need a nice, long sleep and then you'll feel right as rain tomorrow."

I feel my eyes grow heavy again and manage a small nod. "You're probably right."

Hopefully. Maybe. But it doesn't stop the nagging feeling that something is very, very wrong. No matter how much I want Finn to be right. In every possible way.

I burn sage and bless all the corners of the small room at the back of the Inn. Maggie has let me use this backroom for years to hold my covensteads. She returns, holding two mugs of steaming mulled mead.

"I thought you'd need this," she offers a cup to me which I take gratefully. "You'll need your strength for the night ahead."

I give her a small nod. This wasn't my first-time summoning, but I needed to make sure I did everything perfectly.

"May the Goddess bless you, sweet Maggie." I take a sip and the spiced liquid coats my throat. I still see the bruises around her neck from months past, the day that the hunters had tried, and failed, to hang her. I had been one of the women to hear her tapping on the coffin lid, and I thanked the Goddess that the clergy had deemed her resurgence a miracle rather than an act of Magick. How ironic, that their act of persecution had driven her into the fold of my coven for

sanctuary after they'd cast their judgement. She hadn't been a witch the day they'd hung her, but she was when she'd returned.

"I was passing through the Grassmarket today," her face turns grave. "Helen's accused by that gossiping trout Emily. They took her from her house yesterday. Left her bairns screaming into the night."

Helen is not part of our coven, she is a mere mortal, but that wouldn't stop the townsfolk- they are more blood-thirsty and vicious than any demon. That damned monarch, James the witch hunter, half mad in his hunt to kill any outliers, witch or no. I know in my heart there would be no appeal for Helen, just as there hasn't been for any of the countless others. All are tortured, drowned or burned. One can only hope that their deaths are as swift as possible.

I've given all my coven the spells and precautions I've found in the grimoire to ensure their safety. I have only lost one of my sister witches to the hunters and that's because the fledgling had forgotten her spells. Poor soul. She was bound and thrown into the Nasty Norlock. The innocent girl fought for her life, drowning in filth. The only small mercy I could grant her was to numb her mind and soul, so she would rest in peace as the last of her dying breaths bubbled to the surface.

"There will be no end to this, will there?" Maggie asks, bringing me out of my sad reverie.

"I shall see to it that there is," I take another sip. "Before the others arrive, I must speak with you." I turn and place a hand on her arm, "I appreciate your hospitality Maggie, but I feel that we may need to look to move our meetings to a more secluded location."

The Inn has been perfect for our congregations, but now with the ever-present threat of hunters and paranoid, accusatorial townsfolk in the city, a gathering of women in the night was bound to start raising suspicion.

Maggie looks as though she's about to argue, but before she can, I say, "It's safer for all. I cannot risk losing any one of you. Not again."

She gives me a slow nod. "I understand."

I give her arm a small squeeze before moving to pick up my grimoire. "Leave me for a few minutes please, Maggie."

"I'll let the others know to wait until you open the door."

As I hear the lock click, I begin pouring salt onto the stone floor. I trace a pentagram and place a candle on each point of the star. Each demon is bound to an element, and I use the candle flame to focus. To think of him.

I centre myself at the top of the star, closing my eyes and whispering softly. "I summon thee, Tenebris Noctis Daemonium, Night Demon, Devil of the dark, High Lord of Hell. Second to Lucifer. Come to me now."

"Good evening, Sarah," a male voice, dipped in the sweetest honey. "You summon me?"

"I-I did," I open my eyes, to see a tall dark figure. He's cloaked in shadows, as if he can dim the candlelight in his presence.

He looks down at his nails, a gesture so human I have to remind myself once again that he is a demon. He looks at me and my breath catches; whilst he may manifest as a handsome human male, he is anything but. With his inky dark hair that falls over his high proud forehead, his golden eyes burn into mine.

A smirk teases his full lips. "Why do you call for me, Witchling?"

I stand, brushing the dust from my skirts. "I missed you."

"I missed you too, my Sarah," he rushes towards me, bundling me into a tender embrace, pulling away from me to cradle my face in his hand. "My dark little Witchling."

"There have been more burnings," I sigh. "More women tortured and killed."

He looks down at me, "But you're using the grimoire to keep you and your sisters safe?"

I nod. "Yes, but still so many lives are being lost. So many innocents."

He sighs. "I know, but there's nothing that can be done. If I interfere there will be costs. Costs that will be too high for me to stand."

Hell will forbid him from stepping on Earth if he interferes in mortal affairs.

"But how can they expect us, expect me, to not do anything?" Tears cloud my vision.

"That is why I gifted you the grimoire," the smile returns to his handsome face. "Know the rules, so that you may bend and break them."

He always says this for he is a rebel at his core nature. Whilst demons and witches were always bound by arcane laws, there's a fine balance of power that has to be managed. Witches could summon demons for bidding and could offer them bargains, promises, even their very bodies, but never their hearts.

"Ez!" strong hands are shaking me, "Ez wake up!"

I'm quickly dragged from the darkness; I struggle to open my eyes. When I do, I scream, a face stares down at me.

In the dim glow of my bedside light, I forget for a moment that I'd dyed Finn's hair earlier. He looks like someone else.

"Finn?"

"You were crying," he says quietly, his face pinches in concern. "You were having a nightmare."

I sit up straighter, shaking my head slowly to try to loosen the tight grip my dream had on me. I'm in my room. I look down at my green nightdress which is coated in sweat.

Finn clasps his hand over mine, "Ez?"

"I- I'm alright," I manage to answer. "It was just really vivid. I saw a book. A red spell book and- and…"

"Come here," he pulls me into an embrace. "I'll protect you from your bad dreams."

I cuddle in closer to him, breathing in his warmth and comfort. Wishing it were true.

I wake early the next morning, Finn is curled up around me, his arm wrapped protectively over my waist.

The memory of my dream is still so raw and real. It's like I'd been there. I can still feel the weight of the burgundy grimoire, still see the side profile of the stranger's face. He'd been so angelically handsome.

I roll over, snuggling into Finn.

"Mmmhunn," he murmurs as he pulls me in closer.

I lean my ear against his chest, hearing the warm stable rhythm of his heart. A drum that hadn't beat in over seven years. But here he is. With me. I snuggle closer and trace my hands over his toned abs. Sure, he loses time and might be killing people. But you know, no one is perfect.

His hands begin to lift my nightdress up, tracing lazy circles over my hips.

"Babe," I whisper. "We need to get up. I've got to open the shop."

His grip tightens and he hoists me onto his lap.

He places a soft kiss on my throat, and I can't stop my heart skipping a beat. I stamp down three words circling my brain; 'murderer', 'zombie' and 'brains.' Along with the words, 'liar' and 'denial'.

It's then that I look down at his knuckles which are bruised and bloodied.

"Finn!" I sit bolt upright, grabbing hold of his hand. "What happened?"

He looks down at them. They look like he'd been using a brick wall as a punching bag, and he looks as surprised as I do.

"I don't remember." He looks at his knuckles, examining them in the early morning light.

I watch Finn's reaction and he just looks confused. Not guilty. Or murderous. Just perplexed.

He looks up at me with that same look of innocence and sweetness. "Is something wrong with me?"

"No," I plaster a benign smile on my face, even though my insides are turning to ice. "You're perfect."

Chapter Twelve

Nox

The shower beats down on my aching back. My bruised and bloody hands rest on the green tiled walls as I let the scorching water rain down my muscles.

I'd awoken just as the witchling had clambered off me, a strange look of alarm on her face.

"You want coffee, babe?" I hear the harlot call from behind the bathroom door.

"Aye-" I stop myself, remembering I need to sound like this meat puppet twit. "Yes please!"

"Do you want some company?" she asks, and I hear the doorknob rattle. Thankfully I've locked the damn door.

"Not right now," I call back. "Thanks…. Babe."

She's spent the last few days looking at me like I've grown five heads. Now she wants sex. Is she part succubus?!

I hear a sad sigh from the other side of the door. Fine by me. Sulk all you want, you wanton brat!

"Babe?"

This woman really is relentless.

I huff out a breath before calling back, trying to keep the frustration out of my voice. "Yeah?"

"Do you want toast before I head to the shop?"

The shop. If anywhere holds clues about where the witches' descendants have stashed that grimoire it might be in that quaint little shop. Most of the witches in Edinburgh have probably been in there one time or another to pick up crystals, or candles, or some other shit they use in their silly little spells.

"Yeah," I give my reflection a playful wink. "Sounds like a plan."

107

I quickly dress in a black shirt and jeans, buckled with a black leather belt. I look up to see Esme sitting on the edge of her bed, practically drooling.

She's clothed, thankfully, wearing a sage green playsuit and her pastel hair is bundled into two bunches. She's sitting cross legged in front of the TV, ignoring the animated film, absently picking at a croissant and making a mountain of pastry crumbs in her lap. It's hard to believe this woman is nearly thirty, she certainly doesn't act, or dress, like someone her age should.

Her mouth hangs open as she gawps at my appearance.

I point down at the mess she's made. "You missed your mouth."

She smiles shyly, a blush creeping over her cheeks. "Sorry I hadn't realised watching you put clothes on could be as sexy as watching you take them off."

I roll up the sleeves of the shirt, admiring my reflection, before turning my gaze back to her. "You're incorrigible."

She beams up at me, like I've just complimented her. "Thank you!"

I grumble under my breath. "Relentless."

I make my way to the door. "Didn't you say you wanted to get to the shop?"

She untangles her legs and leaves a confetti of crumbs all over the floor. Her expression is full of apprehension. "Er- yeah. But I'm not sure you should be..."

I arch an eyebrow. "Should be what?"

She gives a slight shake of her head. "Doesn't matter."

"Let's get going," I wiggle my outstretched fingers at her. "Don't want you to be late."

She walks towards me, hesitation on her face. "Are you sure?"

I ruffle my hand through my newly darkened locks. "I think I'll be good after your amazing makeover."

"No, I mean," the colour in her cheeks deepens. "You know the whole..."

"I'm not a zombie," I rub my thumb over her knuckles. I'm a lot of things but not a cranium munching ghoul.

"But," she chews her lower lip again. That's what she does when she's nervous. She sucks in a steadying breath and furrows her brow. "Okey dokey."

I swallow down a shudder at the mind-numbing cuteness and

stretch my face into a benign, fake smile for the entire walk.

She leads me to the floral display of the shop. "And we're here," she strokes a hand over the blush painted wood. "Home sweet home."

A flicker of sadness traces her features. She seems to forget that I'm here for a second. Her eyes mist over as though she's lost in a distant memory, but suddenly she snaps herself out of it and turns to beam at me.

"If you get bored you can always go for a wander," she offers as she unlocks and opens the door.

"I'd never get bored of being with you," I have to stop myself from gagging on the words.

She grins warmly at me. "Can I get you a coffee? Tea?"

I walk in, and my breath halts in my chest as I see the flowers on the bookshelves begin to brighten at her presence. It reminds me of Sarah. The way that life would gravitate and bloom around her.

"No thanks," I watch the roses on the shelves transform into the darkest shade of red, almost black.

She watches me and walks towards the roses. "They do this," she strokes the petals of the nearest flower lovingly, "they like to show off for visitors."

"They do it for you," I say before I can stop myself. "They're talking to you."

She brushes her finger over the edge of a rose's petal, so tenderly it makes my heart twist in a strange way. I remember the last time I'd seen flowers speak like this and I remember what black petals mean. Death. Evil. Demon. Fortunately for me this witchling doesn't speak flora.

"They do it for the shop. For Mum," she answers offhandedly, and for a moment the small shadow of sadness returns. "I just keep them alive."

She continues to walk to the back room. "Are you sure you don't want a drink?"

I hear the kettle turn on as I walk around the occult emporium, taking in the floor to ceiling bookshelves, crystals and candles packed onto every inch of shelf space.

"Can I have a coffee," I reply. "Black. No sugar."

I hear the clatter in the kitchen pause. "Sure."

Everything is too cluttered and messy. Almanacks mix with garden herbology. Everything about this shop's merchandising is chaotic. It's triggering.

Esme returns holding two steaming cups. She hands one to

me and I take a large gulp, savouring the bitterness.

"So, what do you think?" She tries, and fails, to keep her tone nonchalant.

"It's warm," I answer, and she blossoms, like her indoor rose garden. "But," I stretch a hand to the walls, "I have to question the organisation of the shelves."

She arches an eyebrow. "Oh?"

Before I can stop myself the words come tumbling out of me. "I must ask, are they ordered in a particular way? By colour? Or perhaps by the title font?"

That delicate flush returns on her cheeks. "I haven't really done the best job of organising them. I kind of left it to Dahlia, as she's way more anal about stuff like that."

"Well, she's not done the best job either!" I laugh. "She's mixed the Samarian and Celtic charms together, and is that an Egyptian talisman next to a Babylonian one? Frankly, that's culturally insensitive, or at least it would have been three, or four, thousand years ago!"

Esme smiles up at me with wonder and surprise, "Babe, I didn't think you'd even know what half of these things are! Let alone how offensive it is to have them together!" She begins moving them around, it still looks like shit but at least she won't upset any ancient civilisations now.

I let out a short laugh and take another swig of my drink.

Fuck. Me. Sideways.

"Oh yeah," I chuckle, trying to style out my faux pas. "I had lots of time to learn. That's all you have when you're dead."

She frowns but doesn't say anything as she steps over to the till, gently moving the climbing rose off the register.

"Is there anything I can do to help?" I give my most charming smile. "I don't want to sit around feeling useless."

She beams back at me. "You're not useless."

"I am if I can't help," I pout. "Please?"

She rolls her eyes, but I see the twinkle in her expression. "Ok. If, you're sure?"

"I insist," I flash my dimples.

"Since you said about the shelves not being ordered correctly," she pauses, waiting for my reaction. "How would you feel about organising them?"

"I'd love to," wow, I can honestly say that. Some degree of calm in this space feels like it would be a blessing. In the most unholy way possible, that is. "Are these all the books in the shop?"

"Well, there's more in the back," she gestures behind her. "But it's kind of a shit show back there…"

I walk past her and head down a little galley corridor. At the end I push open the door. "It can't be that ba-" the word dies in my mouth.

Unholy Hell. This stockroom is a complete disaster. Shelves are apparently optional. Products lay strewn all over the floor, and piled up on an unfortunate table which seems to be screaming under the weight of arcane paraphernalia and biscuits. Why are there eight packets of biscuits? And why are they all open?

Esme wanders up behind me. My senses are being assaulted. My nose by her. My eyes by this catastrophe of a room.

Sweat begins to prickle on my skin. This. Will. Not. Do.

Books, crystals, jars and taxidermied animals all coated in a thin layer of grime, dust and biscuit crumbs.

"Finn?" A warm hand clasps around my forearm, I flinch back from the touch and accidentally drop the mug of coffee on the floor.

"I'm fine," my voice is both taut and frayed, like a hangman's noose. "Everything's fine."

What does fine stand for? Fuck Ups Never End? No, that can't be right…

"Are you sure?" She looks up at me with concern. "Do you want another coffee?"

I want order. I want cleanliness. I want this nauseating, candy-coated woman out of sniffing distance.

"Coffee sounds good, thank you," I manage to grind out.

She leaves, and finally I can breathe.

First things first, floor. I need to find the floor. Which I'm sure is somewhere under all this shit. Down is traditionally where floors are kept. There's a very real possibility the grimoire might be in here; trapped under a sea of occult shit, but I won't be able to find it until I find the ground!

This is my own personal version of Hell. The irony. I'm a demon, I'm supposed to inflict torture, not be subjected to it.

Chapter Thirteen

<u>Esme</u>

Something is wrong. I can feel it. But this time I know it's not me. It is definitely Finn. I don't know how, or what it is, but something about him isn't right.

Dahlia's scepticism might be clouding my judgement. But he doesn't want sugar in his coffee, and he said 'dead' even though that's a swear word as far as he's concerned. He keeps slipping into a Scottish accent, even though he's a born and bred Londoner. He's not using my nickname. He's obsessively fastidious all of a sudden. Although that last one is kind of handy. The stockroom has never looked so tidy. But still, something isn't right.

Finn, who's finished his cleaning frenzy is now reading a book on the history of Scottish Witches. He leans back in the seat, resting one hand on his chin as he absently flicks through the pages.

"I never knew you're interested in history," I try to keep my tone casual. Even though I've been cataloguing his every word and gesture for the past three hours. I continue to reorder the shelves, whilst covertly hunting for the books on summoning. Maybe Dahls and I missed something in our last check?

"I had a lot of time to pass when I was dead," he skims over another page before flicking to the next, as if he's searching for something. "It's quite interesting."

"Are you enjoying it?" I quickly flick the shop sign to 'Closed' as I begin to loosen my bunches, sauntering towards him. If Finn is really Finn, he can't resist when I let my hair hang loose. It was his Achilles' heel back at uni. Or more his Achilles' hard on?

"Hm?" he murmurs, not looking up from the book.

"The book," I make my way to his chair and begin unbuttoning the top of my playsuit. "You seem like you're enjoying it."

"Yeah, it's very informative," he mutters, still focused on the page.

Ok, so talking isn't cutting it. Time to bring out the big guns and by big guns I mean…. I pull the playsuit down to my hips and unhook my fuchsia bra.

He looks up and alarm flashes across his face. "What are you doing?"

"Me?" I look down at him, my eyes wide and innocent. "Just entertaining myself."

"Esme," his voice is full of warning and disdain. "We're in the shop. Someone could come in."

I trail my fingers down my midriff, halting just above the elastic of my thong, watching him become more and more uncomfortable.

"Relax, I flipped the sign. No one will walk in." My fingers move past my underwear. "No one can see us from this angle."

"Esme," he growls, closing the book, gripping it so tight his knuckles are white. "Stop. We're in public."

"You used to like it." I move to sit on his lap, and he pushes back in the seat, like he'd rather be anywhere else than here. "Remember that time in Poison's bathroom when we snuck in after the Freshers' ball?"

I lean in to kiss him and he visibly recoils. Disgust blazes across his face. Like I repulse him.

I sit back. His expression strikes me just as the sting of rejection stabs my chest. "What's wrong?"

He looks at me with exasperation. "Nothing. I just don't want to have sex."

I look down at the very apparent, and extremely prominent, evidence in his jeans. "Since when?"

"Since… I don't know," he stands, practically shoving past me. "I just want to use my brain to think for a few moments. What's wrong with that?"

He's lying. The voice in my head says.

Oh, no shit?! Now pipe down, I'm busy trying to be a sexy detective! I snap at the voice.

Just as I'm about to answer Finn, the front door jingles as Dahlia enters.

"I know, I'm late! I'm sorry!" She rushes in, halting when she sees Finn practically climbing into a bookshelf and me with half my playsuit off. "Whoa, what did I walk in on?"

"Nothing," I answer coldly, pulling on my clothes, fixing Finn with a glare. "Apparently."

I turn and hear an exasperated sigh behind me, before following Dahlia into the backroom.

"What's going on?" she whispers to me as she flips on the kettle.

I check that my ex-ex-boyfriend isn't behind me. "Something is definitely weird with Finn."

"I mean... I already told you that," she says whilst she boils the kettle. "I also said he might be a killer. But you seemed to have ignored that little accusation so you can snuggle up with him and watch Disney movies."

"Look," I move closer to her and whisper quietly so that Finn can't hear me. "I'll admit there was a part of me that just wanted to pretend everything was fine. But now I see it," I look behind me. "Something is definitely wrong with him."

"Besides the whole coming back from the dead thing?"

"It's not that, well it is, but it also isn't," I'm aware of how insane I sound. "It's not all the time, but I can feel it now. He feels different."

Dahlia nearly falls into the cupboard in surprise. "Did you have sex with him?"

"No, of course not," I baulk. "I'm not crazy."

Says the woman who's hearing voices, my new imaginary friend comments.

Just the one voice, I mentally snap. *Singular. One, singular pain in the ass. You. I mean you!*

I got that, it retorts dryly.

Dahlia is now also looking at me like I've grown a second head. Oh good. It's contagious!

"He just keeps doing all these strange things, and apparently he's now an expert on the geographical and cultural origins of charms," I continue, "also he's become a complete neat freak!"

She turns back to the kettle, popping a herbal tea bag into her mug. "So, he's a little odd? It's to be expected since he was dead for so long. Oh when did we get biscuits?" She asks as she points at the mountain of half-eaten and crumpled packets by the fridge.

"He just looked at me like he was disgusted by me when I was topless in front of him."

"What was that meant to achieve?" She stares at me aghast.

"He keeps looking at me like," I grimace, embarrassment flooding my face, "like he hates me."

"So, boobs were your peace offering?" She arches an

eyebrow.

"Well, it used to work," I mutter. "It once stopped us bickering over whether gravy should go on chips and that was a major point of contention."

"Did you actually have an argument about that?" She waves her hand, "Forget it, it's not important-"

"That's what he said."

"He doesn't hate you," she says slowly. "It's not possible!"

"It is!" I urge, "seriously, I don't think he likes me. At least he doesn't today. I practically offered myself up to him on a silver platter."

She arches an eyebrow, a knowing smirk on her face. "Check you out Miss Risqué!"

I collapse down onto one of the wooden chairs, keeping my voice low. "He looked at me like I was trying to... I don't know... molest him or something."

She frowns. "But you two are always like bunnies. I wasn't joking when I said I felt like I needed to get a bucket of cold water to throw on you!"

"Yeah, well," I turn and look behind me, certain Finn is back reading that bloody book. "That doesn't look like that's a problem right now."

Her smirk falters. "Seriously?"

I nod. "I'm serious. Whatever, whoever, is sitting out there right now. That is not him!"

Dahlia and I keep an arms distance away from Finn all afternoon, leaving him to read and apparently, brood, in the corner.

Finn hasn't so much as held a grudge for longer than five minutes, except that one time with the gravy.

Zoe comes in early afternoon, a whirlwind of anxiety, adamant that whoever is following her hasn't stopped.

Finn only looks up from his book briefly as she blusters in, I note that his eyes return to the book, but they haven't moved across the words. He's listening intently to our discussion. I try to ignore him as I reassure Zoe that I will be back in a couple of days to refresh the wards and I remind her to keep wearing the protection pendant.

When it's time to close the shop, we walk in near silence back to the flat. Dahlia and I constantly shoot warning glares at each other.

When it's finally time for bed, I feign tiredness and deliberately slow my breaths to mimic deep sleep.

I feel the mattress shift and hear Finn dress quietly.

I hear him move to the living room. After shoving on my pink docs and a thick cream wool cardigan over my nightdress, I follow suit. I wait until I hear the soft click of the front door being opened and closed before grabbing my keys and heading out into the night like a woman possessed.

I don't know what I expect, but as I watch him swagger down the hill, I know I'm not looking at Finn. He looks like he's on the hunt, and again I'm reminded of what Dahlia said about the dead witch and her missing organs... and I realise I definitely don't have any survival instinct.

I keep my footsteps as quiet as possible, staying in the shadows, pressing against shop doorways when he stops and turns slightly, like he's caught a scent in the air.

We continue down the cobbled road, the only illumination coming from the dim streetlights. I feel the chill air swirl around me, whipping at my bare legs and face. He saunters on, down an alleyway of a darkened stairwell and I follow behind. There are no lights down here, but luckily, I know the steps well, so I tentatively follow.

This is so stupid; I may as well be wandering around with a big neon sign saying "stalker" on it! But if I'm going to get any answer on what's going on with him, I need to follow not-Finn and get to the truth. Because Finn's not telling me. Either because he can't remember, or because he's somehow become one of the best liars in the world.

I reach the bottom step and look down the alley, expecting to see his silhouette, but instead I see nothing.

I freeze when my foot lands on the final cobblestone, holding my breath. Where the hell has he gone?

Immediately I'm shoved up against the brick wall.

Muscled heat flattens me and an inhumanly strong hand grips around my neck. The hand is so hot I feel like I've been set on fire. Another hand grabs hold of both my wrists and pins them above my head.

"Why are you following me, Witchling?" he murmurs into my ear.

He smells like my cinnamon shower gel, but something else... like smoke and whisky. Like danger and darkness.

"F-Finn?" I manage to choke out from beneath his iron fingers, my head is pinned to the wall. I can't move and all I can see is darkness and shadows.

He chuckles. "No," his nose grazes my jaw. "Not Finn." His grip around my neck tightens and I feel my breathing constrict.

116

"Who-who are you?" I manage to choke out.

His face remains at my neck. "Someone… else."

His other hand grips my hip, a hand which less than twelve hours ago was caressing me, now holds me in a painful, vice-like grip.

He kicks my legs apart and my breath hitches before I have a chance to fight back. His grasp is so tight I feel my fingers begin to tingle and go numb.

"You're more astute than I thought," he says, a thick Scottish accent coating his words. "I'm almost impressed."

"Who are you?" I repeat.

He presses into me harder, and I have to try and ignore the frantic beats of my frightened heart.

"Not Finn," his voice is light and mocking.

His grip feels like iron shackles which I try to wriggle free from. "You're hurting me."

"I'm not," he growls, his face inches away from me and that's when I see the fire in his eyes. Blue transformed to molten amber, I can feel their heat and see their flame illuminating the darkness that surrounds me. "But I could," his words caress my neck. "And I bet I can make you beg and scream for it."

"Get off me!" I spit.

He smirks a devilish grin, and I struggle to recognise the features of Finn. Why would he say things like this to me?

He releases me. My arms go numb and hang limply beside me.

I watch as his silhouette swaggers to the opening of the alleyway, whistling a cheery tune. "As for my name," he turns, his voice echoing down the tunnel of tall buildings. "I'm Nox."

Chapter Fourteen

Esme

I've been ignoring the feeling that something is wrong with him. I mean, I've been avoiding the possibility that he's a murderous zombie!

But now? Now my head is being dragged out of the sand, whether I like it or not. The whole time Finn and I have been together he has never behaved like that. He's never spoken to me like that. That was not him.

He left me shivering in the dark alley and went whistling into the night like I meant nothing. I don't know if I'm still shaking because of the cold or because of fear.

I pull my cardigan tighter around my shoulders to stop me from shivering.

A dog barks in the distance, and I practically jump out of my skin. I run a hand through my hair as I stumble back to the flat.

How have I messed this up? I'd followed the spell to the damn letter. I'd done everything right...right? So how has this happened?

Goddess, the way he looked at me, the way he spoke to me, like I was nothing. Less than nothing. Just some tawdry piece of trash.

Those blue eyes were gone and replaced with a terrible fire that Finn, my Finn, doesn't possess. Possess. Something about the word hits me like a poison coated arrow. Could someone, or something, be possessing Finn?

I halt my steps at the crossing of the Royal Mile. The only source of light comes from the meagre streetlamps.

It'd explain his memory loss, personality change, dress sense and strange compulsion to keep everything neat and tidy. Could he somehow have been altered by the resurrection?

"Even I don't believe that," I grumble as I stare up at the sky. "And I'm the one thinking it!"

The wind whistles down the streets, a violent gust that causes me to shudder and close my eyes against the blistering cold. So much for summer! The unseasonal gale catches my hair in the breeze and as I open my eyes to brush the strands away from my face I feel my breath halt in my chest.

The street is transformed. The electric lights have been replaced by sparsely spaced oil lanterns, and instead of the shop fronts I walk past daily there's old-fashioned merchants… butchers, bakeries and inns.

I'm seeing things. It's just because I'm overtired and stressed. That's all. But if it's just my eyes playing tricks on me that doesn't explain the stench. It's so vile that I have to pull my cardigan up over my nose. I look up at the imposing buildings and recognise their silhouette across the sky. It's still the Royal Mile. But not the one I know. There's a golden mist hovering in the sky and it casts the streets in an eerie glow.

I look at my watch, 3am, there's no way it's dawn. Multiple voices shouting and booing erupt around me. The sound is deafening. I look around and still can't see anyone. Where the hell is this noise coming from?

I search up and down the streets, and take a cautious step, but freeze when a blood-curdling scream reverberates down the road. A woman's voice, filled with such terror. I pull my hands up to my ears trying to muffle some of the sound.

There's movement. A faint shape further up the hill. Something round and dark grows larger as it rolls towards me. As it gets closer, I see that it's a big wooden barrel. It clatters down the cobblestoned road at a frenetic pace and gathers momentum.

Another scream and I realise with horror, the sound is coming from inside the barrel. There's a woman trapped inside.

I force my limbs to move, rush to meet the wooden cylinder and put my weight in front of the barrel, bracketing all my strength against it. All too late, I realise it should have just run me over, but it stops. The wood is rough and solid against my shaking palms. My fingers grip the barrel's rough planks. Either I'm hallucinating or having the most vivid dream of my life. Although this is more like a nightmare. As I think this, another scream, slightly quieter, comes from inside.

"Are you ok?!" I call into the barrel. "I'm going to get you out!"

I begin to pry the lid open; the cold and the adrenaline make my hands tremble so much that my fingers struggle to find the rim.

"Help me!" the woman inside pleads, her voice stutters between sobs. "Please! Help me!"

"I'll get you out!" The wood splinters as I give the lid another violent tug and manage to pry the wood apart. My hands scream with the numerous cuts and splinters.

I throw the lid aside and kneel to pull the woman out. It's so dark inside but I see the glinting of sharpened nails hammered in from the outside. No wonder she was screaming. That would have been agony! I reach to pull my phone from my pocket to shine the torch inside, but just as I do a bloodied hand snaps out of the barrel and grabs my wrist tightly.

"Please help me," the woman's voice is barely more than a whimper. "Make them stop!"

Her grip is so tight my fingers are going numb. "I will. I promise. I just need to-"

"What the fuck are you doing?" a male voice from behind me asks.

I free myself from the woman's grasp, tumbling back onto the pavement and clutch my aching wrist. I hit the cobblestones, pain reverberating through my hips. When I open them again, the streets are back to normal. The foul stench has gone from the air, but not from my memory.

I look around to see Finn, on the other side of the road. He's leaning against one of the shop fronts with his arms crossed over his chest.

He's looking down at me with the expression of someone about to chastise a two-year-old. He pushes off the wall and saunters towards me. The streetlight makes his eyes dance with that same eerie glow I'd seen in the alleyway.

"I said," he looks down at me with an uncharacteristic sneer on his handsome face. "What the fuck are you doing?"

I pull myself up into a sitting position, wincing at the pain in my side, another one to add to the collection. Yay. "The woman she- she was screaming. I had to help her."

His eyes are steely but there's a glimmer of curiosity. "What woman?"

I twist towards the barrel, but just as I'm about to point to it, I realise it's disappeared. I turn back and look up at Finn.

"I saw something," I make a move to stand, but my legs feel like jelly, and they buckle. He'll tell me I'm being crazy. I don't need to

120

be gaslit by Finn when he's being a prick. I didn't even know he was capable of being like this.

He looks skyward. "For fucks sake," he grumbles, he holds out an outstretched hand. "Come on."

I look at his hand like it's a poisonous snake. "Why?"

"Well, unless you fancy sitting there until morning, it looks like you need some help getting up," he wiggles his fingers at me. "You can either accept my help or not. I honestly couldn't give two shits, but I don't think your boyfriend will thank me for leaving you on The Mile all night."

"My boyfriend?" I frown up at him, the streetlight above making those golden eyes glow brighter in the darkness.

"Aye," he sighs, crouching down in front of me. "The meat sack you're screwing."

"I'm not…" I look into his face, trying to piece my broken thoughts together. "You really aren't Finn?"

A wolfish smile curls in the corner of his lips, a smirk that I'd never have seen Finn's face show before. "Not at the minute, no."

"How?"

He shrugs, looking completely nonchalant. Like this kind of thing happens all the time!

"I wouldn't worry about it," he brushes a piece of lint from his trousers. "Why are you on the ground looking like you have seen a ghost?"

I let out a humourless laugh. "I shouldn't worry that my boyfriend has multiple personalities, one of which is a colossal asshole?!"

His eyes flash with warning. "I'm not an asshole."

"You're being one right now!" I rake a hand through my hair. "And in the alley way, for fucks sake, Finn!" My voice echoes down the street and I hate how much it trembles.

He holds up a finger, wagging it at me like he's scolding a child. "We already covered this, Witchling. I am not Finn."

I manage to push myself off the pavement. "Right. Whatever," I wave a hand dismissively, sure I'll enable this delusion. I just want to go home. "You're Nox."

"Correct," he flashes his dimples. "So are you going to tell me why you were on the floor or is this just something you tend to do?"

I pull my cardigan tighter around me. "Do you care?"

He arches an eyebrow. "I'm curious."

Goddess, why is he being such an antagonistic twat?

I huff out an exasperated breath. "Alright, fine," I begin

limping down the hill, trying to ignore the way my hips scream in pain. I'm going to have bruises all over me tomorrow. Wonderful.

Finn, or Nox, falls into step with me.

"I thought I saw something," I look up to see his features flicker for a second before settling back into a bored expression. "A barrel rolling down The Mile. I thought I heard screaming and the streets looked all weird," I stomp my feet as we walk, trying to ignore the heat in my cheeks. "Like I was seeing into the past." I let out another brittle, humourless laugh. "Maybe my imagination just ran away with itself," I look back up at him, the dark hair resting above a small frown that puckers on his forehead. "You know, like how yours is right now with your new persona."

He glares down at me. "I'm not Finn."

"You look like Finn."

"Unfortunately," he sighs. "But I'm not him."

"So where is he then?"

He shrugs. "Sleeping, I guess. I'm always a bit woolly about what happens to the humans I possess. I don't tend to give it much thought."

Hearing him say the word confirms my fear. Possess. I've fucked up. I've bollocksed this spell up so much I did a two for one on Finn's body.

"So, you're what," I halt and stare up at him, trying to ignore the wobble in my voice. "A ghost?"

"I remember you asking him this the first time you two were reunited," his smile widens, like this bloody nightmare is entertaining to him. "No."

He steps towards me, too close for my liking, and I take a step back to keep a safe distance away from whoever is driving Finn's body right now. "Guess again."

"I'm not in the mood to play games, *Nox.*"

He sighs theatrically. "Alright, fine. I'm what you humans call a demon."

I stand dumbfounded for a couple of seconds, before a high pitched, unnerved laugh escapes me.

"You're joking!" I manage to splutter between my hysterical outbursts. He looks at me like I've gone insane. Maybe I have?

He waits until my laughter subsides before answering. "I came back when Finn did. I co-own his body. Think of it like a time-share. Sometimes it's him, sometimes it's me."

"Once again I come back to my question, how?"

"You're the one who did the spell, Witchling," he begins

122

walking again, no not walking, swaggering. "It's your spell. You figure it out."

This is why I never push myself to try and do advanced Magick. This shit happens! I try to do one spell and it blows up in my face and I am now talking to a literal demon who's wearing my boyfriend like a suit.

I need to look at the spell and figure out if there's some way I can fix this absolute cluster-fuck of a conjuring without losing Finn. I've only just got him back. I can't lose him. Not again.

The demon turns, his golden eyes glowing. "Are you coming, Sugar?"

Chapter Fifteen

<u>Nox</u>

I resist the overwhelming urge to drag Esme back to her flat, but she eventually begins to follow. She walks a good few feet behind me like a sullen child. I don't have time to babysit but I need to get Little Miss Sugar and No Spice on side, or to keep things civil, at least for the time being. I don't know how capable the witchling is in her powers but if she has a coven, they may be able to help her figure out a way to get rid of me. So, I'll play nice. Or at least pretend to. I look back at her and she glowers at me from beneath the frown perching above her eyes, and it takes all my willpower not to snap at her. She's deliberately dawdling to piss me off.

"Careful," I cast another look behind me at the pink haired nightmare. "Your face will stay like that!"

"At least it's *my* face," she grumbles, kicking at a rock that she could have been aiming at my legs. "I'm not some weirdo who's *apparently* inhabiting someone else's body."

I stifle a chuckle; she's willingly choosing to believe that her boyfriend is having a mental break rather than accepting the truth. It's amusing that her rationale is so far from reality.

"Again," I call back. "This whole conundrum that you and your boytoy are in is not my fault. If you want to be pissed at someone about messing up your spell, I'd recommend taking a good hard look in the mirror, Sugar."

"Stop calling me!" she huffs, a small breeze causes a whirlwind of her candy floss perfume to waft over me. Does everything about her have to be so nauseatingly sweet?

"Well, I could call you some of the names I've heard Finn call you in his head," I tease, enjoying the tension that radiates from her. I bask in witty self-satisfaction when something small and hard hits the

124

back of my skull.

A large pebble clatters to the ground, "Did you just throw a rock at my head?"

She looks at me with a mixture of shock and disgust, "You said that possession means that you don't know what the other person is doing!"

"For the humans, yes," I say, rubbing the back of my head, "if I was mortal that would have hurt. For demons' possession is a little different."

"Oh, my Goddess!" Her hands fly to her mouth, mortification coating her features, "So you were there in the background? Watching everything like a grade A creep?!"

"Doesn't seem like there was that much to watch," I snicker. "Except you giving the Finnster blue balls!"

So much for playing nice with her. Although, in my defence, she's already resorted to violence! I need to diffuse this situation, or she's going to hunt for banishing spells the minute she steps through her sodding front door. Maybe I really have underestimated her? Although judging by the state of this girl, I doubt she's capable of figuring out how she'd mastered the spell, let alone how to adjust it.

"I may be a creep," I bite out, trying to control my temper, "but at least I don't act like a child and throw literal stones in arguments!"

"You deserve it!" She scowls at me, closing the distance between us. Her eyes flash up at me and for a second I almost believe the witchling can fix her fuckup. "You're a pig!"

"Demon," I correct her, I can't help but smirk. Her nostrils flare and her cheeks flush with anger to match her hair colour.

"Demon pig!" Her scowl deepens, before sticking her tongue out at me. Like a five-year-old!

I can't stop the laughter when she overtakes me. It's like being threatened by a chihuahua! Although I must admit, the back of my head does hurt! She's got a good throw on her.

I quickly catch up with her within a few strides. "I apologise," I try to keep my tone sincere. "That was rude and mean of me."

"It was," she keeps her attention locked on the pavement in front of her, deliberately avoiding looking at me.

I step in front of her, halting her frog march. "Can you forgive me?"

I attempt to sound sincere, although it's taking every part of my willpower to do so.

She chews on her bottom lip and looks troubled for a couple of seconds, before she breaks free of my grip and recommences her ascent, albeit with slightly less stamping. "I don't know, I need to think about it."

I stop myself from chuckling. Humans are so predictable. Show them a sliver of remorse and they'll always clutch to it. Particularly this one, she's so desperate to believe I'm not all bad. She's clearly just as hairbrained as I thought. It'd be funny, if it wasn't so pathetic.

I paint on a forlorn expression, attempting to feign regret. I'm going to need to start taking anti-nausea medication to cope with her.

We continue the walk up to the building in silence. I linger on the pavement as I watch her ungracefully amble around the huge flowers at her door. Her delicate fingers shake as she tries to fish the keys out of her cardigan. She finally gets the key in the lock, pushes open the door and turns to look at me as if she's conflicted about letting me inside. Poor girl. I almost feel sorry for her. Almost.

But then I remember the thorn that witches have always been in my side, and any sympathy I feel is quickly snuffed out. I try to keep my face neutral but can't stop the teasing smile on my lips creeping up as I watch her flounder at the entryway.

"I'll save you the turmoil of deciding whether to let me in," I tease, leaning against the lamppost. "Scintillating as our little tete-a-tete has been, I've got an appointment and I'm already late."

Her brow furrows again. "Who the hell are you meeting?"

I can't help but chuckle at her choice of words. "Just a friend from back home," I answer breezily. Smugness surges up in me when I see the look of confusion on the witchling's face, before sauntering back down the hill whistling a cheery tune into the darkness.

Home. The word sticks in my mind like a splinter. I don't know what, or where, home really is. As I slink through the abandoned, nighttime streets of the city, I wonder if I even know what the word really means. The only time I ever felt like I was home was when I was with Sarah. She'd been my home. My sanctuary. Witches and demons rarely form alliances outside of the usual contractual transactions. Eventually one will wrangle more power over the other and they'd need to sever ties. But not her. She bewitched me with her innocence, her honesty and her soul. Many would think a demon would find these traits tawdry but to me, her transparency was her biggest strength and my biggest weakness. A mortal I'd promised to protect, and when it mattered most, I wasn't there. She'd been alone in that barbaric torture and when she'd been in agony, when the flames finally took her, I'd failed her. And now...

I look down the winding street, letting out an

uncharacteristically melancholy sigh. Now I have no bloody idea where she is. I kick a discarded piece of rubbish down the path.

Culum may be a Grade A prick most of the time, but I know he will have at least been thorough in his research. I've known the asshole for centuries and I can trust him. Well. As much as I can trust any demon.

I continue until I stand outside Maggie's. Despite it being well past the last call, I go down the alley, make quick and quiet work on the back door and enter the pub.

Even after all these years it still has that same lingering atmosphere that Maggie had instilled into the building when she'd run it. Or that could just be me being nostalgic. Hell, what's wrong with me? I never used to be such a soft touch.

The pub is as silent as a grave. I quietly grab a bottle of scotch from the top shelf and pull down a tumbler. I pour myself a generous helping and swill the glass. I hold it to my face; the scent of warm spices and the fiery burn of the liquor makes me smile. I run a hand over the bar top. So many years have passed since I set foot in here, yet it still feels familiar. The scent of stale alcohol, hand-rolled cigarettes and the ghosts of countless perfumes and aftershaves linger in the air.

I always loved this pub. Culum, Sarah and I would often sit with Maggie at the back late into the night, laughing and drinking. Enjoying the simple pleasure of company and alcohol. I look to the corner where we used to sit. Three wooden stalls sit around a small circular table. So similar to the one from all those years ago. I can't bring myself to sit at it.

I look down at my watch. 3am. The time in which the veil between the mortal and immortal realms is thinnest, allowing for easy and covert passage.

Where the hell is Culum?

I take a large swig of the scotch and settle down at one of the bar seats, spinning the glass in my hand impatiently. I hold it up and watch the golden light sparkle even in the meagre moonlight.

My thoughts turn to Esme. I don't know what I'd stumbled onto, but when I saw her crumpled on the ground, she looked so scared. I felt compelled to ask what was wrong. Before she'd had time to train her mouth from spilling all her thoughts there was something about what she said that irked me. She said there was a screaming woman.

Edinburgh's streets had once sung with screams and the roads would run red with the blood of condemned women that the church and monarchy had decided were witches. They accused poor innocent outcasts, midwives or medicine women. Those judges, juries and executioners were usually wrong. They would single out any woman who was too strange or too clever. Sometimes it was just because they had shirked the wrong man's advances.

But the witches had been cunning, they hid in plain sight and with the help of Sarah and I, most remained unharmed. Except for Sarah herself, who was tossed into the flames.

I take another large gulp.

Perhaps the pink haired harlot had seen something? A vision of past events. If so, she may be useful. If she can somehow tap into what happened in the past, maybe she can find some clue to where the grimoire is.

I look at my watch. Eleven minutes past three. Culum isn't coming. Strange, I would have thought he'd be chomping at the bit to come back to Maggie's for a drink. Granted, he can be a little unreliable, but it seems odd. Maybe it had proven too difficult to slip away unnoticed.

I make my way behind the bar and grab a knife from the side, before heading to the little circular table. I crouch down and scratch a message into the underside of the table. If Culum does come to the pub, he'll see it. I quickly polish off the rest of my glass and throw a tenner down on the bar.

I'd best head back and try and play nice with the witchling. Hopefully I can get something useful out of her before I throttle her.

Chapter Sixteen

Esme

I don't know how I manage to sleep, but once I feed Ink and lie down on my bed, I fall into a dreamless sleep. I only stir when the warming rays of sunlight caress my face.

"Morning, babe," I feel the weight of someone next to me on my bed and I almost jump out of my skin at the sight of Finn. His onyx dyed hair is damp from the shower and the smell of cinnamon soap clings to him. He holds out a cup to me which looks and smells like coffee. I take the drink gratefully and take a cautious sip.

If Finn is really Finn he wouldn't have done anything to my drink. Nox on the other hand… Goddess only knows.

"Are you, erm," I look at him intently, trying to gauge if there's a flicker of Nox behind his handsome features. "Are you really you?"

A small smile teases at the corner of his lips before he gives a light-hearted chuckle. "Yeah, why wouldn't I be?"

Could it be possible that Finn doesn't know what's happening to him? Surely he'd realise he's losing massive chunks of time?

I take another gulp of coffee, trying to figure out the best way of telling someone that they are possessed and oh yeah, it's all my fault.

I put the coffee down on the bedside table, sit up on the bed and pull his hand to mine. "So what I'm going to tell you is going to sound a little strange."

Understatement of the bloody century!

"When I brought you back, I kind of brought something else with you."

He frowns. "Something else?"

"You're, erm," I suck in a breath. "You're possessed. By something which says it's a demon."

129

Finn's eyes widen in alarm. "What?"

"He says his name is Nox."

"Are you telling me," he says slowly, "that there is a demon possessing my body and you've actually spoken to it?"

"Afraid so," I nod, "and he's a dick."

A dry laugh escapes him, and he looks up at the ceiling, like he's at a loss for words.

I give his hand a gentle shake. "Are you alright?"

"I honestly don't know. I thought I was, but I'm turning into a demon without my knowledge!"

I give his hand a light squeeze. "I'm so sorry."

"Why are you sorry?"

"I messed up the spell and I ended up getting you possessed!"

"Hey," he leans in, cupping my face with his other hand. "This isn't your fault. You did something amazing. You brought me back to life."

"I brought you back, but now there is a demon cohabitating in your body like some kind of messed up time-share!" I feel the tears in my eyes begin to brim. I screwed up. Just like I do with everything. I should have done more research. I should have looked into the spell more before blindly diving in. I didn't think about the repercussions. My Dad's right about me.

"Stop it," Finn strokes my face gently. "Stop beating yourself up."

"But it's my fault."

He gives me a lop-sided smile. "Hey, so there's some complications."

"Complications? You seem to be handling this information unnervingly well!"

"Life never works out the way you expect," he strokes my chin. "Why should death be any different?"

I let out a weak chuckle. "I'll fix it. I just need to figure out some way of getting rid of the prick without accidentally losing you."

"Could that happen?"

I shrug. "I don't know, I brought you both here. If you're linked and I get rid of him, what would happen to you?" my voice falters. The thought of losing him when I just got him back makes my heart twist painfully.

"I might go back to where I was before?" he offers.

I give a small nod.

"Well, then, worse comes to worse, I just have this little

130

affliction, until we figure out how to solve it."

"You have a prick of a demon who's walking around doing Goddess knows what with your body!"

"Is he that much of an asshole?"

"He's a demon. Being an asshole is probably him reigning it in!"

Finn grimaces. "Did he tell you why he's possessing me?"

"No. He was pretty tight-lipped about it."

He nods slowly. "I guess if he's got motives for it, he's going to play them pretty close to his chest."

I scrub a hand down my face. At least Finn doesn't hate me for bringing him back with a demonic passenger. All things considered; he's taking the news pretty well.

Maybe this seems like a small price to pay? It does make me wonder how bad the Afterlife must be. I remember what Nox had said about possessing a body, and how he's always sitting in the background of the person's mind.

"He said last night that when he's in a body he can listen in on thoughts and feelings," I say slowly. "Maybe you can try to do the same with him?"

"You want me to spy on a demon who's possessing my body?" he asks doubtfully.

"Do you think you can?"

"I don't know, Ez," he sighs. "I mean I didn't even realise anything was wrong until you told me."

"But did it not feel odd that you were losing so much time?" I ask incredulously. I've never classed Finn as one of the great thinkers, but I would expect him to notice that!

A small flush rises on his cheeks. "Honestly, I kind of thought that was just normal. After everything that has happened. I just thought I was zoning out."

I try to put a kind smile on my face to hide my concern.

"It'll be ok," I say quietly. "We'll figure it out."

Just as I say this, I hear the clatter of the front door being opened and Dahlia calls from the living room. "Please tell me you're not shagging somewhere I'm about to walk into?"

"We're in my room," I yell back. "Don't worry we're not having sex!"

Dahlia pokes her head around the door. "Huh, weird! Are you two feeling alright? Has the honeymoon already gone stale?"

I give her a dirty look.

She scoffs. "You can't blame me for checking! It used to

131

sound like I was living next to a barn."

I throw a pillow at her. "Don't be gross!"

"Besides," Finn pushes a hand through his hair, "it's not every day you find out you're possessed."

Dahlia's jaw drops so low, she might need my help picking it up. "What?"

"Oh yeah," Finn offers a sad smile. "I'm possessed. Apparently, all the cool kids are!"

"Something went a bit foofy with the spell," I say sheepishly.

She arches an eyebrow. "Foofy?"

"Ez's way of saying something is fucked up without saying fucked up," Finn explains.

"I'm quite aware of Ez's vocabulary, thank you Finn!" She walks over to the bed and sits down opposite us. "How did you find out?"

I take another sip of my cooling coffee. "I met Finn's alter ego last night."

"Oh Goddess, were you having sex?"

"No! What is it with you and sex?" I squeal. "I followed him when he was wandering the streets in the middle of the night, very creepy and ominous."

Dahlia leans forward, her attention rapt. "Oooh! A ghost?"

"Apparently he's a demon called Nox," Finn says dryly.

"A demon?!" Dahlia splutters. That's the reaction I was expecting from Finn! But here he is, looking incredibly calm for someone who has a demon inside him.

"What's he like?" Dahlia asks, her voice full of curiosity.

"A colossal prick!" I lean back against my bedframe and the ivy gives my shoulder a comforting tickle. At least my botanical Magick hasn't blown up in my face. Not yet at least.

She doesn't look taken aback by my answer. "Well, he is a demon."

"So, being a prick goes hand in hand?" I sigh. "Now I have to try and figure out a way of untethering him from Finn."

"Well, given you're now a bad-ass witch, I'm sure that'll be a piece of cake," Dahlia gives me a playful smile which falters when she sees my grave expression. "What?"

"Nox crossed over with Finn," I say. "Which means whatever I do to get rid of Nox might mean…" The words die on my lips again.

"She gets rid of me too," Finn finishes my sentence.

"Ah," realisation crosses her features. "That's crap."

"Super crap," I agree.

"So, what's our plan of attack?" Dahlia asks and I am reminded again how much I love this girl. She's never been someone who let the world smack her down. She'll get up, dust herself off and kick its ass.

I set my jaw in grim determination. "We go to the shop. Time to do some research and I'll speak with Agnes."

"Will she be able to help?" she asks sceptically, "I know she was in your mum's coven, but will she really know what to do about this? Do you even want her to know about it?"

"Agnes knows her stuff." I pull back the covers and throw myself out of the bed. No more wallowing. That never helped anyone anyway. "And if she doesn't know, she should at least be able to point me in the direction of someone who will. OK, let's go."

"Erm, Ez," Finn looks up at me from the bed, that small smile is back on his face. "As much as I love you in your little pink shorts, maybe you might want to put some more clothes on before venturing outside?"

I look down. Finn's right. My pyjamas are definitely not suitable for the general public.

"Fair point." I skip out of the room and head to the shower. "I'll get ready. Just give me ten minutes."

I hear Finn call hopefully from my bedroom. "Want some company?"

"No!" Dahlia and I answer in unison.

I get dressed in record time, throwing on my favourite strawberry print halter dress and pink Doc Martens.

"Your outfits never fail to baffle me," Dahlia drawls as we head out of the flat.

I cast a look at her, despite the heat, she's still head to toe in her funeral black attire. "Just because you're allergic to colour, doesn't mean we all have to be!"

Finn throws an arm over my shoulder as we wind through the busy streets.

"I love how you dress," Finn places a kiss on my cheek as we make our way to the shop. "You look good enough to eat!" he chuckles, "metaphorically, not literally, I promise!"

The streets are already heaving with bodies. The noise and chatter immediately brightens my mood. Sure, shit is going sideways, but at least he's here.

I smile at him. "Thanks babe."

"Goddess, give me strength!" Dahlia grumbles beside me,

casting a disdainful glare at us before popping on her oversized black sunglasses.

"She's just jealous," Finn says loudly so that Dahlia can hear him over the crowds of people. "We just need to find her a nice guy and-"

"I'd rather eat glass than go on a blind date," she smiles sweetly, but I can see the snarl behind the grin. "Besides, they are more Ez's forte!"

"Not anymore they aren't!" Finn puffs out his chest gallantly, "she's officially off the market!"

I fish my keys out from my bag and call back to them. "Can you two stop talking about me like I'm not here?"

"Fat chance of that happening!" Dahlia snorts, "You look like a pink bauble!"

I stick my tongue out at her, before turning to push the shop door open. As we walk in the flowers begin to bloom and their sweet scent rivals the candles and incense.

"Right, when you two have finished discussing my love life can you start looking through the books." I fish my phone out of my pocket. "I'll call Agnes and ask her to come in."

"Ask her to bring cake!" Dahlia demands as she tugs Finn over to one of the bookshelves containing the summoning spells. Which ironically will be much easier to peruse now that Nox has organised them for us. "She owes us at least twenty!"

Agnes picks up the call after several seconds of ringing. "Oh, hello Esme dear!"

"Hey Agnes, how are you?"

"Tell her I want red velvet!" Dahlia demands and I fire a warning glare at her.

"Oh I'm..." Agnes' voice flounders and I swear I hear a shaky inhale over the call.

"Agnes, are you alright?"

"Oh, I'm sorry Esme dear I just... I had a strange call from one of our sister witches, she'd been scrying last night, and she had a vision. She saw... she'd seen another girl. Another dead girl. Poor thing is quite shaken up."

"Oh Goddess, I'm so sorry."

"Yes, terrible business. We're trying to unpick some of the details but it's all a bit scattered. She saw brief flashes, a white room in disarray, and blood, so much blood. She also mentioned seeing a flash of long red hair on a white tiled floor..."

I don't hear anything else that Agnes says for a second. Bile

134

rises in my throat.

"Was the hair... curly?" I ask, my voice coming out in a strained whisper.

Finn and Dahlia stand still; both turn to look at me with confusion on their faces at my strange question.

"Why - I - yes, I believe so," Agnes answers, I'm certain she's got the same expression that Finn and Dahlia are wearing.

"Oh Goddess," I double over, my hands are shaking so much I accidentally drop the phone.

They rush over to me, and Dahlia picks it up, trying to calm the now frantic sounding Agnes on the other end of the line.

My knees buckle and Finn catches me. "Babe, what's wrong?"

"I think it's Zoe," my voice comes out hoarse and strained.

Dahlia's brow furrows as she listens to Agnes repeating the vision, horror slowly seeping into her eyes.

I try to fight the fear that rushes through me. "I think Zoe might be dead."

Dahlia manages to get Agnes off the call. I've tried over thirty times to ring Zoe's number and every damned time it goes to voicemail.

She might just not have her phone on loud. It could be silent, or in the other room or...

Stop! Don't think about it!

We quickly close the shop and head to Zoe's flat. I try to argue against the gnawing fear inside me, insisting that it probably isn't Zoe. Scrying is woolly at best, there's no guarantee the visions are accurate, but I can't shake the dread inside me. I have to go check on Zoe.

We dodge past boisterous tourists who are happily chatting and snapping photos. I have to fight the voices in my head that are arguing about what we'll find.

"I texted Agnes Zoe's address, Ez," Dahls says quietly. "She said she's on her way over as well, so she'll meet us there in case..." She trails off.

None of us want to contemplate what we might be walking into.

"She's fine," I say, cuddling into Finn's arm which is once again slung around my shoulder, taking comfort in his warmth. Even though the late summer sun is beaming down on us, I feel a looming chill. Like we're heading into something cold and dark. "We're just going to check on her."

Dahlia looks like she's about to say something but stops herself. "She's fine. Like you said, we're just checking on her," she says unconvincingly.

Finn gives my shoulder a gentle stroke.

Zoe is fine. She has to be fine. But then I remember how panicked Zoe was when she thought someone was following her.

I quicken my pace, practically running towards her flat. Dahlia and Finn don't miss a beat as they fall into step with me.

All three of us are sweaty, breathless messes by the time we arrive at Zoe's. I hadn't thought about how we were meant to get in. But luckily, or unluckily, someone had left the door on the latch.

We enter without Zoe's neighbours being alerted, which saves us from having to concoct a half-assed excuse.

We climb down the spiral staircase and see her door. My stomach plummets. It's ajar. I have to steal myself before I push the door open wider.

Finn places a hand on my arm. "Maybe we should call the police?"

I fix my mouth in a tight line. "We have to go in before we call them."

"Ez is right," Dahls looks ashen. "We have to check first."

I take another step forward, hating how shaky I feel.

"Zo?" I call down the hallway, only to be met by deathly silence.

I look back at Dahls and Finn, both of them look like they'd rather be anywhere else than here. I feel the same way.

"Ok," I suck in a shaky breath. "Are you both ready?"

"Honestly," Dahls sighs. "No. Not at all. But fuck it. We're here now. So, let's go."

"Okey dokey," I chew on my bottom lip.

"What the fuck am I doing here again?" Finn questions behind me.

I knew he was losing time, but I didn't realise that would mean he'd forget where he was every half hour!

"You ok, Finn?" Dahlia asks behind me.

"Not Finn," the heavily accented voice says and immediately I feel myself bristle with apprehension. "Sugar, be a dear, and introduce me to this dark beauty beside me."

Oh, perfect timing. Just what this day needs. Nox making his guest appearance.

I turn to see that he's now leaning against the banister nonchalantly, a stark contrast to how shit-scared Dahlia and I feel. Although I do catch a flash of curiosity in his features.

"Nox?" I don't even know why I'm asking. I know it's that prick at the driving seat.

"The one and only," he smirks, his gaze glimmering in the dim stairwell light.

Dahls looks at Nox like he's a poisonous snake and takes a wary step back, "I'm Dahlia."

Nox flashes a smile, which would almost be charming. If he wasn't such an asshole. "Enchanted. I'm-"

"She knows who and what you are, Nox. Stop pretending like this is your first time seeing her when you've been spying on us this entire time!" I glare at him. "Where's Finn?"

He shrugs, looking completely unfazed by what's happening. "Beats me."

"Bring him back!" I snarl. "Now!"

"Doesn't work that way, Sugar."

I grit my teeth, "Stop calling me that!"

He inspects his nails. "Maybe I'll be a braver alternative? You two look terrified." He looks up, arching an eyebrow, "What exactly is going on?"

I stalk over to him and poke his chest. "Get Finn back right now!"

"Not happening, *Sweetheart*," those whisky golden eyes flash at me, reminding me of our last encounter in the alleyway. He swats my finger away, and marches forward. "Are we going in here?"

"No, *we* are not! *You* are getting Finn back right now, or... or..."

"You'll throw another rock at my head?"

I let out an exasperated huff. This is just typical. It's like he's doing it deliberately.

"Did you just growl at me?" he smirks, amusement dancing in his face. "That's adorable!"

"Oh, fuck off!" I snap. I don't normally swear at people, but he's asking for it, although he's not technically a person. He's practically begging for another rock in the back of his stupid, smug face. Wait, no, that's not his actual face. Why does he have to possess someone I'm romantically involved with? Goddess, give me strength!

"Ez, breathe," Dahlia holds out her hands between Nox and me, like she's playing mediator.

"I am breathing," I grumble, crossing my arms in front of me. "He's just winding me up."

"I'm a demon, remember, Sugar?" he saunters through Zoe's hallway. "I live to torment, torture and be an all-round badass."

Dahls steps closer to me. "Did he just refer to himself as a badass?"

"He did."

"Maybe he can be useful?" she shrugs. "He's a demon, maybe he's got superpowers?"

"His biggest superpower is being a dickhead," I say loudly to make sure he hears me. "Either way, he's now in Zoe's flat, so I guess we're following as well."

"Looks like that way," Dahlia deadpans. "Lead the way, *Sugar.*"

I shoot her a warning look as I pass her. "Oh, don't you bloody start on that too!"

The crystals in the hall haven't been moved from where I'd put them, so that's good at least, but as I walk into the open plan living room, I have to double check we're definitely in Zoe's flat. It's been completely trashed.

Her normally sterile white apartment is in complete disarray. Upturned chairs, broken crockery, even the window has been shattered and a light breeze causes the white curtain to billow.

"Take it that it doesn't normally look like this, huh?" Nox asks rhetorically.

"Zoe?" I call out weakly. "Are you… are you here?"

I head towards her bedroom. I have to grip the door frame as I take in the sight. Splashes of red slash across the walls, as well as a pool of crimson in the centre of her cotton sheets.

A lump rises in my throat. "Oh Goddess."

Nox pushes past me, letting out a low whistle. "That's a hell of a lot of blood. I like it kinky, but this is extreme, even for me."

Dahlia gasps as she walks in. "Oh fuck."

Nox circles the bed once, before making his way past us. He walks towards the bathroom.

"Nox?" I call after him. "Where are you going?"

"Well, I wasn't going for a piss," he answers.

I make my way towards the bathroom, but he blocks the doorway. Is he bigger? Finn is already tall but when Nox takes over, he's somehow more imposing.

"You don't want to go in there, Sugar," he warns, his tone is so low it almost sounds gentle.

"The fuck does that mean?" I say. "Move your ass out of the way!"

He looks down at me with something like pity. "Trust me."

"Trust you?!" I baulk. "You're a demon who's possessing my boyfriend! I wouldn't trust you as far as I can throw you!" I step closer to him, lifting my chin defiantly. "Now. Move!"

He moves to the side, leaning against the doorframe. "Don't say I didn't warn you."

I give him one more steely glare before pushing the door open and immediately I regret my decision. Blood. So much blood. The white bathroom is painted red.

I look towards the tub, there's crimson handprints across the tiles and the bath is full of coppery orange water.

I step forward and see scarlet hair swirling amongst the water. The water is thick with blood, but I can still see Zoe's face beneath the surface. Her eyes are glassy, and her ivory skin is torn with angry gashes across her stomach, arms and legs. Her neck looks raw, like several layers of skin have been stripped away.

I lunge for the toilet to vomit into the porcelain bowl.

"Oh Goddess!" I hear Dahlia behind me, her voice is hushed and horrified. "What the hell happened to her? Do you think she killed herself?"

I pull myself from the toilet, wiping my mouth with the back of my hand. "I don't think so, look at those cuts… and her neck, there's no way she did that to herself."

I look towards Nox, his face is set with grim resignation.

"I've seen this type of thing before." He walks towards the bath and looks down at Zoe. "She was tortured," he turns to look between Dahlia and me. "By any chance was Zoe a witch?"

"Not a practising one," I answer numbly. "She wasn't even really a fledgling."

"Well, they thought she was," he sighs, looking around the bathroom. "Enough to torture and drown her."

"They?" I ask dumbly.

"Witch hunters," Nox answers flatly as he looks at the still crimson water.

Chapter Seventeen

Esme

"Ez," Dahlia jostles my shoulder. I'm still propped against the bathroom wall, unable to pry my eyes away from Zoe. From Zoe's corpse. Oh no, I'm going to throw up again.

"Ez?" She gives me another shake and I turn away from the crimson waters. I meet Dahlia's gaze; her face is grey, and she looks like she's going to either vomit or pass out. "Agnes is here."

I try to process her words, but my brain is sluggish, like I'm having to translate what she's saying. "Agnes?"

"Aye, remember?" she continues, her tone strangely detached. "She came to meet us. She- she wants to come in."

That's ironic, all I want to do is get the hell out of here. If only I could make my damn limbs move. But if I move away from this wall, I know I'll end up collapsed on the floor amongst the pooled water and blood. Zoe's blood.

Another one of my friends is dead. The memory of Hazel's murder resurfaces, and I can't help but wonder how much grief the human heart can withstand before it breaks.

"You told her?" I ask and Dahls looks towards Nox, who reemerges from the hallway and gives Dahlia a small nod.

"Nox did."

I can't stop my eyebrows from shooting up. The idea that Nox can be tactful seems as likely as me performing brain surgery, or you know, casting a successful conjuring.

"Don't worry," she says upon seeing my reaction. "I was there. He was surprisingly… sensitive. Although he kept looking at her strangely," Dahlia leans in and whispers, "but that could just be

140

because of what she's wearing.

I can't stop the weak chuckle at that, but as I look at Nox, I notice how grave his expression is. I'm getting used to him looking cavalier, arrogant, but there's something lingering in his eyes that almost looks human. Almost sadness. Maybe it's because it's Finn's face? Maybe…

He continues to look at the bathtub. Staring at what lies beneath the surface.

"Does Agnes know that Nox is, erm, Nox?" I ask.

Dahlia shakes her head. "I think we need to tackle one thing at a time. The woman who had the vision is with her. Crystal something…"

I nod absently. Crystal had been part of Mum's coven. When I was little, she would sit apart from the other witches, but she would always be watching. I was always wary of her, the way her hooked nose would crinkle in disdain when she looked at me. Like I shouldn't have been allowed to attend the meetings.

Maybe that look of disapproval will have diluted over time? Maybe she just doesn't like children?

But as the two older women walk in, both gravely quiet, I catch that same look of prickly mistrust from Crystal. Guess it's nothing to do with my age. She just doesn't like me. Oh goody.

Not even the fuchsia dress Agnes wears can brighten the darkness of this room. Crystal gives me a withering glare, before walking over to the bath, pulling her jade shawl tighter around her tiny frame.

She peers closer into the water and doesn't even gag, I can't help but admire her constitution.

Agnes stands a few steps behind her. "Is she the same girl you saw, Crystal?"

"Aye, that's her," Crystal says sadly. "Poor thing."

Nox walks further into the room, standing behind the two women. "Did you see anything else in your vision?"

Crystal turns, casting a sceptical look at him. "They don't work like scripts I'm afraid. I get flashes. I saw blood. White tiles. A flash of this poor girl's face and…" Her expression changes. "Wait, there was one more thing…"

Crystal walks back out of the room and when everyone follows along behind. My legs work without buckling underneath me. I trail behind Nox, his usual swagger subdued.

I peek over his shoulder to see Crystal at Zoe's bed. Again, I'm horrified at how much blood there is on the cotton sheets.

141

"He did most of it here," Crystal points to the bed.

"Did what?" Dahlia chokes out.

"The trials," Nox says. I can't see his face, but I can hear the disgust in his voice.

Crystal gives him a suspicious look before nodding and kneeling beside the bed. She reaches underneath and pulls something out.

"What the hell is that?" Dahlia asks.

"Thumb screws," Nox answers again before Crystal has a chance to respond. "A torture device. They're used on the accused to get a confession."

"Precisely," Agnes looks surprised by Nox's knowledge of torture methods. "The pain is so excruciating it will cause any poor soul to confess to anything, just to make it stop."

I throw a hand to my mouth as the nausea roils up again. How could anyone do this to someone? Especially Zoe. She was one of the sweetest, kindest people I knew. She didn't even practise Magick. She studied plants. She was a scientist. All she had wanted was a quiet life.

I'd always wondered if something like this had happened to Hazel as well. I'd always told myself it was random, but maybe it hadn't been?

"But she wasn't even really a witch!" I can't stop the sob from escaping at the thought of this injustice against Zoe. "She didn't even understand how to do protection charms!"

"Ez is right," Dahlia comes to my side and wraps an arm around my shoulders. "We had to come round to help her do a basic cleansing-"

"Why did you need to do that?" Crystal shrewdly scrutinises Dahlia and me like we're naughty schoolgirls.

"She said she thought she was being followed."

"Did she know who it was?" Agnes asks, her voice uncharacteristically stern.

"No... No," I falter as the guilt pools in my stomach. "Just that she felt unsafe and that she thought someone had broken into her flat."

"Why didn't she go to the police?" Crystal asks, and I have the distinct feeling I'm being accused of something, but I have no idea what.

"I don't know," I answer truthfully. "I guess because there wasn't any real evidence. She just had a feeling that something wasn't right. We came over, placed crystals around did protection

142

spells and-"

"She should have had a full coven to cast the protection spells," Crystal interrupts, her cold glare fixes on me. "Not two novice witches-"

"Whoa!" Dahlia steps forward and I practically feel the anger crackling off her, or maybe it was my own annoyance riling her up. "I don't know who the hell you think you are, calling us novices. We knew what we're doing. She wasn't left unarmed."

"Clearly not," Crystal gives Dahlia the same icy, judgemental glare. "If she'd had the support of a coven-"

"There is no coven in this city!" Dahlia snaps. "You disbanded after Ez's mum died."

Agnes and Crystal exchange a look. As fast as a hummingbird's wing. But I see it.

"You never disbanded, did you?" I glare at Agnes, and she has the decency to look embarrassed.

"We didn't want to burden you, dear. After your sweet mother's passing you took it so hard and we-"

"You didn't want to tell me that you carried on without her," I snap, and Crystal's eyes widen with shock and fear. "Like I didn't deserve to know. Like I don't matter. Like I wasn't even worthy of joining the coven that my mother led?!"

Agnes walks to me, her fuchsia dress swishes around her. "No, that's not what I meant. It's just that after your mother's passing you were so young and so…" her words falter.

"Inexperienced?" I can't hide the hurt in my voice. "What was it you called me?" I look past Agnes to Crystal. "A novice?"

"Witches," Nox sighs. "All secrets and politics. Glad to see some things never change." His comment makes both women bristle.

"You'd do well to hold your tongue, young man," Crystal's clipped, crisp voice is worthy of the most formidable headteacher.

"Wrong on both counts there," Nox drawls.

"Not. Now. Nox." I warn through gritted teeth. The last thing we need right now is Nox being Nox.

Agnes's eyebrows shoot up, alarm on her rounded face. "Nox? I thought your name was Finn?"

Nox looks over at me with mock surprise and feigns a gasp of alarm. The prick.

"Oopsy," he smirks at me, and I have to stop myself from going over and walloping him in the head. Again. I'm not a violent person but he seems to inspire it in me.

He looks at Agnes like she's the village idiot. "Tenebris Noctis

143

Daemonium. Nox for short."

"Daemonium as in…" Agness swallows several times. "As in demon?"

"Catch on quick don't you, witch?" he smiles. "Not the dimmest one in the coven. I sense that honour goes to the old shrew behind you. Also explains how your name keeps popping up."

"How dare you!" Crystal splutters, ignoring Nox's strange comment about Agnes.

"Oh, I dare," he chuckles. "I very much dare. You lot are just as hierarchical as you always have been. I mean honestly, you'd think after all these centuries you'd have twigged that age doesn't always equate to power." He signals towards me, and I wish the ground would swallow me whole. "Take this one here. Sure, she doesn't look like much, but she's got a mouth and a half on her, and she's incredibly adept at spells, especially conjurations. I'd suggest you two old bags hold fire on your judgement, hm?"

The room falls deathly silent. I hadn't expected that. A rallying cry of support. Least of all from Nox.

No one seems willing to break the tension until Dahlia shuffles her feet uncomfortably.

"What do you mean by spells and conjurations?" Agnes looks between Nox and me, a look of trepidation in her face.

I get the oddest feeling that Agnes and Crystal aren't surprised by his strangely backhanded compliment to me. If anything, they look scared shitless.

"Just the usual stuff," I try to dissipate the strange tension in the room. "Protection spells, floral enchantments."

"Bringing back the dead," Nox interrupts and raises his eyebrows at me. "What?"

"Can you stop digging me into a hole please?" I snarl.

Crystal steps towards Agnes, placing a hand on her shoulder and murmurs in a hushed tone that she clearly hopes I won't hear.

"It's happening," she whispers, as she stares at me.

"No," Agnes answers, her expression clouding with doubt. "It's not."

Crystal's face is ashen. "We did not heed the warning-"

"Silence, Crystal!" Agnes snaps and I feel like I've been slapped across the face. I've never heard Agnes speak to anyone like that.

"What's happening?" I arch an eyebrow at the women who both clamp their mouths shut into tight lines.

Agnes shoos Crystal's hand from her shoulder. She walks

towards me with an expression of such sadness my stomach immediately somersaults. "You need to speak to your father, dear."

My dad? Why the hell would I need to speak to my dad? We barely have conversations that are over three minutes long. And when we do, they're always awkwardly strained.

My brow furrows, and I see Nox look between Agnes and me like he's watching monkeys learn how to use tools. At least he's keeping silent. First time for everything.

I look at Crystal, who seems to be terrified of me now. I guess that's an improvement over disdain. Maybe?

"Why do I need to speak to my dad?"

Agnes opens and closes her mouth a couple of times and seems at a loss for words. I'm getting tired of this cloak and dagger bollocks.

"She asked you a question," Nox's amber eyes bore holes into Agnes's face.

Her face takes on a ruddy shade, which I'm certain has nothing to do with the stifling summer heat in the flat.

"It's not my place to say," she says in a hushed tone.

I can't halt the white-hot rage that's simmering under my skin. "Why?"

"I promised your mother," she answers.

Crystal looks like she's on the verge of combusting. "We all promised," she says as she watches me like a hawk, like she's expecting me to set the room on fire.

I look back at Agnes, her face twisted into a mixture of fear and sorrow.

Hurt and disappointment roils inside me. I didn't expect much loyalty from Crystal, I'd barely known her when I was little. But Agnes? She practically became my surrogate mother after Mum died.

"Tell me," I ask again.

Agnes shakes her head sadly. "I really can't. I'm so sorry, dear, I-"

"Save the apologies," Nox snaps. "Being sorry never does anything for anyone."

Silence falls over the room again, and I'll be damned if I give into the anger and hurt swirling through me. If they aren't willing to give me an explanation, I'll find out myself.

Dahlia clears her throat, clearly uncomfortable in the deafening quiet. "So," she says. "What do we do now? We need to call the police. Much as I'm enjoying this little party, it's going to look suspicious."

The police. I fish my phone from my pocket and Dahlia shoots me an alarmed look.

"Ez, what are you doing?"

"Calling them," I answer flatly.

"You can't call them," she says. "You need to go. Now."

"What? Why?"

"Well, for one," she turns and points at Nox, who is once again back to inspecting his nails like they are the most fascinating thing he's ever seen. "You can't have him here. How are you going to explain *him*?!"

"I'll think of something." Even I can't ignore how weak my excuse sounds.

"Fat chance that he'll behave," she looks over at Nox. "No offence, but you don't seem like the type of demon who's willing to make life easy."

He flashes Dahlia a dazzling, dimpled smile. It's so disarming, I almost forget how much of a colossal pain in the ass he is. "Demon's never make life easy. But especially me."

Agnes gives a small nod. "She's right. You two both need to go before anyone else turns up."

"But how are you going to explain why you're all here?" They are a trio of misfits.

Dahlia gives me a look. "Don't you worry about that. You just need to get him out of here before he starts shooting his mouth off!"

"Are you sure?" I ask, Dahlia gives me another look and I know I'm skating dangerously close to getting on her bad side.

She points towards the door. "Go. Now."

Nox lingers in the bedroom, and I notice the look of mischief in his eyes. "I have a knack for charming law enforcement."

"Please, for the love of Goddess, get him out of here!" Dahlia groans as she pulls her phone from her pocket.

"Alright, fine," I look at Nox. "You. Out. Now."

Nox looks at me with a mock puppy dog expression. "Ask me nicely."

I give him a threatening glare. "Out!"

Nox looks over at Dahlia. "Is she this charming to everyone?"

Dahlia gives him a look of surprise. "Actually, No. She's usually sickeningly lovely. A pathological people-pleaser, but you seem to bring out the worst in her."

"Can everyone stop talking about me like I'm not here?" I snap. "Between the murders, secrets and people assassinating my character I'm close to punching someone!"

146

"You've already resorted to violence," Nox grumbles. "I've got a welt on the back of my head to prove it."

"I barely even touched you!" I snap. If he wants a proper injury, I'd be more than happy to give him one!

His dimples flash with mischief. "If you'd like to touch me more, we can-"

"For the love of Goddess, please, please, *please* do *not* finish that sentence!" Dahlia snaps.

"Move it, Demon-boy," I smirk in victory at how much he hates his new nickname. It seems only fair that he gets what he gives.

Mutual irritation. No way that can end badly, the voice in my head quips.

Nox glares as he passes by me, and I stick my tongue out at him. Arrogant prick.

"I'll see you back at home?" I ask Dahlia, ignoring the stares of the other women: Crystal's wariness and Agnes's sympathy. What have they been hiding? Aside from the coven. What would be so important Mum would make them swear to secrecy? And why was it about me? The coven pretty much ignored me when I was younger. Now I'm trying to remember if they all looked at me the way Crystal does.

Dahlia gives me a small nod and a less than half-assed smile. "Aye, sure thing."

As I reach the door, Dahlia's already on the phone. Nox and I step back out into the muggy summer heat.

I jump at the sound of laughter as it echoes down the road. It's jarring to hear someone enjoying life when we've just seen the stark and bloodied opposite.

"Are you alright?" Nox asks.

I turn to look up at him. "Do you care?"

He shrugs nonchalantly. "Not particularly, no."

"That's what I thought," I mutter, as I walk down the slope of the street. The city is brimming with noise and life. How can everything continue as normal when something so horrific has happened?

Images of Zoe's frozen face swimming in the crimson bathtub flash in my mind. Painful memories resurface as I remember the last time I'd seen that expression.

A memory of what Nox had said in the hallway swims to the surface of my mind.

"The fuck am I doing here again?"

Had Nox been at Zoe's flat before? I know Nox has been taking Finn's body for nighttime walks… could he have gone to Zoe's one night? Judging by the state of her, she'd been dead at least a day. He's been making it perfectly clear just how much he dislikes witches.

"What's going on in that head of yours?" Nox taps the top of my skull and I bat his hand away.

"None of your business!" I snarl up at him. "Also, how about we have a 'no touching' rule?!"

He saunters alongside me as we dodge around the clusters of tourists gathering outside a busy souvenir shop. I keep a wary eye on him: he's a demon after all, maybe it was him?

"What did you mean by being there again?" I watch him like a sniper tracking their target. Waiting to see if there's any change in his expression to signal his guilt. "When we were at Zoe's. Have you been there before?"

"No," he answers breezily, giving me a casual glance. "Just got a little turned around, that's all."

His face remains completely stoic, but it doesn't dispel my suspicions. As he rubs a hand down his chin, I'm struck by how different Nox is from Finn, and I'm annoyed it took me so long to notice. Finn's presence is as warm and welcoming as a bubble bath… but Nox is as cosy as a tub filled with razor blades. His handsome features become weapons. Polished and sharpened to be as deadly as a dagger. Then there's his eyes. The fiery storm is a jarring contrast to the calmness of Finn's baby blues.

I prickle as he watches me. He knows I'm suspicious of him, I can feel it.

However much I don't want to engage in conversation I can't stop myself. "What?"

"Well, you and pretty boy seem to be incapable of leaving each other alone." He winds around a gaggle of schoolgirls who stop talking to gawk at him. "But with me-"

"You and Finn are nothing alike."

He chuckles, giving the girls a dazzling smile. "Oh, trust me. I'm aware."

You and me, both. I let out a sigh. "I want to talk to Finn."

I'm unnerved by the way he navigates the winding streets with familiar ease, heading directly towards the shop.

He finally speaks once we reach the floral window display. "Well, as the great Jagger says, you can't always get what you want, Sugar."

I fish my keys out of my bag. "You need to stop calling me that or...." I push the door open. "Or I'll keep calling you Demon-boy."

He rolls his golden eyes. "Very mature."

"Hey, you started it," I snarl. "I just figured if I have a nickname, it's only fair you have one too."

Nox walks over to a bookshelf, tracing his hand along the spines in a way which makes my skin crawl. "Maybe I'm just being kind and letting Finn have a rest? Those blue balls you keep giving him are exhausting for the poor boy!"

"Do me a favour," I grind my teeth. "How about you don't talk about Finn?"

"Why would I do that?" he sniggers. "It's funny as hell watching you get all worked up about it. I bet I can make your face the same colour as your hair."

"You're such an asshole!" I glare at him as his damned smirk grows. "Can you just stop talking for a minute? I need to think."

"You're going to take longer than a minute," he chuckles. "I'll put the kettle on whilst you try to form a thought process. Maybe there's a nice novel or crossword puzzle I could do to pass the time."

"Try not to scald yourself!" I shout as he heads to the backroom.

Hopefully he'll have some tragic accident with a kettle. Maybe I could enchant the flowers to strangle him? Although one murder per day is enough.

Images of Zoe flash in my mind and memories of Hazel resurface... How can this be happening again?

I chew on my bottom lip and my finger hovers over a number I really, *really* don't want to call. I press the dial button, sucking in a breath as I wait for Dad to answer.

It continues to ring when I hear a clatter from the back room. Maybe Nox has managed to have a nasty accident with a kettle... one can only hope.

"Ez?" Finn's voice comes over the sound of kettle boiling.

I hang up on the call when it goes to voicemail. At least that's one good thing. Nox has taken the hint and buggered off.

Finn walks into the room and I quickly search his face. His blue eyes are full of confusion. "When did we come back here?"

Oh right. His last memory was being in the stairwell at Zoe's.

"Er, not long." I pop my phone down on the counter and make my way over to him. He's shaking. I search his face. "Do you remember anything?"

He shakes his head. "No, nothing," a slight flush creeps up

149

his neck. "I'm sorry."

My brow furrows. "Why are you apologising?"

"Because… I…" he falters like he's at a loss for words.

Guilt twists inside me. It's my fault he's stuck in this mess. He didn't ask for any of it.

"It's not your fault," I say gently. "I'm the one who should apologise. I promise I'll fix this."

He's about to say something, but just as he opens his mouth, my phone rings on the counter. Dad's name flashes on the screen and I grimace.

I run a hand through my hair and try to keep my tone casual. "Hey Dad."

"Esmerelda," he says curtly. "Is everything alright?"

"Fine thanks," I lie weakly. How the hell am I meant to ask him about a secret that he and Mum are hiding? I can barely even talk to him about the weather. He's more closed off and tight-lipped than a nunnery.

I clear my throat. "Are you home?"

Silence and then he finally answers, "No. I'm at work. Why?"

"No reason," not technically a lie. There are multiple reasons. "I just wondered if you kept any of Mum's old grimoires? I remember she used to have piles of them," I attempt to keep my tone innocent.

Silence falls over the line and I have to check the screen to make sure that we've not been disconnected.

"No," he finally says, "I got rid of all of them."

A sense of betrayal roils through me, and I can't stop myself from asking, "Why didn't you check if I wanted them?"

"Because," I hear the sound of shuffling paper, "I didn't want you to get exposed to any of that stuff. That world was your mum's-"

That stuff. He means witchcraft. He seems to forget being a witch isn't a choice. I was born with these gifts. They might be meagre compared to Mums, but still.

I bite my tongue. There's no point having this argument again.

He's at work, the voice in my mind reminds me.

This might work in my favour. Maybe I can find clues whilst he's out of the house? I have a feeling Dad's not going to tell me anything. I'm more likely to find it myself.

"Esmeralda," wariness returns to his tone. "Is everything alright?"

No, it's bloody not alright, I bristle. But I doubt you'd help me anyway.

150

"Everything's fine," I try to keep my tone breezy. "I'll come by Friday."

Friday. Mum's anniversary. My heart twists painfully in my chest. Just how many secrets did she keep?

More silence before Dad finally says, "See you Friday."

The line goes dead, and I can breathe again.

I look over at Finn, who looks like a lost puppy. All I want to do is cuddle him and tell him everything's going to be ok. But we don't have time.

I look at my watch, half past one… we have a window. Albeit a small window. Four hours before he gets home. Not ideal. Especially since I don't know what the hell I'm looking for.

"How do you feel about a little bit of reconnaissance?"

Finn's handsome face takes on a concerned expression. "Why does this sound like breaking and entering?"

"It's not breaking and entering," I flip the sign on the shop and give him a reassuring smile, "I've got keys!"

Chapter Eighteen

<u>Esme</u>

I stare up at my family home like I'm looking at a stranger. The three-bedroom terrace in the middle of Leith gazes down at me with its large bay windows. There hasn't been laughter in that house for years. Not since Mum died.

I walk through the tidy front garden, and the familiar scent of lavender planted by Mum makes my heart ache. Lavender is resilient. Much like most of the flora she had cultivated. These flowers are tenacious. They'd have to be, to cope with Dad.

I push open the door, feeling like an intruder, despite the fact I've walked through it thousands of times. Besides, I have a key. I'm not doing anything wrong. Technically.

I step into the buttery yellow hallway as the afternoon sun dapples across the oak floorboards.

Finn closes the door behind me as quietly as possible. "So what is it we're looking for exactly?"

I march up the stairs towards the study. I might as well start in the room which has the most books. "Clues."

Finn lets out a resigned sigh, "Right."

"Something about this feels wrong. I don't know what Agnes and Crystal aren't telling me, but at least I know they aren't telling me something. What's Dad hiding?"

I push open the study door and the scent of my father's aftershave greets me. The floor to ceiling shelves is full of books and a large oak desk sits in front of the bay window looking out over the back garden.

"Dad knows something. Something he's not telling me. So that's why we're hunting for clues. Mum used to have piles of grimoires and she wrote in her own ones every day. There's no way

152

Dad would have thrown them all away." I begin scouring the shelves. "I have a couple of them, but I think there might still be some in the house."

"This might be a stupid suggestion," Finn follows me into the room, rubbing a hand down the back of his neck, "but why not just ask your dad?"

"Dad said he'd thrown them all away, which I bet was a lie." I thumb through a green leather-bound journal, but it's just a place where he keeps his receipts. "Besides, you do remember my dad, right? He'll find anything to avoid having a frank and honest conversation."

"I remember," Finn grimaces. Dad had not been his biggest fan when we'd been dating in uni. "So where do we start?"

"If you search in here," I gesture around the study. "See if you can find any purple or gold leather books. Those were always the colours of her grimoires. They'll probably look quite old, and the spines have a floral design down the side."

"You and your mum always did have a thing for flowers," Finn gives a small smile which I return. Whatever my parents may be hiding, at least I know one truth. Mum used to say: "People lie, but plants never do." That's why she loved them so much.

I give him a quick peck on the cheek. "I'll be just down the hall… alright?"

Finn continues to look uncertain but gives me a small nod.

"If you spot anything suspicious give me a shout." I make my way down the hallway. I halt when I see a colourful glow peeking through the door that hangs slightly ajar.

I hover at the threshold to my childhood bedroom. I'm greeted by the pink walls, warm oak floorboards and the delicate peony chandelier that, under Mum's guidance, I'd conjured on my sixteenth birthday.

Dad kept my room the same. Right down to my moonstone dreamcatcher and the collection of 'Powerpuff Girls' memorabilia which still sits on the windowsill. My eyes catch the family photo on my old bedside table: Mum cuddling a newborn me in hospital. Dad was never in the pictures; he was always the one behind the camera. In fact, as I look up and down the hallway at the family pictures that decorate the walls, they are all of Mum and me. Never Dad. My heart twists painfully as I realise, he was never in the pictures because he was making sure the precious moments were captured.

I close the door to my room and the memories of my childhood. There's no way the grimoires are in there.

153

I head down the hall to my parents' room and I'm met by mustard yellow walls, sunflower print bedding and I can't help but smile.

Mum had embodied summer and sunshine. She made sure that even though Dad could be a miserable arse he'd wake up to golden rays on every surface. She's gone but the room, Goddess, this entire house… it's still filled with her.

I trail a hand over one of the pillars of the four-poster bed. I can almost pretend that Mum is just downstairs. I can't stop the tiny seed of hope sprouting in my chest that maybe I'll hear her call me from the kitchen and ask me to come down for tea.

Just as I make my way over to their walk-in wardrobe, I hear a rattle at the front door. Maybe it's the postman? There's a jingle of door keys and the sound of it being opened. Nope, definitely not the postman! Unless he and Dad have become a lot closer since I moved out… which seems unlikely!

Finn nearly crashes into me. "Your dad's home early."

I barely stop myself from colliding with him. "You think?!"

Finn's on the verge of shitting himself from fear. I knew he was always nervous being around Dad when we were younger, maybe bringing him wasn't the best idea.

His eyes are as wide as saucers. "What do we do?!"

I grab hold of his sweat-slicked hand and drag him into the wardrobe. I have a memory that they used to be a lot bigger. Or maybe it was because I was smaller? It probably doesn't help that Finn and I are tall. He's a complete wall of muscle and I have to drape myself all over him so that I can get the door closed.

"Don't panic! We just need to stay quiet and wait until he goes back to work," I say in a hushed tone, whilst I try to avoid accidentally jamming a coat hanger up my arse. "Can you move back a bit?"

"How?" he splutters. "Also, this might not be the best time to mention it, but I am a little claustrophobic."

I clamp a hand over his mouth as I hear the soft pad of footsteps coming up the stairs.

Bugger, bugger bugger! If Dad catches me here…. I can almost see how this conversation is going to play out.

"Oh, hey Dad, this is Finn… remember the guy who died when I was at uni? Don't worry, we weren't fucking in your wardrobe! Oh, and by the way, what secrets have you and Agnes been keeping from me?!"

Finn accidentally stands on my foot and a small squeak of pain escapes. I grind my teeth. It's fine. It's not like I need toes.

"Can you scootch back just a bit, please?" His giant foot is still on mine and it's taking all my self-control not to jump out from the wardrobe. Finn looks at me nonplussed, but I realise it's because we're so squished together that he doesn't register he's turning my foot into a pancake. Paincake, more like!

I successfully yank my foot out from under his mammoth black boots and tumble into a big brown leather suitcase that falls on top of me. I push it back on top of the precariously balanced mountain of cardboard boxes.

Goddess, when did Dad become such a hoarder? I freeze when I hear footsteps coming into the bedroom that halt just outside the wardrobe door.

Shit! Fuck! Shitty fucksticks!

I brace myself for our impending discovery, but thankfully the footsteps wander back out of the room.

"Why the fuck are we in a dark box that smells like lavender?" The unmistakable lilt of a Scottish accent drifts over my skin. Nox has taken control. Again.

"Ssh!" I place a hand over his mouth, and he glares at me like he's contemplating biting my fingers off. His eyebrows furrow and his expression is full of exasperation.

I pull my hand away, fearing for its safety. "Can you stay quiet? Please?"

"Maybe, if you answer my question," he grumbles but keeps his voice low. "What the hell are we doing here?"

"Finn and I were looking for books at my parents' house and he... well..."

That damned smirk is back on his face. "He buggered off again like a scared little mouse, didn't he?"

"No!" I whisper. "He just doesn't cope well with stress or-"

"Any situation that requires a pair of bollocks?"

"That's so sexist!" My voice is steadily growing pissier. "Having bollocks has nothing to do with how well you can handle stressful situations!"

"Clearly," he retorts. "The Finnster is a prime example of that!"

"Don't talk about him that way!"

We halt our bicker at the sound of footsteps returning. Both of us freeze and look at each other in alarm.

"Don't. Say. Anything," I warn.

"I'm. Not. The. One. Still. Talking!" he answers, and I have to resist throwing one of the suitcases at him.

Sod it, Dad can find me! It'll be worth it if I can get Nox to shut up!

After a few more seconds in silent stalemate, I hear Dad make his way back down the stairs and open the front door. It's only when I hear him locking it that I finally let out the breath I've been holding in.

Nox pins me with his whisky eyes before he drawls, "Are we staying in here?"

"You can!" I shove the wardrobe door open, relieved to get some space.

"So why were you and the Finnster snooping around here then, eh?" He's still standing in the wardrobe and thumbing through some coats. "Looking for a new place to screw? Is the romance getting a little stale?"

"You really are such a pig!" I sneer. "All you seem to think about is sex!"

He chuckles, rummaging in the back of the wardrobe some more. "That sounds like that's more your wheelhouse than mine, Sugar!"

"Will you get out of there? If you're not going to get Finn back, can you at least be useful?"

"Probably not." He shoves the suitcases out of the wardrobe.

If I can't figure out a way to get rid of Nox, I may end up accidentally sending Finn back to the Afterlife when I throttle them!

He finds an old black leather jacket and throws it on. Which is impressive given how small the space is. "Why were you hiding in a wardrobe?"

"Because I didn't want my dad to know I was looking for something."

He turns, raising an eyebrow at me. "Is this because of what those old windbags said? You decided to go snooping on your dear old Daddy? Honestly Sugar, that's not very nice!"

I flop onto the bed. "Neither is being lied to."

"You're so dramatic!" More rustling comes from the wardrobe. What the hell is he rooting around for now? "So, what was it you were looking for?"

"Grimoires."

The rustling stops.

"Grimoires?"

"Books for spells, conjuring-"

"I'm familiar with what a grimoire is."

I don't know if I'm imagining it, but I swear it sounds like Nox

156

practically spat those words out. Strange to hear someone get so hostile over some old books.

He rummages again, and I let out a huff of exasperation. "Can you come out of there? We need to keep looking."

"There's books in here."

I sit up. "What?"

Nox turns, pulling out one of the large cardboard boxes and dumps it at my feet. Inside there's got to be around thirty books, all in various stages of age and damage. I recognise them immediately. They're all grimoires. I knew it! Dad had lied about throwing them away. I just don't understand why.

"Judging by the stunned look on your face, I take it these are what you're hunting for?" He wanders over to the full-length mirror, appraising the vintage leather jacket he's wearing. It hasn't seen sunlight in decades but somehow, he makes it look like it was designed for him. The prick.

He looks at me from the mirror, that bloody smirk growing. "Guess this Demon-Boy isn't as useless as you thought, huh?"

I persuade Nox to carry two of the boxes back to the flat for me. I'd done a quick comb through of the remaining ones, and the rest were too disintegrating or illegible.

"Are you hoping to uncover some great family secret then?" Nox asks as we walk up the hill towards the flat.

"I just want to see if I can find out what's going on without having to speak to my dad about it."

"Ah daddy issues," he chuckles. "Why am I not surprised?"

I scowl. "I don't have daddy issues."

He pauses as I unlock the door. "Whatever you say, Sugar."

I grind my teeth. "I already told you, stop calling me that."

"No chance," he lets out a low laugh. "Annoying you is my entertainment."

"Fine." I bristle but try to keep my tone deceptively jovial. "Come on in, Demon-Boy."

Now it's my turn to be amused as I skip to my flat front door. "It's funny."

He's still frowning. "What is?"

"How much you hate being called that."

"Names have power." He saunters past me once I get the door unlocked. He makes his way into the living room where he drops the two cardboard boxes on the coffee table with a loud thud.

I scoff dubiously, "Yeah, sure."

157

"It's true." He leans over and begins pulling out grimoires from one of the boxes. "Name's have always been used to control, to oppress…" a ghost of a smile teases his lips as he studies my face. "To summon."

I squirm under his scrutiny. "I didn't summon you."

"Like I said, Witchling," he carelessly flicks through the grimoire. "It's your spell. It's not my problem."

I snatch the book from him, he grins and drapes himself gracefully over the sofa.

I stare down at him. "If you don't give a shit why bother helping now?"

He shrugs. "I've not decided whether to help you or not yet." He pulls out another book from one of the boxes and I continue to glare at him.

"Then why are you so interested in looking through the grimoires?"

"I'm not." He scours the pages, before haphazardly throwing it back in with its brethren. "Just curious."

He's still staring at the boxes, like he's itching to rummage through them. What interest could he possibly have in them?

"I don't believe you."

He laughs. "I don't care if you believe me or not."

I huff out an exasperated breath. "Ok, if you don't care then why help me carry them?"

"Seemed the easiest way of getting out of there."

I wait for him to continue. He doesn't. He just sits there. As stoic and impenetrable as a brick wall.

I narrow my eyes. "Why did you defend me against Agnes and Crystal?"

"I hate hypocrisy," his control finally breaks. He tries to cover it up by leaning forward and pulling out a lilac grimoire. "I've seen it far too often and it always pisses me off."

My curiosity peaks, if I can catch Nox off guard a bit maybe he'll give me some kind of clues as to why he's here.

I sit down opposite him and begin thumbing through the pages of the grimoire, trying to keep my tone casual.

"You sound like you have a lot of experience with that," I comment as I skim through the book.

Silence. Too long a silence. I look up and catch Nox staring at me with a fiery glint.

I chew on my bottom lip. "What?"

"Stop."

"Stop what?" I ask, trying to sound innocent and failing miserably.

"Trying to get to know me." He leans forward and his stare burrows into my skull. "It won't help you."

"Help me with what?"

His eyes twinkle with amusement. "You really are awful at lying, Sugar."

"I don't know what you're talking about." I cross my legs and turn my attention back to the elaborate handwriting. This is going to take days to decipher.

"A word of advice," he stands, brushing a hand down his shirt. "Don't try to bullshit me. It won't end well for you."

He walks down the hall, towards the front door.

"Where are you going?" I call after him.

"Out," his tone is clipped, all notes of the casual arrogance gone. "Don't wait up for me. Or Finn."

Before I have a chance to contest, the door slams shut. I feel a knot of unease at the thought of Nox wandering around and getting Finn into trouble.

Sure, he likes to present a facade of devil may care nonchalance, but I can see underneath his bullshit. I saw it in the hallway at Zoe's.

I sit reading for the next hour, trying to make my way through a particularly text heavy edition by a witch called Moira Smyth from the eighties.

Mum had added little yellow post-its into each of the grimoires. Some had names and dates, but others are so old Mum had just written question marks. So many grimoires. She'd collected and preserved them all. Some are as old as the 1800's. Many are impossible to read with their washed-out text; I'm going to need a torch and magnifying glass to decipher them.

To save my eyesight, and sanity, I start with the most recent grimoires. I'm really not looking forward to using my piss poor Latin to decipher the spells, but as I begin pouring through Moira's book, I realise I'm not going to have much of a choice. Nearly all of them are either in Latin or Gaelic… this really is going to take forever.

I plop Moira's book down and make my way to the fridge. Wine. I need wine. I look back to the mountain of grimoires. Ok, scratch that, I need vodka.

I roll my shoulders, grimacing at the crunchy sound as I stretch. I really need to work on my posture when I sit. Although it would help if the handwriting wasn't so teeny tiny!

I open the fridge and spot an unopened bottle of Prosecco. That'll do for starters! I quickly pull it out and use my hip to shut the door, which causes me to wince in pain. Stupid injuries!

Retrieving a wine glass from the cupboard, I begin my next mission: trying to get the cork out of the bottle.

I hear the jingle of keys and the front door unlocks. Guess Nox gave up on whatever mischief he was planning and decided annoying me would be more fun.

"Can you give me a hand please, Demon-Boy?" I call out to the hallway.

Dahls walks in, a tired expression on her face. "Hey."

She looks as emotionally exhausted as I feel. "How was it?"

She scrubs a hand down her face and leans against the island unit. "Awful. As expected."

I give her a sad nod. I can't even imagine how horrible her afternoon has been dealing with the police.

I continue to tug on the bottle's cork. "What happened?"

"Statements," she says flatly, "many, many statements. But it's done." She points at the Prosecco, "is that mine?"

I give her a sheepish grin. "Sorry, I…"

"Gimme!" She holds out an outstretched hand. "You suck at getting them open!"

A small laugh escapes me as I hand her the bottle.

She returns my smile, but there's still a haunted look in her eyes. "Get me a glass as well, would you?"

I turn and hear the pop of the cork behind me. I grab another glass, bring it over to the sofa and flop down next to Dahls.

"So," she fills the glasses to the brim. "How was your afternoon?"

"Oh, you know," I take a big gulp, trying to stifle a hiccup from the bubbles. "Snuck into Dad's, found a bunch of grimoires which he'd kept hidden… argued with Nox. A lot."

Dahlia gestures to the coffee table that strains under the weight of the boxes. "I was wondering why you were trying to pressure test the leg strength of our furniture!"

"Mum kept all of them." I hate the sadness in my voice. I should be pissed off. I am pissed off! But I can't ignore the pang of disappointment at my parents and Agnes.

She lets out a low whistle. "Your mum had all of these?"

"I guess she figured their spells and secrets were worth preserving." I take another gulp, not even trying to hide the bitterness in my tone. "Seems like that's what she was good at."

"Ez," Dahlia chews her bottom lip, "I don't think your mum meant to hurt you by hiding stuff-"

"I think she hoped I'd never find out." I take another gulp, emptying the glass in record time. "Afterall, I'm barely a novice-"

"That's bollocks, Ez!" Dahlia snaps. "You're strong. Stronger than you give yourself credit for. I mean, you brought Finn back from the dead!"

"I brought him back wrong-"

"And you can make it right. You can fix it," she leans in and gives my hand a squeeze. "*We* can fix it, alright?"

A wave of gratitude sweeps through me. "Thanks Dahls."

"Don't mention it," she shoots me a warning glare. "Seriously. Don't mention it, you'll ruin my reputation. Although I'm in danger of losing my title of 'resident badass' to Nox?"

"He's the biggest ass, that's for sure!"

"Speaking of," she takes another sip. "Where is his unholiness? Off kicking puppies or changing wine back into water?"

"I accidentally got his panties in a twist, so he went out."

"I dread to think about his panties!" She pulls a face, but her eyes suddenly go wide. "We should go out!"

I splutter, nearly choking on my wine. "What? Why?"

She shrugs. "Because we should. We've had a shitshow of a day, we're alive, we're young, we're single-"

"Technically I'm not single," I hold a finger up. "Remember Finn?"

"Your part-time sweetie, who's playing sidekick in his own body? I'm aware. So where is he?"

"Right now," I slump back in my seat, "playing sidekick in his own body."

Dahls takes a large gulp of her wine. "Exactly. So," she stands grabbing the bottle. "We're going out. We only have one life Ez, might as well go out and live it!'"

Chapter Nineteen

Esme

'Poison' is heaving. Considering it's a weekday, it's impressive. Maybe I'd underestimated the appeal of a cocktail bar with a sleazy rock soundtrack. Or maybe it was the two-for-one cocktail happy hour? Which wasn't so much an hour but the entire evening.

I'm standing at the bar, squished in between two other patrons, attempting to order. I try to get the attention of Dahlia's manager, Bri.

Despite the club being packed, she projects an air of calm control. Her bleached blonde ponytail is pert and bouncy, and her painted scarlet lips are set in grim determination. She's the embodiment of rockabilly cool, and I can't help but feel a twist of jealousy at the way she commands everything and everyone in here.

"You sure you can't just go whip us up some daiquiris?" I call behind me to Dahlia, who is currently draped over a guy that's covered in tattoos and oozing bad boy energy... Or at least he's trying to. When I first saw him snake an arm over Dahlia's shoulder, I had to stop myself from snorting at the juvenile bravado. The guy is trying so desperately to impress her it's kind of sweet. Laughably sweet.

"No can do," Dahlia continues to sway in the guy's embrace; he's wrapped around her back like a limpet. "Tonight's my night off!"

I roll my eyes. "What's the point of coming to a bar you work at if you aren't going to get us free drinks?"

Another unwelcome shove comes from one of the men next to me, who would definitely be better off going home instead of ordering another drink.

162

"My night off, remember?" Dahls calls over the loud bass. "Just smile at Bri and she'll serve you." She gives me a cheeky wink, "She's got a sweet tooth."

"No!" I groan, "no more of that!"

The guy behind Dahlia stops swaying and looks up from nuzzling her neck. "What?"

"She has a nickname," Dahlia smiles wickedly. "Don't you, Ez?"

I grit my teeth, "No."

The guy perks up. "What is it?"

Dahlia grins like an evil Cheshire cat. "Dan, meet *Sugar*!"

Dan's grin turns sleazy, and I immediately regret wearing my favourite lilac dress. Whilst the hem pools around my calves, it has a big slit down my thigh which flashes my ivy tattooed legs whenever I move. The low neckline also means my boobs are front and centre of the outfit. I take a wary step back in my rose gold heels. This guy is a letch, and why Dahlia is even bothering to interact with him, Goddess only knows.

Dan's attention lingers on my tits. "Cute nickname."

I turn, trying to suppress a shudder. Dahlia's taste in men borders on masochistic.

I lean back on the bar, attempting to ignore the gawking from drunk and drunker. I give my dress a slight tug up to prevent them from looking down at my cleavage.

Why did I let Dahlia talk me into this? I could be home right now. In my pyjamas, drinking wine, eating ice cream and watching Disney films. Not having to fend off the less than chivalrous advances of some of the grossest men in Scotland.

I manage to catch Bri's eye, who gives me an apologetic smile. "Hey Ez, sorry. It's been one of those nights."

"Don't worry about it," I say breezily, trying to ignore the less than subtle groans of the other patrons waiting to be served. "Can I get two strawberry daiquiris, please?"

She flashes me a quick grin. "Sure thing."

I turn to look down the bar and catch a glimpse of dark hair and a very familiar leather jacket.

Oh Goddess, not him. Anyone but him.

Even from the other end of the room, I see the fiery glow of his eyes. He's not being subtle at all, but he doesn't seem to give two shits. Neither does the blonde girl he's cosying up to, apparently.

I wave a hand at Bri, my attention wandering back over to the scene down the other end of the bar. "Can I get two shots of vodka as well please?"

Fuck it. If Finn's body is going to be pressed up against some random girl all night, I'd rather not be able to see it.

Bri gives me a sceptical look. "Are you sure, Ez?"

I give her a short nod before turning just in time to see Nox brush the hair from the blonde's shoulder. "Abso-fucking-lutely."

The girl leans in. Wrapping her body around him. I'm going to need a drink to stop myself from throttling her. Or him. Fuck it, I'm feeling generous, both of them!

Bri brings me over four drinks and I begin to reach for my purse.

"On the house," she smiles.

I furrow my brow. "You sure?"

She gives me a wink. "Abso-fucking-lutely."

I give her my most dazzling smile, before haphazardly grabbing hold of the glasses.

I meander through the crowd and make my way back to Dahlia and Creepy Dan, who are now on the dancefloor. The centre of the club is a mass of limbs, body heat, sweat and sugary sweet alcohol.

A heavy drum bass pounds from the speakers as I head towards them. Their dancing is borderline pornographic.

Dahlia signals to my smorgasbord of alcohol and leans in and shouts, "Are you thirsty?"

"Nox is here!" I shout back into her ear.

She pulls back, concern crosses her face. The music is so loud I can't hear but I see her mouth form the words, "Are you ok?"

I shrug, passing her two of the drinks. I quickly neck my shot of vodka and try to avoid shuddering. Bleurgh, this stuff is foul!

I look through the crowd to see Nox lean in and stroke his hand up and down the blonde's arm. They are making their way over to the dance floor. Fuck. Me. Sideways.

Dahlia leans in, prying away from Creepy Dan's meaty hands to shout, "We can go if you want?"

I shake my head, taking a sip of my daiquiri. It'll be worse if I leave. Then I'll just be imagining all of the scenarios of Nox's abuse of my boyfriend's body. Goddess help me!

I take a big gulp of my drink. The strobe lights flicker, making the bodies sway and swerve in time with the bass. The beat triggers something in my lizard brain as I recognise the song. It's something I used to dance to at Uni.

I look over at Dahlia, who gives me a small, guilty smile.

"Figured you'd appreciate it!"

I try to spot Nox and the blonde, but they seem to have been swallowed in the sea of bodies.

I let the rhythm work its way through my limbs. My hips begin to sway, and I feel myself slip into the song. For a moment, I'm lost. Lost in a warm drunken haze. Lost in the music. My brain switches off and my body takes control.

My movements only falter when I feel a strong hand grab a hold of my waist and pull me back against a wall of muscle and heat. For a second I dread that it's Creepy Dan, but I look over to see he's still attached to Dahlia.

I swirl my hips, before attempting to pull myself from the steely grip of whoever is behind me. But the hands don't loosen. I feel a hot breath on the back of my neck. "Do you always dance like that, Sugar?"

I don't say anything, instead I continue to dance.

I lean to the side, not turning to look at him, I can't bear to look up to those eyes right now. "Like what?"

"Like you're begging to be fucked?"

I reach down to the hand around my waist and scratch at his fingers. My nails dig into his flesh and for a second I feel his grip loosen.

I turn to smile up at him with a flash of venom. "Not by you."

His hands remain locked around my hips, and he continues to move me in time with the music. I can feel every hard line of him. Every. Single. Thing.

His left hand trails up my side and his fingers delicately trace my bare skin; they land on my throat and my skin pebbles with goosebumps. "Doesn't seem that way."

I grind my hips back and hear a sharp intake of breath behind me. "Likewise."

"Trust me sweetheart, you have zero effect on me."

I spin and drape my arms around his neck. "Now who's the liar."

His hands creep down my waist again, they trace the lightest circles along the base of my spine, and I hate how much I enjoy it.

It's Finn's body, I remind myself. That's all.

His stare heats me with the fire of molten amber. "I could ruin you and make you scream my name."

I scoff, trying to maintain my crumbling bravado, "Unlikely."

He smirks. "But like I told you before, Witchling," his hand moves up to my face and strokes down my cheek, before tucking my hair behind my ear. He leans in and I inhale sharply. "You're not my type."

Sparks shoot up and down my skin and I remember our rule. "I said no touching," I try to wriggle free of his hold, but his grip remains firm. "Finn's the only one who gets to. If you do that again, I'll-"

The strobes etch across his face, that damn smile dances in the light. "What will you do, Sugar?"

I sneer, quickly finish my daiquiri and shove past him. I push through the mass of writhing bodies and eventually reach the bar. I'm disappointed to see that Nox is standing right beside me.

"Can't take a hint?" I smile sweetly at him. "If a girl walks away from you, it means she doesn't want to talk to you."

"That's handy," he leans closer, and I'm hit by the scent of whisky and cinnamon. "I'm not particularly interested in talking."

"Where's the girl gone?"

He raises his eyebrows. "What girl?"

Bri catches my eye and holds up one finger.

"The blonde," I want to make that smirk falter but all it does is grow. "The one you had your hands all over?"

His smile twinkles with mischief. "Oh, her," he gestures towards the dance floor. "I think she's in there somewhere."

"So, this is what you meant by 'going out'?" I can't stop the words tumbling from my lips. "Grinding up against strange girls?"

"Why, Sugar," he leans in. I hold my breath at his unexpected proximity, "are you jealous?"

My skin prickles in annoyance. "I'm worried that Finn might catch something from whatever you end up fucking."

Nox raises an eyebrow, his hand winding around my waist. "You really do sound jealous."

Bri walks back over, bringing me two daiquiris and two shots. She seems to sense the tension and lingers. "You ok Ez?"

I glare up at Nox. "I'm fine."

"Are you sure?" I can hear the concern in her voice.

I shift my gaze from him. "I'm fine, don't worry."

I can still sense Bri hovering for a couple of seconds before she makes her way back up the bar to serve the other customers.

That bloody smile hasn't moved from his lips, and I want to smack it off his face.

Nox leans in and murmurs in my ear, "It's quite sweet really."

Dammit, I can't stop myself from asking, "What is?" I blame the alcohol.

166

"How everyone always rushes to protect you."

I glare up at him. "I don't need protection."

I try to grab a hold of the drinks, but Nox's grip is making it difficult for me to move away.

"Oh, trust me," he says quietly but the amusement in his face turns serious. "I know you don't."

I pause, his eyes feel like they are prying into my soul, and I don't like it. Not one bit.

"Just be sure that if you do fuck her," I try to keep my tone casual, "that you wear protection. I don't want Finn coming back with anything-"

"I can help with that, I can get rid of his blue balls for you," he chuckles. "Or he could learn some new tricks?"

"How would Finn learn new...?" Realisation hits me. How can I have been so stupid.

I lean in and my voice barely contains my rage. "Don't you subject Finn to your bullshit. He's innocent. He's good. Not like-"

Nox's eyes turn to lava. "Not like me?"

"You're a demon, afterall."

"Appearances can be deceiving," he leans in again. "You look delicately sweet but all I see is steel and fire."

"Well, what can I say," I finally manage to wriggle out of his grip and snatch up the drinks. "You bring out the worst in me."

I walk away from him before he has a chance to offer up another smart-ass retort. I shove through the mass of bodies and rejoin Dahlia. Oh, fuck I forgot about Dan.

"You ok?" Dahlia asks as she takes both of her drinks.

"Fine," I snap. "Everything is fine."

I look behind me to see Nox lingering at the bar, his back propped against it and his hands spread behind him nonchalantly.

Dahlia looks between us. "Whatever that was. It didn't look fine."

I down my vodka shot and can't stop the shudder that courses through me.

"I handled it," I shout over the music.

Creepy Dan looks up from nuzzling Dahlia's neck. "Is that guy your ex?"

"Something like that," I answer vaguely. I look behind me and Nox has disappeared again. He's probably gone off to find that blonde. Not that I care. Maybe if he has someone to distract him, he'll stop being such a colossal prick to me.

I sip my drink and wrinkle my nose, my tolerance for bullshit

167

tonight has reached maximum. A bath, sofa or bed would be preferable to this. I want to go home.

I lean into Dahlia. "I'm going."

Her brow furrows. "What? Why? It's barely ten, we can go somewhere else, or-"

I place a hand on her forearm. "Trust me, all I want is to go home, put my pyjamas on and eat ice cream."

She continues to give me a dubious look.

"Trust me," I say earnestly. "I'll be alright, I just want to go."

"I can-"

"You can stay here and enjoy your night." I give a wary glance behind her at Creepy Dan. "Just don't fuck him!"

She slaps my arm. "Ez!"

"I mean it," I wrinkle my nose. "The dude is weird."

"He's cute!'

"Yeah, sure, in a Ted Bundy kind of way!" I shoot her a serious glare. "I'm telling Bri to look after you, so you don't end up getting murdered!"

She falls back into Dan's embrace. I know a lost cause when I see one. I roll my eyes and return to the bar. Bri makes her way over immediately.

"You've already drunk the cocktails?" Her question is equal parts alarm and pride. "You girls are going to drink me dry!"

"I'm going home," I shout over the music. "Can you make sure Dahls doesn't end up going home with *that*?" I gesture towards the walking felon behind me.

"I mean, I can try, but you know when Dahlia really wants something-"

"She's going to have sex with it?" I finish her sentence. "Can you look after her for me, please?"

"Sure thing," Bri lingers opposite me. "Need me to call you a taxi?'

I shake my head. "I could do with the walk."

"You sure?"

"If you ask me that again, I'll start asking you for my money back!" I warn.

She waves her hand at me. "Alright, fine! Head home and leave me to babysit!"

I head towards the exit through the melting pot of bodies. I escape the stifling heat of the club and retrieve my headphones from my clutch bag. Music will help speed up the walk home.

I lean against a lamppost to pull off my shoes; I decide

barefoot is safer for my ankles than attempting these treacherous heels.

Making my way up the hill I feel a prickle of trepidation as I hear footsteps behind me.

I turn, and the streets are eerily deserted. Huh. Guess I should add vodka to the list of drinks to avoid.

Pulling my phone out I start the Spotify playlist featuring all of Mum's favourite songs and I'm reminded again about earlier.

I feel that same tingle, like there's someone behind me, I glance back and see Nox, leaning against one of the streetlights halfway down the hill. I yank a headphone out of my ear.

"Stalking is illegal, you know?" I call down at him, I hear a small quiet chuckle echo off the buildings.

He strolls up, his hands tucked neatly into his pocket, and he halts in front of me. "Aye, and so is assault."

"When did I assault you?"

"Numerous times, Sugar," he smiles, and I have the weirdest sensation, like he is seeing through all my bravado. And I hate it. "How come you're leaving?"

I turn away and continue walking.

"I'm tired."

Nox easily falls into step with me. "You didn't look tired, you looked-"

"Spare me from your low opinion of my dance moves, Nox-"

"Effervescent," he interrupts. "You looked effervescent."

A weird floaty feeling bubbles up inside me at Nox's compliment. I don't care what he thinks. He's a demon for Goddess' sake.

"I've had enough of your mind games for tonight, Demon-Boy."

"You're upset," he observes.

Not a question. Not a weird cryptic response. Just a statement. And he's right. I am upset. In so many ways.

I try to squash the feelings down. "I don't want to talk about it."

"Talking might help?" His tone is oddly sincere, and I have to double check the colour of his eyes to make sure it's not Finn.

"Says you," I snap snarkily. "Any time I try to talk to you, you either give me a smart-arse answer, evade me or walk away!"

"That does sound like me," that damned amused tone is back in his voice.

"Aye, that's you."

My feet sting from the rough pavement, but I'll be buggered if I'm going to put my shoes back on. I'm not in the mood to fall flat on my face in front of Nox.

I can feel him looking at me, and dammit I will not turn to look up at him. I will not.

"Did my talking to that girl bother you that much?" he asks.

I continue the ascent, relieved the flat is near. Just a few more minutes, then I can put an end to this conversation.

"Not you…" I flounder. "Just seeing you, *as* Finn It's just bizarre."

"Possession is bizarre," he laughs softly. "But it is what it is."

"You sound like him," I glance up at his face. "Finn. He said something like that earlier."

"Just so you know, that's not the compliment you think it is, Witchling."

"It wasn't meant as one," I sigh, frustrated that the dancing has done nothing to loosen the tension in my muscles. "It just reminded me of him. That's all."

I fish my keys from my bag. "Can we stop talking please? I'm so tired. I just want to go to bed." I continue to put the keys in the lock, ignoring Nox's presence behind me.

"Would it help if I told you I wasn't planning to have sex with her?"

I nearly drop my keys in surprise at his candour. "It looked like you were going to."

"Leaving 'Poison' should be a big clue that I wasn't going to. Do you care?"

I spin on my heel, annoyed by this whole conversation. By him. "I care because I have to stand there and watch my boyfriend's body grinding up against some random girl!"

A low chuckle escapes him. "I'll keep my grinding on strangers to a minimum in future. That better?"

I wiggle the key into the lock just as my vision begins to fog. Everything blurs and my limbs suddenly grow heavy. Oh Goddess, no… not now…

I can hear Nox behind me, but his voice is muffled. Distant. "Witchling, I-"

Everything goes pitch black as I feel my body fall. My consciousness slips away like sand through my fingers. I don't even have time to get my hands up to protect me from the ground as it rushes up to meet me.

When I regain consciousness, I realise I've been tucked into my bed. My vision has stopped making me feel seasick. I test my theory by focusing on my dresser in the corner of the room, which thankfully appears to stay still. I wiggle my feet and immediately Ink's sharp little talons latch onto my toes.

"Natural born killer that one," a Scottish drawl comes from the doorway.

Nox is leaning against the doorframe, his arms crossed, amusement twinkling in his eyes as he looks down at the kitten.

I sit up and feel a throb on the side of my head.

"What happened?" I settle back down into the pillows.

Nox pushes off from the doorframe. "Too much alcohol and too little food." He wiggles his fingers in front of Ink, who tries to pounce at his outstretched hand.

"I passed out?"

"Collapsed," Nox tickles Ink under the chin, a strangely affectionate gesture. I thought he hated cats. Well, all living things really. "The hydrangea took the brunt of your fall."

I look down at my pink polka dot pyjamas. "Did you put me in these?"

Nox grimaces as he continues to stroke Ink. "I had to. You were covered in mud and flowers."

"Oh," I feel strangely shy at the idea of Nox undressing me. "Thanks, I guess."

Nox gives Ink one final stroke before moving back to the door. "Don't mention it."

He's still in Dad's jacket. Why's he still wearing it?

He points towards my bedside table. "You need to eat and drink. Get your strength back up." A big cup of tea and two slices of white toast slathered in butter and strawberry jam sit beside me.

"Eat and rest," his expression stern. "And maybe next time don't double fist your drinks on an empty stomach?"

I give him a small nod and take a bite of the toast. He'd used my favourite jam. Weird.

"Are you going somewhere?" I try, and fail, to keep my voice casual.

Nox finally looks at me. "I've got to head out for a bit."

I lean back into the bedding, now it's my turn to not meet his gaze. Right. The blonde in the bar.

"Have fun," I can't hide the bitterness in my voice.

"Always do," he chuckles as he leaves.

I throw back the blanket and begin munching on the toast. As

I stand, I'm relieved that the world is no longer topsy turvy.

Wandering into the living room I hear the pitter patter of Ink following along behind me. I look down at his big jade eyes as he looks up at me. "Guess it's just you and me then, buddy."

He lets out a loud meow.

I sigh, trudging over to a pile of the grimoires, grabbing a handful of them and returning to my bedroom.

If I'm going to be stuck here on my own, then I'm going to do something productive.

I settle cross legged on my bed and lay them out in front of me.

I'll find out what is being kept from me, even if it means I end up reading all night.

Cracking open the grimoire I'd been reading earlier releases the smell of old books and I'm greeted by the tiny little writing crammed onto the pages. This is going to be a long night.

I take a sip of the tea. It's just how I like it. Five sugars and lots of milk. He remembered. Weird. Very, very weird.

Chapter Twenty

<u>Nox</u>

"She left. I don't know what else to tell you," the haughty woman behind the bar answers curtly, before she shoves my double Jameson towards me.

"The pretty blonde?" I continue, trying to fight against the other patrons clambering for alcohol. "Tight dress."

The barwoman signals around 'Poison'. "You might need to be more specific!"

I chuckle, she's not wrong, the club is packed to the brim with pretty, nubile flesh. Just not the flesh I need.

"The one I was talking to before?" I signal to the corner where I'd been speaking with Cassie, who'd been trying her best to charm me.

The barmaid pours a beer. "I don't keep track of what the customers do. They come, they drink, they go."

I grind my teeth. I'd been close to getting a lead from Cassie, I was sure of it. She was visiting from Glasgow, and she'd accidentally let slip that she was part of a small, newly formed coven. It's amazing how loose-lipped people become if you ply them with cheap liquor. I could smell the Magick coming off her, a sweet subtle perfume that had drawn me in from the cold streets, but the second Esme stepped through the door, her honey sweet aroma had taken my breath away. I'd never noticed it until tonight but there was no denying her scent. It was intoxicating and fucking infuriating.

Then she started to dance in that tight lavender dress. Her gyrating was more suited to a strip tease than a nightclub. Despite liquor heavy on her breath her movements on the dancefloor had been graceful. A siren song and I'd been powerless to resist. Then came the bitter retorts and sour barbs, such an opposition to how

173

delicious she appeared. Those big eyes had flared with such anger and her full lips pouted sullenly.

I pry myself away from the memory and take a sip of whisky. Fuck what's happening to me? I'd tried to be her goddamn knight in shining armour, walk her home and put her to bed. Hell, I'd even made her tea and toast.

"What the hell is wrong with me?" I take another gulp, savouring the burn.

"Oh Nox," a voice from behind me drawls. "I've been asking that same thing for a very long time."

A grin spreads across my face as I glance up at the mirror behind the bar. Culum. Dressed in a white t-shirt and black hoodie, ever the embodiment of the delinquent youth. He pushes the hood back and runs a hand over his freshly buzzed skull.

I signal to the barmaid. "Another whisky when you get a second?"

She scoffs, "Aye. I'll get right on that!"

I turn and look at Culum. "Took you long enough."

"Not my fault, boss. The powers that be have been a little twitchy about everyone's comings and goings. Had to make sure I could pass over without anyone realising."

I take another swig. "What's causing them to get so tied up in knots?"

"Oh, I don't know," his eyes trail to the gyrating swarm on the dancefloor. "Maybe the fact that one of the most infamous demons they had imprisoned down there has slipped through their security."

A cocky smile creeps across my lips. "Serves them right for underestimating me."

He slaps a hand on my back. "Damn right!"

The barmaid slides a whisky down the bar to Culum, who takes a hearty swig.

"So," his focus remains locked on the crowd. "Why are you here?"

"Research."

Culum smirks. "And you practically fucking that pink haired girl on the dancefloor classifies as research, does it?"

"It's not like that."

"It never is…" his voice trails off and that smile seems to dim.

I grind my teeth, "Like I said. It's not like that."

Culum gives me a small nod, but I see the scepticism in his expression. "Got it."

I'm going to grind the enamel out of this mortal's teeths.

I place a hand down my chest, "She's the one who brought this meatsack back."

Culum lets out a low whistle. "That's impressive Magick for such a sweet, little thing."

"Trust me, she's not that sweet. Plus, she's a fucking liability."

A low chuckle rumbles from Culum. "You always did like the feisty ones."

I throw back my drink, suddenly annoyed by the bodies and noise. "Let's go somewhere quieter for another. I'm bored of this place."

Culum quickly downs his drink and slams it back down on the bar. "Lead the way, boss."

I smile at the barmaid as I slam my glass down, and she gives me a small wave before continuing her duty in the trenches.

"So," Culum holds the door open for me as we escape the heat of sweaty bodies and pheromones. "Where do you fancy?"

I begin walking. "Maggies? I'm feeling nostalgic-"

He chuckles, throwing an arm around my shoulder. "Boss, you're getting sentimental in your old age, I swear-"

We both stop walking as we catch a whiff of something. The scent of Magick lingers in the air but it is overshadowed by something stronger. The coppery, iron smell of blood and lots of it.

Culum tilts his head in the aroma's direction. "Can you-"

"Smell that? Aye." I move towards the macabre perfume. "I'm old. Not dead."

We track the scent to an alley between two restaurants.

Tangled, bronzed limbs coated in blood that pools along the pavement.

I crouch down in front of the body to flick the blonde hair away from her face. A face that a few short hours ago had been making moon eyes at me. Cassie. Dammit.

Culum mutters behind me. "Damn, she was hot. Such a waste."

I circle the body, careful to not tread in the puddles of blood. Sharp angry slashes criss-cross across her back. I look up at Culum, who scrubs a hand down his jaw.

"The second dead witch I've seen today."

Culum arches an eyebrow. "Someone's been busy."

"Apparently," my jaw clenches so tight my eardrums pop.

I tug at my hair. Goddammit. I look up and down the alley. "Cassie was with me less than two hours ago."

"And this is how you left her?" Culum deadpans.

I give him a fiery glare that slaps the humour off his face. Why the fuck was this happening again? All these dead girls, tormented and left in bloody piles… this is far too familiar.

"Let me guess," Culum sighs. "You want me to go back and see if I can find anything?"

"Speak to the witches," I say through gritted teeth. "See if they'll talk to you."

"Boss, the only person those witches hate more than me, is you."

I hear drunken laughter from down the other end of the alley. "Time to go." I shove my hands in my pockets and begin walking down the tunnel. My footsteps are unnervingly loud.

"Hey boss?" Culum calls after me, "what should I tell them?"

"Tell them that Scotland's witch hunters are back," I reply, not missing a beat in my steps. "They'll be a lot more cooperative once they realise their descendants are being tortured and killed."

Chapter Twenty ~ One

<u>Esme</u>

By the fifth grimoire I'm close to throwing them all back into the box and calling it a night. The handwriting has gotten smaller. That or my vision is getting blurrier. Maybe there's a spell to save me from going blind?

I collapse back on my bed, shoving a pillow over my face both to avoid unleashing the frustrated scream perched in my throat and looking at words that could have been written by ants!

"This is going to take forever!" I grumble into the pillow.

Tea. I need more tea. And maybe an extra brain.

I throw the pillow aside and make my way into the kitchen. I flick on the kettle and load up my mug with six sugars. Maybe caffeine will help my eyes read faster? Or fuel my self-discipline and prevent me shredding the books. Or maybe do it more effectively?

I finish stirring milk and sugar into my brew and throw the spoon into the sink. A sink that is now scrubbed and sparkling clean.

"Whatever," I trudge back down the hallway. "He's still a jerk."

I return to my room, just in time to see Ink balancing precariously on the shelf above my bed. Nearly knocking my pink quartz scrying orb off with his overzealous tail.

"Ink! Down!"

The kitten continues to wind around the shelf and gives me a loud meow. Maybe that's "Fuck you, Esme!" in cat? Ink's tail flicks again at my orb.

An idea suddenly hits me: scrying! Sure, I'm no whizz at it, but it's worth a shot. I pop my tea on my bedside table and give Ink a small tickle under his chin. He meows at me again.

"Okey dokey," I sigh. "Let's go with your idea then."

Scrying is something I rarely dabble in, as I'm usually just met with swirling grey images and not a whole lot of answers.

Ink decides chasing after a piece of lint near my windowsill is more fascinating than watching me scry. I don't blame him. I cross my legs and place the globe in my lap.

Clearing my throat I say. "Quaeso dea, videam post vela secreti."

I beseech thee Goddess, let me see behind the veils of secrecy.

I stare intently into the rosy, pink sphere, visualising the image of a gossamer veil being draped over a shadow. The veil blows enticingly in my mind's eye. It's so close. Close enough for me to reach out and grab it. I imagine gripping the silky material and as I do this, the orb begins to change and swirl to a dark indigo.

The image shifts and the swirling mists in the orb begin to take shape. I peer closer into the globe to see two figures I recognise. Mum and Dad. My heart leaps in my chest at the sight of Mum, but that feeling quickly dampens at seeing her so angry. They are silently yelling at each other. I can't tell what they are saying, but their faces are red with anger; it's bad. Really, really, bad. Weird. They never argued when I was younger. I can't even remember them squabbling. Dad is pointing at something Mum's holding. It's blurry but I can make out the faintest outline of a book. It's sage green with gold etching down its spine. A grimoire.

"Bingo!" I murmur quietly.

My focus returns to Mum. It's nice just to see her alive. Even if it is only a memory and even if she does look murderous. Why would she be so angry with Dad?

They blur and fade; a pang of sadness twists my heart as the image of my parents' dissolves and the orb returns to its pastel pink hue.

I blink, looking up to see that Ink has stopped his lint hunt and is now sitting on the windowsill staring at me intently.

"Ok, fine, it was a good idea!" I grumble as I uncross my legs. Now all I need to do is find that grimoire. There are no green books on my bed, so there's only one other place it can be. Hopefully!

I head to the fort of cardboard boxes in the living room and carefully sift through them. I see a sliver of that same ivy green in between the other books, about halfway down in the largest box.

"Double bingo!" I prize the book out. "Please don't be filled with teeny, tiny writing though!"

I flip open the first page seeing Mum's post-it note, "Beatrice Smyth, 1954." I bet Beatrice had been some fifties pin-up with scarlet lipstick and a big poofy poodle skirt; she'd probably have given Bri a run for her money in retro glamour!

Thankfully Beatrice's handwriting is normal sized, and I begin skimming through the pages. It's all in Latin but I can decipher most of the spell's titles. I stop when I see a small flash of yellow that catches my eye. Just a solitary little post-it, looking perfectly harmless, but as I pull it back my blood turns to ice. In big italic writing are the words. "*Exponentia facere magam mundanam*".

Cloaking Magick: Make a Witch a Mundane.

"What the hell…" I pull out a notepad beside me and begin writing down the translation. With each word that I write in English I feel myself getting colder and colder. My stomach feels like it's being weighed down with rocks and being drowned in a lake.

"*This spell was first written by the sister witches of Edinburgh during the infamous trials and tortures of the city's condemned souls during the 1600's. This curse is to only be used in the most desperate times, when a witch must be hidden. She will live a half-life, as her Magick and lifeforce will be tempered due to the dilution of her gifts. The essence of a witch's father can be used by the coven to cloak the witch's full power. The spell will last until the witch's thirtieth year. To make the spell permanent the witch should marry a Mundane and take their surname. Once she takes the betrothed mundane's name, she too, shall become a mundane-*"

"What the actual fuck?" Horror spreads through me at the dawning realisation. It all makes sense. Such horrible, twisted sense. My hands shake so much I drop the book and I crumble in on myself.

They'd done this to me, and Dad has been trying for years to make it permanent. Was this his warped way of trying to protect me? No… not his. He couldn't have done the spell if he'd tried. This was Mum. All of it. She'd put a spell on me to make me weaker. To control me. Contain me. And to marry me off to a Mundane to make it permanent.

Anger and hurt swirl through me like a storm and I feel it start to envelop me. White hot rage crackles under my skin, making me feel tingly and hot.

I glare at the piles of grimoires. Mum had given more care and consideration to these dead witch's texts than to her own daughter.

Smoke emits from the grimoire that had hidden the spell and a flame sparks from the corner.

It takes me a couple of seconds to register that the flames are growing and spreading. I spring into motion grabbing hold of my cold

179

mug of tea and dowsing the grimoire to extinguish the flames.

And now I have a new problem: it is covered in sticky and extremely sweet tea.

"Oh, sodding hell!" I take the soggy book over to the sink. "Uh! Tonight sucks!"

I carefully peel the pages apart; the right corner is burnt but luckily didn't destroy the text... apart from a couple of words on each page. The bigger issue is the ink running when I tilt the book to the side. Ok, so no tilting then! I carefully peel the grimoire apart, separating the pages out and laying them down flat to dry.

Easy peasy! Now I just need to figure out how I can now set things on fire by glaring at them. I guess Mum's spell is wearing off. Goddess only knows what else I can do...

Chapter Twenty - Two

Nox

The streets are full of raucous, drunken laughter. Some things never change. This city has always been able to ignore horror and yet again there are dead witches popping up all over the place. Witch hunters were always relentless, but I thought that by now they'd have died out. I suppose I have to give them some credit, at least this time they are actually killing witches. Speaking of, I've got to deal with the pink haired drunkard now.

I groan as I open the front door to the flat, hoping that the witchling is asleep. The last thing I need is another argument with her. Granted, it is amusing to see her little face go red and flustered, but I really am not in the mood.

I need to look at those damn grimoires without her interrupting me every two sodding minutes.

Fuck. It's awake. I can hear her muttering like 'Rain Man' in the living room. Why can't I get one moment's peace? It almost makes me miss Hell. At least in Hell there aren't witches everywhere I go. Don't get me wrong, there are a lot of them but at least they have their own neighbourhood, far away from mine.

I shove past the hanging crystals with disdain. Another benefit of Hell: there isn't pink, sparkly shit everywhere.

Speaking of pink and sparkly, I see the strangest sight of the night: Esme laying down sheets of soggy paper all over the floor in a decoupage tableau.

"Did you get a burning urge for arts and crafts, Sugar?" I lean against the kitchen table. "Or are you in need of a refresher on toilet training?"

She looks up long enough to give me a withering glare and a very unladylike hand gesture.

There's got to be around a hundred pages all stretched out across the tile floor and the kitchen unit. They are all covered in large loopy writing and a light brown tint.

She continues to scrabble around on all fours like a feral pixie. Her hair is scraped up in a messy bun and her cheeks flushed with irritation.

She stretches out another sheet across the floor. "Did you go back to the club and find the girl you were flirting with?"

I can't fight the smile on my face when I hear the note of jealousy.

"A gentleman never tells," I answer smoothly, and she huffs out an angry exhale. "So, what are you doing?"

"I had an accident," she grumbles.

"I was joking about toilet training." I step over the paper to the sink and see a soggy book cover propped against the washing up liquid. "Want me to pop out and grab you some incontinence pants?"

She pulls a face. "Don't be gross."

I pick up the sodden cover. "This is a grimoire."

"Well done, Captain Obvious," she snaps behind me. "Like I said, I had an accident."

The corner is burnt and all the pages on the floor have the same damage. I take a closer look and notice how sticky the cover is.

"Did you drop an entire mug of your tea onto it?" I ask, turning to look at her.

She sits back on her heels and huffs as she pushes back some of the sweat-slicked tendrils from her face. "I had to."

My eyebrows shoot up as I wait for her to explain further.

She chews on her bottom lip. "I accidentally set it on fire."

Pyrokinesis is incredibly rare amongst witches. I'm a little impressed that she was able to wield it. Albeit it sounds like it was more fluke than design. "Accidentally?"

"I found a spell in the book," she stands and carefully makes her way over to one of the pages near the counter. Closing the distance between us, she points with a shaky finger.

I lean over to read the page and try to ignore the distracting way she floods my nostrils. I look at the blurry words and manage to make out the title of the spell.

"How to disguise a witch as a Mundane?" I lean closer, there's a substantial disclaimer above how the spell should only be performed in the direst circumstances. I remember it well, I'd warned Sarah about it; that it's a dangerous spell, with serious side-effects. Seems neither her, nor her coven heeded my warning about documenting it. Fucking witches. I continue to read but catch sight of Esme. She's shaking and as I translate the words, I realise that her trembling is not from annoyance at me. That makes a change.

"I think, no, I *know*," she clenches her hands into little fists. "My mum used it on me."

So, she's figured out what the old crones were alluding to earlier. "Interesting."

"Interesting? Interesting?!" She snaps, "I've had a spell on me to hide my abilities and I've been lied to my entire life!"

"The spell was originally created for protection," I say slowly, hoping my logic lands in her emotional state, the last thing we need is more pages catching fire. "It was used to help witches hide from hunters."

"It can also be used for control!" She closes her eyes, "I don't even know why I'm trying to explain this to a demon, it's not like you can possibly understand!"

I let out a humourless laugh. "I can't understand what being controlled feels like?"

My entire existence I have dealt with the bureaucracy of Hell and the Magick of Witches.

She takes a step back from me, almost as though she's afraid of me, which is probably one of the first sensible things I've ever seen her do.

"Well, you know," she falters, and her rage evaporates, quickly being replaced with trepidation. "You're a demon. You're all about temptation, corruption… generally bringing the worst out in people…Right?"

I glare at her. Technically, she's not wrong. That is what people think demons are. That's what they've been indoctrinated into believing. There's no point trying to rationalise this with someone who's entire personality is a candy-coated delusion. I've only ever had one mortal look at me like I was something other than evil.

I let the silence hang in the air. I'm too old and too tired to argue against this dogmatic bullshit.

She has the grace to at least look shamefaced. "Sorry. I'm just upset."

Her expression twists as she fights back sobs. Her eyes brim with unshed tears and she's close to blubbering all over the paper.

If one more drop of liquid lands on these pages there will be no saving them. And sod's law that this might be the one that has the information I need.

I peel a sheet from the pile by the sink and lay it down across the floor.

"So, we go get answers," I say matter of factly and I look back to see her face scrunched in confusion.

"Answers?"

"From your father," I shrug, picking up another sodden sheet. "We go and ask him about the spell." Who knows, he might even be useful.

She frowns. "Why would you help me?"

I keep my expression innocent, but I see the lingering wariness in her eyes. "Call it curiosity," I flash her a wide smile. "Also, I'm incredibly persuasive."

"Oh no," she points a finger in my direction, "No, none of your demonic tricks on my dad!"

I laugh. "So just your witch Magick then?"

She scowls at me. "I just want the truth. I don't like being lied to."

"Your father has been lying for the last thirty years. He's gotten a lot of practice," I pick up the last sheet and lay it alongside its tea-soaked brethren. "I don't imagine the truth will come easily to him. Will you be able to control that temper of yours?"

"I don't have a temper!" she snaps as she crosses her arms over her chest.

"Now look who's lying!" I flash my dimples at her. "Also, do we need to bring a bucket of water with us, in case things get heated?"

The flush spreads to her cheeks. "I can control it."

"If you say so," I say, "a word of advice, I'd suggest you get some sleep."

She's about to argue, but I hold a hand up to her. "Sleep deprivation and a heightened emotional state are a recipe for disaster. Go to sleep. I'll tidy the rest of this up."

She shuffles for a few seconds. "Are you sure?"

"I can tidy the kitchen without setting fire to anything," I begin straightening the sheets of paper draped over the back of the dining chairs. "Which is more than I can say for you."

"Thank you," she mutters begrudgingly as she jumps around the drying sheets on the floor. "You're still an asshole."

I stifle a chuckle as I watch her nearly lose her footing around the sofa. "You're welcome. Sleep tight."

I hear more grumbling from her as she heads to her room. When I hear the click of her bedroom door closing, I make my own journey to the boxes of grimoires.

184

Whilst the one she'd attempted to set alight and then drown didn't contain anything surrounding banishments, that doesn't mean the others will also be fruitless. Maybe somewhere in this pile of leather and parchment would be the one. My one.

I begin to sift through them impressed at their overall condition; the witchling's mother had done a hell of a job in preserving them. Finally, the hoarding of witches has worked in my favour.

I will have to go through every single one of them. I begin skimming through the pages, careful not to damage the old binding. The first grimoire is filled to the brim with spells, but none are useful; page after page of love spells and glamor's. This witch is so sickly sweet she could give Sugar a run for her money. Although I'm starting to wonder how true that is. The anger I saw moments ago is testament to that, her fiery rage was undeniable. She couldn't disguise that. Nor the new power she's developed. Pyrokinesis is normally much darker Magick, not wielded by those who grow flowers.

I continue reading through the grimoires and as the golden sunrise begins to creep through the bay windows, I am onto book fifteen of the pile. So far, they've all been useless.

As I reach for the next one, my control of the mortal's body slips, and I'm pushed backwards into the space in his mind. For fuck's sake. What a great time for the Finnster to grow a backbone.

Chapter Twenty - Three

Esme

I snuggle deeper under my blanket. It can't be morning. Not yet. I barely feel like I've slept. I pry open one eye and see the sunlight that glimmers through the partially opened blinds.

"No," I tug the duvet over my head. "Go away!"

"That's a first," I hear from behind me and register the weight of an arm around my waist. I'm hoping to Goddess that it's Finn. I don't think Nox is capable of cuddling someone. Let alone me.

I lay completely still. "Finn?"

A soft laugh rumbles behind me. "Morning babe, you ok?"

"Er," I roll over to look at him and his arms remain wrapped around me like a comfort blanket. He searches my face, and his smile wanes a little. Am I ok? I don't feel as sparkly as I normally do when I wake up next to him.

His brow furrows, "What's wrong, Babe?"

I puff out a breath. I genuinely don't know where to begin. Finn has lost so much time I don't know where to start.

"What's the last thing you remember?"

"Being trapped in your dad's wardrobe," his mouth turns downward. "Why?"

Well, I suppose that's a plus, at least he doesn't remember the blonde girl grinding up against him. Or Nox and me dancing together.

The unwanted memory of that smirk and his eyes heating with… Nope… not exploring that thought any further! I quickly squash the memory down.

"Oh boy, ok, so," I chew on my lip. "My parents put a protection spell on me when I was little to cloak and weaken my powers. The whole reason my dad is so dead set on me getting

186

married is because if I marry a Mundane I would become one as well. Permanently."

Finn's fingers interlock around my back. "Huh."

I arch an eyebrow at him. "Huh? What does 'huh' mean?" I'd expected 'Oh Ez, that's awful!' Not blasé indifference.

"Well, would that really be such a bad thing, Ez? It seems like being a witch is dangerous. I mean Zoe was murdered, maybe it wouldn't be so bad to be normal?"

I pull back from him, I can't believe what he's saying. "Normal?"

"Yeah, you know, just like," he pauses, considering his choice of words. Unfortunately, he's picking all the wrong ones. "We can have a normal life together. We wouldn't have to worry about any more bad things happening."

"If I was 'normal' I wouldn't have been able to bring you back, Finn," I try to keep my voice level but it's getting louder and angrier. "Bad things happen, that's life. What I didn't expect was that one of those 'bad things' would be my parents lying to me for my entire life!"

"You said the spell is for protection," his tone is so patronisingly calm, it makes me want to punch a wall. "It sounds like that's what they were trying to do?"

"They stopped me from being me!" I snap. "They stifled me and tried to make me something I'm not!"

"Or they were trying to keep you safe, Ez. Seems a lot more goes wrong than right with Magick…" he tails off, as if realising he's said something he shouldn't, but I catch it. I knew it. I knew he was harbouring that against me.

I try to wriggle out of his grasp, but his hands hold firm. Trapping me.

"I knew you blamed me!" I keep my voice barely above a whisper, but it doesn't hide my hurt and anger. "Let go of me, Finn! Right now!"

His hands remain tight, and I feel that strange tingling sensation simmer just below the surface of my skin.

Uh oh… ok, think calming thoughts. Oceans. Sunsets. Libraries. Definitely nothing on fire!

"Finn," I try to escape again but he's not releasing me. "You need to let go of me!"

His embrace has always been my sanctuary, but now it feels like a cage. I try to keep my mind tranquil, but his fingernails dig into my skin.

His grip is painful. "Not until you let me finish-"

I try to calm the anger at Finn's unwanted touch.

It's fine. Everything's fine.

No, a cold voice in my head says. *No, it isn't.*

Anger swallows me whole and I can't see anything other than blinding white light for a couple of seconds. My skin prickles and I feel like there are rays of power shooting off me like sunbursts.

"Oh shit!" Finn exclaims, finally releasing me when he jumps from the bed.

I open one eye and see there's a small fire on the bottom of my rose print duvet. Before I have a chance to clamber out, Finn grabs hold of a glass of water on the table and tosses it over the flames.

I grimace, I need to work on controlling my temper with this new power. "Oopsy."

"Wait," Finn stands frozen, still holding the glass, with a look of complete shock on his face. "Did you do that?"

I watch his face transform from confusion, to alarm to… fear.

"It's a new power I have," I try to keep my tone casual, but he's still looking at me like I'm a bomb about to detonate. "I can, erm, kind of set things on fire now."

"See! This is exactly what I mean, Ez!" He points at the soggy bedspread, "Spells, fires, possessions! It's all too much!"

"What are you saying?" I frown at him. This is the first time I've ever heard Finn talk to me like this. "You sound like you don't want to be with me?"

"No, I'm," he flounders, placing the glass on the table and sits down next to me. "I'm saying that maybe your parents were trying to help you. I don't think they meant to hurt or upset you."

No, they might not have. But they also hadn't tried to understand me. They'd stifled me. As I look into Finn's eyes, I realise he agrees with them. That all they want is for me to not be… me.

"But that's not love," I say. "Love is supporting someone, no matter who they are. You accept them."

I see that hesitation lingering in his face. I'm certain mine echoes the same wariness, but for the opposite reason. I don't doubt that Finn and my parents care for me but… but I don't think they understand me. Not really.

Something settles in my chest, and I feel like for a moment I'm seeing him clearly for the first time. The lust-filled haze is clearing, and his expression is clouded with fear and wariness. Of me.

"How long have you felt this way?" Part of me doesn't want to ask. Shouldn't ask. I'm terrified of what the answer is going to be.

How could he want to be with me when there's such a big part of me, he doesn't like or understand?

He reaches over, clasps my hand in his and brushes his thumb over my knuckles, "Ez…"

Whatever he is about to say is cut short by the sound of keys and a very loud, and probably still drunk, Dahlia wailing from the hallway like a banshee from hell.

She bangs into something, hopefully it's not breakable. "I've got to tell you about my night!" She stumbles into my room but halts in the doorway, looking between Finn and I. "Whoa, what did I just walk in on?"

"Nothing," Finn answers abruptly. "I'm going to take a shower."

He quickly brushes past Dahlia who is looking at me with such scrutiny I squirm.

"What?" I ask.

"Nothing, just," she pauses for a second and sniffs. "Why does it smell like smoke in here?"

I walk past her to the kitchen and grimace at the sight of the tea-stained pages all over the floor and kitchen side. Getting to the kettle to make a coffee just got a whole lot more interesting. Once I traverse the paper laden terrain, I flip on the kettle and twist my head to see Dahlia flop down on the sofa to pull her heels off.

"So how was the rest of your night?" I smile back at her.

"Fun," she smiles, unusually coy. "Dan's an absolute animal, I don't think we stopped all night-"

"Please don't tell me about your sexcapades!"

She fixes me with a cold glare. "How many times have I had to listen to you and Finn screwing?"

Luckily the sound of the kettle boiling muffles whatever Dahlia is slurring behind me whilst I brew coffee.

"Wait, what's with all the paper?" Thankfully they've now dried, and the writing has remained relatively clear.

"I had to dry out the pages of a grimoire."

She gives me a slow nod as I hand her one of the coffees. "Riiiiight. So, from the smell of smoke and the burns on the pages, I'm assuming it involves fire?"

I collapse down on the sofa next to her. "There's no getting anything past you Dahls."

She gives me a wink before taking a gulp of her coffee. "As Dan can attest to last night, I am a woman of many, many talents!"

189

Finn gives me the silent treatment the entire walk over to Dad's. Despite the summer sun, his clothes match his mood: black jeans and a black fitted t-shirt. His brooding could give Nox a run for his money. I catch our reflection as we pass a shop window. We're polar opposites. Finn is all darkness and I'm wearing my pink beret and my favourite daisy print dress.

"How long are we doing this not talking thing for?" I tease, trying to lighten the mood. "Just because if you're going to keep looking at me like I'm a rabid Pit bull it's going to make it super hard to convince Dad to talk to me."

"I'm not not talking to you, Ez," he sighs, running a hand through his hair. "I just don't understand why you're so angry at me when I might have agreed with your parents on something."

I roll my eyes, my bullshit-metre is going off the scale.

"Finn, just be honest."

His mouth is a tight line, "I am being honest. I didn't mean to make you feel-"

"I changed my mind. Actually, I'd prefer the silent treatment for a little bit longer," I huff, crossing my arms as we pass by a group of elderly tourists taking pictures outside of one of the kilt shops.

Finn falls into step behind me, but I can still feel his bad mood following. Oh goodie. Nice to know grouchiness is contagious.

"Oh dear," a thick Scottish drawl purrs from behind me. "Do I detect a lovers quarrel?"

For the love of Goddess. Not now. Why now? In my past life I must have been a monster, like someone who kicks puppies for sport!

I keep facing forward. "No."

"I think someone's lying," Nox says in a sing-song voice.

This possession sucks, either one of them is being mardy, or the other one is being a smug prick, but both of them are pissing me off!

"What happened to Finn?" I call back to him, as we meandre through a busy street.

Nox takes on his familiar swagger and gives me a wry smile. "He didn't want to stay out and play. So," he shrugs, "I took the driving seat."

Finn relinquished his body? He'd rather have Nox take control than deal with me? I knew he hated conflict, but I never thought he'd be that much of a coward.

I turn to look back at Nox. "He really decided to hide rather than be with me?"

Nox's expression oozes with faux sympathy. "Sorry, Sugar,

guess he wants a little time out."

"Time out?" I splutter, "he's not a toddler! What the hell?"

"Don't take it too personally, it's not that he wanted to give me control; the less he wants to keep it, the easier it is for me to take it." He jogs to catch up with me and drapes an arm around my shoulder. "But on the plus side, you get to hang out with me!"

"Oh good," I try to wriggle out from under his arm, but he just pulls me closer. Fuck my life. "Maybe on the way home I can squeeze in a root canal and really complete the day!"

"You know, I've been told by everyone who knows you that you're this bundle of sunshine," he drawls, "but all I ever see is this sullen spitfire."

I escape his clutches and narrowly avoid stumbling into a lamppost. "What can I say, you just bring it out of me."

He chuckles and I bite my tongue. The bad mood I caught from Finn really isn't going anywhere.

We walk in silence, amazingly Nox seems to recognise he's in danger of physical violence if he continues to provoke me.

As I push open the gate to my childhood home, Nox gives me a wink. "Aw don't look at me like that, Firestarter! Today's going to be fun! I can feel it in my bones!"

I glare, "Don't call me Firestarter."

"Why not?" he asks. "It's accurate!"

I'm going to throttle him. I knock on the door. "Can you please behave for an hour? Can you be, you know... not you?"

"Sweetheart, I'm incapable of being anything other than the intelligent, dashing, charming, devilishly alluring-"

"Do you ever shut up?" I'd take two root canals over this right now.

"Occasionally," he ponders. "When do I get to experience this sugary sweet ball of sunshine everyone says you are?"

"Up until very recently," I sigh. "I was never anything but."

He looks me up and down and I don't like the scrutiny of his gaze. "Interesting."

"No, it's really not," I shuffle. "Also, stop looking at me like that!"

His smile transforms to a smirk, which seems to elicit a strange sensation in my core. "Like what?"

"That." I feel myself getting flustered. "Just stop that. That look!"

Before he has a chance to utter a classic smart-ass response the door swings open. Dad looks like he wishes he was opening the

191

door to a pack of feral Jehovah's witnesses.

"Hey Dad!" I smile, putting a little extra wattage behind my grin.

"Hello Esmerelda," he gives me a curt nod.

Heaven forbid he smiles, or hugs me…

He looks at Nox like he's trying to remember him. Maybe the hair dye wasn't enough of a disguise for Finn? Although the idea of Dad remembering any of my friends or my boyfriend from Uni is incredibly unlikely.

"Good morning, Mr McCleod," Nox smiles warmly and with anyone but Dad that would have worked. "I'm Nox."

Dad keeps scrutinising him for a few more seconds, pushing his glasses up his nose before saying, "Nice to meet you, Nox. That's an interesting name."

Nox chuckles lightly, "I had interesting parents."

Do demons have parents? My mind starts reeling through scenarios of Nox as a child. I kind of thought he hatched from an egg as a fully formed jerk.

"Please come in, I just boiled the kettle," Dad leaves the door open, and we follow him inside. "Go into the living room and I'll make us all some tea."

Nox bows at me like some leering butler and I watch him warily as I pass. He closes the door and is immediately right behind me. He leans in too close as he whispers. "Why does your dad talk to you like he's giving a tour?"

I ssh him before Dad overhears. "Tea sounds lovely, thanks Dad."

The living room hasn't changed since I was little: pale green walls, bottle green sofas that face each other. A dark green glass coffee table sits beneath the twinkling green chandelier that shimmers in the morning light.

Mum had insisted the house was filled with colour, but rather than mixing them, each room stuck to a restricted palette. Unimaginatively, when I was little, I always referred to this as the 'Green Room'.

Nox makes his way over to the fireplace to look at the pictures of my family. "Oh wow," he picks up a photo of a ten-year-old me in my school uniform. "You didn't always have that hair colour."

My naturally dark auburn locks had been combed and scraped into two plaits. I hated that picture. I loathed my school uniform so much it had given me an aversion to blue gingham that I

192

still have to this day.

"Although," he looks me up and down. "It suits you better now."

"Is that a compliment?"

"I was stating a fact," he continues to peruse the photos. "It's just odd to see you not covered in pink and glitter. It's unnerving."

I lean forward, making sure Dad can't overhear. "Not anymore unnerving than having a literal demon in my family home!"

His attention lingers on the photo of our cottage in the Highlands. Mum used to hold her Solstice celebrations there. I remember dancing and singing all night long, with the smell of bonfires and summer, blooming roses and lavender. I don't even know if Dad kept the cottage after Mum died. He'd rarely even gone up there when she was alive, so it seems unlikely that he would keep it.

"This is a beautiful picture," Nox says quietly as his attention moves to the photo at the centre of the mantel. He's so quiet it's almost as though he's talking to himself. "The beauty of a candid moment."

Mum and Dad on their wedding day. Maybe one day someone would look at me like that. I used to think that's how Finn would always look at me, but after this morning I don't know. My heart twists painfully in my chest at the thought of him. How could he not understand how much this upset me? We'd always seemed like we were on the same page but now... now he feels like a stranger.

"Uh oh," Nox grimaces when he sees my eyes full of unshed tears. "You've got that 'someone kicked a puppy' face again. Knock that off. We need game faces for this."

Dad walks in with a tray weighed down with a teapot, a bowl of sugar cubes, mugs and a pile of biscuits. The man is as emotionally warm as the North Pole, but he'd rather be caught dead than be called a bad host.

He puts the tray on the coffee table and begins placing cups out in front of us.

"Dad," I clear my throat, "I wanted to talk to you about something."

He passes us each a mug before settling down on the sofa opposite. Nox walks away from the fireplace to sit down beside me.

He leans forward, grabbing the sugar pot, dancing it tauntingly in front of my face.

I glare and he stops swaying it and promptly pulls off the lid. Before I have a chance to add it myself, he proceeds to drop the

193

cubes into my cup. Five sugars. He remembered.

"If you don't get your daily quota, you'll start getting ratty with me," he answers my quizzical look.

"That's got nothing to do with sugar!" I clench my jaw, "it's just dealing with you!"

Dad looks between us. I quickly backtrack, the last thing I need is him getting even more suspicious of Nox.

"Erm, thanks," I hate how flustered I sound, why am I bothered that he remembered? It's just tea. It's not some grand gesture of friendship, but it still throws me. Especially after this morning. I'm a bundle of raw nerves and emotion. Perfect time to try and confront Dad. Who is sitting, stirring his tea and looking between Nox and me with an assessing expression.

"Dad, the reason I'm here is because..." I trail off, how the hell am I meant to ask him about this? It's hard enough to have a simple telephone exchange with this man, but now... I've got to figure out a way of asking him about why he's lied to me for years.

"I think it's quite obvious, Esmerelda," Dad continues to stir his tea before tapping the spoon on the side and placing it on the saucer. "You've come to introduce your new suitor."

Suitor? Have I walked into a Jane Austen novel?

"Oh no, Dad, it's not like that," I fumble for words. "Well, it kind of is, but-"

Nox places a hand on my knee, and I have to resist the urge to slap it. "Mr McCleod, my relationship with your daughter isn't the reason why we are here," he says smoothly.

"What was that rule we had about no touching?" I whisper and he gives my knee a patronising pat.

"We uncovered something quite disturbing," Nox continues, ignoring me. Jackass. "And we felt it was best to hear it from the horse's mouth as it were."

Dad's eyebrows shoot up into his hairline. "I'm the horse in this scenario?"

I give Nox a sideways glance. His grin is perfectly amicable, but his eyes burn with the heat of Hellfire. I don't like that look. Not one bit.

"Four words Mr McCleod," Nox takes a sip from his cup, "ever heard of the *Exponentia facere magam mundanam*?"

Dad blanches, "Pardon?"

Nox leans back on the sofa, extending his long legs in front of him. I feel him drape an arm behind me and instinctively I move away, but he doesn't seem to notice.

"Come now, Mr McCleod," Nox chuckles, "I may not be a mind reader. Or a witch like your daughter or your dead wife."

Dad's eyes flash angrily at Nox, but he doesn't say anything.

"But I know a thing or two about Latin and spells," he continues, tapping his fingers on the back of the sofa behind me like he's playing a tune. "And that particular spell is very powerful, and might I add, very dangerous. It's a spell to dampen the power of a witch."

"I don't know anything about it," Dad says quickly. Too quickly. It's amazing I never noticed up until now, that he sucks at lying. Small beads of sweat creep from his furrowed forehead and a muscle in his neck ticks.

"I found the grimoire, Dad," my voice feels strangely disconnected from me. "Actually, I found *all* the grimoires. You know, the ones you said you'd gotten rid of? Turns out that was a big fat lie and you've been telling a lot of those."

"Don't come into my house and start accusing me of things, young lady," his snaps and he wipes the perspiration on his face. "You don't know what you're talking about."

"Enlighten us," Nox says conversationally.

Dad seems so flustered. I've never seen him like this. He gives his face another wipe but as he does, more perspiration appears.

"Dad?"

"He's fine," Nox answers before Dad can say anything.

I frown. "He doesn't look fine."

"He just needs a little persuasion," Nox says casually and gives my dad a wink. "He's alright, aren't you, Pops?"

Disbelief courses through me. "Are you using persuasion on my dad?"

Nox shrugs. "Just a little push. Don't worry about it."

"Don't worry about it?" I splutter, "don't worry about it?! You're brainwashing my dad!"

Nox sighs. "Will it be better if I make him forget afterwards?"

My mouth hangs open. How can Nox be so callous about this? He's mind-controlling my father like this is nothing.

He pinches his nose, a gesture I always do. "Look Sugar, I know you want to have some deep and meaningful heart to heart with Daddy dearest, but I think Hell has a more likely chance of freezing over than you getting a straight answer from him."

I look at Dad, who is still wiping at his face and I'm starting to worry about him becoming dehydrated.

"Are you," my voice is quiet, hoping Dad can't hear me. "Are you sure he's ok?"

Nox crosses his chest. "Scouts honour."

"You're not a scout."

"Ok, demon's honour."

"Do demon's have honour?"

"For fucks sake, Sugar, do you want the truth or not?"

Nox's stare bores into me, like he can see the ugly truth: I want answers. Real ones.

I give a small nod.

"Wonderful," Nox returns his focus to Dad. "So, I asked what you know about *Exponentia Facere Magam Mundanam*?"

A couple of seconds pass and Dad starts to tremble as if he's overtaken by a fever.

"Why's he shaking and sweating like that?" My worry begins to increase.

"Like I said," Nox's tone remains blasé, "he's fine. He's just stubborn."

"Eve found the spell," Dad finally chokes out, like he's fighting against each word that escapes his mouth. "She said it would act as protection."

My scrying had worked. It had been true.

"Protection from what?" Right now, my curiosity outweighs any concern I have for my father.

Sure, I may be a shit daughter, but I want the truth. I deserve the truth. If people aren't going to give it to me willingly, well, then, I'll have to take it.

"Hunters," Dad's jaw tightens. "Witch hunters."

"When did she do it?" I lean forward, ready to snatch the words that are pried from his unwilling mouth. I'm asking a demon to manipulate my father for answers, but as Nox says, maybe this is the only way to get to the truth? It's messy, cruel and exploitative, but in my defence, my parents did it to me first.

"You were eight," Dad splutters. "You had just begun to show signs that you were... like her. Like your mother. Three of her friends had been murdered just before your birthday and she said the spell could keep you safe."

His words unlock memories in my mind. Mum standing by the kitchen sink sobbing on the phone. Mum stood in a cemetery walking to three different tombstones on a cold winter morning. Mum's eyes red-rimmed and her skin a weird mixture of pale and blotchy red from hours of sobbing. Like mottled strawberries and cream.

I swallow. "Why do I have to get married before I'm thirty?"

"Protection," Dad bites out. "Eve said that the spell would weaken over time. She said by marrying someone normal... it would help keep you safe."

Realisation hits me that Dad doesn't know what the spell actually does. Not really. He's in the dark. Maybe not as much as me but... but he doesn't understand the ramifications of it. Dad wasn't really trying to control me, but had Mum?

"Did Mum not tell you that if I got married to a Mundane, if I took their name, that I'd become a Mundane as well?"

His face twists and I recognise the twinge of shame and embarrassment in it, "She didn't go into the specifics about it. She just told me that it was beyond me. That she was powerful enough to make sure that you'd be kept safe."

I guess I wasn't the only one who was lied to then.

Anger flares inside me. "She stopped me from being who I was meant to be-"

"She did what she thought was best," Dad splutters. "We both did."

"She lied to me," I counter, wiping the angry tears. "You both did."

"We were going to tell you once you finished Uni, but then," his eyes bulge behind his glasses and he swallows hard trying to stop the words. "Eve was murdered."

"Yes, I know," I remember Agnes coming into my room late at night and waking me to tell me something horrible had happened. That my life was now irrevocably changed.

"No, you don't," Dad is straining against the words. "I lied about how she died. I'd said it was a hit and run... but... but.... it... was..."

"A witch hunter?" Nox's tone is grave.

Dad shakes his head fervently but can't stop his mouth from shouting. "Yes! A witch hunter murdered her!"

Hurt and betrayal roils through me, a tempestuous pyre that wants to set the whole world aflame. "Why didn't you tell me, Dad?"

Nox senses my anger, like a match ready to be struck, or a bomb about to explode. He places a cold hand on my arm and before I can bat it away the change of temperature on my skin seems to quell the heat in my veins. A soothing balm to the wounds of Dad's words.

Dad's eyes bounce around the room until they land on the mantelpiece, the picture of him and Mum on their wedding day. "I didn't want your memory of your mum to be tainted by that. The police said it was a suicide, but Eve wouldn't do that. I thought it was easier to think it was a random, horrible accident rather than what it was."

My stomach twists at the thought of Mum being tortured and killed. That whoever did it could still be out there.

"You hid so much from me," I glare at Dad. He's lied to me so much and for so long, I don't know if I'll ever be able to trust him again. "Both of you."

"I did it to protect you!' Dad spits out, his shoulders shake from the force of trying to keep the truth contained.

"This cloaking spell," Nox continues, oblivious to the fact my life has been an entire lie. "Can it be used on just living witches?"

"What? I don't know," Dad's jaw ticks. "All I know is she took Esmerelda to that cottage. She used it for all her ceremonies and when they both came back, Eve said she'd taken care of it."

Nox leans forward, practically on the edge of his seat. "These grimoires you had hidden in your wardrobe," anger flashes on Dad's face as he realises, we've been snooping around his bedroom. "Are there more?"

"I don't know!" Dad splutters.

"Ok, let's try a different question," Nox strums his fingers on his chin. "Where would Eve keep her most powerful grimoires and possessions? If not here, where else might they be?"

I round back on Nox. "What? Why does that matter?"

He shrugs. "Don't you want to figure out if there's a way to undo the spell that's been put on you? Whether or not your parents have any more skeletons in their closets?"

"I mean, yeah, but you read what the grimoire said. It's a spell with some serious Magick behind it, I don't have that kind of power."

"Which is why," Nox speaks to me like he's talking to a toddler, "I'm asking about other grimoires and artefacts. Look, all I'm saying is what's the harm in trying to find out? How often are you going to get the opportunity to get the truth from your father?"

I clamp my mouth shut.

"I'll take that silence as agreement." He turns back to Dad. "So, where would Eve keep all her big bad grimoires and little trinkets? If not here, or the shop, then where?"

Dad's eyes bulge, "The cottage. She'd have them in the cottage!"

Nox points up at the mantelpiece. "That one?"

Dad splutters, "Yes!"

I look at the picture of the little chocolate- box house with its

198

thatched roof, lilac front door and cheery climbing roses. It's hard to imagine Mum storing powerful, sinister Magick somewhere that idyllic.

Although the same could be said for Mum: she looked like sweetness and light, but clearly the woman was keeping a hell of a lot of secrets.

"I just can't believe this," the teacup in my hand is shaking so badly I nearly slosh tea onto the hardwood floor. I look down to see Nox's hand is still on my arm, cooling energy radiating through his touch. Calming the boiling temperature still crackling under my skin.

"It's the truth," Nox's voice softens. "I can tell. He's not lying to you, Sugar."

My hand continues to shake, and Nox realises I'm on the verge of dropping my cup. He gently takes it from me and places it on the table.

I stare at it. I want to shatter it. I want to destroy everything in this room just so it is as broken as I feel inside.

For such a small family we seem to have racked up a mountain of secrets. Why would Mum perform such a dangerous and extreme spell on her only daughter? Why do something that should only be a last resort?

I study my father's face. "Why would she put the spell on me but not on anyone else? Why not on herself or the rest of the coven?"

Dad's breathing begins to heave in short, sharp breaths. "Enough! Stop asking me questions!" His expression twists into terror, "Please, Esmerelda!"

His skin begins to take on a blotchy complexion. He clutches his chest.

"Nox!" I rush to my dad, kneeling down in front of him to grab hold of his hand. "That's enough! Stop it now!"

"Are you sure?"

Dad's skin turns a deep shade of scarlet, like he's choking. I'm terrified he's going to have a heart attack.

"Nox! Stop it! Right now!"

I hear a sigh of disappointment behind me. "Sure thing, sweetheart," his tone makes me shoot him a withering glare.

Dad collapses back in the chair; his expression relaxes, but his eyes are wide with horror at the realisation of all these secrets he's revealed.

All these lies. They may have wanted to protect me, but I can't ignore the sting of betrayal. I want to burn this entire house down.

I stand, making my way to the front door, not looking back at

199

my dad. I can't face looking at him for one more second.

"Make him forget." I wish Nox could make me forget as well. But I know I need to remember this. Whilst my parents may have wanted the best for me, they'd controlled me. Stifled me. Hidden who I was, even from myself.

I don't even know who I am anymore, but the only way I can is by acknowledging and accepting this pain.

Chapter Twenty ~ Four

<u>Esme</u>

"I can get time off work," Dahlia stands in the doorway of my bedroom. "I can ask. I've covered so many people I'm owed a few nights off."

I squash down my suitcase, zipping it up before it explodes. "You can't. You know Bri depends on you and I need someone to keep running the shop whilst I'm gone. Besides, I'll be fine!"

I've packed a week's worth of clothes, including some hiking gear in case I need it.

When I had been standing outside Dad's yesterday, after multiple bombs of secrecy were detonated, I'd decided I was going to have to go up to the cottage.

I have to find out if there are any more dirty little secrets Mum's got stored up there. It's weird to think of her being this secretive, she'd always seemed like such an open book to me. I guess you can never really know someone.

"Are you sure?" Dahlia continues to linger in the hallway, chewing her bottom lip as worry etches her features.

"Dahls," I sigh, placing my hands on my hips. "It's fine. I'm going up to a quaint village to do a little recon. It's perfectly safe. No biggy."

"I just hate the idea of you going alone, Ez," Dahlia's voice is full of concern. It's disconcerting.

Now it's my turn to feel apprehensive. "I won't be alone."

"Finn's going with you?"

"I guess so," I give a noncommittal shrug. "I can't leave him here. You're going to be busy either at the bar or at the shop and he's not really safe to leave alone in the flat so…"

"So he's going with you," she finishes my sentence, I can't

201

ignore the amusement in her voice. "Are you going to be able to do any investigating or will you end up shagging all the time?"

I grab my leather jacket from my wardrobe, avoiding her eyes. "We aren't all over each other all the time you know!"

She scoffs. "Since when?!"

Since the morning, he let slip how much he disliked something about me that I don't want to change. Nothing is more of a mood killer than having someone look at you like you're a danger to society. We haven't really been intimate since he came back.

I keep my thoughts to myself and head over to my full-length mirror, applying more strawberry scented lip balm.

Finn and I have been like passing ships in the night since the argument yesterday morning. He's tried countless times to apologise but every time he does, I shoot him down. His apologies feel insincere. They are bitter, like sucking on an old penny.

Despite my stormy mood, I've dressed for the late summer sunshine. My head might be bursting with secrets, but my suitcase is bursting with clothes, and I may as well try to enjoy myself.

I glance down at my outfit of denim shorts and my newly rediscovered blush pink camisole top with a cute sweetheart neckline. I forgot I even had it until I was hunting for my suitcase, and it felt like it's a sign to wear it. Plus, my car's air conditioning doesn't work, so I need to wear as little as possible to survive the drive up to the Highlands or I risk fusing to the car seats!

Mum's cottage is three hours away in a cute little village just outside of Inverness. I'm dreading setting foot inside of it. Every memory I have of that place is happy, warmed by the sunshine of solstice celebrations but now... Now, I'm worried it's going to be tainted by what Dad has said.

Will the cottage now be full of the shadows and secrets that they've kept from me? Would I ever be able to feel the same way about my Mum as before? Or would the sour taste of deception and betrayal overpower the sweetest memories of my childhood? Which wins out? Sweet nostalgia or the bitter truth?

I clear my throat. "Can you feed Ink whilst I'm gone?"

Dahlia rolls her eyes. "No, I was going to let the little shit starve to death, Ez!"

I give her a glare that she immediately baulks from.

"I was joking, Ez!" she sighs, plonking down on my bed. "What's got your panties in such a twist?"

I keep looking down at my suitcase. I hadn't told Dahlia about Nox manipulating Dad. Part of me doesn't want to acknowledge it, but the overwhelming truth is that I feel guilty. I'm ashamed that I let a demon use mind-control on my father. But there's something even more unnerving about it: I'm ashamed, but I'm not sorry. I did it to get the answers I deserve. If I had to, I'd do it again. The weight of the realisation sits heavy in my stomach.

"Nothing's got them in a twist." I tug my suitcase off the bed and almost topple over from the weight of it.

Some things never do change- like the fact I can't pack for shit. Whether I go away for one night or a week, I always have enough clothes to fill a charity shop. Finn and Dahlia would always tease me. I'd usually have to go through at least ten different outfit options before settling on the first.

"Guess I have to try harder then," Nox pokes his head round the door and gives me a look that makes me accidentally drop the suitcase on my foot.

Dahlia flops back on the bed theatrically. "I suppose that's a relief at least. I don't have to watch you two go at it all day and night!"

"What does 'go at it' mean?" Nox looks between Dahlia and me, that irritating smirk playing on his lips. He knows full well what she means, he's being deliberately provocative. Jerk.

"Knock it off, Nox," I scowl at him as I drag my suitcase behind me. Thank Goddess for suitcases with wheels. "We've got three hours in the car, and I can't cope with you being a smart-arse the entire time."

Nox, being Nox, blocks the doorway, stopping my progress to the hall. I drop the handle and look skyward.

Goddess, please give me the strength to not strangle him.

He takes another step and I end up backing into the dresser by my door in surprise. The crystals on the top shelf clatter. He moves closer and my ass presses up against the wood. Alarm surges through me as he lowers his face to mine. He's too close. His mouth lightly brushes my ear, making goosebumps prickle on my skin and my breathing hitch.

Don't overthink it, I reason. It's just because he looks like Finn, that's all!

He pulls back but keeps his body close to mine. There is only a few centimetres between us. His face twinkles at me in amusement. He definitely knows what he's doing to me. He leans back down again, his nose brushing mine. Those golden eyes heat with hellish fire. Warmth courses through my veins and I wonder if Nox is doing that nifty mind-control trick on me. That'd explain my completely unwanted physical reaction to him.

"If you want to see my arse," he leans down further, his head journeying lower, but he continues to look up at my face, which is now blushing furiously. That smile teases across his lips, and I have to stop my legs from buckling. I feel like I'm drowning in golden pools.

He lowers his focus to tie my shoelace. Then he stands, reaching around me and grabs the handle of my suitcase. "All you have to do is ask nicely." He gives me a wink, before wheeling my luggage out to the hallway.

"Wow," Dahlia lets out a low whistle behind me. "What was that?"

I try, and fail, to keep my voice steady. "What? Nothing! What?"

She arches an eyebrow at me. "Ez, I've known you for a long time and many things have changed, but one thing never has."

I turn to see her draped along my bed languorously, playing with one of the vines of my ivy.

"What's that?"

She gives me a mischievous smile, "You still can't lie for shit."

"I need coffee," I sink lower into the passenger seat. Nox is taking the first shift of driving. He'd told me with a sardonic smile that he drives in Hell. Apparently, that's where they first invented motorways. That was a bit too much for my brain to deal with this early in the morning.

After I'd given Dahlia a list of instructions, both for Ink and the shop, we finally hit the road just after nine and the streets are crammed with angry commuters.

"You can have one once we get out of the city," Nox expertly navigates the winding roads. He smoothly swerves around a haphazard cyclist, who dives out in front of us without a care in the world. I hate to admit it, but he's a good driver.

"I need caffeine or I'm going to get cranky," I cross my arms and scowl out of the window before giving him a scathing glance.

His dark hair blows from the morning breeze of his open window. "More cranky?" He looks over at me. "Alright we'll compromise. I'll stop at a drive-through. If-"

I arch an eyebrow. "If?"

"If you tell me why you looked so flustered earlier?"

I squirm in my seat. "When?"

The dark heat from him immediately warms my cheeks. "Just before I was your bellboy."

No amount of coffee is worth this.

"I wasn't flustered," I open my own window, hoping the air will cool my heated face. No such luck, the temperature is already starting to ramp up. Please don't be blushing, for the love of Goddess!

"Hmmm," Nox hums as he navigates a junction. "I don't believe you. I can tell when you're *flustered*."

Despite my desire to talk about practically anything else, curiosity pricks at me. "How?"

He laughs again, so easy and care-free. He could almost be human. I remind myself again that he's a demon underneath it all. That I don't like him. I especially don't like him when he gives me a grin so dazzling it makes my stomach somersault.

"I can smell it," he pulls out onto the main road, his attention leaving me momentarily.

"Pardon?" I splutter.

"I can smell it," he rests his arm along the centre console and my eyes are drawn to his fingers, they track up his broad forearms, muscular biceps... get it together, Esme! It's just because he looks like Finn! "More specifically you. I can smell you from a mile away."

"So what? Demons have superior smelling skills?" I chew on my lip.

"I have many skills," he purrs as he shifts the gear.

I swallow. "What do I smell like?" Why am I asking? I don't even know if I want an answer to that!

Nox pauses for a moment, as if he's carefully choosing his words in his head. "You smell like," he looks over at me again, "sugar, rose, vanilla, warm oats and Magick."

A laugh escapes me. "So, like a cake?" I shuffle in the seat, "except for the Magick part." I lift my forearm and inhale. All I get is the scent of my vanilla body spray, "What does Magick smell like?"

Nox rubs the back of his neck. "Magick smells like the air just before it rains on a summer evening. It's like seeing mist rise across the highland mountains or the moment you realise you're falling in love with someone. Maybe it's less of a scent, more of a feeling."

"So that's how I smell to you?"

"Most of the time, but I can also smell when you're angry, sad, happy or even when you're," he winks at me, "*flustered*."

"So, it changes depending on how I'm feeling?"

He gives a small nod. "I can tell if you're pissed off with me by how strong the smell of Magick is compared to sweetness! Although recently it's changed slightly... there's a smokiness to it. Like whisky, cinder toffee and bonfires."

"Maybe that's because of my new superpower?" I wiggle my

fingers theatrically.

"You may be right there, Firestarter."

I groan, "Just what I need, a demon sniffer dog. Can my life get any weirder?"

He pulls up to a Starbucks. "It's not that unusual. Demons and witches have always been aware of one another. We can sense each other easily."

"I don't think I can," I sigh, leaning back into my seat. "I can grow and bewitch flowers, fuck up the odd summoning and accidentally set things on fire!"

Nox parks and turns off the ignition. He holds his arm in front of my face.

"What are you doing?" I arch an eyebrow at him.

"Try," he lifts his arm in front of my face. "See if you can scent me."

"We're not dogs in a park!"

Nox continues to barricade me with his arm, I finally relent when I realise, I can't get my coffee until I fulfil this weird request.

I sniff, his skin smells warm, like the cinnamon shower gel Finn has taken to using. "You just smell normal."

"Try harder, Esme."

I look at him in surprise. That's the first time he's ever actually called me by my actual name. I think Nox realises this at the same time as me and his eyes widen slightly in surprise. He trains his expression back to nonchalance, "If you don't try, no coffee for you!"

"Are you threatening to take away my wallet?"

His face remains stoic.

"Alright, fine!" I lean forward, my nose nearly touching his arm. I close my eyes and inhale deeply. Warm skin, summer sun... I take another. The scent transforms as I inhale again. Sandalwood, smoke, autumn leaves, ambrette... sex.

I take another deep breath, feel my pulse quickens as my nostrils are flooded with something forbidden and utterly bewitching. Images of amber, taut muscle and dark intentions flash through my mind. I bite my lip as a low moan escapes my throat.

"See what I mean?"

I snap my eyes open to see Nox looking over me, his stare aglow. Their heat eclipses the morning sunlight.

"Erm," I clear my throat. "Kind of."

"Demons and witches have scents that always draw the other close," Nox watches me, awaiting my reaction. "Like the opposite poles of magnets."

I squirm in my seat, wishing he'd release me from his gaze. "Interesting."

"So, do you want it hot or cold?" he says.

"Pardon?" I'm still trying to pry my mind away from the hot and heady images that linger in my mind.

Nox offers me a teasing smile. "Your coffee?"

"Oh!" Fuck! "Iced please! With extra vanilla and cream on top?"

He arches an eyebrow. "I thought you wanted coffee, not a dessert?"

"It is coffee! I just don't like it to be bitter!"

"Coffee is meant to be bitter," he deadpans.

"Look, all I'm saying is if you try it my way you might like it more!"

Nox gives me a look of disgust before exiting the car and heading into the coffee shop. I watch as he leaves and have to mentally kick myself. Here I am getting all hot and bothered by a demon. A demon who is possessing my boyfriend's body. A boyfriend who doesn't even seem to like me. The memory of Finn's wary expression flashes in my mind, but it is suddenly replaced with the image of amber eyes. My core tightens again. What the hell is wrong with me?

I throw my hands over my face.

Maybe Nox can get a vat of ice from Starbucks to throw over me?

We escape the chokehold of the city and as the roads open up to the lush green of the Highlands, we both relax into the drive.

Nox leans back into the seat as one arm hangs out of the car and he taps his hand to the music.

"Who is this?" he continues to pat the door in time with the beat.

"Taylor Swift," I take a sip of my coffee. "Do you like it?"

"It's alright," he answers noncommittally. I notice his hand is still moving in time to 'Style.'

"I knew you were a Swiftie," I hide my smile behind my coffee cup. "I can always sense when they are nearby. We can sense each other too!"

He looks alarmed. "What the hell is a Swiftie?"

"Someone who is a fan of Taylor Swift," I say breezily.

"I'm not a fan," Nox splutters. "I said it's alright."

"Alright is code for 'I love this and only want Tay-Tay from now on!'"

He raises an eyebrow at me. "Tay-Tay?"

"Taylor," I take another sip of my frappuccino. "All must bow before Mother."

"You make it sound like it's some kind of cult."

"It kind of is," I shove my wrist about in front of his face, jingling my beaded bracelet, "but we get jewellery, so that's pretty cool!"

Nox pinches the bridge of his nose. "You mean to tell me this singer has a cult following?"

"We don't call ourselves that," I beam brightly at him, "We're just Swifties! And now you're one too!" I hold out my fist to him.

Nox looks down at my hand like I'm waving a dead fish in front of him. "What?"

"We bump fists," I grab hold of his hand and make it tap against mine.

"Why did we just do that?"

"Because."

"Because?"

"Yep," I pick up my coffee again and turn the music up louder. "Just because."

I'm still making my way through my drink when we make it to our first swap over spot an hour later.

We park up at the side of the road and I admire the sweeping mountains. The streams intertwine between the rocks like lovers holding hands. I roll my shoulders and enjoy the cooling breeze over my exposed skin.

I walk around to the front of the car, leaning my weight against the bonnet and swilling my cup. It's pretty much just dissolved cream, but there's still enough flavour to keep me happily sipping on it for another half an hour.

After a couple of minutes, I hear the driver's door open and Nox joins me.

"It's beautiful here," I sigh, not even trying to hide the awe in my voice. I'm a city girl through and through, but I have to admire how breath-taking the scenery is.

Nox gives a small shrug. "It's alright, I guess."

I pull a face at him. "Alright Glum-Bum, now whose panties are in a twist?"

Something passes across Nox's features, and I see a shadow

of sadness mar his expression. "I lived here for a while."

"Oh?" I try to keep my tone casual whilst my brain starts listing questions it wants to ask.

"Aye," he looks towards the tops of the mountains. "I was a farmer. Call it teenage rebellion."

"I can't imagine you as a farmer," I chuckle, swilling my coffee around to make the remains of the ice clatter against the cup.

"Believe it," Nox drawls, "I had my own land. Raised sheep and cattle. It was... quiet."

I crinkle my nose. "Seems like an odd act of rebellion!"

"Demons aren't meant to have quiet lives," he sighs, looking up at the craggy rocks. "Needless to say, the folks back home weren't happy about it."

I can't imagine Nox in a rural setting. He seems like the type who needs extravagant luxury. I mean, he struggles just slumming it in a two-bed flat!

He snatches my coffee from me. "Let's see what all this fuss is about!"

I try to grab it from him, but he just holds it above his head. "Give it back Demon-Boy! I have an addiction!"

"To sugar?" he chuckles. "Trust me, I'm well aware!"

I jut out my bottom lip. "Give it!"

"Let me try it first, then you can have it back," he sniffs it warily.

"It's vanilla syrup, Nox," I say dryly, trying again to rescue my coffee. "Not poison! It's perfectly safe!"

He takes a sip and immediately recoils. "Bloody hell! It's disgusting!"

I stretch my arm out again. "Give it back then!"

He bats my arm down and takes another sip. "Fucking hell, Witchling, how do you drink this crap?"

"I don't!" I lunge towards him, "not when you've stolen it!"

I end up accidentally sprawling across his lap in my attempt to rescue my drink. It's only then that I realise how revealing my top is in this position. My tits are practically falling out of it. I guess that explains why I haven't worn it for so long!

Excellent outfit choice Esme! Tomorrow, assless chaps!

"Why Witchling," Nox smirks down at me as he takes another gulp of my drink, "if I'd known you wanted coffee that badly I would have-"

"It's safer for you if you don't finish that sentence!" I crawl back to my side of the bonnet and hoist my top up higher. "Please may I have my coffee back?"

"I quite like you asking me for things nicely," he takes another sip and as I look at the cup there's barely any of it left. "It makes a nice change."

"I won't ask you nicely in a second," I growl. "Give it back!"

He tilts his head, emptying the contents into his mouth. He swallows, a big shit-eating grin on his face. "Oopsy!"

I hop off the front of the car. "Asshole!"

"Oh," he's still chuckling to himself as I open the car door, "and Sugar?"

"What?"

"You may want to pull your top up a bit more."

The mountains continue to roll past us. We drive by various campsites and farmland. I coo over the Highland cows we pass who are happily munching on grass.

"So," I tap on the steering wheel in time to *'I Knew You Were Trouble'*.

"So?" Nox mimics me from the passenger side, as he busies himself looking through my glove compartment. Not too sure what he's expecting to find. There's no escape hatch from this conversation in there!

"Why did you decide to possess Finn?" If I'm going to get any answers out of Nox now is as good a time as any. Hell, it's better than any, he's got nowhere to go! He's literally trapped with me!

"It was too good an opportunity to pass up," his voice sounds drawn, like he'd rather be talking about anything else, or be anywhere else.

"Is that the only way demons can get to Earth?" I ask, trying to keep my tone breezy and casual. "They have to possess someone?"

Nox stops rummaging and becomes as still as a statue. "Not normally, no."

Silence stretches between us before I break. "Are you going to elaborate on that or just leave it hanging there?"

Nox scrubs a hand down his face. "I was banished. So possession was the only way I could get back here."

"Why were you banished?"

Again, another silence.

I wave a hand in front of his face. "Helloooooo? Earth to Nox!"

"I loved a mortal."

"Oh," now it's my turn to be silent. I didn't even really think

210

demons could love.

Nox's biggest character trait seems to be how little he cares about humans.

"She was a witch," he says quietly, like he's talking to himself. "She was clever, stubborn and beautiful."

I wriggle in my seat, trying to unstick my thighs from the pleather fabric. "So, loving a witch is forbidden?"

He chuckles next to me. "In some circles. Relationships between demons and witches are meant to be purely transactional. Usually, witches will summon demons to give them more power, more wealth or beauty. But," he lets out another low laugh, "she was different."

"Why was she different?"

I look over at him; he's peering out of the window, lost in his thoughts. "She wanted to get to know me. She wanted to be my friend," his voice is tinged with sadness. "She was a new witch, barely out of her fledgling state when we first met. She summoned me and when I asked what she wanted from me, she said she just wanted someone to talk to."

"Sounds like she was lonely."

"She was," he sighs, "she wanted someone to confide in. Both her parents had died. When she was a child, she'd spent most of her life living on the streets. A kindly landlady had taken her in, who also happened to be a witch. In exchange for food and shelter, she would clean the pub and help at coven meetings. It was during that time the woman noticed there was something different about her. Her power. She could wield Magick outside of a coven. She'd summoned me by accident. The night we first met, she'd only been cleaning the altar and made a wish," he laughs again at the memory, "so naive."

"She must have been incredibly powerful to summon someone without meaning to."

"Not just someone," he points at himself, "a demon. A high lord of Hell. She'd brought me forth against my will. When I first saw her, I had to resist the urge to drag her back with me for her arrogance. It was only after I saw her, trembling and apologetic that I realised she'd done it by accident," his voice softens. "She seemed so genuine. So sweet. Not like other witches I'd dealt with. Craven, vapid things."

"You really don't like witches," my shackles raise as I remember how often Nox has looked at me with disdain.

"Well, would you? If all someone ever wanted from you was what you could give them, it isn't an endearing quality. But not her.

211

She was so different. It was refreshing. She was refreshing."

"How many times have you been summoned?"

"Countless," he sighs. His head remains locked on watching the scenery we pass. "Always the same thing. It's such a bore."

"I've never heard about witches doing that," I feel my cheeks heat with embarrassment for being so ignorant about my own history. No wonder he hates us so much, if all we've ever done is demand things from him.

I sense him looking at me and I steal a quick glance at him. "Well, you wouldn't have would you, Sugar? After they banished me, the grimoires that contained the summoning spells were all destroyed."

"Because of you?"

"Because," his jaw muscles tick, "I did something I shouldn't."

"What?"

More silence. Oookay.

"I gave her something," he finally mutters. "Something I shouldn't. My heart and… something else. Something personal to me."

"But why would that matter?"

"Do you remember what I said about names?" His eyes are golden storms gazing out onto the craggy mountains.

"That they have power."

"It was believed she was syphoning my power. There is an old code that witches and demons should not fraternise beyond their business agreement," his tone is clipped. "It is forbidden. Witches shouldn't have access to that level of power for too long."

"Did she?" I can't stop myself from asking, "did she, erm, syphon from you?" The word feels foreign in my mouth and conjures up images of when people steal petrol at fuel stations. I suppose it's something similar.

Nox fixes me with a fiery glare. "No, Sugar. She didn't need to. She had all the power within her. She just needed help believing in herself, that was all."

I wriggle in my seat again, trying to escape his scrutiny. He finally takes pity on me and returns to the window.

"Eventually she began to see herself the way I did," he continues. "She became so powerful she was crowned the youngest witch to ever lead a coven in history. The old crones didn't like that," he chuckles darkly, "not one bit."

We drive in silence for a few minutes as we pass by a large loch.

"So, what happened?" I ask, as we finally leave the Loch behind and continue up the winding road.

"What always happens to mortals," bitterness coats his tone. "She died."

Nox leans forward and turns the volume up on *"All Too Well"* so loud it reverberates around the inside of the car.

Chapter Twenty ~ Five

Nox

I slip into silence; it's all I can do to avoid spilling my soul out all over the floor of her banged up car.

Uncharacteristically she seems to have taken the hint, and instead of pressing me for any more details, she sings loudly along to the music blasting from the tinny speakers. Seemingly oblivious to the emotional carnage she's just wrought on my soul.

For a couple of minutes, I thought she was going to ask me for more information about Sarah but seems to stop herself. Thank Lucifer for small mercies.

She's a surprisingly good listener, but I don't feel like splitting myself open any more than I need to. Some wounds heal over time, but talking about Sarah just reminds me how deep these cuts run.

Esme is still performing her one-woman concert by the time we arrive in a village. The chocolate box houses, and old-fashioned tea rooms are stuck in the fifties.

We pass by an ancient looking pub with a sloping roof and a haphazard sign swinging precariously in the highland breeze. 'The Gallows Inn' looks as welcoming as the rest of the residences, but I can't ignore the subtle inference of the name.

"They used to hang witches, you know," I point at the pub's sign.

Sugar wrinkles her nose disdainfully. "I'm sure it's just a coincidence."

"Oh, aye," a dark laugh escapes me, "because that's always the way."

"Not everything has to be so doom and gloom you know, Demon-Boy!" She sticks out her tongue at me, "sometimes a pub is just called a name because it makes it easy to remember!"

I raise an eyebrow at her, "If that's the case, then what's that?"

She stays silent, pretending she doesn't hear me. Good luck with that, I've just spent the last hour and a half listening to her sing and unfortunately this car doesn't come with noise cancelling headphones. I'd spent enough time rummaging around in her glovebox, trying to find something, anything, to drown out the sound of that inanely chirpy music. Although after a certain point, I must admit, it had started to grow on me.

"That looks like a noose to me!" I point at the ominous rope hanging above the door frame.

She chews on her bottom lip. "Maybe it's a joke?"

"Hilarious," I deadpan.

The car nearly stalls as we work our way through the village centre. The road is growing progressively narrower the further we clamber up the hill. Finally, we break away from the main road, turning right past a tiny church and a dilapidated graveyard. After a couple more minutes and many, many more fields, we turn left and chug to a halt at the familiar white cottage which I recognise from the picture. It looks exactly the same as the photograph which must be at least twenty years old.

The music mercifully stops once the engine is turned off and Esme steps out of the car. I make my way to the boot and begin pulling out our suitcases.

"I thought your dad said he doesn't come up here?"

She closes the door behind her, stretching her arms above her head before bending to touch her toes. I swear she wore that top to deliberately tempt me.

"He doesn't," she straightens, and I can't fight my smirk as she self-consciously adjusts her top.

I look back up at the well-maintained cottage with its orange climbing roses that wind around the lilac front door. "Well, someone is."

I take a step forward and Esme nearly jumps out of her skin when I stand beside her.

"Kind of twitchy aren't you, Witchling?"

"No," she frowns up at me, a flush creeping over her cheeks. "Well, maybe, it's just been a long time since I've been up here."

"Lucky you have a big, strong demon to keep you company then," I sling an arm around her shoulders, and she gives me a grimace. She wiggles free from my grasp and walks to the front door. She bends to retrieve a key from under the doormat and again I have

215

to look away.

She springs back up, holding a key high above her head. "Found it!"

She quickly unlocks the door and bounds inside.

"I'll bring in the bags then, shall I?" I call dryly as I begin wheeling in the two suitcases.

She turns to look at me from the duck egg hallway. "I thought you said you're all big and strong! I'm sure you don't need any help from little, old me."

I drag the suitcases into the porch and close the door behind me.

"There's something called feminism, Sugar!" I remark dryly. "So, you can carry your own suitcase."

She sashays away from me. "Why would I do that when I have you around?"

Is she deliberately baiting me? I scowl after her, watching her trace her hands lovingly along the walls and for a second I feel a twinge of jealousy towards an inanimate object.

The house is full of the same Pagan paraphernalia as Esme's flat, although there are a few additions to the mix. Alongside the usual crystals, assortment of flowering plants and trailing ivy across all the ceilings, there's a rich array of botanical illustrations covering the walls.

"I take it you inherited your love of plants and flowers from your mum then?" I call down the hallway.

To the left is a cosy little sitting room where sunflowers sit on top of the mantle of a roaring, cheery fire which is crackling away.

"Why is the fire lit?" I call to her.

"It's nice to have an open fire, even in the summer."

"It's not the time of year that surprised me," I shout.

"Oh, I see! It's enchanted, it probably lit the minute we walked inside."

Mustard coloured sofas and armchairs encircle a coffee table where a pack of cards are shuffling themselves.

"Aye," the witchling calls from the other end of the hallway. "She always loved plants and flowers."

I leave the living room and return to the hallway and venture into the kitchen covered in pastel blues and pinks. Daisies and tulips sprout from the indoor window boxes as Esme strokes their containers. The flowers seem pleased to see her and thread through her fingers as more sprout from the soil, reaching towards her.

"They seem like they missed you," I signal to the flowers. I

216

have no patience for plants. They remind me too much of my time farming… and my time with Sarah. I wince at the memory twisting its knife in my chest.

"They miss *her*," she gives one of the tulips a gentle caress. "I just remind them of her."

She walks back down the hallway, "I'm going to get changed, I feel gross after the drive. You can have my room and I'll take Mum's," she grabs hold of her suitcase and begins lugging it up the stairs.

I quickly snatch the handle and overtake her. "We've only just arrived, let's not destroy the stairs and wake the dead on the same day!"

She lets out a small, surprised laugh. "If I didn't know any better, I'd think you're being nice to me!"

"I'm trying to save myself from a migraine," I head up the stairs. "I've had to deal with interrogations and singing for the last three hours!"

"Hey! I saw you bobbing your head a couple of times!"

"Yes, due to your driving, not to the music," I quip, turning briefly to see the spark of annoyance in her features. I halt once we reach the landing. "Which room are you sleeping in?"

"This one," she walks around me, overwhelming my senses and I have to steal myself against the strange sensation. How does the Finnster cope? Just as I think this, I feel my control slip for a second; the boy is trying to wrangle control from me. But that can't be possible. He's mortal, there's no way he's strong enough to overpower me.

"You ok over there?" She raises an eyebrow at me. "You had a weird, glazed expression for a second?"

I give my head a shake, trying to clear the remains of the strange fog that clouds my vision. "Fine, just a little light-headed. That's all."

"Are you sure you're alright?" She takes a step towards me, placing a hand on my arm.

A ghost of a smile crosses my face. "What was that rule about no touching?"

She chews on her lip again.

She releases her grasp on my arm. "Forget it," she turns and points in the direction of the closed door ahead of us. "Can you drop the bag in there, please?" She points with a shaky hand behind me, "That's my old room, you can sleep in there. The bathroom up here doesn't have hot water, so you'll want to use the one downstairs.

217

Unless you like cold showers. So, erm, yeah. This is it."

I continue to peer at her, watching the flush on her neck creep up to her jaw and I have to resist the urge to touch her skin to see if it's as warm as it looks.

"Ok, so," she grabs hold of the bag, tugging it from my grasp. "I'm going in there," she points at the door and begins backing up towards the bedroom. "You can go in there, or, you know, wherever you want!" The crimson of her cheeks continues to deepen, "but erm, shall we go out for dinner in about an hour to the pub? We can pick up some bits for breakfast tomorrow as well?" She's not paying attention to her surroundings, which is abundantly clear as she bangs into the doorframe.

"Are *you* ok, Sugar?" I can't hide the teasing tone in my voice. I don't know what's come over her, but it's bloody entertaining. I take a quick inhale and my nostrils don't deceive me; she's most definitely flustered. I'm just not entirely certain what's causing it. Unless… Did she just scent me? It's unlikely but given the speed with which she's developing new powers, it could be possible. Unlikely, but possible.

She brushes a hand over her brow. She's sweating. Beads of perspiration are rolling down her neck and trailing down between her cleavage.

She clears her throat. "Fine, I just erm, got a bit hot all of a sudden." She reaches around behind her to open the door, promptly yanking the bag and herself in before abruptly closing it.

A soft chuckle escapes me. "Do you need me to get you some water?"

Rustling from behind the door. "No! I mean, erm, no thanks!"

I shake my head, completely dumbfounded. I turn the handle and open the door to my new sleeping quarters for the next few days. Only to be met with a wall of boxes and no bed in sight. Fucking priceless.

I return to the room Sugar is hiding in and gently knock on the door. "We may have a slight problem."

I hear the scrabbling halt. "What? Why? What?"

I let out an exasperated sigh. "Can you open the door please? It will be easier to talk to you without a chunk of wood between us."

Silence fills the space at my accidental innuendo.

The door cracks open slightly. "What's up?" Her face is still as red as a strawberry.

"Well, you know the whole sleeping arrangement thing?" I try to push the door open a little further but it's not budging. She's barricading the entryway and seems to be in a state of undress. It takes an inordinate amount of willpower for me to keep my attention trained on her face. "It's kind of hard to do that when there's no bed?"

Her brow furrows. "Pardon?"

"There's a distinct lack of bed in the bedroom," I say, watching as her face becomes horrified, "so you know, there's nowhere for me to sleep?"

"Shit!" She chews on her lower lip, before pushing past me in a state of half undress.

She shoves the door open. "Shit!"

I scrub a hand down my jaw. "Indeed."

She spins on her heel. "What are we going to do?"

I look behind me at the big double bed, covered in clean white sheets and lilies blooming around the brass frame. "Well, that looks big enough for the both of us so we could..."

"I am not sharing a bed with you!" She baulks, as her hands clench into fists. "You can sleep on the sofa!"

"Believe me, Sugar, I'm not going to fit on those!"

"We can't sleep in the same bed!"

"You sleep with Finn," I counter, wheeling my suitcase into the room. "In fact, didn't you used to do a lot more than sleep with him?"

She scurries around me, trying to block my progress, but I easily brush past her and recline on the bed, propping myself up on one elbow and giving her my most dazzling, shit-eating grin.

"That's different," she grumbles, crossing her arms under her chest and accidentally pushing her cleavage up. "He's my..." she flounders, chewing on her lip again.

"Judging by the state, and scent of you, Sugar," I cast a look up and down at her. She's trembling and it's not solely from anger, "he's not doing a very good job."

She turns on her heel and stalks out of the room. "We're not sharing a bed, Nox!"

A dark laugh escapes me as I hear her scamper down the stairs. Just before she has time to slam the bathroom door, I call down to her, "Do you want the left or right side?"

After laughing until my ribs hurt, I take pity on the witch and vacate the bedroom. I scour the house and find a bottle of Old Pulteney and a crystal tumbler.

I take the glass and bottle out into the garden. The summer sun is beginning to lower across the skyline, painting it a blush hue. I take a sip of the whisky, savouring that familiar burn and warmth that reminds me so much of home.

Many people think that Hell is a land of damnation and torment, the last stop for those who were evil, bad, or simply not "good enough". But to me it was where I was raised. My pretence at a normal, benign mortal life had been blown to pieces as soon as Sarah summoned me. I'd begrudgingly taken up the title as High Lord of Hell, but I hated it. I hated it all. I'd been ordained to rule since I was a child, accepting that it was all my existence was going to amount to until Sarah, who ironically, became my biggest rebellion.

I turn back to look at the house and take a big swig of my drink. It feels like there are answers here. Somewhere behind the sugar-coated appearance of this cottage, I'm certain that the witchling's mother has hidden secrets here. Secrets that may help me. If not, I'm shit out of luck. Culum's research has turned up empty and all the avenues I explored in Edinburgh are proving fruitless; this may be my only hope.

I roll the glass in my hand, warming the amber liquid and catch a glimpse of a silhouette in the upstairs bedroom. Esme. There's a reason I use nicknames: I know the significance of names. The weight and power they hold. Her mother knew that. Besides, compartmentalising her to a mere nickname helps me keep my distance. I stare up at the window, catching a glimpse of soft curves and rose gold hair and it's then that I realise I'm playing a dangerous game.

"Do you even know what you're doing anymore?" I mutter to myself, swilling the golden liquor. "Do you even know what you want?"

I stare back up at the window, the feminine shape spinning and twisting in the dim bedroom light. She's probably dancing and singing. She always seems to be doing that, even when there's no music playing. It's annoying, relentless and strangely adorable.

I scrub a hand down my jaw. "Get it together, Nox."

I feel something warm slink up against my leg and look down to see an ivory cat winding itself around my ankles.

"Sorry, kitty," I look down at the huge emerald eyes, "but white doesn't really go with this ensemble." It's covered me in white fur up to my shins. I look like I've been wading through the North Pole. I try to nudge the cat away from my legs, but the little shit seems to take this as an invitation, and it starts purring.

"That's Snow," I hear from behind me as Esme joins me in the garden, wearing a long green dress with a modest neckline and pretty scallop sleeves. She almost looks demure. Her hair has been curled to frame her face which is regrettably, blush free. At least for the moment. "She was Mum's."

I try to gently nudge the cat away from me. "Charming. How old is it then?"

Sugar arches an eyebrow. "She. Snow is a *she,*" shrugging she leans down to pick up the pearlescent feline. "To be honest, no one knows. One day she just showed up here and that was it, we had a cat."

"Why don't you take her back to Edinburgh?"

The witch nuzzles into Snow, who proceeds to purr even louder, whilst keeping a wary eye on me. "She's born to live in the countryside, she loves to hunt the frogs and mice in the fields. I couldn't do that to her! It'd break her spirit; she was happiest when she was with Mum." A flicker of pain flashes across her features, "and nothing embodies Mum more than this house."

"I can't imagine what you're going through," my tone softens. "But she's still your mother."

She holds up a hand, halting me. "Please, Nox. Not tonight. I can't deal with it tonight. It's…" She nuzzles her face into the cat's fur as her eyes fill with unshed tears. "It's too painful."

I give a small nod, before taking another big swig from my glass. She respected my boundaries earlier; it seems only fair I return the favour.

She looks up from cuddling the cat. "Pour me one?"

I give her a lopsided grin, sloshing a generous helping into the crystal glass. She takes it, giving me a gracious smile, before placing the cat back on the ground. She walks further down the garden. There is no fence cordoning off the perimeter of the cottage, it just slopes down onto the lush moors, before sweeping back up to the heights of the mountains.

She takes a sip, signalling towards one of the points on the landscape. "That's where Mum used to hold her solstice celebrations. We'd all help to build a big fire and I'd run around the woods and gather up wildflowers for garlands and headdresses."

"Sounds nice," I say, taking a hefty pull from the whisky bottle.

She gives me a sideways glance. "Don't you want a glass? Seems a bit uncouth to drink straight from the bottle?"

"I'm a demon remember," I take another swig, anything to try and distract from the strange feeling in my chest as I look over at her. Every fibre of my being wants to reach out and… I don't know what. I clear my throat. "Uncouth and debauched are my middle names."

She tilts her head at me. "Do you actually have a middle name?"

"Actually yes," I take another swig, "but I prefer not to tell people."

"Why?"

"It's embarrassing."

"Ok, well, now you have to tell me!"

"I really, really don't."

"I'll tell you mine, if you tell me yours!"

"No," I scrub a hand across my face, "because I'm certain yours is something like

'Sparkles' or 'Glitter' or 'Hope'! Whilst they may be marginally cringe-worthy, nothing will compare to mine."

She looks up at me and gives me a frown.

"You know one of these days your face will stick like that!" I warn, holding the bottle out and offering a salute to the mountain. "Here's to memories."

Sugar lifts her glass to the Highlands. "To memories. Both good and bad."

Chapter Twenty - Six

Nox

'The Gallows Inn' is crowded with bodies, most of whom smell distinctly like agriculture: sweat and fertiliser. I force myself to breathe in through my mouth when we enter the pub.

The interior is as macabrely decorated as the pub's name alluded to; strange iron signs of old laws are nailed into the dark maroon walls along with large crucifixes strategically hung so you would see one in every direction you looked. Despite the cheery atmosphere of the drinkers, I can't ignore the threatening undercurrent of the decor when we step inside.

The pub is packed with people, and many are having to stand, but somehow Sugar finds a small table near the back by the fireplace, which thankfully has not been lit.

"What do you want to drink?" she asks over the shouts of the other patrons.

I sit down in the overstuffed Chesterfield armchair. "Scotch, double, no ice."

She gives me a small nod before making her way through the crowd.

As she navigates around the tables, chairs and patrons I notice how many of their conversations halt. They all return her warm smile but watch her with either curiosity or fascination. In the entire pub I'm the only one who's immune to her charms. She looks like a fairy wandering through a grove, a drastic contrast to the weather-worn faces of these mortals.

As she reaches the bar, she gives the young man standing behind it a dazzling smile, and he is immediately besotted with her and practically sprints to make her drink.

She's completely oblivious to the effect she has on people;

she is the object of infatuation for everyone in here. To her, this is just normal. When she tries to pay for the drinks the barman shakes his head and I see him mouth the words, "On the house."

I shake my head, dumbfounded. "Un-fucking-believable!"

A woman standing near to our table turns to glance at me and gives me a look of surprise. She's different from the other patrons; her appearance looks out of place here: orange paisley dungarees, auburn hair tangled wildly around a ruddy face. She offers me a wry smile before taking a sip of her gin and tonic.

Sugar returns to the table just as the woman who had been regarding me lets out a loud squeal.

"As I live and breathe," the woman gasps. "Little Esme McCleod, my how you've grown!" The woman grabs hold of her and pulls her into a tight embrace.

"Aunt Clara!" Sugar hugs the woman whilst managing to keep hold of our drinks, although they look dangerously close to being dropped.

"Why didn't you tell me you'd arrived?" Clara clucks her tongue like a mother hen. "If I'd have known I'd have been round at the cottage to welcome you!"

"Don't worry, we were needing to unpack and settle in," I stand and take hold of the glasses before they end up watering the floor.

Clara releases Esme and gives me an assessing look. "Well, well, well..." she looks me up and down, taking in my all-black attire, which is a far cry from the rural appearance of the rest of the patrons. "And who might you be?"

"I'm Nox," I flash a smile and her expression turns curious.

"Lovely!" Clara returns my grin although she continues to look at me warily, "are you Esme's boyfriend?"

"More like associate," I answer as Esme shoots me a warning glare.

"Sit with us!" Esme squashes onto the arm rest of my chair as I give her a withering look. At least her scent cloaks the other patron's odours. Clara takes the seat opposite us and looks between us.

"So," Esme takes a sip of whatever pink, sugary concoction she ordered at the bar, "how have you been?"

Clara lets out a small laugh, "I've been fine dear, keeping busy and all that! Business has been slow, but other than that I can't complain!"

"Clara runs the tearoom we passed on the way in," Sugar explains. "I used to go in there all the time when I was little."

"She'd always order the same thing," Clara chuckles, "a strawberry milkshake and an iced bun. Even when she was a teenager, she would always have that exact order!"

"Speaking of things being exactly the same," Sugar says, "I assume I have you to thank for looking after the house?"

Clara gives a modest smile and nods. "It's almost the same," Clara sighs, looking around the pub. "Sadly I had to pack up your old room, a lot of the stuff your Mum had in Edinburgh had to be moved back up here. Your father said there simply wasn't space for it at his house."

"That's strange," I say quietly.

"Well, I believe some of the items are too, erm, valuable, so needed to be kept in a more remote location," Clara looks around nervously, as if expecting someone to eavesdrop.

"It's like he wanted to get rid of anything that reminded him of her," Sugar sighs. "Like she wasn't a-"

"Botanist?" I interject when I notice a couple of the older men in the corner casting curious glances our way.

Whilst Clara doesn't appear to be fazed by the attention our little meeting is generating, I am. They all appear to be human, but I wouldn't put it past some of them to be something else in disguise. The more we're noticed, the greater the chance I'll be discovered.

Clara and Esme stop talking when they realise, I'm watching the three men opposite us. I put a little more heat behind my glare and they all shift uncomfortably, turning their backs on us and moving towards the other end of the pub.

"Was that necessary?" Sugar snaps at me.

"They were bothering me."

Clara regards me. "You're not all you appear, are you?"

I flash my dimples and raise my drink to her. "Likewise."

"He may have had the right idea there, dear," Clara leans in closer to us and we mirror her movement. "There have been some rather alarming things happening the past few weeks."

"Such as?" I look around the pub, no one appears to be listening to us now.

"You remember your Aunt Helena, dear?" Clara takes a big sip of her drink, as if bracing herself for what she's about to say next. "She was found dead last month. It was the strangest thing; she was discovered hanging in her kitchen. Poor dear committed suicide."

"Aunt Helena killed herself?" Sugar's question is a strangled whisper.

"Apparently, although she didn't leave a note," Clara sighs. "I guess you never can know what's going on in a person's head. I'd spoken to her the day before and she'd seemed fine, bright as a button and talking about her next holiday with her kids and grandchildren. They were all going to go to Lanzarote... or was it Tenerife? Poor things."

"Why did they think it was suicide?" I ask. This all feels too familiar.

"Because of the way she was found, dear," Clara is looking at me like I've had a bump to the head. "She hung herself."

I pinch the bridge of my nose. "But you said there was no note."

"And you said she seemed fine before that?" Sugar pipes up beside me. "She wouldn't kill herself if she was excited to go on holiday with her family, would she?"

"Well, I don't know, dear," Clara looks between us. "We weren't as close as we used to be when your mother was still alive. We all drifted apart after her... her accident."

We both notice the moment of hesitation as Clara says the last word.

"Clara," Sugar leans over the table to place a hand on her arm. "I know what happened to Mum."

Clara's looks between the both of us in alarm. "I don't know what you mean, dear!"

"Aye, you do," I say flatly. "Now we know too."

Clara slumps back in the seat, her shoulders dropping as though a heavy burden has been lifted. "I'm so sorry. Your father, he made me swear, made us all swear, that we weren't to tell you what had happened. He thought it was for the best."

Sugar lets out a shaky breath. "I understand. I mean, I don't like it, but I get it. You were just following Dad's wishes."

"Not just your father's dear, your mother's. She'd given us all strict instruction in the event of something happening to her."

"She knew?" I ask. Sugar's eyes are practically on stalks.

"She had her suspicions," Clara says slowly. "She wanted us to be prepared."

Hurt and anger crashes from Sugar in waves like an ocean battering the shore.

"Why don't you come by mine tomorrow evening, say around seven?" Clara offers when she realises the silence isn't going to be broken by my companion.

"Tomorrow sounds good, thank you, Clara," I offer a benign smile.

"Right then," Clara stands, finishing up the rest of her drink. "It was lovely seeing you Esme dear. You've grown into such a beautiful young woman," she turns her attention to me. "Nox, lovely to meet you."

"Likewise," I stand and offer a hand to Clara, who looks at it hesitantly before shaking it. Her eyes widen; she's powerful, she recognises what I am, and to her credit she doesn't flinch. She makes a speedy exit out of the pub, and it's only when I hear the jingle of the bell above the door, I turn my attention back to Sugar.

I look down at her and place a hand on her shoulder. "You doing ok down there, Firestarter?"

Her shoulder trembles for a second before she looks up at me. To my surprise, she's laughing. "I just don't know how much more of this I can take."

"You're a lot stronger than you think," I offer, giving her shoulder a light squeeze. "Don't set fire to anything in here. We still need to order food."

The ghost of a smile traces her lips. "What was that rule about no touching?"

I pull my hand away. "Sorry. Not sure what came over me then."

"I think that's called being a nice person."

"Not a person."

"Ok, a nice demon."

"Demons aren't supposed to be nice."

"For Goddess' sake, Nox! Just take the damn compliment!"

"Doesn't sound like a compliment to me," I grimace as I sit down in the seat Clara vacated. "It sounds like I'm going soft."

"I don't think you're soft," crimson flushes her cheeks. I'm pleased to see her blush return, despite the circumstances. "You know what I meant."

"Certainly," I pull free one of the laminate menus from the holder between us. "Now what shall we have? I'm in the mood for something breaded, battered and deep-fried."

Sugar picks up the menu, crinkling her nose. "I think those are the only options available here."

"Do I hear judgement from the woman who ingests sugar like it's a food group?"

"I don't have that much," she grumbles, "I just like sweet things."

"You like everything sweet. Food, drinks… people."

She looks up at me over the top of her sheet. "You're not

227

sweet."

"I'm also not technically a person," I continue to scour through the menu and find something that sounds like it may have been haggis in a past life. The pictures all look very sad and incredibly beige. Even the photos look like they have been dipped in grease and fried.

I look up to see Sugar is still peering at me over the menu and that flush has reappeared.

"Did you just say you like me?" I ask.

"No," she looks up at me shyly. "Well, maybe, you're kind of growing on me. Like a fungus."

"Charming."

"Ok, something nicer than fungus," she backtracks as her blush deepens.

"Like?"

"I'm trying to think of something."

"Ok, so whilst you do that, I'm going to the bar." I signal to her glass, "Same again?"

She gives me a small nod, "Yes please."

I make my way back over to the bar and signal at the young lad who has spent most of his shift fawning over Sugar.

"Same again, pal," I tap on the bar and point up at the whisky.

"Sure thing," he says, managing to pry his focus away from our table.

Every red-blooded male seems to end up falling head over heels for her. Fortunately, I'm neither, so I remain immune. I do feel a little sympathy for the lad as he clatters into the glasses, distracted by his newfound love.

"Might be easier to pour the drinks if you look at them, mate," I try to keep my tone light.

He laughs, embarrassed. "Sorry," he reaches up to grab the scotch. "It's just we don't get many girls like that in here."

"Aye," I look back to see Sugar stroking a dog that one of the farmers had brought in with them. The big slobbering mutt is clambering all over her and licking her face, which she doesn't seem to mind. She lets out a musical laugh which makes something twist in my chest.

"At least not many that are like her," the tone in his voice is practically awe-struck.

"Aye," I turn back to retrieve the drinks. "She is a rare one."

I make my way back through the crowd, just as Sugar gives the dog one final stroke before the owner tugs it away, apologising for the drool the witchling is now covered in.

"Is there anything on the planet which is immune to your charms?" I ask as I sit back down in my seat and hand her the lurid pink cocktail.

"Actually, yeah," she takes a big sip of her drink. "You."

"Soooo, I was thinking of something that grows that'sh less gross than frungus!" Sugar slurs as she stumbles along beside me on our way back to the cottage.

"Do you mean fungus?" I ask.

"That's what I said!" she baulks.

After we'd braved the dinner of all things fried and breaded, we'd moved onto making our way through the cocktail menu. I don't know why we'd thought that was a good idea. Maybe after the stress of the past few days and the need to thaw our constant bickering? Either way it culminated in us getting pissed. But I'd underestimated the witch's ability to drink and remain lucid. As the night air hits the both of us, it becomes apparent we are just equally drunk.

"Oh, aye?" I drawl as I narrowly avoid walking into a lamppost. "What that's then?"

Sugar skips about and halts to spin on her heel. "You're kind of like," she hiccups, "a rose."

"A rose?"

"Aye, you're kind of beautiful,"

"I look like Finn," I grumble, shoving my hands into my pockets.

"Your eyessss aren't," she slurs. "Your eyes are different. Anyway! You're like a rose. Beautiful but covered in thorns."

"So, I'm a bit of a prick?"

"Thorns aren't like pricks," Sugar frowns. "Well, I suppose they are, but like lotssss of little ones."

"There's an image. I suppose a rose is better than mould," I stagger up the high-street. Casting a look at my companion, I slur. "You're like glitter."

"Because I'm so sparkly?" She drunkenly beams at me.

"No, because once you're here it's impossible to get rid of you!"

She sticks her tongue out at me, "That doesn't sound very nice."

"I'm a demon, remember?" I shout after her, nodding politely at the alarmed elderly couple who are passing in the other direction. We meander past the lop-sided church, which looks like it's sloping even more than earlier.

"Sooooo what do demons actually look like?" Sugar pretends to walk on a tightrope along the pavement, her arms flailing to stop her from toppling over. "Does that mean you have horns? A tail?" she giggles as she slips off one of the cobblestones, "A pitchfork?"

I overtake Little Miss Drunkard. "No, I don't have horns or a tail."

"Do you look human?" she hiccups, "that's kind of boring."

"Well, it'd make it a bit difficult to wander around on Earth if we looked the way you mortals think we do!" My body feels heavy and sluggish. I used to be able to drink sailors under the table. A pitcher of cocktails shouldn't affect me like this!

Sugar sprints towards the cottage, her pink hair whipping around as her dress spills out behind her like leaves on a breeze. "So, you do look all boring and normal then?"

I catch up with her when she's fumbling to unlock the front door. "I wouldn't class myself as boring."

She pushes open the door and practically falls into the hallway. She manages to stop herself before smacking onto the checkerboard floor tiles. "What would you rate yourself?"

"Rate myself?"

"Aye, you know," she hiccups again, "on a scale of attractiveness?"

"Why?"

She shrugs. "Just curious. It's weird that I don't know that much about you, that's all! You really could have horns or some shit."

I look over and see the earnestness. She's trying to get to know me. To be friends. Someone who's head is filled with sunshine and sparkles shouldn't be around a soul as dark and damaged as mine. Especially one who keeps stealing her boyfriend's body.

"You know all you need to know," my voice is clipped and firm. But as I say this, I try to soften the edges, I don't want to be cruel. Strange, because I enjoy cruelty. Being in a confined space with her means I need to set clear boundaries. I can't have her prying out more information about me or why I was so eager to come up to the cottage with her.

"Fine," she huffs and lurches towards the kitchen.

"Where are you going? The bed is upstairs!"

"I need a hot chocolate!"

"No," I stagger behind and find her rummaging through the cupboard, balancing precariously on one of the chairs to try and reach the top shelf. "What you need is a big glass of water, to go to

230

sleep and pray that you don't have a hangover tomorrow."

She groans. "Why are you so boring? I want hot chocolate; it'll help me sleep!"

"I think the ten pitchers of liquor will do that for you," I offer an outstretched hand which she begrudgingly takes, narrowly missing whacking her head on the cupboard door. "You go upstairs, and I'll get you water."

She glares at me before trudging past and grumbling the words, "demon-boy", "boring" and "fucking water." I hear stomping as she makes her way up the stairs. This must be what it feels like dealing with a sullen teenager.

"Lucifer, give me patience," I grab two tumblers from the shelf and fill them with water from the tap.

My vision blurs as I fill one of the glasses with water. My consciousness shoved back as Finn shoves forward. I'm no longer in control of my body. This body. His body. I push back with a powerful force, but Finn digs in deeper. The glass drops onto the floor.

This isn't possible. He's mortal, he has no strength, especially compared to me. I push forward, taking back the control he's trying to steal. I feel his resistance, but he eventually settles back into the shadows of our shared mind again. How the fuck did he do that? Has he developed superhuman strength? I give him one final push down to ensure he stays subdued before picking up the shards of glass.

I fill the second glass and make my way up the stairs. I keep the light on in the hall to illuminate them, so I don't crack my head open as I make my way up the lop-sided staircase.

The upstairs hallway is still pitch black but there is a golden light spilling from the bedroom. I nudge the door open to find Sugar sprawled facedown like a drunken starfish across the bed in a state of undress. She's managed to get some of her clothes off but is still in her pale blue underwear. It looks like she's attempted, and failed, to take her bra off as one of the straps is hanging off of her shoulder coquettishly.

I pry my eyes away from her ivory skin and resist the irrational urge to count the freckles that sprinkle across her back and shoulders.

I kneel beside her, giving her shoulder a gentle shake. "Sugar, you need to drink this before you go to sleep."

"Hmphruhhg," a groan comes from the pillow.

"I know, but you need to drink this, or you'll feel like shit tomorrow."

Her head lifts and one almond eye opens. "Finn?"

231

"Nope," I say in a clipped tone as I place the glass of water on the bedside table. "The other one."

"Oh," her brow furrows, "you brought me water?"

"Just like I said I was going to."

She lifts herself up, her head lolls dangerously close to the bedside table when she tries to sit. I catch her before she can give herself a concussion. She sits upright but my hands remain threaded through her hair, their soft tendrils encircling and ensnaring me like the sweetest siren song. My fingers instinctively twirl around a rogue curl. I try to move away but I can't.

"You're not as mean as you think, Demon-Boy," she gives me a lop-sided, drunken smile and nuzzles into my hand.

"And you're not as sweet as you think you are, Sugar," my hand moves down from her head to grip the back of her neck. I tell myself I'm doing it so she doesn't end up accidentally slamming her skull. That's the only reason.

She leans into my touch before steadying the lolling of her head. Her expression turns serious as she scrutinises me. "I like the way you look at me."

My thumb instinctively begins to circle at the nape of her neck. "With frustration?"

"No," she keeps her gaze locked on mine as she bites down on her lower lip. I'm drawn to the gesture before trailing back up. "Your eyes. The colour of them. It's like I'm being dipped in honey."

"You're definitely pissed," I chuckle.

She scowls. "I'm not."

"Whatever you say, Sugar, but you're drinking that water then going to sleep."

"You're so bossy!" She huffs out an exasperated breath. "Fine," she wriggles forward and grabs hold of the glass with wobbly hands and, to my surprise, she chugs the entire glass.

"Happy?" she mumbles before flopping back onto the bed.

"Ecstatic," I stand and make my way towards the door and flick off the light switch. "Sweet dreams, Sugar."

"Wait," her voice is tiny and timid. The weight of the world is carried in that one word. I freeze in the doorway.

I turn to look behind me, her body shadowed in darkness, but I can still make out the pink waves of her hair cascading over her shoulders. That earnest expression. She doesn't sound drunk, but that doesn't negate that less than two minutes ago she was close to concussing herself on every solid surface in the room.

"You need to sleep," I say, willing my body to leave the room.

232

Just go downstairs. Ignore the strange pull to this woman. She's no good for me and I'm definitely no good for her. Especially as we're both shit faced. But still, however much I will myself to go downstairs, I don't move. Maybe it's Finn? Has he somehow taken back control of his feet?

She looks up at me shyly, the perfume of her nervousness has a slight citrus note. The air smells like freshly baked lemon pie. Even when she's worried, she still smells like dessert.

"Can you stay?" She edges to one side of the bed. "Please?"

I scrub a hand down my face. Why does her saying please make me feel something? Something I shouldn't feel. "Are you sure?"

She pats the other side of the bed. Her face is so vulnerable, and I don't have it in me to deny her.

My limbs seem to move independently of my intentions as I return to the bed.

I curse as Sugar pulls the cover free from under her and nestles deep under the cream sheets. I peel the shirt from my taut shoulders and as I unbuckle my belt, I swear I hear her swallow audibly.

"Just so I'm clear," I unbutton my jeans, pulling them free from my legs and willing my body to remain indifferent to the sea of curves and ivory skin beckoning to me. "We're just sleeping."

"Aye," she gives me a small nod from under the duvet. "Sleeping."

I clamber into the bed, immediately feeling like I'm being enveloped in sweetness. She scoots closer to me before thinking better of it, halting her movement. She edges her back towards the wall, putting distance between us. I can smell the lingering citrus scent along with the heady mixture of toasted marshmallows. Her body may be responding to me, but her mind is still calling the shots. Smart girl.

A low chuckle escapes me. "I don't bite, Sugar."

She rolls over to face the wall, her shoulders bathed in the buttery light from the hallway, and I hear her fight against yawning. "I don't believe you, Demon-Boy."

"Sugar?"

"Mm?"

"Go to sleep."

Chapter Twenty ~ Seven

Esme

Twin amber flames hold steady above me, looking down at me with such ferocity I feel like they could set me on fire. The rest of his body is cloaked in smoke and shadow, but his presence overwhelms me. He surrounds me. The scent of sandalwood, autumn leaves, ambrette and sex.

He lowers his head, those whisky eyes pinning me.

I'm a writhing, squirming mess of need as my chest rises and falls in a frantic rhythm. I want him. No, this goes beyond want. I *need* him. I need him like the air in my lungs, or the blood in my veins, both of which quicken as he descends between my thighs. I squirm.

"Open up for me, Sugar," his voice is as rich and smoky as the liquor he drinks.

His shadowed hands press at my knees and tease my legs apart.

My breathing hitches, and my heart feels like it's going to escape my chest as his hot breath washes across the top of my thighs and moves lower.

His eyes remain locked on mine as my legs move of their own accord.

"Sugar, vanilla and Magick," he purrs.

I squirm and buck beneath him.

I grind against his mouth craving more friction. "More," I whimper. "I need more, I need-"

"Good morning, Sugar."

My eyes fly open to see Nox staring at me. His face full of mischief and a knowing smile teasing at the corner of his lips. "Did you have sweet dreams?"

234

I look down and realise I'm only in my underwear.

Oh no, oh Goddess no!

"Where are my clothes?" I squeak. I wriggle back from Nox, who is far too close to me. His arm is draped over my waist. My treacherous body wants to lean into the touch but luckily Madame Logic has finally taken the wheel.

"I said no touching!" I splutter, scrambling back so fast my back slams into the bedside table.

Nox's chest rumbles with a low laugh of amusement. "I wasn't the one who initiated it. You were grinding up against me, Sugar."

"I was asleep!" My cheeks feel like they are on fire.

He smirks. "So, what were you dreaming about?"

"Nothing!" I pull the cover up higher trying to hide the flush on my face.

"Well given the moaning and grinding," his smile grows wider, to the point where he's practically beaming. "It was a sex dream."

"Please stop talking!" I pull the duvet over my face.

"Who was it about?"

"No one," I mumble from under the duvet. If Hell could open up and swallow me whole right now, that'd be great. Actually, fuck it, someone get me a shovel, I'll dig my way down there.

Nox laughs. "Was it about Finn?"

"N-Yes! Yes, it was!"

Note to self, Esme, learn to lie faster and better.

Silence hovers between us and for one hopeful second, I think Nox has left the room, but then I hear. "I think someone's lying."

"How do you figure that?"

"Because you said my name, Sugar."

I burrow down deeper until my fabric fortress. "Why did you ask then?"

"Just curious what you'd say."

Someone, anyone, kill me now.

Nox takes pity on me when he realises, I'm not going to come out from under the duvet until he leaves the room. I finally emerge from my cocoon once I hear the door click shut.

I tentatively stand and my legs wobble like a new-born deer.

What did I drink?

I catch a glimpse of myself, smeared lipstick across my cheek, smudged glitter eye makeup and my hair looks like I've been dragged through a hedge backwards.

Maybe the bigger question is what didn't I drink?

235

I grab the oversized purple hoodie from my suitcase and shove it on, fortunately it covers my ass.

Not that it matters, says the voice in my head. *Nox literally saw everything whilst you dry-humped him in your sleep.*

It's not my fault, I argue back. *It was the alcohol. Or his scent. Pheromones. Or proximity. I'm not attracted to him. I don't even like him.*

You don't have to like someone to want to ride their face, the voice in my head slyly retorts.

I scrape my hair into a bun and shove my pink bunny slippers on before I begin the cautious journey downstairs.

Why can't the upstairs bathroom have hot water? Maybe I can just get dressed and forfeit the shower, but I catch my reflection again. Nope, I need a shower, and a lobotomy to get the memory of that dream out of my mind. The way he'd been smirking at me, I'm certain he knew full well what the dream had been about, and that he'd had the starring role.

I tiptoe into the kitchen to find Nox sitting at the table, a smug expression on his face as he lifts his coffee to me in a mocking toast.

"Look who managed to finish," he takes a sip from his mug, a dirty smile dancing across his lips, "waking up."

"Leave me alone," I scurry towards the bathroom and narrowly avoid tripping over my own feet. "I'm hungover, gross and need coffee."

Just as I'm about to close the door I hear Nox call. "Want some company?"

"No!" I slam the door.

Scrap that, I don't just need one lobotomy, I need two! One for me, and one for the jackass in the other room who looks like all his Christmass' have come early!

After I finish a scalding shower, trying and failing to scrub away the memories of this disastrous morning, I resign myself to the fact I'm going to have to brave Nox. That, or I'm going to have to live in this bathroom.

I wrap a towel around me and tentatively open the door. I take a step out and see Nox is still sitting at the kitchen table with his head in his hands.

"Looks like someone's hangover finally caught up with them," I giggle, skipping over to the Cafetière to pour myself a coffee as big as my head.

I turn and notice he's still not moved, his hands threading

through his hair as a pained groan erupts from him.

"You alright over there, Demon-Boy?" I find the sugar pot and begin plopping cubes into my mug.

He finally looks up, his eyes crystalline blue.

"Where are we?" he asks with a lilting English accent.

"Finn?"

He sighs, he sounds so tired and despondent. "How long have I been out?"

I sit down opposite him, cradling my coffee mug. "A couple of days."

"It feels longer," he looks up at me expectantly, as if hoping I can give him some kind of comfort. When I don't say anything, he lowers his gaze, spinning the empty coffee mug. "Why did you ask me about a hangover?"

"I went out drinking," I squirm in my seat, feeling strangely guilty. "With Nox."

He lets out a humourless laugh. "So, whilst I'm being trapped in the back of my own mind, you're becoming drinking buddies with the demon who's stealing my body?"

I wince at the look of disappointment in Finn's face. "It's not like that. Nox has as much control in this as you do."

He tugs an exasperated hand through his hair. "Is that what he told you? Jesus, Ez."

"Well, I don't know, do I?" I chew on my bottom lip. "It's not like I'm an expert on possession."

"I thought the whole plan was to try and find a way to get rid of him?" Another angry spin of the coffee mug. "Not befriend him."

"I'm working on it," I grind my teeth, trying to remind myself that whatever is going on between Finn and me, he's allowed to be annoyed about this situation. "But it looks like you and Nox are kind of a package deal. If I get rid of him. You go as well."

Finn pushes the mug away, laying his hands flat on the table. "Maybe that'd be for the best."

My mouth falls open. "You can't be serious."

"Well, it seems like I'm not really living anyway, Ez. More and more of my time with you is just being taken by *him*. Whenever I do manage to take control, you barely want to talk to me, let alone touch me. It's like you don't want anything to do with me."

"That's not true," I say. I don't even sound believable to myself. My doubt hangs between us like a big, ugly cloud. Finn supporting my parents' efforts to quash my powers has been a bitter pill to swallow.

"It's just been a lot to come to terms with. All these secrets my parents kept about my abilities." I hate how my voice begins to tremble. "And after what you said. You can't accept something about me that I don't want to change."

He leans across the table, offering his hand to me. I stare down at it for a couple of seconds before tentatively taking hold of his outstretched fingers. "I'm sorry for being such a dick about all the stuff with your powers, Ez. I just want things to go back to the way they were. Like when we were at uni."

"When we were at uni we didn't know who we were. We were kids. Things change," I sigh. "I've changed. I am changing. It's like I'm waking up."

"But you don't know what these powers could do," his jaw tics. "It's dangerous. You don't understand-"

"I understand," I move to untangle our fingers, but he just clasps them tighter. "I really don't want to talk about this again, Finn."

"Well tough, Ez," his thumb rubs roughly along my knuckles. "Because there's two of us in this relationship." A small sad smile quirks at his lips, "Well I suppose, technically three."

"Nox isn't involved in our relationship," I attempt to move my hand away. "I appreciate you apologising, I do, it's just..."

He searches my face. "Just what?"

"Magick isn't just something I can switch off," I suck in a breath. "It's who I am."

"But how can you really miss it, if you never had it?" Finn searches my face again.

I sigh, "I never felt like I was good enough. I always felt like I was a failure. In my career, in my abilities. In myself. But now I know why."

"But Ez, all of these new powers you're developing they're dangerous. I mean, you nearly set fire to the bed."

Nearly?! The voice in my head scoffs. *A couple of inches to the left and this bastard wouldn't have had eyebrows!*

That's not helping, I argue back.

"But this power isn't new," I try to keep my voice level and ignore the smartass remarks bouncing around in my brain. "They've always been here. Inside me."

"Yeah, but," he gives an exasperated huff. "Your parents kept them hidden for a reason."

"I know and I know they were trying to protect me," I answer.

238

"But it stifled everything about me. I've always felt like something was wrong. I've always felt like a failure and now I know why. For the first time in my life, I feel like me."

And now he's trying to stifle you too, the voice states.

Finn bites on his bottom lip. "Ez, they wanted to keep you safe-"

And stop you from being who you truly are.

I manage to wriggle my hand free of his grasp. "I know Finn, but that's not all they did," I stand as I feel my anger begin to crackle under my skin. "I'm going to get dressed."

As I stalk out of the kitchen, Finn calls behind me, asking me to come sit back down. My control of my temper is slipping and if I don't move, I'll end up setting something on fire in the kitchen. Maybe even Finn, that would stop him trying to control me. No. It won't, it'd just add more fuel to flames... pun very much intended.

I stomp up the stairs, trying to calm my breathing.

I can still hear Finn calling, "Babe," from the hallway. He's too much of a coward to come find me. I refuse to deal with someone who's afraid of climbing stairs to talk to me.

I'm already hungover, I don't need to feel any crappier than I already do. I've got enough of that going on in my head as it is. All anyone has ever done is either underestimated or controlled me. Including myself. I didn't need Finn reminding me how little control I had over my powers, I'm painfully aware of it.

I'm tired of not believing in myself and people not believing in me. Finn doesn't believe in me. The thought unlocks something in my mind. He wants everything to remain the same even after my world has been changed. I don't want to pretend to be someone I'm not.

I tug my hair into two plaits. I'm in such a bad mood, I almost ignite my daisy print playsuit as I try to scrub out a coffee stain.

Ok, deep breaths. Calming thoughts. Ocean. Summer rain.

Images of my dream simmer at the corners of my mind. Flashes of gentle but firm touches, shadows and those eyes...

Nox says that scent is what draws demons and witches together. Maybe that's all it is? Nothing more.

I finish buckling my silver flat Mary Janes and resolve I will not think about Nox in that way again. If I need to, I'll just stay awake to avoid any more of those dreams.

My phone vibrates on the bedside table, and I smile as Dahlia's name flashes up.

A text appears along with an image of Dahlia looking pissed off with scratches all over her arms. *"Your cat is an ass hole."*

239

"Why are you all scratched up?"

"Because the little shit got covered in wine, so I had to wash him!"

"Why did he get covered in wine?"

"I threw it at him when he attacked my foot."

I call Dahlia and she picks up immediately.

"What do you mean he attacked you?" I ask as I pull open the door to the spare bedroom. "He's a kitten, he's just playful."

"He's a prick!"

"He's a kitten!"

Clattering sounds down the line and I can hear the faint jingle of the shop door's bell. I check the time on my wrist, 8am. "You're opening up early?"

"Aye, well after dealing with that little psychopath last night. I didn't sleep in case he tried to smother me!"

"I think you're overestimating the vindictiveness of a kitten," I chuckle as I navigate around Fort Box. Cardboard fills the entire room and there's barely any space to move around them.

The piles nearest the door are labelled up with little tags; 'Grimoires', 'Crystals', 'Charms'... oh my!

But many them are just tatty and unlabelled.

Goddess only knows how long it's going to take to go through all of these!

I hear Dahlia flip on the kettle and the distant sound of water bubbling. "I think you underestimate the level of vengeance that little furball has. He keeps trying to kill me!"

I pull one of the boxes down from the tower near the window and pry away the masking tape. "How are things going with whatshisface from the club?"

"Oh. Him," Dahlia sighs. "Over it. He stopped messaging after our last hook up. Speaking of all things pelvic, how's things up there? Managing to get anything done or are you and Finn too busy getting busy?"

"Not so much fucking, as just fighting," the box is full of pressed flowers and stale herb bundles. I crinkle my nose at the dried sage which is disintegrating in the daylight. "I'm still pissed at him."

"Ez," Dahlia's tone turns concerned, "you didn't actually say why you're so pissed at him?"

"He thinks me not being able to access my Magick might actually be a blessing in disguise."

"Seriously?"

"Deadly serious," I sigh, pulling down another box.

240

"Apparently Finn and my parents have something in common; they'd both prefer me to be a Mundane."

"Ez, you couldn't be a Mundane if you tried."

I chuckle. "I can't tell if that's a compliment or an insult!"

"Trust me, it's a compliment," she says begrudgingly. "I don't like that many people and the fact that I can still stand you, despite the amount of pink and sparkly shit you're covered in… that says something."

Warmth blooms in my chest at the unexpected compliment. Dahls is never one for being forthcoming with her emotions, so getting her to say something like this is normally like getting blood out of a stone.

"Are you just giving Finn the silent treatment then?" she continues, trying to move away from sounding sentimental.

"Well, he's not been around that much, Nox drove up with me yesterday and then we went out for dinner and drinks last night-"

"Did you go on a date with him?"

"No!" I flounder. It does sound awfully date-like. That's not even factoring in the whole one-bed and sex dream fiasco. "We needed to go out for food, so we went to the pub!"

"Well, just so long as that's all it was!" Her tone is mocking. "At least the cottage has two bedrooms, so you don't have to share a bed with him."

Silence falls between us.

"Well, my room kind of got turned into storage for Mum's stuff," I can hear the guilt in my voice.

"Are you sharing a bed with Nox?"

"He's too big to sleep on the sofa so…"

"I bet Finn is getting so jealous!" Dahlia giggles mischievously, "Nox is getting all the privileges! Just make sure you don't accidentally end up screwing him instead of Finn!"

I won't be screwing anyone for a long time, I think grimly. Finn and I haven't been intimate since his return.

Images of whisky eyes between my thighs resurface and I quickly stamp them down again.

Whilst Finn and Nox may be sharing the same body, their energy, auras and general personalities are as different as night and day.

"No chance of that happening," I answer, unpacking another box and wondering whether I should use the upstairs bathroom for an ice-cold shower.

241

Chapter Twenty - Eight

Esme

"Anything good in your box?" I call over to Nox's corner of the room. I close the one I'd been inspecting. It was full of massive jars of dead rats, mice and one I'm certain contained a stoat or ferret. At least I hope it was… It might have been a cat.

A chuckle comes from behind the stack of cardboard. "Shouldn't I be asking you that?"

I huff out a breath. Goddess, give me strength. I wonder if I'm powerful enough to turn him into a toad.

He's just trying to wind me up. Just don't rise to it. Be the bigger person and don't engage.

"How's your box? Anything you want me to help with?" That damned mocking tone comes again, something in it makes my skin tingle and unwanted images of that dream flash through my mind.

I pull down another one labelled 'Charms'.

I grind my teeth. "No, thank you."

"Are you sure about that? You seem flustered," his voice drips with amusement.

I'm going to climb over and strangle him. Sparks ignite under my skin, and I feel the same prickle of Magick spike through my core.

"Your flaps are on fire," he comments.

"Look you've had a free pass up until now because you're in Finn's body, but I will kill you-"

"No," he points down. "No, I mean the box. It's on fire."

"Oh crap!" I bat at it, trying to smother the flames. But my flailing spreads it further.

There is a flash of movement behind me as Nox throws a blanket over it. The blanket smokes for a couple more seconds before stopping.

242

Nox's quick thinking had stopped Fort Box from turning into a bonfire.

"Thank you," I say begrudgingly.

"No problem, Sugar," he chuckles. "So, what's got you so hot and bothered?"

He's too close. The warmth of his body. The scent of his skin. He's causing my heart rate to quicken. I look up and immediately regret it.

Those eyes trap me. I'm as powerless as a fly caught in a web, and this spider looks like it wants to devour me.

He leans forward, closing the space between us. Sandalwood and ambrette envelop me. Images of my dream resurface, and I have to press my legs together and try to stamp down this unwanted need. Bad. Very, very bad.

Or very good? The voice in my head says lasciviously.

You. Are. Not. Helping! I snap back.

"Or should I say," his smile twinkles with amusement. "Who?"

Before I have a chance to think up a lie, a loud bang comes from downstairs. I shove past him and sprint from the room with my tail between my legs. Another loud bang comes from the door.

"Alright, already," I call down. "No need to break the bloody door down!"

I unlock it and I'm greeted by a police officer, who is probably three or four years older than me.

"Good morning, Miss," his handsome face slips into an easy smile.

"Morning," I clear my throat, taken aback by his presence.

"Apologies but I've had a couple of calls from the locals saying that they'd seen someone up here, so I wanted to introduce myself."

I try to keep a polite smile on my face. "Well, it's my house, so... I don't see why it's causing any commotion."

He chuckles. "It's a small village. People talk"

Meaning, everyone in the village is a grade-A gossip.

I sigh. "Like I said, it's my house. I'm just clearing out some bits."

His eyebrows lift and his face shifts into surprised recognition. "Esme?"

"Yes?"

He points at himself. "Mark Morris, remember? I used to look after you sometimes when your mum was busy with her..."

"Meetings?" I offer. My grin grows wider at Mark's

243

awkwardness. When I was younger, he'd been the epitome of cuteness and coolness. His chocolate brown shaggy hair that had been longer when we were young is trimmed into a neat, grown-up style. The colour still matches his eyes which now have fine wrinkles crinkling the corners. He always had the best pick n mix, and he would always share.

"Aye," he scrubs a hand down his face, a flush creeping across his cheeks. His gaze trails up and down. "I gotta say you look…" he clears his throat. "You grew up."

I laugh, "Well I did try not to, but time had other ideas!"

"I just," his focus trails up to my face, "I can't believe you're the same geeky girl I used to babysit."

"I was not geeky!"

"You were! Always carrying those big books around," he smiles. "I half expected you'd collapse under their weight one day! Every time I'd offer to help, you'd be all stubborn and say you could carry them."

I match his smile. "I remember."

When I was younger, I'd wanted more than anything to be as powerful as Mum, so I would try and study all the spells I'd seen her do. Not that it did any good. My powers never went past plant enchantment.

"If I'd known you'd grow into…" he clears his throat again, his cheeks practically beetroot red. "So, you said you are clearing out the house?"

I give a small nod. "I haven't really done much with the cottage since Mum passed. So, I thought I'd come up here to do a bit of a clear out."

He lets out a low whistle. "That's a whole lot of house to work through. Are you sure you're going to be alright doing all that on your own?"

"She's not on her own," Nox reaches a lecherous hand around my shoulders, and I have to fight every impulse to wriggle free.

"Oh," Mark's eyebrows shoot up. "Sorry I didn't realise you're up here with your boyfriend."

"Nox isn't my boyfriend," I manage to finally shirk his arm off.

"No, but," he leans forward, his scent washing over me. "I'm close friends with her boyfriend. He's very jealous and extremely possessive and he needed me to come up here to make sure that this one," he points down at me, "stays out of trouble. Isn't that right, Sugar?"

My cheeks are on fire. Both from embarrassment, rage and Nox.

"Anyway," he smiles at Mark, "we better get back to it. Lots of tidying and clearing to work through. Not all of us have so much time we have to look for things to do."

Mark scowls at Nox. "That's not why I'm here."

Nox gives him another smile, but this one doesn't meet his eyes. "Sure, seems like it, officer."

Nox begins closing the door and I have to forcibly keep it open with my foot.

"Nox," I grind my teeth. "Mark and I are talking."

"Weird," Nox smirks at me. "Looks like Mark's hitting on you whilst he's on duty," he clicks his tongue and gives Mark a chastising shake of his head. "That's not very professional."

"I was just checking on the cottage," Mark puffs out his chest in defiance. I'm impressed by a Mundane trying to hold his ground against a demon.

"Well now that you've done that, you can go," Nox says amiably.

Mark gives Nox a glare before turning to me. "If you want to grab a drink whilst you're in the village, let me know. My house is next-door to my parents so-"

"Why don't you hold your breath until she gives you a call? Bye now!" With that Nox wrangles the door free from my foot and promptly slams it on Mark's face.

I whirl on him. "There was no need to be rude!"

Nox points at the door. "The guy was hitting on you."

"Why do you care?" I place my hands on my waist and scowl up at him, "That's none of your business."

"It is when we're in the middle of fucking nowhere and our plan is to look for clues, not fraternise with the locals."

"Mark was my friend when we were little," I spit. "Not that it concerns you."

"He's a creep," Nox retorts. "The whole time you were talking he was staring at your chest."

"Again, I have to ask, what's that got to do with you?"

Nox takes a step forward, backing me up against the doorframe. He places a hand on either side of my head, caging me in.

"It has everything to do with me when we're working on a deadline," he growls.

I tilt my head up and glare back at the fire reigning down on me. "Are you jealous, Nox?"

His expression heats to molten lava. "If you want to screw random guys, do it on your own time."

I have an overwhelming urge to either throttle or climb Nox like a tree. My brain is too fried to know which is stronger.

"Although the way you're looking at me right now," he leans down and tucks my hair behind my ear. Tingles erupt from his touch. "Maybe it's not a mortal you want at all. That little smoke show upstairs was proof enough of that."

"All that was, was proof I wanted to set you on fire," I answer tartly, stamping down whatever my stupid body is trying to get me to do. "It wasn't a positive reaction."

"Your reaction was because I get under your skin," his smile grows as he leans out to tug on one of my plaits and I bat his hand away. "Which I find amusing."

I duck under him and clamber up the stairs. The smell of burning cardboard still lingers in the air. I open the window and when I turn back around, he's leaning against the doorframe, that sodding smirk still on his face.

"Ok, time for a refresher!" I scowl, "One, I said no touching. Two, I need to not set fire to this room. So, if you could refrain from pissing me off for the next couple of days, that'd be great!"

Nox raises his hands in mock surrender. "Ok, Sugar, whilst we're in this room I will try and behave."

"You mean you'll stop trying to wind me up?" I glare at him.

"I'm not trying to," he smirks. "I just am. It's not my fault that my presence provokes a reaction in your little Witchling body."

"Nox!" I grind my teeth again. My molars are going to turn to powder from the tightness in my jaw.

"I'm not technically in the room at the minute-"

"Nox!"

He steps beyond the threshold. "Now I'm on my best behaviour."

"Good," I point at his corner. "Now you go back over there and don't make any more smartass comments."

He opens his mouth to say something, and I point a finger at him. "Actually, scrap that! How about we just search in silence? Yes? Yes! Now, go over there!"

He smirks again and mimes zipping his lips before returning to his search.

I huff out another breath, frustrated at our constant bickering and the tingling sensation that wantonly remains in my core.

The mind can't fight what the body wants, the voice in my

head taunts.

We stop as the dusky sunset begins to coat the room in a pink hue.

I roll my shoulders, wincing when I hear the crunch of my shoulders. We've been hunting for hours.

As I stand my knees click from being sat cross-legged for so long. I'm covered in dust from hunting through ancient boxes and a disintegrated pile of motherwort that fell all over the top of my head when I'd tried to pull it down. Nox, thankfully didn't say anything when it happened, but I think I heard him chuckle.

I dust myself down, but I swear I'm still going to be finding this for days...

Nox pokes his head up from the box he's searching, one hand holding what looks like a taxidermied crow. "Since you're stopping, does that mean I'm now allowed to talk?"

I give him a wary look. "That depends." I stretch up and wiggle my fingers trying to dispel the aches. "Are you going to be nice to me?"

His gaze bores into my soul. "I'm always nice." He stands and somehow doesn't look remotely dishevelled, despite having combed through some absolutely revolting boxes. One of which stunk because a shattered mugwort jar had rotted the bottom of the box. "Ok, how about I cook dinner?"

"That depends," I narrow my eyes. "Are you going to try and poison me?"

I poke at the saucepan bubbling on the stove. Nox has taken control of the kitchen and there's an array of ingredients I didn't even realise were in the fridge.

"Where did all of this food come from?" I ask as I look at the fully stocked pantry.

"I went out before you woke up and got stuff from the shop."

"What are you making?" I give the ominously brown concoction another poke with the wooden spoon.

"Stew," Nox steers me out of the way. "Unfortunately, we'll have to forgo the dumplings as I didn't think to pick up lard."

I crinkle my nose. "Ew!"

"What's ew?" he looks at me with confusion.

"Lard!"

"Lard doesn't come just from ewes, you usually get it from cows," Nox speaks to me like I've got a head injury. Ironic, since I'm

247

on the verge of giving him one.

"No. Lard is disgusting," I pinch the bridge of my nose. "That's why I said ew!"

"So ew means disgusting," he says slowly.

"Correct."

His brow furrows. "Why does it mean disgusting?"

"I don't know, it just does," I grind my teeth. I feel like I'm speaking to my grandfather.

"The world has changed so much," he tuts whilst he heads back into one of the cupboards.

"Lard isn't something I tend to eat."

"Your palette isn't that discerning," Nox looks me up and down with scepticism. "I've seen some of the crap you've eaten."

"I do not eat crap," I clench my jaw.

"You bloody well do!" Nox murmurs from inside a cupboard. "If it's not smothered in butter or drowned in sugary chocolate you don't eat it."

"That's not true!" That ominous tingling is back again. Oh bollocks.

"It is," he continues, oblivious to the fact my blood pressure is rising at an alarming rate. "If you could, you'd just eat sugar cubes."

Red spots start to prick in my vision. It doesn't help that the sodding voice in my head is chuckling at his comment.

"Nox..." I growl, my voice is so fuelled with annoyance I barely even recognise it.

"Sugar, all I'm trying to do is make sure you eat something with nutritional value!"

"And lard is the way to go about that?" I snap.

"No, I told you, I don't have any lard-"

"I fucking know! I meant-" I cut myself off early and take a deep breath. I try to calm down by turning away from him and stirring the stew.

Nox leans in behind me. His unnerving closeness and breath on the back of my neck sends my emotions into hyperdrive. The floaty feeling his scent causes within me makes my Magick bubble over and the pot and its contents to suddenly explode.

Nox pulls me back just in time, narrowly preventing us both being showered in vegetables and hot gravy.

"Oopsy!" I grimace. "Pub?"

Nox glares at me. Then at the state of the kitchen. "Aye. Pub."

248

Chapter Twenty ~ Nine

Nox

"Pub's that way, Sugar," I point down the hill towards our unfortunate local.

"We'll go to the pub afterwards." Pink hair swirls behind her in a cloud as she heads up the hill. In the opposite direction.

"Afterwards?"

"Aye," she bellows back at me. "It's seven o'clock. We need to go to Clara's."

"For fuck's sake."

"Pardon?" She whirls on me with anger flashing in her feline eyes. I remember the incident earlier. Best to not poke the beast. Especially when the beast can quite easily set me aflame.

"Nothing."

She twirls back around, continuing her ascent of the hill. "That's better."

She stops stomping once we arrive outside the front of a ramshackle looking little cottage covered in climbing ivy and dreamcatchers.

I jog in front of her to open the white picket gate. "After you, my lady," I say gallantly.

She gives me a sceptical look. "Thank you?"

"You're welcome?" I mirror her rising inflection, which is met with a glare that could melt glaciers.

She swans past me, with an air of hostile scepticism.

Sugar taps on the jade green front door before calling through the letterbox. "Clara?"

There's no movement from inside, but the witchling continues to wail through the tiny gap in the door like a banshee. My vision pulls back, and again there's that strange feeling of being shoved into the passenger seat of this body.

I place a hand on her shoulder, her warmth grounding me, and I feel myself regain control. She bristles like a cat being stroked backwards. "Sugar, I-"

She whirls on me. "You're touching me again! What is it about the concept of 'no touching' you don't understand?

"Sorry..." the apology dies on my lips.

How am I meant to explain touching her was an act of survival? That she's a life raft to a drowning man?

Her eyes narrow to slits. There's wariness, but also a shadow of something else.

Something that looks like concern.

"You don't sound sorry. You sound..."

I tug at my hair, annoyance at her scrutiny as she attempts to pull back my carefully constructed mask. "I sound what?"

The concern on her face lingers, "Are you alright, Nox?"

"Never better," I start walking back up the cobbled path. "Look, Sugar, she's either not here, or she is here and is ignoring you. Or," I point down the hill, "she's in the pub. Where we should be."

She crosses her arms and looks like she's considering forcing a confession out of me.

I don't understand it. Touching her stops me losing control. That'll be enough to make her set some kind of Magickal restraining order on me. Then she can get her precious, boring boyfriend back and I'll be stuck in the passenger seat whilst they play house.

It's my turn to walk away from her and I bellow back behind me, "Are you coming, or what?"

Sugar's scrutiny continues through another dinner at 'Gallows Inn'.

If she ever wants a job in Hell interrogating the damned, I'll write her a bloody letter of recommendation. Unfortunately for her, this isn't my first time dealing with incessant questioning. I had to deal with Culum on a five-day shift at work. Talk about torture.

When she finally realises, she isn't going to get an answer out of me, she decides to start talking to the table opposite us. I think that her childish logic is that ignoring me will get a rise.

Despite personally finding her bubble-gum sunshine demeanour nauseating, the Glum Family quickly warm to her as she compliments their mangy dog and pulls faces at the chubby baby, eliciting a flurry of gurgling laughs and snot bubbles from it. Delightful.

"So, are you going to ignore me for the entirety of dinner then?" I ask as I begin tucking into my cottage pie. "Not that I'm complaining. This may be the most peaceful dinner I've had in weeks."

"Well, I can," she says, chewing thoughtfully on a piece of overcooked carrot. "But first you need to tell me what's going on."

I toss down my fork. "Nothing's going on."

"You keep getting this look on your face," she continues chewing the carrot for longer than should be necessary. Which must at this point be the same consistency as the putrid swill that the toddler is mashing into his plastic bowl. "Like you're lost in thought."

"Aye, that's one way of putting it." Lost is the right word. I'm completely rudderless and there's no light at the end of this damn tunnel. Possessions tend to be short and shocking for maximum impact. I'd never really thought about what would happen if I overstayed my welcome in a mortal's body.

She leans over the table, placing her hand on mine. Part of me wants to question why she's allowed to touch me, but not the other way round? But I bite my tongue when I feel her concern burrow into me. No one has looked at me like that since…

"Are you thinking about Sarah?"

"What? Oh, aye, yes," I sigh. "Sarah."

She continues to study me.

For fuck's sake, maybe if I say something she'll stop looking at me like she's trying to use the power of sight to drill into my mind.

"I miss her."

She's still bloody watching me.

"A lot," I bolt on. "She's important to me."

"She sounds like she was an amazing person."

I flinch.

"I'm sorry," she rubs my knuckles with her warm hands. "I know what that feels like. When people use past tense." Another stroke of her fingers over my knuckles, like I'm a pet. I hate that I don't hate it. "It feels like a punch to the gut."

I laugh weakly. "Aye, you're not wrong."

But she's not right either. Sarah's missing. Being dead doesn't matter. I just need to find her and stop wasting time bickering with Sugar.

She rubs her thumb over my knuckles again. I look up at her face as a flush appears in her cheeks.

251

"I thought you said, 'no touching'?" I ask darkly.

She quickly pulls her hand back and immediately I feel the hollowness in my chest return; thankfully, this time I don't lose control.

Sugar looks around the room and puffs out her cheeks. "Clara's not here."

"Clara's not here," I agree, nodding sagely as I tuck back into my bowl of beige. How are the carrots and peas beige as well? I shudder to think how fresh these ingredients are.

She glares. "That's what I said."

I shrug. "Maybe she's at another pub. Or gone for a walk?"

"Or," she chews her lip, that anxiety pricks at the corner of her face again. "Or something happened to her."

"Sugar, be realistic," I lean forward, and she mirrors me. "What's the likelihood that she probably just fell asleep early? She's old. Old people sleep a lot."

"Not through someone banging and screaming through their letterbox-"

"She might not have heard you," I reason. "Old people are hard of hearing."

"She's not *that* old."

"She's old."

She scowls, her eyes turning a vibrant green. "She's not as old as you."

"Technically this body is younger than her. But true," I smirk when I see that flush rise in her cheeks again. "Although she's not as pretty as me."

She huffs before excusing herself to go to the bathroom, once again saying hello and smiling to every bloody patron in the bar.

I watch as she passes that same table of sinister looking men from yesterday, still huddled in the same corner. They watch her, like a hungry pack of wolves sizing up a vulnerable lamb for slaughter. Their expressions are a mixture of lechery and anger.

Sugar smiles brightly at them, completely oblivious to their hostility. I wouldn't be surprised if they had pitchforks and torches under their table.

I focus on the surly group of gentlemen and make sure my glare carries with it the embers of Hell.

After a couple of seconds, I see the men register me and they begin to fidget uncomfortably. They may not see anything out of the ordinary in me, other than my stylish dress sense and inhumanly good looks. But they feel the threat in my gaze, and they definitely feel the heat of my anger.

252

I don't know why the way they look at her bothers me so much. Seeing a bunch of strangers' stare daggers at someone who is so sweet just pisses me off.

The man nearest me squirms in his chair and begins to rub the back of his neck like tiny pincers are pinching into the back of his skin. Exactly the image I've imprinted into his soft, malleable mortal mind. I shoot other images into their subconscious… just the usual existential horror. I make them bear witness to the cosmos heaving in denial before it breathes its final, cataclysmic breath, and then throw in some spiders. Everyone hates spiders. They all turn pasty white, one of them drops his drink. Another wets himself. I've still got it.

The man with bloodshot eyes and a gnarly beard sputters and wheezes as I flash the image of him being kicked in the stomach. He grasps at his beer belly like he actually felt it.

A dark smile spreads across my lips as I continue to project violent, threatening visions into their drunken imaginations. It's like shooting fish in a barrel. Very dumb, drunk fish.

"What are you doing?" Sugar asks.

Shit. When did she come back to the table? Clearly, I'm having too much fun.

I flash her a devilish smile before returning my focus to the other table. "Nothing."

"It doesn't look like nothing," scepticism coats her tone. "It looks like…" she flounders.

"Like I'm sending images of torture into the minds of the dirty old men who either want to kill or fuck you?"

"What?" She gasps, grabbing at my hand across the table and stopping me from sending a particularly nasty vision of red-hot pokers being shoved up their aged and wrinkled assholes. "Why are you doing that?!"

I pull my gaze away. The men let out a collective gasp and begin shaking from shock… and I hadn't even gotten to the really good bit with the eels yet.

I turn to meet Sugar's face, which is pinched in anger and concern. The expression she's been wearing for most of dinner. So, no real change there then.

I arch an eyebrow at her. "What?"

"What do you mean what?" She's still scowling at me, like she's trying to project her own images into my skull. "They're just normal people, they don't deserve you doing…" she wiggles her fingers in front of her head, "weird things in their minds."

"They weren't weird things," I drawl, "just your everyday

psychological hellish torture."

She pinches the bridge of her nose, "Have you any idea how wrong that is?"

"Wrong?" I scowl. "What was 'wrong' was the way they were looking at you like they wanted to have you hung, burnt or fucked three ways from Sunday."

I look back over at the table and all the men are now looking at me like I'm Lucifer. Closer than they realise, but still a bit far off, I'm at least three job titles (as well as extended annual leave and a much heftier bonus scheme) below the Prince of the Fallen.

"Why the hell did you do that?"

"They were looking at you," I bite out, jabbing my fork into the remnants of my pie. I'd much rather be jamming a fork into the eye sockets of those fuckwits.

Sugar sucks in a theatrical gasp. "So?"

I throw my fork down and cross my arms. "I didn't like it."

"So, you thought mentally torturing them was a good way to smooth over any tension?" Sugar is rubbing her temples. "What part of trying to keep a low profile whilst we search Mum's cottage do you not understand?"

"That'd be easier to do if you weren't floating around looking like Princess Bubble-gum!" I grind my teeth. "Smiling and chatting to everyone and getting all their life stories."

"It's called gathering intel," she snaps snottily, puffing her chest up with self-importance and it's very hard to not look down at that scooping neckline. "What's the best way of finding out about the comings and goings of a quaint little village then talking to the townsfolk?"

"Alright then," I smile brightly at her withering glare, "what have you found out?"

She points towards the end of the bar, where a matronly looking woman, who would be better suited to be sitting in front of a fireplace knitting and reading bedtime stories, is nursing a hefty slosh of brandy.

"That lady there is Marie Cloche. She's friends with Clara," Sugar leans closer to me and whispers conspiratorially. "She was meant to meet Clara for a ramble, but she never showed."

"Like I said earlier, old people sleep."

She pulls a face at me. "At two o'clock in the afternoon?"

"Maybe she really, really needed a lie in?"

She leans back in her chair like she's just won an argument. "Now look who's being wilfully ignorant?"

"Alright fine," I clap my hands on my knees, "what do you suggest?"

I don't like that look. It's one of mischief, determination and grit. A far sight from the sugary princess who was pulling faces at the table next to ours.

"We sneak into Clara's."

"You cannot be bloody serious!" I snap at her heels as she begins marching back up that bastard hill again. I've stuck to her demand of no touching, but I'm tempted to throw her over my shoulder and cart her back to the cottage. "You can barely walk in a straight line, let alone break into someone's house!"

"One," she huffs her breath as she doesn't slow her pace, impressive given her impractical choice of footwear. "It's not breaking and entering, if I know where she keeps her spare key. Two-"

"Why didn't we use the key earlier?"

She turns to look at me, "At that point I wasn't as convinced that there was something wrong. I remember where it is…. I think."

"You think?"

"Yes, I do, Nox," and she smiles at me with saccharin sweetness.

"For fuck's sake."

She shoves open the picket fence to Clara's and makes her way to a very smug looking gnome ornament and proceeds to lift him from the rockery and peer at his ass.

I don't like gnomes. We have them in Hell, and we usually give them admin jobs like weaving cosmic dread and photocopying. They are slippery little shits at the best of times. I stare at the statue half expecting the bastard to start moving or enjoying having the witch shoving her fingers up his backside.

"Having fun over there, Sugar?"

She shakes the gnome and I hear the jingle of something metallic clattering inside. "It's in here. I just wish I had a key to get the key out… Do you know what I mean?"

I shake my head. "Not even a little bit," I hold out a hand and wiggle my fingers expectantly. "Give it here."

She shoots me a dubious look before handing it over. "Be careful with it. It's really old. She's had it as long as I can remember."

I arch an eyebrow. "As old as I am?"

"Aye," she continues to watch me warily as I fiddle with the garden ornament. "And infinitely cuter and more agreeable."

"I could attest to that," comes a high squeaky voice.

255

I looked down at the ornament to see the face transform from the eerily painted cheery demeanour to a disgruntled looking menial labour worker from Hell. The little shit is alive after all.

Sugar leaps back and practically fall into a pile of cosmos. "It's alive!"

"If you call standing in someone's rockery for the last thirty years living you've had a worse time of it than I have, Doll face!" the gnome grumbles.

Sugar gasps, "Did that gnome just call me Doll face?"

I grin at her disgust. "Apparently. Can you blame him?"

After a quick glare at me, she regains her composure, steps forward and looks down at the animated gnome, "Erm, right so, sorry to bother you Mr....?"

His face brightens. "Salacious Dong."

I smirk but don't say anything.

"Well, it's nice to meet you Mr. Dong. I'm Esme and he's Nox. We erm, are needing to get into the house, but you see the key is well..." she flounders.

"In my forbidden wallet?" the gnome offers.

"I was going to say key ring?" I pipe up, I don't miss the slight tilt at the corner of her lip.

"Either way, it's in you, so, erm," Sugar clears her throat. "Would you mind if we retrieved it?"

"Well, that depends," the Gnome casts a cheeky glance between the two of us. "Who's the one retrieving it?"

"Ideally if you could, erm..." she falters again, and her cheeks are the deepest shade of scarlet. She looks to the sky, as if asking for some higher power to help her finish the sentence. "Would you mind grabbing it yourself? Please?"

"I will for you, Doll face," he gives her a cheeky wink. "But under two conditions."

Her brow furrows. "Okay?"

I grind my teeth. Sweet, merciless Lucifer, it's amazing this woman hasn't been kidnapped or murdered yet. "Don't agree to something until you know what he wants, Sugar!"

Salacious scowls at me. "That's no way to speak to a lady."

"It's alright, I'm used to it. He is right though, Mr Dong," she smiles warmly at him, and I swear I see his little porcelain cheeks flush. "Can you tell me the conditions first please?"

He holds up his small index finger, "First, I will need you to turn around. I'm shy. Well, I think I'm shy. I've only really been alive for two minutes." A second finger pops up. "Two, I would like you to

256

place me nearer the windowsill, preferably angled towards that rather nice-looking kitchen."

Sugar smiles brightly, "Agreed."

She holds out her pinkie finger and the gnome takes hold of it with both hands and shakes it enthusiastically.

"Much obliged, Doll face, now if you could pop me back down on the rockery and turn around for two minutes, I'll have a quick root around and recover the key that your pretty heart desires so much!"

I place the gnome on the ground, and he promptly waddles back towards the rocks.

"Can you please do me the courtesy of turning around so a poor gnome can have some dignity whilst he rummages inside himself?" he commands with all the pomposity of a town crier.

"Well, there's a phrase I didn't think I'd hear today," I sigh, turning to look back down the darkened hill.

"Oh, come on Nox, you need to have a little fun and a little faith that things will just work out," Sugar smiles up at me, with all the sweetness and sparkle she usually gifts to random dogs or babies. "Sometimes you just need to see the best in people and see that-"

"The gnome is running away," I interrupt, pointing at the small porcelain figure trying to sneak around us. "Unsurprisingly, two minutes of being alive does not gift you with honesty, stealth or brain cells."

Chapter Thirty

Esme

Nox and I launch ourselves at the gnome and after much cajoling we finally get him to perform 'operation key retrieval'.

"Keep that thing away from me," I wrinkle my nose as Nox proudly holds the key out in front of me.

"It's fine, it's not like he's got a normal arse anyway," Nox says breezily. "It barely smells of anything."

"It doesn't matter if it smells," I shudder. "I know where it's been!"

The image of Salacious' elbow deep in himself will haunt me forever.

Nox moves to the front door, a confident swagger in his step. "Stop being such a baby. It's just a key-"

"That was in his arse."

"His arse is porcelain," he reasons, unlocking the door and pushing it open, "Practically pristine."

"That may be the case, but," I close the distance between us, whispering in case the gnome overhears. "His eyes went crossed when he did it and he let out that groan and-"

"You're wondering if he hit his 'G-Spot'?" Nox looks at me with a devilish grin. "And by G, I mean gnome."

"Please stop. I'm begging you!"

We step inside Clara's house. It's just as I remember it growing up. Dark, moody and the antithesis of what most fairy tales would have you believe. Every room is painted in varying shades of plum, black and crimson and full to the brim with taxidermied animals and rustic pentagram charms.

"You lot never change," Nox clicks his tongue as he regards a very stuffed, and very dead, crow perching on the end of the banister.

258

"Hoarders. Every single one of you."

"Not all of us want to live in sterile minimalism, Demon-Boy!" I shoot him a smile as I step into the wine-red living room. Clara did always have a flair for the dramatic when it came to her interior decorating. "Clara, are you here?"

Silence greets me and despite the cosy gothic interior something feels wrong. Dread settles in my stomach as I sense it. Despite the cloying summer heat, the cottage feels cold. Too cold.

"Nox?" My voice comes out croaky. "I...."

"I know," he says behind me, his body close enough that I can feel his heat. A strange sense of comfort washes over me knowing he's nearby. "Let me check the rest of the house."

I turn to look at him and his mouth is drawn in a tight line.

"I can go check upstairs," I offer weakly, "if you go look down here-"

"No," he cuts me off. Finality in his tone. "You need to stay here. I'll do it."

"But-"

"Sugar," his voice is stern, but I can't ignore the softness. A blade sheathed in velvet. "Stay here."

I give a small nod. When he accepts I'm not going to ignore his request, he leaves me, making his way back out into the hallway to search the rest of downstairs.

I sit down on the overstuffed sofa; the maroon velvet fabric feels like it's trying to swallow me whole.

The room is crammed with more taxidermied animals. A dead fox by the fireplace regards me. His head tilts sideways and the glass eyes sparkle with curiosity. I look around the walls and see pictures of solstice celebrations. Coven pictures which have been bleached from years of sunlight exposure, but I can still make out the happy faces of the witches. My attention catches on the one just above a collection of crystals beside the fireplace.

A picture of the spring equinox. Over twenty witches stand in front of a massive bonfire with spring garlands tangled in windswept hair. All of us wear the same long flowing white gowns that look like old-fashioned nightdresses. My attention snags on the figure at the front of the picture. Me. Thirteen years old, beaming with a big goofy smile, standing right in front of Mum and Clara, their hands resting proudly on my shoulders. All our faces glow in the firelight, our cheeks rosy from dancing around the fire pit. Happier times.

I hear Nox make his way back past the living room, his footsteps disappearing up the wooden stairs.

I extricate myself from the big squishy sofa and move towards the wall of pictures, my eyes still drawn to teenage me. I lean closer to peer at the grainy image. Something catches my eye. I'm wearing a necklace, a large amulet with a heavy looking charm in a big oval shape resting on my chest. The jewellery looks too grand for a thirteen-year-old to wear for dancing around outside.

Remember, the voice in my head says. I jolt at the sudden intrusion. I hadn't heard the voice in a while.

Remember, it says again.

A memory of playing with the necklace, throwing it around haphazardly whilst talking to Clara that night. Mum had grabbed my wrist painfully tight, the warning in her tone when she said. "Don't play with it, Esmerelda."

I asked her why, pouting sullenly. She'd been telling me off all night. And I'd warred against every request she asked of me. Everyone else was allowed to have fun, but I had to behave. She'd been so stressed. Her sunshine demeanour was clouded by the responsibilities of organising the solstice. She'd reminded me countless times to behave, to not play with the necklace and to stay silent until after the ceremony part of the gathering finished.

"It's too big!" I whined as she'd draped the necklace on me. "It's sooo ugly and it smells funny!"

I twiddled with the golden banding that encircled the oval. There's a strange cap on the top which makes it look like a perfume bottle.

She reached forwards, pulling my hands away from the necklace, her eyes flashed with hidden meaning. "Some things aren't for playing with."

I hear footsteps descend the stairs, and I turn to see Nox in the hallway.

"We need to go, Sugar," he says flatly.

I frown. "Is Clara not upstairs?"

"We need to go," he repeats, he opens the front door. "I'll explain when we get back to the cottage."

"Nox," I walk towards him, "what's wrong?"

"Nothing," he looks uncharacteristically nervous. He's too keen to get me out of here and it makes my dread increase tenfold. "I'll explain once we get back home."

My nerves start screaming at me and I dodge around him to bolt up the stairs. He reaches out but fails to stop me.

I take the steps two at a time as he shouts my name from below. Three closed doors greet me.

I open the door opposite me, a deep navy bathroom with crystals hanging from the ceiling over a clawfoot bath.

I go to the door to the left of the bathroom, a small purple study filled to the brim with grimoires and an ancient looking computer covered in a thick layer of dust.

"Sugar!" Nox calls, his footsteps getting louder as he starts climbing the stairs. "Get down here. Now. Please!"

Please? Nox never says please to me, I realise dimly.

Before I have a chance to register his plea I go to the furthest door. My body is moving independently as I push it open.

A plum-coloured master bedroom with a large double bed sitting in the centre of the room. On top of the blood red bedding lies Clara. Her face, puffy and purple, frozen in fear.

"Clara?" my throat is so dry the question comes out like a rasp.

I walk towards Clara; her bloodshot stare is wide and unfocused in a beseeching plea.

"Sugar," Nox says softly behind me.

I reach out to take hold of her outstretched hand, hoping that if I touch her, she'll wake up.

Strong warm fingers take hold of my shoulder, halting my progress.

"What are you doing?" Nox asks.

"I need to check if she's alright."

"Sugar," his voice is so quiet. So calm. "She's dead."

"She can't be dead," I can't break the staring match with Clara, "she can't be…"

"Sugar," he moves past me, moving as silently as a cat. "Look at her neck."

He points at the swollen, bruised flesh. A delicate piece of metal digs into it.

"She was strangled," he stands and moves in front of me, blocking my view of Clara. He places his strong hands on my shoulders, locking me in place. "We need to leave before anyone knows we've been here."

"Why?" My voice sounds so far away from me. Distant and alien. My vision blurs as my breathing becomes laboured.

"Because whoever did this," he continues, with the same soft tone. "Might come back, and if they do, we shouldn't be here."

"Why?" I ask again. My limbs begin to shake; rage and sadness crash through me. I blink, trying to get the image of Clara's outstretched hand and bruised body from my mind. They are tattooed into my brain no matter how much I try to push them away.

Nox peers down, forcing me to meet his gaze. "Because whoever did this, is a witch hunter."

"Drink this," Nox holds out a steaming mug to me. "It'll help."

Nox had practically carried me from the house, completely ignoring the 'no touching' rule. His presence on the walk back to the cottage had been a comfort and even though the summer heat is heavy, my limbs feel like they've been doused in ice water.

Clara's dead.

Not just dead, the voice says. Witches used to be tortured and killed that way.

I shudder. The image of Clara's puffy purple face and that fucking wire digging into her flesh swim in my mind.

That's not helping! I snap back at the voice.

I clear my throat and lift the mug to my face; I'm hit with fiery alcohol and cloves. "What is it?"

"Poison, obviously," Nox looks down at me like I've had a head injury when I don't react to his joke. "A hot toddy."

Maybe I have, that'd explain the voices.

A humourless chuckle bubbles up and escapes my chest.

I take another sniff and wrinkle my nose. "I don't want it."

He rolls his eyes. "Can you at least try it?"

I sigh, lift the mug up to my mouth and take a tentative sip. Spicy, fiery liquid coats my tongue. I give an involuntary shudder.

"It's not sweet," I offer the mug back to Nox. "I'm not drinking that."

"For fucks sake," Nox grumbles. walking to the cupboards.

"What are you doing?"

"Hunting for something sweet," his disgruntled voice comes from inside the cupboards. "Since that's apparently the only way to get you to drink anything."

He makes a small sound of triumph when he finds a jar of honey, brandishing it in front of me.

"Can I not just have sugar in it?"

His scowl deepens. "You can't have sugar in a hot toddy. It'll ruin it."

"It's already ruined by tasting like that!"

"You'll have honey, not sugar," he grumbles. "You bloody heathen."

"Fine, but just so you know, I'm not happy about it."

He adds three large tablespoons, but upon seeing the pout

262

on my face he adds another.

I take the mug again once he finishes stirring the concoction. He leans against the counter, his head tilting quizzically when I take another tentative sip.

He raises an eyebrow. "Better?"

"It's no strawberry daiquiri," I take another sip, hugging the warm mug in my cold hands. "But it doesn't suck."

"High praise indeed," he says dryly.

I take another sip, letting the warmth of the drink work its way through me. "Thank you."

He looks down, shuffling his feet. "No problem."

As I live and breathe, I could swear he looks bashful.

I take another gulp. My hands are shaking so much it's amazing I've not sloshed any of the drink down me.

"We need to call the police," I lean back in the kitchen chair, hating how the trembling is coursing through the entirety of my body.

"No. That's a very, very bad idea," he looks at me like I have a concussion. "Whoever did that to Clara. They know about witch torture and the last thing we need to do is draw attention to the fact that you're here."

"But nobody in the village knows I'm a witch," I frown down at the steaming golden liquid.

"Possibly, but maybe they do. How long has Clara lived here?" Nox asks.

"Years. She's been since before I was born."

"So why is it only now since we turned up that she's been murdered? Either a suspicious local has noticed us or someone has followed us up here."

His words hit me like a hammer.

"But why would they want to hurt Clara?" tears well as I look up at him. "She baked cakes for the village fete, she fed stray cats… she was kind and good."

"And she was a witch," Nox says. That same cold, detached tone returns to his voice.

"Being a witch doesn't mean she's a bad person," the shaking continues, as shock begins to give way to righteous rage. Clara had been like an aunt to me, a kind soul who loved animals and would never hurt anyone. I feel the fire begin to crackle beneath my skin.

"I know that, Sugar," Nox pushes off from the counter, making his way to stand in front of me. He kneels in front of me. "Believe me. Whilst I don't always have the highest opinion of witches. I understand that Clara is…was,"

263

I flinch, but he continues.

He raises his arm, his hand lingering above mine. Close, but not touching. "She was a good person." His hand remains hovering, "and so are you."

The tears that have been threatening to escape finally fall. Rivers of sadness, grief and rage travel down the landscape of my face.

"I didn't think giving you a compliment would reduce you to tears," Nox's mouth lifts in the smallest smile.

"I can always gauge how bad things are by how nice you're being to me." I shuffle in my seat, backing away from his potential touch and taking another steadying sip from my mug.

"Aye, well," he stands, backing away. Creating distance between us again. "Don't get too used to it."

I let out another small laugh and a small spark in my chest reminds me I'm still here. I'm still me. Even though grief, anger and rage want to swallow me whole.

"Thank you for that as well," I clear my throat. "For the unexpected compliment."

"Like I said, don't get used to it," he says gruffly. "But going back to what I said, no police. We can't draw any more attention to ourselves than we already have."

"We haven't," I reply sheepishly, "I just talked to a few people in the village. That's all."

"Trust me, Witchling," he returns to his position, leaning against the counter. "You drew a lot of attention." His lip quirks again as he looks at me, "whether you meant to or not."

I squirm uncomfortably under his gaze.

"We just need to keep looking for clues," he looks heavenward, and I realise he is gesturing towards the box room. "There's got to be something in there."

I drain the remaining dregs from my mug. The warmth from the drink is quickly eclipsed by the return of icy apprehension.

I shut my eyes. Trying to push away images of the faces of those I've loved and lost. Clara. Zoe. Hazel. Mum.

So much heartbreak and so many secrets, the voice says.

I look up at the ceiling. The more I uncover about Mum and myself the more lost I feel. How much more can I take? And do I even have the courage to find it? Life used to be so much simpler.

You can't hide from who you are, the voice says. *No matter how much you may want to.*

"Hopefully you're right," I answer to both Nox and the voice, even though a part of me doesn't really believe it.

Chapter Thirty - One

Nox

We pass the rest of the afternoon combing through boxes in the small, cluttered bedroom.

The atmosphere is as sombre as a grave. She's quiet, too quiet for her, but I don't push. Her grief is evident from the distracted looks, lapses in concentration and silences that drench the room. She has the scent of melancholy. Her grief is so palpable- I can taste it in the air. I find my mouth opening to ask her about it, but that's not why we're here. Not why I am here.

We had only taken a brief break from the boxes for dinner. The grandfather clock downstairs chimes seven times. She moves from her corner, staggering to the doorway as she mutters about having a shower and going to bed.

Her mood permeates the house and soaks into the walls; even the flowers seem sad.

I step outside, breathing in the fresh summer night air, relieved to escape the atmosphere inside. Mortals always get so maudlin about death.

Reclining on the rickety wooden bench in the garden, I bask in the dwindling summer sun as its chokehold on the landscape loosens.

Finn grows restless and I give him a violent shove. He's been agitated the past few hours, but I keep squashing him down. He has been pushing too much and I'm not in the mood.

I swirl the amber liquid in my glass, staring out across the lush fields and hear the birds' evening songs. Their cheerful tune feels like a mockery against the hollowness in my chest.

The cavern inside me expands as the minutes pass. I'd hoped that today's search would be fruitful, but once more, my path meets another dead end.

A falcon's song calls across the mountains, echoing over the hills. An echo that I feel in my heart.

"Where are you?" I sigh, watching the pillowy clouds creep across the burnished skyline.

One slip, one moment of thoughtless action and now I must suffer the consequences for eternity. The scales of judgement in the afterlife have always been extreme, but this? This feels especially unfair. All because of that damned grimoire. I should have heeded the warnings, I should have-

"*Sing me a song of a lass who is gone,*" the soft lilt comes from the bathroom above. "*Say, could that lass be I?*"

I look up to see a silhouette in the window. Her soft pastel hair is a blur and her elegant limbs swirl around her as she showers.

"*Merry of soul, she sailed on a day, over the sea to sky,*" her willowy voice continues to carry across the garden, travelling to pierce my soul with a sharp blade.

"A pretty tune, from a pretty voice," someone emerges from the shadows beside me, snapping my attention from the window.

Culum steps out from the darkness, his handsome features carved in moonlight.

"Evening boss," he drawls, his hands stuffed into his low-slung jeans. Culum's ability to pass for a mortal is incomparable. To any onlooker he would just seem like an ordinary human.

But to those attuned to demons? They'd feel his power. It crackles off him like the energy before a thunderstorm.

"Took you long enough," I take another swig of my drink. "Remind me again to give you a lesson on the definition of urgent."

"I didn't want to waste your time without information," he retorts, taking a long pull on his cigar. Culum, a poser until the last.

"And did you?" I arch an eyebrow. "Get any information?"

He exhales smoke from his nostrils like a dragon, "Afraid not, boss."

I down the rest of the glass, savouring that familiar burn, but it does nothing to ease the emptiness in my chest.

"*All that was good,*" Sugar's voice haunting melody carries across the garden. "*All that was fair, all that was me is gone.*"

"I asked around. If anyone does know anything, they are keeping tight-lipped about it," Culum nods towards the window, his focus on the shapely silhouette. Irrationally it makes me want to punch him in the throat. "Maybe she knows something?"

"Trust me," I sigh. "She's of no use to anyone."

Culum's smile takes on a mischievous glint, "Oh I don't know about that." He puffs on his cigar. "I could come up with a few ideas."

With that the bathroom window opens and a cloud of steam escapes into the summer night.

Sugar moves away from the window oblivious to her audience.

"*Sing me a song of a lass who is gone,*" her voice continues, a slight waver in her melody. "*Say, could that lass be I?*"

Culum leaves before Esme finally emerges from the bathroom. I remain in the garden, savouring the cooling air. Its breeze is a balm to the burns on my soul.

I belong in the shadows, away from all the light and sweetness that emanates from the cottage. Away from her.

The witchling takes a tentative step out into the garden. Her bare feet tread as delicately as a fawn through fresh snow.

Her eyes widen as she searches the garden until she discovers me in my hiding place, tucked away under the apple tree. Like Adam fallen from grace, lamenting under the fruit that cursed him and all of humanity. He always was such a buzzkill.

"Why are you sitting outside?" she pulls her lilac dressing gown tighter as her scent washes off her like waves on the shore. Her ivory skin pinked from the hot shower.

"I thought I'd feel more at home in the darkness," I say as I kick at a fallen apple. The flesh of the fruit is soft and bruised, already beginning the journey to decay.

She takes another step towards me, her feet sparkling as her nail polish twinkles in the twilight. "And do you?"

I press my head harder into the bark of the tree. "Not really."

Her focus returns to me, wide and searching. Emerald pools filled with an unspoken plea, "Can we go inside?" She shuffles again, another look towards the house, "Please?"

I lean forward, moving my face out of the shadows. I study her face, "What's wrong?"

She chews on her lower lip, "Nothing, I..." she takes a shaky inhale. "Something feels wrong," she points towards the cottage. "In there. It feels... I don't know. Like something doesn't want me to be here. Something dark. Something dangerous."

"More dangerous than the demon under the apple tree?" I drawl.

She tugs again at the collar of her dressing gown, pulling it closer to her throat. The light catches her delicate neck, and an angry red mark encircles it.

I stand in one swift movement and bundle her into my arms. Before she has a chance to bat my hands aside, I gently cradle the back of her head, whilst my other hand holds her chin to tilt it gently upwards. She winces as I study the wound.

A raw, scarlet band wraps around her milk white throat, I recognise it immediately. I've seen them countless times in the past.

My tone is a hushed whisper, "What happened?"

"I," she croaks, it's only then I realise her voice has an unfamiliar raw and husky quality. "I-I don't know. I was just washing my face and then I felt something loop around my neck. Something rough and strong. It was so tight, and I couldn't do anything. It just pulled me back," tears fall from those jade eyes. "I couldn't do anything. I couldn't stop it," a small bubble of a sob escapes her.

"I couldn't call out for help," she sniffles as her shoulders begin to shake. "I couldn't call out… to you."

I move my hand from her chin to delicately trace her jaw, a feather light touch across her throat.

Sure enough, I see them. Rope burns so deep and angry on her flesh that I can make out the pattern of the twine on her skin.

"What do you think it was?" my focus remains locked on her neck, "A spirit?"

"I-I don't know," her voice barely above a raspy whisper. "But whatever it was, it felt cold and wrong and… evil."

She wipes away the tears that streak down her face. "Will you come inside with me," her eyes are pleading. Like I'm her guardian angel. Ironic.

Her bottom lip quivers on that damned word once more, and once more I'm powerless to resist. "Please?"

I release her, but as I do this her knees buckle.

I grab hold of her again, steadying her and she leans into my touch. "I know we have a rule about no touching, but given that you can barely stand, I'm going to suggest that we pause that, just for tonight."

She gives me a weak watery smile, a ghost of her normal dazzling grin. "Just for tonight."

Before she has a chance to argue, I scoop her into my arms. Her trembling frame presses close to mine as we journey back inside. We pass through the oak door frame to the cottage like a married couple crossing a threshold.

She curls closer to me. "Please don't leave me, Nox."

My hands instinctively clasp her tighter. "I'm not letting you out of my sight tonight, don't worry."

I tread carefully up the stairs, cautious that whoever, or whatever, has harmed her may still be here. I feel no presence or dip in temperature. The house is silent and benign. As quaint and chocolate-box sweet as it had been upon our arrival.

I push open the bedroom door. But again, there is nothing. Just an unmade bed and the witchling's clothes all over the floor.

I gently place her on her side of the bed and pull the covers up around her, but as I move away, she grasps my hand tightly.

"Don't leave," she says again. "Please. I don't want to be alone."

A small smile tips at the corner of my mouth, despite the atmosphere. "Don't worry, Sugar. I'm not going anywhere; I just need to take my shoes off."

She watches me as I kick off my boots, like she's terrified I'll disappear if she blinks.

Her focus doesn't waver as I move around the bed and climb under the duvet.

Without asking permission I wrap her into an embrace, resting her trembling body on my chest. She doesn't protest, instead she threads her arms around me.

My hand begins to absently weave through her still damp hair. "How did you get the shower to have hot water up here?"

She gives a small shrug. "I don't know, I just kind of looked at it and wished it'd be as warm and comforting as it used to be when I was little and then," she gives a small chuckle, "it turned on and hot water came out."

I continue stroking her hair. "So, it seems you're capable of charming not only plants and fire, but now water?"

"I wonder what I can do with earth and air," she mumbles as she stretches and wriggles her toes.

"Is there much demand for controlling earth or air?" I ask, continuing to stroke her head, coaxing her into sleep, "outside of mining and aeronautical industries, anyway?"

"Earth could be handy if I'm gardening. I suppose I'd need to take better care of my garden at the flat…" she murmurs absently into my chest. "Air's a bit redundant, considering how much you produce-"

"Sugar?"

"Hm?"

"Shut the fuck up and go to sleep."

I jolt awake. I'm alone in bed.

The warmth of her breath and body had lulled me into a dreamless sleep. Now without her, I feel adrift.

The bedding is knotted and tangled towards the yawning bedroom door.

Any lingering drowsiness evaporates as dread settles in my stomach, and I lurch from the room.

An unfamiliar sensation courses through me as I remember the bruise around Sugar's neck.

I dimly register what the feeling is. Fear. Fear for her safety.

The attack earlier had been so fast she wasn't able to call out to me.

I track the scent of warm oats and Magick like a bloodhound, halting at the entryway to the box room.

Relief washes through me when I find her.

Her lithe frame is statuesque in the moonlight.

As I take a step into the room she begins to sway. She rocks from side to side like a pendulum. Her face and body are painted in strokes of alternating darkness and what little light comes from outside.

I look down to see her feet are bare and muddy. Strange.

The shadow of the branches from the oak tree at the bottom of the garden stretch out across the floor as if reaching to come inside. As if reaching for her.

Her swaying continues, and as she does, the shadows lengthen across the floorboards.

Her eyes stare vacantly through the doorway. Through me. "Witchling?"

Her expression remains unfocused and distant whilst her body sways like a flower in the breeze.

I take a small silent step forward and as I do, she begins to whisper. Her voice barely above a breath. I halt midstep, my throat strangled by the lyrics I hear.

"Cummer gae ye before, cummer gae ye," her voice that same gentle, haunting cadence I'd heard earlier in the garden.

"Gin ye winna gae before, cummer let me," her voice grows louder as she reaches the last word in that melody.

"Ring-a-ring-a-widdershins, linkin lithely widdershins, cummers carlin cron and queyn, roun gae we!"

Her rocking grows more pronounced, see-sawing faster from one foot to the other. Her voice grows louder and more fervent. Despite this, her face remains in a dreamlike trance.

"Cummer gae ye before, cummer gae ye," her voice is as

crystalline and piercing as the sharpest dagger. Its blow is lethal. Devastating.

That melody has haunted me since the first trial. It's a cursed song and it has followed me. A grim reminder of what was to come. A grim reminder of Sarah's fate.

"Cummer gae ye before, cummer gae ye," Sugar begins again. The pace quickening in time with the beat of my heart and her rocking, *"Gin ye winna gae before, cummer let me, Ring-a-ring-a-widdershins, linkin lithely widdershins, cummers carlin cron and queyn, roun gae we!"*

"Cummer gae ye before, cummer gae ye," she's shouting. Her tone is shrill and filled with panic. The speed of her swaying increases in time with the cadence of the song. But still, her face is calm. So eerily calm.

I move closer but freeze on my next step.

Beneath her melody is another voice, one with rich, honeyed tones. An echo that feels like a jagged mockery to Sugar's frightened voice.

"Sugar," I suck in a breath, "can you hear me?"

Closing the distance between us, I place a steadying hand on her shoulder, which soothes her slightly.

The rocking and singing continue, but they are subdued. As if lulled by my touch.

"Ring-a-ring-a-widdershins," she backs out of my grasp, moving towards the corner of the room and making her way to the window seat.

"Linkin lithely widdershins, cummers carlin cron and queyn, roun gae we."

She crouches down, her back to me as she kneels in supplication to the window. To the moon. She stares vacantly at the glowing orb as she places her hands in front of her, her fingers interlinking with the shadows of the branches. They move as one, as if the darkness is guiding her hands. They both halt when they snake around one of the floorboards and she begins to pry it free of its brethren.

"Cummer gae ye before, cummer gae ye," and still she sings, whilst yanking on the splintering wood. I wince as I see angry wounds appear on her fingers, they fill with splinters, but she continues unperturbed.

The floorboard lets out a defeated groan as it cracks and finally succumbs to her strength. It clatters to the side when she discards it.

I move closer, concerned for the damage she's done to her delicate hands.

"Ring-a-ring-a-widdershins," I see her hand reach into the space between the floorboards and hear the unmistakable jingle of metal.

She pulls a large gaudy stone out from the secret hiding place, it glitters and shimmers in the dim moonlight.

She holds the chain above her head, towards the window, causing the stone to pirouette as gracefully as a ballerina.

Esme's voice returns to a gentle whisper, *"linkin lithely widdershins, cummers carlin cron and queyn, roun gae we."*

Chapter Thirty ~ Two

Esme

"Is there any more sugar?" I grumble, pulling open the larder door to peer inside. I've gone through every single cupboard in the cottage and the only thing left is that ancient jar of honey. I draw the line at putting honey in my coffee. Even I have my limits.

"There was some in the back of the cupboard behind the tea," Nox says, prodding at the pancakes sizzling on the stove with a copper spatula. "I mean yesterday there was; it's possible you ate it all. It has been twelve hours since I last looked!"

I lunge for the shelf to push aside the boxes of herbal tea to find the sugar pot and cling to it like a poisoned woman holding a vial of antidote. I tear open the lid only to have my hopes dashed.

"It's all gone!"

Nox gives me a blasé shrug, "Oh well."

I scowl. "Oh well? No sugar is not an 'oh well' scenario!"

Nox's continues to cook but I don't miss the quiet chuckle as he flips a pancake with unnerving prowess.

I move to stand next to him, "Don't laugh at me, Demon-Boy! Sugar withdrawal is serious! I'll get cranky!"

He gives me a sideways glance, "Crankier than you already are?"

I glower as his smirk grows and a dimple appears that I'd never noticed before.

He rolls his eyes and hands me one of the plates, a tower of thick fluffy pancakes with chocolate chips. My mouth immediately waters.

I look back up at him, "These look delicious, but pancakes just aren't right without syrup-"

"Then it's a good thing I hid some behind the mountain of

274

dried pasta and lentils, isn't it?" He hands me a ginormous bottle of maple syrup which is over half full.

I snatch hold of it and skip over to the table with my teetering tower of breakfast. I begin drowning the golden discs until they are disintegrating under the weight of syrup.

I pop a mouthful of the pancake into my mouth and have to stop myself from letting out a moan. They taste like heaven.

"That was mean of you!" I say around my next mouthful.

"If I hadn't," Nox pulls out the chair opposite me with a plate of his own, "we would be eating dry pancakes, and you'd have diabetes. I did it for the greater good!"

I take another bite and my toes gleefully wiggle under the table.

I polish off my first one with feral passion and begin tucking into the next, "Where did you even get chocolate chips from? I didn't even know you could bake! Can I have the recipe?"

Nox chuckles again and that dimple appears teasingly in the corner. Strange, I've watched Finn laugh countless times and he never had one before.

"Which question would you like me to answer first?"

I'm chewing another mouthful and before I can swallow, there's a loud knock at the front door. I stand automatically and walk towards the hallway but Nox steps in front of me.

He points back to the table. "You keep eating and I'll go get the door-"

"But-"

"Your pancakes are already on the cusp of liquidising," his voice is a mixture of gentle sternness. "You eat and I'll deal with whatever hellion decides eight o'clock is an appropriate time to interrupt someone's breakfast."

I go back to my plate, "Please don't murder someone on my doorstep!" I call, before shoving more fluffy pancakes into my face.

"Only if they deserve it," he answers from the hallway.

I continue eating but try to eavesdrop on the conversation between Nox and the unexpected visitor.

Their voices are too quiet, so I pick up my plate and edge closer to the doorway.

I chew quietly but can only snatch crumbs of their conversation, so I begrudgingly stop eating and lean in closer.

"As I said," the stranger's voice says, "we're just doing initial house calls to find out what happened-"

"And as I said already," Nox's tone is clipped and barely

275

controlling his annoyance, "we don't know anything about what happened. We've been clearing out the cottage the past few days."

"Some of the patrons had seen you and Esme talking to the victim in the pub the night before."

"Since when was it the business of the police to pay attention to drunken gossip?"

"The police have to investigate all possible leads," Mark sounds just as pissed off as Nox.

"No matter how irrelevant?" Nox retorts.

"Like I said, if I can just speak with Esme-"

"She's busy," Nox snaps, cinnamon and ginger fill the air as I sense his anger.

"I won't take up much of her time," Mark says, his voice filled with grim determination. I remember that stubborn streak. When we were little, he'd dig his heels in and wouldn't budge.

I quickly shove the final pancake into my face and place my plate on the counter. I mentally prepare to break up the macho pissing contest that's happening on the welcome mat.

I swallow the huge mouthful just as I reach the door. "Morning Mark!"

"Hey Ez," Mark's face turns to a bright smile when he sees me. "Like I was saying to your friend, I need to ask a couple of questions."

"Er, sure," dread settles in my stomach. "What about?"

Mark's scrutiny makes my cheeks flush, he smiles down at me before saying, "It might be easier to discuss inside, may I come in?"

"No," Nox says flatly.

I glare at the demon, before training my face into a congenial smile and looking back at Mark. "Of course," I say, as I try to ignore how nervous I feel.

Nox glares at me, "but we're having breakfast."

I give him a sweet, benign smile, "I finished mine!" I give Nox a subtle shove back into the house. "Why don't you go eat and I'll have a chat with Mark?"

He looks like he's trying to hex me, but all it does is make my grin broaden.

He grinds his teeth, before stalking back towards the kitchen. "Fine. On your pretty head be it."

I clear my throat, beckoning Mark inside, "Please. Come in."

He gives me a grateful smile, "Appreciate it, Ez."

"Can I get you a coffee? Tea? Or some water?" I try to keep

my tone casual.

"No thanks," Mark props himself by the sink.

I return to my seat and look up at him, clearing my throat before saying, "So, erm, how can I help?"

"I'm sorry, I'm here with grim news," Mark's face fills with sympathy, "but we discovered Clara last night. We'd had a call from one of her neighbours saying they hadn't seen her, so we went to investigate and we found her dead."

"Oh no!" I gasp, trying to feign shock, "that's terrible!"

"Indeed," Mark sighs, his attention trails back over to Nox, who is now clasping his coffee cup with knuckles so white it's amazing the mug hasn't shattered. Mark continues, "So we are now asking her neighbours about the last time they saw her and if there was anything odd about their encounter."

I shrug, "We only saw her in the pub briefly. We caught up a bit on how she'd been. Everything seemed normal. She seemed healthy and happy. Why are you asking for statements?"

"Because of the nature of her death," Mark shuffles his feet, as if uncomfortable discussing how he'd found Clara.

I fight against a shudder at the memory of her bruised and puffy face. Her face frozen in a silent plea.

"How did she die?" Nox takes a sip from his mug, watching Mark like a cat hunting a mouse.

Mark meets Nox's glare, returning the same expression of hostility, "I can't disclose any information right now. We are waiting on forensics to arrive. But unofficially, it's bad."

My hands come to my face, "Oh no! Poor Clara!"

If you're going to pretend that you don't know anything, the voice in my head snips. *Can you at least try to seem a little more convincing?*

Be quiet! I snap back, *also your little quips aren't helping!*

If you can't make your reactions genuine, he's going to leave with more questions! The voice in my head warns. *Try to be less high-school theatre and more subdued.*

I clear my throat and try to squash the voice in my head's advice on acting tips.

"What does bad mean?" Nox asks, as if this is the most normal conversation to be having over breakfast.

Although maybe it is to him, I think numbly.

Mark's tone turns grim, "The nature of her injuries couldn't have been self-inflicted."

I grimace at the image of Clara in my mind again.

"Like I already said," Nox sighs, sounding almost bored. "We only spoke to her in the pub."

"One of the patrons said that they overheard you making plans with Clara to visit her last night?"

I accidentally spill hot coffee all over my lap. Crap on a cracker!

Stop doing that with your face, the voice snaps. *Keep crying, that actually works!*

"Jesus, Ez," Mark rushes forward, "are you alright?"

I quickly grab my napkin and dab at the coffee. My thighs are now as red as my face probably is. Why had I decided to wear shorts today?

Why are you incapable of fine motor skills? The voice asks sarcastically.

Mark grabs hold of a tea towel and begins dabbing at my legs and I swear I hear Nox growl.

"I'm fine!" I say, even though my legs are on fire. I smile and quickly stop when I realise my mistake. "Well, no, I'm not fine. Obviously. My friend is dead!" I wince. I must sound hysterical.

"She's clearly in shock," Nox fires me a warning look. "Your news has overwhelmed and upset her."

Mark peers up at me from his knees, "Are you ok, Ez?"

I clear my throat, "Nox is right. It's just erm, a lot. Clara was like an aunt to me and I'm in shock."

"See," Nox stands with alarming speed and moves to my side, placing a hand on Mark's shoulder. "She's upset. The poor girl needs a lie down."

Poor girl? I sneer up at him, but Nox shoots me a pointed look.

Mark looks between us, "Shall I come back later then?"

Nox hauls Mark to his feet and frog-marches him out of the kitchen, "I think that would be best. Give her time to process."

"Oh," Mark mumbles, his voice growing quieter as Nox continues shoving him out of the cottage, "shall I come back this evening?"

"Aye, this evening," Nox says as I hear the cottage door open and snap shut. "Or never. The latter would be preferable."

I rush to the sink, turning the cold tap on full blast. I drench the towel Mark had been dabbing me with and soak my legs, which are starting to blister.

Nox walks back in; a bad mood crackling off him.

"What's the matter with you?" he snaps. "You practically gift-wrapped yourself as a suspect!"

"I did not," I carefully dab at my bright red thighs. The coffee has soaked into the crotch of my shorts as well. I can feel a burn in my nether region.

I look up to see Nox's nostrils flare, "You need to go take a cold shower."

"Rude!" I baulk, "I washed this morning."

Nox casts his gaze heavenwards, whilst he continues to grind his teeth, "You poured scalding black coffee all over your lower half. You need to go wash it off and cool your skin. Go in the shower," he points to the bathroom. "Now."

"Alright," I grumble, waddling my sodden legs to the bathroom. "Stop being so bossy!"

"Stop making me," he snaps as I slam the bathroom door on him. "Throw your clothes out here so I can soak them," he calls.

"Wait," I crack open the door, giving him a sceptical assessing look. "Do you know how to do laundry?"

Nox fires an exasperated glare at me, "Sugar, now is not the time to rate my level of domesticity. Take your clothes off now."

"If I had a penny for every time I heard that," I tease, despite the fact I'm nursing burns so hot I can fry eggs on them, "I'd have a whole lot of pennies!"

"Witchling!" Nox warns.

"Alright!" I close the door and suck in a stealing breath as I unbutton my shorts and begin peeling the soggy denim from my thighs. The fabric feels like it's fused to my skin.

"Fuck!" I let out a yelp as I try to wriggle them down my hips.

The bathroom door flies open as Nox swoops in.

"Erm, excuse me!" I squeak. I try to yank my shorts back up which causes another yelp of pain to escape my chest. "I'm getting undressed!"

He arches an eyebrow, "You're screaming like you're being murdered!"

"No, I'm screaming like my legs are burnt!"

Nox lets out an exasperated sigh as he straightens up. "New approach," he moves to the shower and turns it on, moving the taps to change the temperature from warm to cold. "Get in."

"But I still have my clothes on," I answer weakly, batting a stray tear away.

"Aye," his jaw twitches, "but you need to get them off and the easiest way to do that will be when the fabric is cool. So," he beckons me forward with an outstretched hand, "get in."

My cheeks heat, "I'm not showering with you."

"I didn't suggest that," amusement colours his tone. "But I'm going to stay in the bathroom in case you need any help. The last thing we need is Mark hearing you scream bloody murder."

I chuckle weakly, "Poor choice of phrase there, Demon-boy."

"Stop joking and start soaking!"

I shuffle forward and let out a yelp when I try to lift my leg to step into the clawfoot tub.

"For fuck's sake," Nox scoops me up with alarming ease and plonks me down in the shower. "Get on with it."

"Alright!" I pull the shower curtain around the bath.

"If you need any help," I hear him drawl from near the shower. "Ask. I don't want to deal with any more locals accusing me of attempted murder. One is enough for this morning."

I tentatively put an arm under the water to check it's not too cold. I step under the stream and begin shimmying the denim down my hips. Surprisingly Nox's advice works and peeling the fabric away from me, whilst still painful, isn't half as bad as it was. I throw my shorts out of the shower and turn to remove my top.

I pause when I hear a clatter behind the shower curtain, like something has just been knocked out of the cabinet.

I open the curtain tentatively, aware that I'm only dressed in a skimpy vest and a tiny pair of briefs.

"Nox?"

I pull the curtain back a little further and see him leaning against the sink, he is gripping it tightly and breathing heavily.

I clear my throat and speak a little louder, "Nox, are you ok?"

"So," he looks at me through the bathroom mirror, "you're showering with him now?"

I grimace, "Oh hey, Finn."

He scowls at me, and I notice it lacks the fire and brimstone that Nox manages to shoot at me on a daily basis.

"Don't 'hey Finn' me," he snaps, "how long has this been going on?"

I frown, pulling the curtain back and crossing my arms. I don't care that I'm standing under the shower in my 'Hello Kitty' pants and probably look like a drowned rat. The look Finn is giving me makes me feel like I'm some kind of harlot. I glare at him, "How long has *what* been going on?"

"You and Nox," he scowls. "If you're screwing him Ez, I have a right to know!"

"I'm not screwing him," I snarl back. "Nox is just..."

280

Just what? What is Nox to me? I don't know if I'd class him as a friend. We can barely go an hour without bickering, but he has helped me. More times than I count.

"So, I'm supposed to just believe you're showering and he's just in here to brush his teeth?" His eyebrows shoot up, "I'm not an idiot, Ez!"

"I dunno, this reaction suggests you might be!" I gesture down at my scarlet thighs, "See these? I burnt my legs and couldn't get my shorts off, so Nox suggested I have a cold shower to make it less painful. Honestly, it's perfectly innocent."

"That demon was just looking for an excuse to get your clothes off so he could seduce you!"

A small giggle escapes my chest before I have a chance to stop it.

"You think I'm a joke?" Finn scowls, "you two probably laugh about it all the time. Stupid Finn not being able to satisfy you-"

Before I have a chance to say anything he stalks out of the room. I try to clamber out of the shower and let out a hiss of pain as I raise a leg out of the tub.

Well, that went well, the voice in my head says snarkily.

Do you ever say anything helpful? I argue back as I lower my foot onto the fluffy green bathmat. As I lift my right leg my vision blurs and my world turns sideways.

Mind your head, the voice warns, as my vision fades to black.

"Confess!"

My eyes slowly focus on golden torch light and the tall shadows that crowd me.

I try to move but my hands are tied tightly behind my back.

I smell dried blood and realise I'm coated in it. Both from old and new wounds. My body screams in pain.

Ice cold water is thrown in my face, and I splutter for breath.

"Confess!" the man's voice, full of hatred bellows at me again. He holds out a black leather-bound bible in front of me.

"Please," I gasp, "please stop!"

"Confess, witch!" he commands, and a chorus of voices scream behind him.

"But," my breath comes out in ragged gasps. "But I didn't do anything wrong!"

"You consort with the devil!" he spits in my face. I feel the spittle land on my bruised and swollen cheek. "Everything about you is wrong and evil!"

281

The crowds around him erupt in feral glee. Shouts and hooting surround me on all sides, threatening to swallow me whole.

"Witch!"

"Harlot!"

"Demon!"

"Burn her!"

The man steps back, giving a grim nod to a figure behind me.

"Muzzle the witch," he orders. "Maybe once she is unable to speak her tongue will loosen from the lies of her evil deeds!"

I struggle, trying to break free from the bindings on my wrist.

"No, please!" I drop to my knees, "please I beg you! Have mercy!"

"Mercy is only granted to God's children," he looks down at me, disgust twisting his features into an ugly expression. "You are a whore of the devil. You will receive no mercy!"

"Please!" I manage to cry out before my head is yanked back and an iron grip traps me in place.

"Don't forget the mouth bolts!" barks the man. "You must keep that conniving tongue from wagging!"

Another shadow stands before me, blocking the view of my accuser. A metal bar is shoved into my mouth. The spike pierces my tongue and blood begins to flow from my mouth.

I gurgle and try to cry out but as the final lock clinks in place I can no longer scream. All I can do is whimper, try to swallow the blood that now gushes down my throat and pray that death will take me before the flames do.

"Ez!"

I hear a voice calling to me from so far away. Like they are at the end of a tunnel.

"Ez," the voice says again, closer now. "Ez, wake up you have to wake up!"

I pry open one eye and take in the strong arms encircling me, cradling me close to him like I'm precious. Instinctively I relax in his embrace.

"Ez, are you ok?" he asks again, his voice pinched and anxious.

"I- I hit my head." I feel around where it hurts, a welt blooms on the back of my skull.

"What happened?"

"I- I had a vision," I mumble, wincing as I continue to prod at my head.

282

"Jesus, Ez, we need to get you to a doctor?"

My mind slots puzzle pieces into place. Finn is holding me. Disappointment twists in my chest.

Nox would know what to do about the vision. Sure, he'd offer some kind of smartass comment but ultimately, he'd help settle the storm in my mind.

But Finn? I know how Finn will react to this stuff. Brush it under the carpet and ignore it.

"No," I try to lift myself up but my body flops back uselessly onto him. "No doctors."

He's about to say something when I hold up a hand, halting him. "Please Finn, just trust me on this. It'll only make things worse."

He still looks like he wants to argue but he clamps his mouth shut and gives me a small nod, "If that's what you want, Ez."

"Thank you," I give him a small grateful smile. "C-Can you help me up please? I need to lie down somewhere that isn't a tiled floor?"

"I can do that," he bundles me up and carries me carefully through the cottage, into the living room and places me on the sofa. So gentle. So sweet.

I shiver, between my scalded thighs, my injured head and my vision I'm an absolute fucking mess.

Finn reaches around me to grab the emerald, green blanket and as he does I hear something clatter to the floor.

He reaches down and retrieves a necklace: a large vial made from rose quartz, with a design of intricate rose gold ivy wrapped around it. It's still just as bright, beautiful and ostentatiously opulent as it was all those years ago.

"Huh," Finn studies it with indifference, oblivious to the fact that my heart feels like it's just fallen out of my chest. "Weird. Why would Nox be wandering around with this?"

I reach out and Finn drops it into my hand. I'm hit by a wave of belonging. This is mine. Why the hell did Nox have it?

Chapter Thirty ~ Three

Esme has been sulking the whole afternoon. I regained control of our shared flesh and bone at noon but fuck only knows what happened whilst I was gone. All I know is that since I was last here the atmosphere has transformed, a palpable sense of hostile tension fills the cottage and now I feel like an unwelcome guest. I suppose I was always unwelcome, but now, even more so.

I don't know how this mortal managed to push me so far down that I had no awareness of what was going on. It's only when he relaxes slightly that I'm able to take hold again.

Whilst Sugar isn't my biggest fan, she usually talks to me, or at least argues with me. But for the last four hours all my questions and deliberately provocative jabs have been met with stony silence. Her green eyes flash with hostility every time I open my mouth to speak.

"So, are you going to tell me what I've apparently done wrong?" I begin sifting through another musty box. The label has been ominously scribbled out, so it's a potluck of whatever shit I'm going to find. "Or are you going to continue looking at me like I've unleashed fire eels up your arse?"

That's a job usually reserved for interns, but occasionally I like to step in and lend a hand. What can I say, I'm a giver.

"Hello? Earth to not-so-sweet Sugar!" I reach into the box and throw a charm of, well, I don't know what it is, but it smells like mouldy cheese. "Are you not going to talk to me all day, Witchling? Because I'll just keep talking *at* you if necessary! I can tell you about the tortures I used to inflict on some of the poor fucks in Hell. One of my

284

personal favourites was to take a big bag of feral badgers riddled with smallpox and put them into a catapult. Then-"

"Alright!" she bites, and I feel a surge of satisfaction from finally getting a reaction. She whirls around, her face flush and her pink hair swirling around her like a strawberry cyclone. "Enough with the monologues! You want to know why I'm not talking to you?"

"Ah! Finally! A conversation!" I smirk. "You're talking to me now, that counts as a victory. Please enlighten me. What have I apparently done that is so abhorrent that I now must deal with your glittery wrath?"

She huffs out an exasperated little growl, which treads the line of endearing. "The reason I'm not talking to you is because you've been lying to me!"

I keep my expression neutral, despite how my heartbeat quickens.

She pulls out the shiny necklace from her jeans pocket and waves it above her head like a trophy. "This!" She dangles it in front of my nose. "You found this, and you didn't tell me!"

"So what? I liked the look of it, so I kept it, what's the big deal?"

Her scowl deepens as distrust colours her features. "Why would a demon be interested in a necklace? All it's ever been used for is carrying some herbs and perfumes."

"It's shiny," I return my focus back to the disgusting box I was searching, "demons like things that are shiny."

She scoffs, "What? Like magpies?"

"That's a bit hypocritical coming from a human disco ball," I scoff before pulling
out an ominous jar of what looks like petrified mice. At least it looks like mice. They had tails. Once. That, or there's also a collection of dried worms at the bottom. "Every single one of these boxes has some kind of bullshit trinkets in them."

"The big deal is," her voice trembles, "this is mine!"

"Isn't everything in this cottage technically yours?"

"Technically, yes, but," her voice begins to lose its bite, her anger wavering, "this was mine from when I was little. This is important!"

"Well, that explains why at arse-crack o'clock you decided floor renovation was a good idea-" I cut myself off. I've avoided telling her about that night. It had been alarming to see her attacking the floorboards like a demented beaver. Not to mention the echo of that strange voice beneath her creepy singing. There's only a couple of reasons why that might have happened, and none of them bode well for the witch who looks like she's two seconds away from ripping my head off.

Silence hangs between us for a couple of seconds before she begins to vibrate.

"What?" Her eyes flash like jagged emeralds.

"I-" I clear my throat. "Nothing."

The heat of her anger prickles my skin and dances across my body as her stare bores into me.

"Stop. Lying. To. Me," she bites out. Her voice is as venomous as a viper. Rage crackles and sparks from her like embers from a pyre.

I move to stand, "Just take a breath and-"

"Don't tell me to calm down!" she snaps. She stamps her foot and as it slams on the wood panels, my knees buckle beneath me. An unseen ferocious grip holds me in place.

Well, that's new.

She continues to glare at me with the heat of a thousand suns.

"You need to calm down, before you set the whole cottage on fire." I try to stand again, and again I'm pinned down. Held against my will by a powerful grip.

She glares at me, "if you won't tell me the truth," her jaw ticks. "I can't trust you."

"Sugar-"

The grip on my shoulders loosens only to tighten around my torso and yank me upright. The force drags forward, even as I try to plant my feet. Instead, they trail behind me uselessly.

I try to grab a hold of the door frame, but my hands just brush against the wooden panes, as they are forced to ball into fists. I'm hauled from the room, and I tumble down the staircase. The front door snaps open, eagerly awaiting my descent. As soon as I fall unceremoniously outside, it slams shut behind me. I stand and reach for the doorknob, but as I do, I'm shoved back again, nearly falling flat on my ass.

You can't come back in, until you tell me the truth! Sugar's voice shouts inside my head. Anger scorches every word that's bellowed into my mind.

Fine, if she won't let me use the front door there are other ways to get inside. I stalk around the cottage and discover a wayward path of brambles and blackberry bushes. I push through them and shred my shirt, much to my annoyance.

286

Once I navigate the prick of all prickly bushes the small, cobbled path clears and is littered with pretty, well-tended flowerbeds and hanging baskets. I accidentally bang my head on one of them, causing the fuchsia flowers to rain petals down on me. I clamber through the flower beds, stamping on the heads of cheerful violet bundles of delphiniums and lupines. I decapitate several flowers as I stagger to the small stained-glass window that peers into the kitchen.

"You can't keep me locked out here forever, Witchling!" I shout with enough force to cause most mortals to shrink in fear. "You'll be stuck going through those boxes for twice as long!"

Better that, than having to deal with someone who lies and steals!

I deliberately squash more flowers- their cheery prettiness irks me. "I hope the boxes topple over and you get trapped in there!"

"Mr Nox! That's not a very nice thing to say," a small voice chastises from behind me.

"Well, I'm not very nice so-" I whirl around to see the diminutive figure of Salacious Dong, his arms crossed over his portly stomach. "For fuck's sake."

I traipse past him to the front of the cottage, collapse on the doorstep and rest my back on my periwinkle barricade. Despite my foul mood, I still appreciate the warmth of the summer sun as it dapples over me.

I close my eyes, hoping that the gnome will take the hint and bugger off.

I open one eye cautiously to check but the sodding garden ornament is uncoordinatedly tottering over to me.

"I fear I did not make the best first impression," he clambers up the step to sit beside me with his stumpy legs dangling over the edge.

My eyebrows shoot up, "What gave it away?"

"I shouldn't have done that," Salacious says solemnly.

"You should have started with one finger and worked your way up?" I ask dryly. The image of him elbow deep in himself gave me an idea for a new torture at work. I could call it the Oroborarse-

"I shouldn't have lied," he lets out a sorrowful sigh.

"Aye, well," I roll my neck, hearing the muscles crack and pop. "I wouldn't worry about it so much. Lying is as natural as breathing. I do it all the time."

"Wow," Salacious looks up at me with awe, "but why?"

"I'm a demon," I drawl. "It's what we do."

"Why?"

287

"Why do I lie or why am I a demon?"

"Yes," he smiles brightly after a moment of deep consideration.

"Why do you ask so many questions?"

Salacious looks down and ponders, "I don't know. Maybe because I have only been alive for a few days?"

"Hm," I look down at him. He's looking at the flowerbeds and vegetable patch like they're the most magical, mysterious places imaginable. "Strange that being alive for such a short time has instilled you with such a strong moral code."

"Mr Nox is it all this beautiful?" he says in a hushed reverent whisper.

"What?" Oh, fucking wonderful, this one-word questioning is contagious.

"This," he gestures to the unkempt garden like he's Adam admiring Eden. "The world. Life."

"This is just a front garden," I point past the driveway. "There's more stuff down there."

His mouth hangs open before his expression shifts to one of pure delight.

Stuff. I use the smallest word possible to encapsulate all the joys and horrors of existence. I think of the countless souls in Hell and Earth, the wonderful and terrible acts they have committed in this life and the hereafter. Every change they have wrought on existence, and I call it 'stuff'.

A butterfly, painted in the deepest shade of jade, lands on the head of one of the crushed lupines I'd trampled. "No, it's not all wonderful."

"Strange," his tone is wistful. "It all seems so beautiful."

"Most horrible things are."

He points, "Is she?"

Before I have a chance to answer, a soft purr rumbles beside my leg followed by a soft bump on my shin. Snow, the pearlescent white feline, lives up to her name: her fur shimmers effervescently in the afternoon sun. She's so bright I see a prism of colour ripple over her glossy coat.

I lean down to stroke under her chin, and she rumbles with appreciation.

She looks up at me with her wide blue eyes and nudges my hand with a silent demand for me to continue. Once satisfied, she gives me one small meow of gratitude, before stalking towards the butterfly still perched on the bloom.

Her attack proves unsuccessful, as the insect flies off unscathed and free to fly another day.

"Mr Nox?"

"Hm?" I look back at Salacious, his eyes full of child-like wonder. "Is Miss Esme like that? Horribly beautiful?"

I let the question hang in the air, lingering like the sweetest perfume. I watch as Snow lunges for another butterfly. This time she squishes it with her delicate paws.

"Almost certainly."

Salacious continues his asinine questions for what feels like an interminable amount of time. I've tortured people like this. Endless questions with no answer that is ever satisfactory. But after the hundredth question I find myself thawing to the naive creature.

The sun hangs low over the horizon, and I dimly register that Sugar is still holding firm in her fortress of solitude.

He swings his legs off the step, like a toddler perched at the edge of a swimming pool. "Am I really alive?"

"That I don't know."

"What is alive?"

"Alive is something that lives, grows, breathes and…"

"Dies?"

I knock my head back against the door, "Aye. It dies."

He frowns, "So something is only alive because it dies?"

My own brow furrows, "I suppose."

"Are you alive?"

"Sort of."

"Can you not die?"

"Technically, yes," killing a demon has been known to happen. But it is rare. Although in this stupidly fragile body I imagine it's much easier. Especially with how much my control has been slipping.

The gnome kicks his feet higher, "Then that means you're alive then."

"You may be right," I chuckle.

"What about love?" Salacious asks, "do you have to be alive to love?"

I think of Finn and feel guilty. But I'm not meant to feel guilt. I'm a demon. I don't feel guilty about anything. I rub at the spot on my chest as it clenches. His heart. This mortal body that I am stealing. He loves. I feel its presence linger whenever I take hold. He loves, in his own misguided mortal way. He loves her.

289

"I wouldn't know," I lie.

He tilts his head quizzically like Snow. Eyes filled with wonder and curiosity. Fuck, when was the last time I ever looked at anything like that?

A wave of sugary sweetness strokes across my nape.

She's nearby.

Are you ready to be honest with me?

I raise my hand and gently rap a knuckle on the door.

One knock for yes, two for no.

A small laugh escapes me, "I make no promises."

"Then you can stay out there and starve," she says through the letterbox, her breath gently kissing the back of my neck.

I shift my head to peer through the mail slot. I meet those wide, almond eyes with sceptical surprise, "You cooked?"

"Goddess no!" she splutters, "I ordered in!"

I narrow my eyes, "It's going to be cookies or ice cream or some kind of shit, isn't it?"

"No, I ordered something with vegetables," she huffs through the gap between us.

"Miss Esme!" I catch a flash of movement as Salacious bounces next to me. He's jumping so high it's like he's attached springs to his feet. "So lovely to see you. You are incredibly beautiful, like a garden!"

"What the fuck? How are you getting that high off the ground?" I look down at him to see that he's dragged one of the flowerpots over to help him reach the letterbox. "Stop doing that! You're going to ruin the flowers!"

"But you were doing it before?" Salacious says innocently. "You were stamping all over the ones around the side of the house. I just assumed that's how we say hello?"

Sugar's glare could melt icebergs.

"What was that about my flowers?" she growls.

"I thought we were talking about dinner?" I ask conversationally, trying to steer away from a topic that will result in me sleeping outside. "What are we having?"

Those viridescent eyes flare, "My foot up your arse if you don't tell me what you've done to my flowers-"

The gnome is still bloody bouncing; the daisies in the pot are now practically mulch, "Please Miss Esme, Mr Nox meant no harm. It is only because he thinks you are horribly beautiful."

I can only see her eyes, but I can tell how much that amuses her, "Does he now?"

"Aye! He says the most beautiful things are the most horrible!'

I cringe inwardly. Dong giveth, and Dong taketh away!

I swiftly pull his makeshift trampoline out from under him. He lands with a thwack on the doormat, which is accompanied with a muffled "Ow!"

"It's a figure of speech, all the demons in Hell say it," I clear my throat. "Can I please beseech your kindness and seek shelter in your humble abode?" I flutter my eye lashes.

"Please, Sugar," I whisper into the letter box. "I don't want to sleep outside. I don't want to be bed buddies with Salacious."

A small, exasperated groan comes from the other side, and the letterbox snaps shut just as the door slowly opens.

"You can come back in," Sugar crosses her arms, trying, and failing to look intimidating, "under two conditions. One," she holds up a finger, "you tell me what happened the other night and two," another finger goes up, "you're honest about the necklace?"

"Ok," I suck in a breath, "I'll try."

And I mean it, I don't know why, but some part of me just wants to accept the olive branch she's offering.

"Chips don't count as vegetables," I watch as Sugar tears into the greasy paper with feral glee. "They are just boiled and fried potatoes. Potatoes do not make a meal!"

"They do when you add the sauces," Sugar bundles up the two sweaty bags of chips along with five different condiments. She waddles into the living room, plonking one of the parcels on the seat beside her, before opening her own bundle with insurmountable glee.

I hover in the doorway, "Do we not at least get plates?"

She frowns, "Do you like washing up?"

"Well, no. Nobody does, but-"

"Exactly," she pops a chip in her mouth. "Sit down. Eat your dinner, and stop being such a whiny demon!"

I hesitate at the doorway. These jeans are expensive, at least they would have been if I'd paid for them. I dread to think what this meal will do to them.

Sugar's voice fills with warning, "If you don't sit down right now you can go sleep outside with Salacious. I told you, Demon-Boy," she begins squirting an inhuman amount of ketchup over the grease-sodden monstrosity. "You need to tell me what happened last night with the necklace and why you have it?"

I acquiesce and lift the heavy parcel from the sofa, before sitting beside her. "You found the necklace," I peel back the paper and grimace at my own mound of squashed carbohydrate. How the human body can consume this, Lucifer only knows. It explains why we have so many damned souls admitted early with high blood pressure as their cause of death. I wrestle one of the sodden chips from its brethren and give it a tentative sniff. "You were in a trance."

She freezes, a chip poised in front of her mouth, "A trance?"

"Aye, vacant stare, standing in the middle of the spare room," I nibble at the end of the chip. "Creepy shit."

She scoffs, "That's rich coming from a demon!"

My memory flashes back to the sight of her haunted, harrowing demeanour. Like she was no longer there and someone else had taken over.

I look over at her, "Trust me, Sugar. It wasn't good."

She gulps, "So, what happened?"

"You started swaying, and singing-"

Her brow furrows, "Singing?"

"Aye, you sang an old song…" I take another bite, trying to distract myself from the melody playing in my head. "A very old song."

"What was it?"

I shove the rest of the chip in my mouth, trying to delay the conversation for as long as possible. I swallow, but she's still staring at me with rapt attention. "The Witches Reel," I finally manage to choke out.

She shrugs, "Never heard of it."

"It's one of the oldest songs ever recorded in Scotland," I watch her face closely, seeing if there's any spark of recognition. "It was written during the first witch trials."

Her face remains adorably blank.

"You were singing it, and then you went over to the window, tore up the floor and pulled out that necklace."

"But I don't know that song," she whispers quietly. "And why would I start pulling apart the floor? I'd entirely forgotten about it until I saw it in that old photo…" she flounders.

I narrow my eyes at her, "What photo?"

"Erm," she picks absently at her dinner, shifting uncomfortably. "It was an old one from when I was younger."

"And you didn't think it would be wise to mention this little nugget of information?"

She scowls, "It takes two to tango! You've hardly been honest with me."

She doesn't know the half of it.

My jaw tics, "I'm being honest right now."

She opens her mouth to argue, but I reach over and shove another chip in before she has the chance to say anything.

"Anyway, you were singing," I sigh, leaning back into the sofa. "Very animatedly, and that's not to mention the chorus behind you."

Sugar claps a hand to her face with so much force I worry she's given herself a concussion. "How can I not remember this?"

"Witchling," my voice is hushed. "You're experiencing a lot of changes at the minute. You're getting stronger. More powerful. You can set things on fire." I point at Salacious who's shoving chips into his face with glee, "You brought that bloody gnome to life. Hell, you forcibly cast me from the cottage and stopped me from coming back in." I tap my forehead. "That's not even mentioning the whole telepathy thing."

She leans forward and I lunge across to save her chips from falling to the ground.

"Oh Goddess," she whispers. "What's happening to me?"

I pick up the chips from her lap and place both bundles onto the coffee table. I don't understand it, but I want to reach for her. Hold her. Comfort her. And I ask myself that same question: what the hell is happening to me?

"I think you're waking up," I place a tentative hand on her knee. "These aren't new powers. You always had them. They were just hidden away."

She shudders and after a couple of seconds, she regains control of her breath.

She turns her steely emerald eyes to me, "And why did you have the necklace?"

Again, I'm lost for words as to why I didn't give it straight to her. Last night when Magick held her in its chokehold, an overwhelming need to protect her had washed over me. Seeing her devoid of her light, that sparkle which makes her who she is, felt alien. Wrong. The way she'd burrowed through the bedroom floor to find that thing was unnerving. Like it was calling to her. Something just felt horribly wrong. No. It isn't safe for her to have it.

But there was something else: some selfish craven part of me felt like it was a clue. When I held it, I felt a spark of hope, like I'd finally found a breadcrumb. Some minute clue which might lead me to the grimoire. After much cajoling, I opened the vial to find nothing but the remnants of dried leaves and dust.

"I don't know," I answer weakly, and I hate myself just that little bit more for playing the fool, so I offer up one feeble token of truth, "but I know nothing good can come from it."

293

Chapter Thirty - Four

Esme

I soar above the heather like a bird in flight. Lilac fields blanket the ground beneath me. The sky is a swirl of amber and coral. The hills below look like ocean swells, only occasionally broken by green peaked mountains. I'm free and untethered.

I move lower to the ground to catch the scent of the warm soil and wildflowers. I dive into a forest. I wind gracefully around the ancient trees. I dodge between their tall trunks and watch the golden rays of sunset peak between their leaves.

I bask in peace as I am enveloped by Nature's beauty. It's a feeling I haven't felt in so long.

I burst through the forest canopy and leaves follow me like a wave cresting the ocean. I feel a tug. A beacon beckoning me.

I fly for a long time, following the gentle request.

Another soft pull as I catch sight of a crystalline expanse of water. The loch is nestled amongst mountains, and I see something shining beside it: a structure, painted in the same shade as the rose-tinted sky.

"Witchling," a distant voice calls across the mountains.

I look down to see that the shoreline is empty.

"Witchling," the voice says again.

No, not from the ground, I realise dimly. The voice is everywhere, reverberating around the wilderness.

"Witchling!"

I jolt awake. Nox's amber eyes glow as he leans over and shakes me forcefully. "We need to get out now," his voice is full of warning.

"Nox?" I bat one of his arms away and rub at the sleep in my eyes. "What are you doing? It's the middle of the night!"

294

It's then I realise. Nox's scent has addled my drowsy brain, but I catch it. Smoke.

I straighten, all vestiges of sleep wash away like I've been doused in water. I see tendrils of smoke coiling beneath the bedroom door.

"What's happening?" I choke out.

"Fire," he lunges for me, grabbing my hand. "We need to get out. Now."

He pulls me from the bed, and I untangle myself from the sheets. I let go of his hand to rush to the corner of the room.

I pull on my lilac hoodie, shove my feet into my pink converse and grab hold of my satchel.

"Sugar, what are you doing?" Nox snaps. "Now is not the time to start packing. We need to get the fuck out of the cottage, unless you want to burn to death?"

I wave my bag in his face. "The necklace is in here. I'm not leaving without it, especially since we don't really know what it's for."

"Ok, now you've got that, we need to go," he commands. "We need to get out before we can't use the stairs."

His hand hovers above the door handle, his eyes asking the question before it escapes his lips. "Ready?"

I suck in a breath and give a small shaky nod.

His other hand reaches out to me and instinctively I take hold. "Whatever happens," he says, as my fingers interlink with his. A jolt of electricity sparks between us. "Do not let go of my hand, got it?"

"Okey dokey," I chew on my lip and for the first time today, I'm in no mood to argue. "Let's avoid getting cooked!"

His lip quirks minutely, "That's the spirit."

With that, he tugs the door open, and we're immediately engulfed in smoke. We both splutter as it whooshes in.

"Follow me," he gasps in a choked breath. He pulls me forward and the heat from downstairs surges over me. I can't see anything except the dim shape of Nox.

A coughing fit racks through me as we stagger across the landing.

"Stay calm," Nox's voice is hoarse. "You need to try to slow your breathing."

I splutter, "How would you kn-"

Stop arguing and listen to him, the voice orders. *And trust him.*

Easier said than done, I snap back. *He's a demon after all.*

A demon who's trying to keep you safe.

295

Nox begins to descend the steps, and despite my brain screaming at me to go the other way, I follow behind.

The smoke grows thicker, if that's even possible, and the heat begins to swirl around me with every step.

My childhood is in flames and all of Mum's treasures and secrets are burning around us.

Stop thinking about the past, the voice shouts over the crackle of the fire. *Focus on getting out, so you can have a future!*

Nox reaches the front door and tries to pull it open, but it doesn't budge. He releases my hand to tug on it with all of his strength and still it doesn't open.

"Could the wood have swollen in the heat?" My voice is rough and ragged.

"We're trapped," he shouts, his voice strained and wheezy. He takes hold of my hand again and drags me past the living room which is completely engulfed in flames. The heat sears my skin and makes my eyes water.

"Where are we going?" I gasp as he pulls us in the direction of the kitchen, which is swallowed in smoke.

Goddess, how could this have happened? If Nox hadn't woken me, I would have-

Stop thinking about that and focus! The voice orders.

I try to think about potential exits, when the realisation hits me. The kitchen window!

I overtake Nox; it's my turn to tug him forward. "The window," I splutter, "we can get out of the window!"

The kitchen looks like an immersive modern art exhibit or a really shit nightclub. I accidentally stub my toe.

"Be careful!" Nox wheezes.

"Oh sure, I'll just take a leisurely stroll whilst everything is on fire!" I snap back. Despite my retort, I do as he says; I slow my pace and try to see through the smoke for the stained glass.

There! The voice proclaims, halting my search.

I squint, and then I see it, the faint glimmer of rainbow glass.

I tug Nox's hand, "This way."

My head begins to fog, and I feel like I've had ten strawberry daiquiris on an empty stomach. I wheeze, my breathing is so shallow and weak.

He pushes me out the way so he can move closer to the glass, "Stand back!"

I do as he says, as my head begins to swim.

He smashes his elbow into the glass. Once. Twice. The

shattered shards paint the floor. He grabs at the rose pattern curtains to knock out the remains and creates a clear exit.

He turns to me, "You first."

Before I can protest, he shoves me through the gap. I wriggle out and tumble onto a flower bed. I suck in a breath. Air. Fresh and clean, wonderful air. Oxygen surges into my scorched lungs and for a moment I go light-headed.

Nox looms above me and I clamber out of the way just as he inelegantly flops into the squashed flowers. His right arm is a mess of soot and blood. The glass has shredded his forearm and there are several angry gashes. Small pieces of multicoloured glitter dapple the blood and I register dimly that it's glass. Blood flows and pools from his wound to mingle with the soil.

"Nox," I croak. "We need to get you to a doctor. Your arm-"

"Miss Esme?" a small voice calls near the bush of brambles.

I struggle to stand and have to clasp the windowsill to stop my knees from buckling beneath me.

"Miss Esme?" the voice says again.

Nox tries to pull himself to a sitting position but fails, his left arm hanging uselessly beside him. I crouch to lift his torso and prop him against the wall.

He offers me a weary, pained half smile, "Thanks, Sugar."

"Miss… Esme…" the voice is pained and hushed. I take a tentative step on my shaky legs.

"Salacious?" I croak out and take a step forward. I follow his voice to find shattered pieces of porcelain littering the ground.

"Miss Esme," Salacious' decapitated head smiles warmly up at me. "I knew it was you. I recognised your voice."

The gnome's limbs are broken and scattered like ivory confetti amongst the brambles.

"What happened?" I try to keep my voice level.

"I tried to stop the fire; I saw… I saw a figure by the front door. They were doing something strange…" his eyes grow wide with curiosity. "What's another word for strange?"

"Suspicious?" I offer weakly. I barely recognise my own voice.

"Suspicious! It sounds like my name! What a horribly beautiful word," he beams up at me with the remains of his chipped and broken teeth. "He was sticking something to the door, but before I could stop him, he threw something into the window and then… and then everything caught fire."

He looks behind me and I realise Nox is standing there.

"Mr Nox," the broken gnome says, "I think I may be alive after

297

all!'

"Why do you say that, Salacious?" I manage to ask.

"Because he's dying," Nox interjects before Salacious can answer.

"That's right," the gnome's smile is wistful. "I tried to stop them and when I did, they grabbed me and hit me against the wall again and again. Then they threw me over the hedge!"

I see the remnants of his broken chest attempt to puff out in pride, and I manage to whisper, "You were so brave, Salacious. Thank you so much."

"It has been my honour, Miss Esme," his voice grows quieter. "You and Mr Nox have been so kind. You are the best friends a gnome could have!"

A tear escapes and I bite down on my lip to stop a sob erupting.

Salacious looks above us at the twinkling stars.

"It's all so..." he blinks slowly, his gaze awestruck. "So... horribly beautiful."

His expression turns vacant, and my tears burst free.

I wipe at my filthy face, "What did he mean about someone sticking something to the door? Do you think he meant that they'd barricaded it?"

"Stay here," Nox staggers through the brambles.

"But," I begin to follow.

"Sugar," his eyes flash with warning. "Stay here, for Hell's sake!"

I prop myself against the garden wall and look back at the inferno. I should just be glad to be alive, but I'm mortified. How many memories lay destroyed and in ashes? Irreplaceable. Precious. All consumed by the flames. There's no way I can salvage them; I wouldn't even know where to begin.

I look up at the night sky, and another tear traces down my cheek. "I'm so sorry, Mum."

Nox returns through the side entrance, his face white with fear. No, not fear. Rage.

"Sugar, I need you to get to the nearest house and call the police," he grinds his teeth. That golden glare is filled with the fire of a thousand suns.

I frown. "Why? Aren't you coming with me?"

His hands ball into fists as blood drips from his injured arm onto the flower bed.

"Nox," I step forward. "What aren't you telling me?"

298

"Please, witchling." He never pleads. Panic sets in my chest. "Just get to a neighbour-"

"What did you find?" I dodge around him, as he unsuccessfully tries to tackle me with his one good arm. I run down the narrow alleyway beside the house, ignoring the snag of brambles on my bare legs, the burn in my lungs and my shaking limbs.

My heart stops when I catch sight of what Nox is trying to protect me from.

Snow.

Her body is nailed to the front door and her beautiful white fur is drenched in blood.

I let out a howl of grief and anger. My last connection to my mother. My beautiful Snow.

I scream again, and hope that whoever did this hears me, and that they know what I'll do to them.

White hot fury clouds my vision just as everything goes black.

Chapter Thirty - Five

Nox

"Sir, we just need to inspect the wound," the young doctor attempts to hide the nervousness in his voice. It's not working, although I am giving him an extremely heated glare which probably isn't helping. A not-so-subtle warning to hurry the fuck up. "Once we've c-c-cleaned the wound we can give you stitches?"

I arch an eyebrow, "Are you asking or telling me that's what you're going to do?"

He lets out a frightened squeak.

I'd begrudgingly acquiesced to being admitted to the local hospital. Although calling it a hospital may be a bit of a stretch-there's five rooms and one of them is a broom cupboard. There are only three staff: two very frazzled nurses and this man-child doctor.

"Where is she?" I growl.

"The woman you came in with?" the boy pushes his glasses up his nose as sweat begins to stream from his brow. "Sh-She's resting."

"Resting?" I attempt to stand, only to be manhandled by one of the nurses. With her broad shoulders and bulging biceps she looks like a boxer. I peer around the giantess, "She fainted, I'd hardly call that resting."

Sugar is the only reason I'm here. Her scream tore through me, and before I could reach her, she was already out cold. Before I could scoop her up and bundle her into the car, one of her neighbours had already called for help.

She'd been swiftly carted into an ambulance, and I'd had no choice but to follow along behind. I've had to endure Dr. Juvenile inspecting my arm with the same level of skill and expertise as a two-year-old doing long multiplication.

300

"Mr," the man-child scours his clipboard. "Smith? Mr Smith, she's been through a traumatic event. You both have."

Traumatic, that's one way to put it. Fucked up is more accurate. This is now an everyday occurrence: wherever Sugar goes, chaos follows.

"I need to see her," I add more heat to my words. "Right now."

He stares down at the clipboard, deliberately avoiding my gaze and staring at my chart like it's the most fascinating thing he's ever seen.

Smart move.

"Look at me when I'm talking to you, boy!" I command.

He does as he's told, and begins to speak, but no words come out. Sheer terror fills his eyes, and he sees me for what I really am: the horror in the shadows, the bump in the night. I should reign it in but it's working.

"Where is she?" I demand.

"Room Two," he whimpers. I look down to see a dark stain appear on his cargo trousers. I wrinkle my nose in disdain, both at him pissing himself and his dress-sense. Whoever allowed smart casual to be appropriate work attire should be hung, drawn and quartered.

"And you," I glare at the nurse. "Get your fucking hands off me before I break them off at the wrist and make you eat them."

I fill her mind with the images of a thousand suns exploding.

She gasps and drops her hands as though she's just been scalded. Which technically she has, my skin crackles with fury and fire.

"Thank you," I give her a charming grin, flashing my dimples as I leave them both trembling and terrified.

I saunter out of the room, ignoring the pain in my arm. Nothing matters except her. I stop in my tracks, questioning the thought.

Nothing matters, I correct myself. *Except finding out what she knows about the grimoire.*

Satisfied, I continue down the hallway, the neon yellow making me wince. It's like the staff deliberately picked the most obnoxious colours, as if to say, "You'll get better, whether you like it or not!"

I step into Room Two. There are four single beds, all of them empty, except the one at the corner by the window.

Lying eerily still, Esme is tucked under sterile white sheets and a monitor beeps beside her.

301

The room is muggy and the puny air-con machine on the wall is doing a piss-poor job of combatting the heat.

I walk towards her. All dirt and grime from the fire has been washed away. Her pink tendrils spill out around her like a rose gold halo. It reminds me of the first time I saw her- tucked in bed and breathing heavily, punctuated only with the small whimpers and sighs that escape her lips.

"No," she whispers, a small frown creasing her forehead. "No... No, I don't want to."

I sit beside her on the orange chair, placing a hand on her arm to wake her. Her fingers claw into the thin sheets wrapped around her.

"No," she whimpers, a tear escapes from her fluttering eyelids. "I don't... don't make me."

I place my hand on top of hers, "Witchling?"

Her head shakes slightly. "No," a shudder ripples through her as the room grows cold. "Stop."

The temperature drops as she exhales. Goosebumps coat our skin and her body shivers.

The room feels freezing and the ancient air conditioning unit sputters and grinds to a halt.

"No," she pleads again, her chest heaving in panicked, frightened breaths. "Stop!"

I give her hand a shake as the shivers claim my body. Frost coats every surface in the room.

"Sugar," I say louder, "wake up!"

"No..." she whimpers, "I can't. Don't... don't make me!"

"I fucking can, and I will," I growl. I've tried the soft and gentle approach, which clearly doesn't work. I allow the flames inside me to erupt and heat my skin.

"Stop!" She's still asleep, but she sits bolt upright as her body shakes violently. "Stop it now!"

"Witchling" I bellow, my face inches away from hers. "Wake the fuck up! Now!"

She's convulsing and instinctively I wrap myself around her, dowsing her skin in fire. My Fire. Her unconscious body latches onto me, climbing into my lap for warmth.

"Wake up!" I bellow into her ear.

Just as I'm about to shout again, she relaxes and begins to thaw. She wraps around me in an embrace so desperate that I reciprocate.

"Finn?" she murmurs into my neck.

302

My heart twists, "No…"

She stiffens, "Nox?"

"That'd be me."

She loosens her grip, untangling her legs from around my waist and runs a hand down her flushed neck, "Erm," she clears her throat. "Sorry."

"Are you sorry about climbing into my lap or sorry that I'm not Finn?" I can't stop the question or ignore the way her eyes flash as I say his name. Why should I care that she hoped I was him? The prick flashes a very graphic image into my mind, one of Esme in his lap with significantly less clothes. I am taken aback; can he see what's happening? It takes a moment for me to collect myself and stamp down his smugness.

She shuffles back, her face as red as a summer sunset, "I didn't realise…" her words die.

"How many times are you going to end up clambering all over me when you're unconscious, Witchling?" I ignore my envy and smile at the little green-eyed monster in front of me. "I only ask, because I'm starting to lose count now."

She self-consciously pulls her hospital gown higher. Not that it matters; I've seen her undressed multiple times. My mind has wandered back to those memories more times than I'd like to admit. Finn gives an indignant shove and I push him back down again. I don't have time for this bullshit.

"What were you dreaming about?" I rub at the back of my neck, trying to ignore the barrage of images Finn continues to blast into my mind.

She lowers her gaze, tucking her legs up to her chest and stares at her knees.

"No, I…." she chews her lower lip. "I dreamt of a pool of water surrounded by mountains. A place so deep in the wilderness, but there was… a pink house beside the shoreline and there were these creatures around the water's edge… calling to me. But… but they looked like horses," she looks up at me. "But also, not horses. They kept changing into people."

I manage to smother Finn just as my heart skips at her words.

She clears her throat, "Such a weird dream."

"Were they black?" I ask, my tone sharp.

Her frown deepens, "It was nighttime in my dream."

"Aye, but," I place a hand on her knee. "But were they dark horses?"

303

Confusion spreads across her features. "How did you-"

So, her dream wasn't just a dream. It was another vision.

"Kelpies," I answer. "They're fucking Kelpies."

The Kelpies and I have a long running feud. It started centuries ago when they'd commanded floods to swallow the land, hoping to drown the mountains in their watery depths. They'd asked me to join them, to combine our power to reclaim the land from the humans.

I'd politely declined the offer by pissing in their holy waters and telling the Prince of the Kelpies to go fuck himself.

"I thought they were just myths," Esme heaves a strained breath beside me. We've been hiking for ten minutes and already she's buckling under the exertion, although I'm not doing much better. With my injured arm and increasing exhaustion I feel like shit, I need a week's worth of sleep. I'd forgotten how insect-ridden the woods around a Loch could be. We are just walking Happy Meals to these little bastards.

The sun mercilessly beats down on us as we journey deeper into the trees, I'm relieved that they shroud us in their emerald canopy.

"Afraid not." I continue to ascend the rocky terrain. "Kelpies aren't just cautionary bedtime stories for little girls to teach them to watch out for good looking men. They are very real."

She lets out a small chuckle behind me, "Are they really good looking?"

I give her a warning glare, "it doesn't matter how handsome they are. They'll still drag you into that bloody Loch and drown you."

"So that's a big fat yes then!" mischief sparkles across her features. She climbs over an uprooted tree. A rogue ray of sun licks at her exposed thigh and my eyes trace where the light touches. She misinterprets my leer as a sneer and tugs at her clothes.

I wince as my arm brushes against a branch and hiss involuntarily.

She looks over at me, "You should have gotten that looked at."

"I was a bit preoccupied with trying to make sure you didn't lose your toes to frostbite!" I look down at the gauze and bandages that smother my forearm.

I'd quickly tended to my injury as the hospital staff issued us an early discharge.

Much to Esme's annoyance, who has been chastising me

since we left.

"Just don't fall for it," I watch her as we walk. "Kelpies will lie just to get what they want, and they are very persuasive, particularly to the naive."

"What's that supposed to mean?" her footsteps halt.

"Just that you have a tendency to always believe what people say."

"Why do you keep looking at me like that?" Annoyance flashes across her face, "You make it sound like I'm an idiot!"

"I didn't say that."

"At least I don't go around acting like everyone's shit on my shoe," she says snottily. "What did they do to you to make you sound so bitter?"

I glare at her for a couple of seconds. "I had a little falling out with them. We agreed to disagree and leave each other in peace."

Sugar gives me a sideways glance. "Maybe it's time to let bygones be bygones. Kiss and make up?"

"Not everything can be solved by saying 'Oopsy!' batting your eyelashes and carrying on as normal," I retort and her nostrils flare in annoyance. "Besides, I don't think you'd say that if you realised what the Kelpies tried to do," I overtake her. The ground levels out and I see the crystalline expanse of the Loch below.

She sighs, "What did they try to do? Not label everything or forget to take the bins out?"

"There's nothing wrong with order," I bristle.

"I think your idea of tidying borders on obsessive," she answers dryly.

I ignore her jab and walk towards the Loch, my usual swagger nowhere to be found. I'm as enthusiastic as an eight-year-old going to the dentist. "They tried to drown the world."

"I would have thought you'd be all for that," she scoffs. "Being a demon and all."

"Shockingly enough, Hell doesn't want the world to end," I answer. "We need Earth to keep spitting out more damned souls. If there's no humans, then there's no more Hell."

The ground levels as I begrudgingly make my way to the edge of the shore. The Loch is beautiful, breath-taking even. It's a shame that it's about to be spoiled.

Sugar stands beside me, resting her hands on her hips as she catches her breath.

"So how do we, erm," she waves a hand at the expanse of glittering water. "Command or summon them?"

305

"They usually respond to the wanton desires of a busty harlot," I give her a sideways glance, noting the heave of her chest. I flash my dimples at her. "Do you fancy unzipping that top and showing those Kelpies what nature gifted you, do you?"

She scowls and zips up the hoodie.

I shrug, "Spoil sport." I begin unwrapping my bandaged arm.

"Wait," her face contorts into alarm. "What are you doing?"

"There are other ways to summon them," I grit my teeth, peeling the bloodied gauze from my forearm. "They are suckers for two things: breasts and blood."

"Shouldn't that be three things?" she asks. She winces as she watches me.

"Technically yes," I hiss. I squeeze at one of the biggest wounds, causing blood to pool and ooze down my arm. I hold it out and the blood drips into the sparkling water. It dissolves quickly like it's been greedily devoured by whatever foul beastie dwells in there. But I'm after one specific beastie. I just hope he's less of a colossal dick these days.

"Why blood?" Sugar picks up a pebble and skims it across the Loch's surface. It bounces once, twice before plopping under.

I shrug, "Blood is life. Stories of bloodshed have carried through the centuries. Hunting, wars, even sporting events." I pick up my own stone, caressing its smooth surface. I throw it and watch it soar across the expanse of water, as elegant as a falcon soaring across the skyline. Its trajectory begins to dip after about twenty metres, bouncing and gaining speed every time it touches the water. It bounces ten times before finally being swallowed under the surface.

I turn to the witchling, "Even you, Sugar. Underneath all that sweetness, there's something primal and blood thirsty. Strip away all that glitter and niceness and you'll see."

Just as she opens her mouth, I see movement behind her. The Loch ripples and bubbles, I pull her close to me and keep my eyes trained on the water.

"Do not say anything," I warn. "Kelpies are incredibly dangerous and charming, don't believe anything especially-"

"Especially?" A drawl comes from behind me, and I recognise it immediately. He'd silently snuck up and caught me unawares. Stupid mortal hearing. I was also too distracted bickering with Sugar.

I didn't use to be so careless.

"Calder," I give him a smile which is more of a snarl. "You're looking well."

He saunters closer. His youthful features are eerily smooth, his ivory skin unmarred by age. A proud brow that sits above dazzling blue eyes that resemble the Loch. His clothing is deliberately untidy. He wears a black suit with no shirt, to expose his pale taut stomach, and his tapered trousers hang loosely over his bare feet.

"You do well to remember your place, human," a female voice sings from the Loch. Sweet and lilting, but with the barb of threat running beneath.

Muir, Calder's forbidden mate, sashays to us. She flicks us a judgemental sneer before linking her fingers through his. She looks ethereal in her black floating gown, with strips of fabric covering her chest and waist. Her attire is like Calder's; their clothes could either be discarded rags or snatched from a catwalk. I've never been a fan of laissez faire dress-sense: it always looks like you can't put clothes on properly.

"You should bow when you're speaking to royalty," Calder sighs, sounding bored.

Muir tilts her head. "Something isn't right," her melodic voice bounces across the shoreline. "Something isn't where it's meant to be... one plus one is two, but one plus two makes three..."

"What's she doing?" Sugar whispers, her scent tinged with nervousness.

"Counting and singing, apparently." I watch as the doll-like Kelpie skips towards us. Muir glares up at me. "I'm not bowing to the Prince of Puddles," I scoff.

Muir's dreamy expression sharpens. Calder looks between us with amusement, like this is the most entertainment he's had in months.

"Nox," Esme whispers beside me, her voice full of warning. "Maybe don't piss them off when we need a favour from them?"

Calder's eyebrows shoot up in surprise, "Nox?"

I sigh, "Thanks for that, Sugar," I look back at the eerily youthful couple. "Nice to see you again, Calder." I give Muir a mocking salute, "A pleasure as always, Muir."

"Why are you here, Demon-Boy?" Muir asks.

Esme laughs but covers her mouth quickly.

"You were to remain in Hell. You're banished-"

"And you two were meant to be parted until the end of time," I point down at their interlocked fingers. "Clearly, we all found loopholes."

"Loopholes, but not absolutions," Muir gives a forlorn sigh. "You shouldn't be here-"

"But why are you here, Nox?" Calder interrupts, his tone is

casual, but I catch the jagged edge underneath. The warning. "I'm sure you didn't come to this Loch to admire the scenery?"

I shrug, "Fancied catching up. It's been a long time. How about we bury the hatchet?"

"I'd much rather take that handsome mortal body you're wearing and drown it," Muir says wistfully. "Or," she turns her focus to Sugar. "I could take her? She's so pretty, I bet she'd look beautiful in the blue."

The witchling takes a step back from them. It appears Muir's madness hasn't dulled over the centuries.

"Good thing I wasn't talking to you," I say in a clipped tone to Muir.

Calder moves closer to his mate, pulling her behind him, a gentle command to be silent. I turn my attention back to the prince, "Calder, my friend, it really has been too long."

"I cannot deny your presence does interest me," Calder says. "I'm assuming, given our last interaction, it has something to do with the witch?"

Sugar shifts nervously beside me and I shoot her a warning look.

"Potentially," I say nonchalantly. "I wanted to know if you'd been made aware of anything... unusual?"

"Aside from a banished demon parading around in a skin suit?" Muir's lilting tone asks. "You're killing his mortal flesh. I can smell the reek of his dying soul."

"Don't be so dramatic, Muir," I chuckle, trying to ignore the look of horror on Sugar's face. "He's fine, he's... sleeping."

Muir looks at Esme. "His heart cries out for freedom and release, he is a tormented prisoner in his own body. He wishes-"

"That's enough of that!" I point a finger at Muir. I look at Esme, trying to keep my tone placating, "Finn is fine." I glare at Muir. "Stop stirring shit when there's no need."

I look back to Esme, but her attention is entirely on the insane Kelpie, "Is it true? Is Finn in pain?"

"Constant agony," Muir nods gravely. "You must free him... free him by letting him come..." Muir glances briefly up at the prince, whose mouth twitches in amusement and encouragement. She turns back to the witchling. "Let him come with us."

"See?" I wave at the Kelpies, "They'll tell you exactly what you want to hear-"

Esme looks horror-stricken, "I don't want to hear this!"

"Oh Nox," Calder drawls. "I see some things never change.

Still lying-"

"She's the one who's lying," I point at Muir who gives me a look of smug satisfaction.

"Some things really never do change," Calder tuts. "Remember when-"

I glower at him, "We're not here to talk about that."

Muir lets go of her mate's hand and spins in a circle. "Of course you are. That's what you always say every time you come here."

I grind my teeth, quickly losing my patience. "I've never been here before."

The craggy rocks and lapping water are as pretty as any painting of The Highlands. The heather clad mountains hug the skyline. The crest of one mountaintop so high it looks like an outstretched hand beckoning the sun to sink lower. No. I have never been here.

Before I can say this aloud Muir interrupts me by saying, "Of course you have." She nestles into Calder's shoulder, who lovingly wraps an arm around her. "You always come back here."

I pinch the bridge of my nose; I don't have the patience for Muir's madness today. I turn my attention to the Prince, "Calder, have you heard anything unusual? Any uprisings or strange oddities within your realm?"

He shrugs, "Nothing I'd be inclined to tell you, *friend*." The last word comes out in a snarl.

"Well, this was pointless," I sigh and make my way back towards the forest. "Come on, Sugar. We may as well head back to civilization, I've had enough of this rural bullshit, and I think I'm being eaten alive by insects."

"Wait," Calder's command booms across the forest.

I halt but allow myself a moment of smugness. So predictable.

I spin on my heel, "What am I waiting for exactly, Calder?"

"There have been whispers," he looks between Sugar and me. "Rumours of an uprising. An alliance between forces which," Calder's gaze lingers on the witch, "are forbidden."

"Oh, not this shit again! Why can't we all just get along?" I sigh, trampling back down the incline. "What's so wrong with people making friends?"

"Friends?" Esme's voice is full of disbelief. "Do you have friends?"

"You know why," Calder snaps. His power crackles from him

309

like an electric storm. "It is forbidden."

I smile wickedly down at him, "Aren't all the best things?"

Calder shakes his head, "Poor Nox. Always so short-sighted."

"I wasn't the one who tried to drown the world," I wag a finger at him. "Talk about throwing your toys out the pram! Just because Daddy dearest decided you needed to be punished, you figured a literal pissing contest is the way to go!"

"As I recall, I wasn't the one who did all the pissing. Besides, I had my reasons," he snarls. "You of all people should understand."

Sugar's attention ping-pongs between the Prince and me.

"No point bringing the up past, *friend*," I growl.

"Future, present and past," Muir begins to sing. Always with the fucking singing. "What once was first, will always be last."

Esme pulls a face at Muir, but has the sense to keep her voice quiet, "Does she always sing in riddles?"

Calder smiles lovingly at his partner, "Only when she's happy."

"She's happy right now?" the Witchling raises an eyebrow.

"She enjoys change," and I swear I see Calder swoon, his tone full of wonder and awe. "She always has."

"Plus, destruction, murder and mayhem," I drawl.

The female Kelpie continues to spin in circles, her black rags trailing behind her like smoke on a breeze.

"There's beauty in bloodshed," Muir sings.

Esme gives me a wary look, "I've been hearing that a lot lately."

"The answers you seek," Muir twirls, as graceful as a ballerina before pointing across the Loch at the opposite shoreline. "Lie there."

"I don't see anything." I grind my teeth and try to stave off the urge to throttle her. She's just as infuriating and insane as she's ever been.

"Look closer," Calder says, his attention locked on Esme. "You can see it, can't you?"

The Witchling squints as she tries to focus. "I see," she murmurs, "something."

Calder looks pleased, "You have the sight."

"The sight?" I ask, but everyone is ignoring me. Rude. Esme's attention is on whatever the fuck she can see in the distance. Calder and Muir stare at her like she's the most delectable prey they have ever seen.

"Is that..." Esme moves closer to the water, her feet dipping into the lapping Loch. "Is that a building?"

"Hurrah!" Muir claps and cheers like a demented cheerleader, "I knew she would see it!"

I move closer to the water's edge; I see a picturesque landscape and nothing more.

"Sugar," I say quietly. "Can you actually see something?"

She tilts her head, "I think it's a pink house?"

"Your mother," Calder answers. "She hid it from you until the time was right."

"The time was right for what?" Esme asks.

Muir answers before Calder can, "The truth."

Chapter Thirty ~ Six

<u>Esme</u>

Nox gives the Kelpies a perfunctory goodbye before he grabs my hand and starts tugging me back towards the trees.

"She said he was in pain," I wheeze out as we hike. Nox's pace doesn't slow, like he's desperate to get away from the loch.

"What?" his jaw tics.

"Muir," I glare up at him. "She said that you are rotting his soul?"

"I also said Kelpies lie," he bites out.

"Nox," I tug his hand, halting him. "Was it the truth?"

Something flickers across his face.

"Nox?" I ask again.

"He's not in pain," he finally answers, but I see a shadow of uncertainty tracing his features.

"You said he's sleeping?" I prod again.

"Kind of," he lets go of my hand and continues to stalk up the incline.

"What does that mean?"

"Recently, he's been a little more," he pauses to think whilst he clambers over an overturned tree trunk, "exuberant."

I arch an eyebrow, "What does that mean?"

"He seems restless," he answers slowly, like he's choosing his words carefully.

"I want to talk to him," I demand, trying to hide the waver in my voice.

Nox pulls a face, "Why?"

"Because I want to check how he is," I answer. "I shouldn't have to justify wanting to speak to my..."

My what exactly? My estranged possessed man-friend? Finn

312

and I still haven't really talked about what's going on between us but I need to know he's alright. Well, maybe not alright... how can he be alright with all this shit going on... but... to check he's safe. That he's not... dying.

Nox reaches a hand out to me to help me climb over the fallen tree, "Does my word not count for anything?"

I look between his hand and his face. Would Nox tell me if something was wrong with Finn? When it comes to honesty he's not at the top of the class.

You're one to talk. The voice says snippily.

Since when did you become Team Nox? I ask.

Since he's not one of the many people trying to control you, it answers.

Isn't he? I ask. *He didn't give me the necklace straight away and I feel like he's not being completely honest about Finn.*

"I want to talk to him," I ask again.

Something like hurt flickers across his face.

"Fine," his jaw ticks. He closes his eyes. For a moment he's completely still, then suddenly, a muscle spasms in his neck and he sputters and coughs. A wheezy rattling breath erupts from him like he's drowning.

I lunge over the tree to grab hold of him, "Nox!"

He shudders just as he falls to the ground. "Nox, answer me!"

He convulses again and inhales like he's choking on something.

"What's happening?" I search his face which is contorted by some unseen pain. "What do I do?"

He stills and opens his eyes. Golden pools lie beneath me.

"Nox," I lean over him, "what happened?"

"He," Nox sits up, running a hand through his hair. "He wouldn't come out?"

My brow furrows, "Wouldn't?"

He stands and dusts the leaves and dirt off his clothes. "I tried to make him, but he wouldn't come out."

"What does that mean?"

He begins walking and I see another shudder ripple across his shoulders. "I don't know."

Nox has been silent, actually sulking, for the twenty-minute journey back to the car. Every time I try to check if he's ok, he shoots me a warning glare.

His lithe form stalks ahead of me as graceful as a panther

through the forest. Silent, deadly and almost certainly grumpy. I know I upset him by asking him to bring Finn forward, but I hadn't expected him to react like that. The image of him writhing in the dirt flickers in front of me.

I caused that by asking him to do it… He was in pain. Because of me.

I jog slightly to catch up with him and his focus remains locked ahead as he deliberately ignores me.

"So," I wheeze out. "Are we going to talk about why it got so tense back at the Loch or are we just going to pretend nothing happened?"

Nox continues to march forward.

"Ok," I scoff. "I guess we're keeping up with the silence."

His pace quickens and I have to double my efforts to keep up.

"My name's Nox," I lower my voice and thicken my accent. "I'm a demon. I don't like to tell people if I'm ok, even when they're worrying about me. I'm super grumpy. I'm all bad and mysterious-"

Nox halts as anger crackles from him, "Do you ever just shut the fuck up?"

"Not when I get this kind of reaction," I giggle in amusement. "I was just trying to lighten the mood." I decide distraction is the best approach. "You really didn't enjoy talking to Calder and Muir, did you?"

"There's no enjoyment being in the company of Kelpies." Nox turns to continue walking through the forest.

"So," I jog a little behind him to catch up. Man, when he's in a grump, he's really in a grump. "I have a question."

"Is that the question?"

"You said that Kelpies are men," I look up and see his eyes narrow. "But then there's Muir-"

"Muir wasn't always a Kelpie," his tone is grave. "She was human. Once."

"But then how come she-"

"She renounced her humanity," Nox's tone is clipped. "Hundreds of years ago, something happened to her. Something so bad that becoming a Kelpie was more appealing."

I feel a surge of sympathy for Muir. I can't imagine what she'd gone through to make that decision.

"Is that why she's, erm…" I flounder, trying to find the correct term.

"Crazy?" he offers as a smile returns to his face.

"I was going to say eccentric," I mumble as I stumble over a

314

large rock.

"No, she's crazy," he sighs, kneeling to pick up the rock I nearly fell over. He rolls it in his hand. "Changing from human to Kelpie did something to her. It's like when a sculptor carves a statue from a piece of stone. It might look like a person, or an animal, but it's still a stone."

I give a small nod, "Did Calder change her into a Kelpie?"

He doesn't answer. The car comes into view, nestled in the clearing and Nox makes his way to the driver's side.

"Kelpies shouldn't have mates," he says once we're both inside and buckled up. "They are to seduce maidens to their watery graves, not form attachments."

"So, what happened?" I ask. The scenery rolls by as we begin driving down the dirt road.

"He got attached," Nox sighs, turning the wheel to navigate a particularly vicious bend. "Love at first sight."

"What's wrong with that?" I open the glovebox to find my emergency stash of strawberry laces and pop one into my mouth. "Do you have a problem with love?"

"It wasn't love," he shakes his head and when I offer him the bag of sweets, he flinches. I can't tell if it's the topic or the candy that makes him grimace. "Love takes time to grow, it needs to be nurtured, cultivated…"

"It sounds like you're comparing love to a flower?"

He regards me closely. "It's a metaphor that works. True love isn't instantaneous infatuation."

I look out the window, "I dunno… they seem fairly happy."

"Except that Muir is batshit and Calder's father hasn't spoken to him since he changed her into a Kelpie," he deadpans.

"But they have each other," I offer. "That has to count for something."

"It has to count for something because they literally have nothing else," he answers grimly. "If all you have to define you is your relationship, then it's not a relationship, it's your identity."

I chew as I process his words and become aware of how heavy the silence is in the car. I turn on the music. Taylor Swift sings loudly and deafens my thoughts, but I catch two things in my periphery: Nox's face still looks like thunder, but he's tapping his fingers along with the beat.

We don't speak as we drive to the other end of the Loch. The sun lowers over the horizon turning the sky a peachy blush. Nox pulls

315

up near the shoreline and I stare up at the house that's sitting prettily beside the water's edge.

It's painted in a shade of coral that rivals the warmest sunset.

I step out of the car, clutching the necklace close to my chest.

"Can you still see it?" Nox asks dubiously, meeting me in front of the car.

My feet involuntarily move, and I wander towards the house.

It's big, at least three stories with two large turrets swirling upward.

"Can you really not see it?" I ask as I stare up at it.

He's not allowed to, the voice in my head says before Nox can answer. *Only those with Magick in their heart and veins can.*

I guess that explains why the Kelpies can and demons can't.

Nox huffs beside me, "How am I meant to get inside if I can't bloody see it?"

My legs continue to pull me forward just as I see Nox halt midstep.

Only you can, the voice commands. *He cannot come.*

I try to stop my legs from moving, but I can't; I'm no longer in control of my limbs.

"Oh wonderful!" Nox grumbles behind me, "so I'll just stay here then, shall I?"

"I won't be long," I call back to him. "Will I?" I ask the voice quietly.

It will take as long as it takes, the voice answers cryptically.

"Great," I whisper nervously. "I'm really looking forward to going inside a house that only I can see, with a necklace I don't really remember and to try to find answers to questions that I don't understand."

When I reach the door, I see a big heavy padlock hanging from it that promptly snaps open and drops to the ground when I reach for it.

"Erm, I didn't do that?" I ask the voice.

No, you did not, the voice sounds amused.

"Did you?" I ask, hating the reedy hopefulness in my tone.

The house did, the voice says. *It knows who you are, and why you are here.*

"Glad someone does," I twist the doorknob which clicks open and swings on creaky hinges. "Oh, also, this isn't creepy in any way!"

Silence, the voice commands. *Be silent and listen.*

"Listen to what?" I spin in the empty alcove. "There's nothing bloody here?!"

316

The house inside is an empty shell. I walk into what should have been a room, and its shape is a strange pentagon. The scaffolding looks like it's barely holding the house together and there are huge gaps in the ceilings and floors.

I hear a crow caw above me and see it fly past through a gap in the roof as the sky behind it begins to dim.

Wait, the voice says.

Just as I am about to ask what the hell I'm waiting for, dust falls from the big heavy beams above me. I absently wonder whether it could be asbestos.

The light catches the dust which glitters in golden sparkles. But the dust doesn't settle, instead it begins to swirl in circles like a miniature tornado in front of me.

The dust begins to take on the shape of bodies and I see the glittering forms of at least four figures.

I'm about to ask the voice what's happening, but then I hear words whisper around me. I concentrate and snatch a couple of them from the air. Featherlight and almost silent, I have to hold my breath to hear them.

"We shouldn't be doing this," a woman's whisper warns, "it's against Nature."

"Nature?" Another voice comes from the figure in the centre of the room. I move closer to it and see a woman crouched over as she places something on the ground. "What I am doing is natural."

"This isn't the way," the first voice says, their tone beseeching. "See reason, Eve. This is dangerous Magick."

Eve. My knees buckle in front of the memory of my mother.

"I am one of the most powerful living witches," Mum's voice becomes crystal clear and the dust that forms her silhouette grows more distinct. She lifts her head and I see her gentle face set in grim determination. "I can do this."

"Can, and should, are two different things. What about the price?" another figure says near the boarded-up window. "Whatever we put out into the world. We get back. Threefold."

"Then leave, if you're so worried about the scales of Magick. I am aware of the price." Mum looks down at the floor. "I have no choice, Agnes. I have to do this. If you don't want to be here to help, fine, leave."

Agnes, my heart twists. She was here with my mother, doing Goddess only knows what, but whatever it is… Agnes was nervous, and it appears the other figures were too.

"But the balance-" the third figure says and again I recognise

317

the voice.

"The balance?" Mum's voice is so desperate and angry. She doesn't even sound like my mother. She was a warming, wholesome presence. She would never raise her voice.

People can be more than one thing, the voice in my head remarks.

"What would you have me do, Crystal?" Mum snarls. "Take more of this pain? This heartbreak? I can't take it anymore; I have to do something-"

"But this?" Crystal asks. "Does it have to come to this?"

"I have no other choice," Mum sounds resigned. Tired. "I understand if you need to leave."

Silence hangs between them and I hold my breath waiting for it to break.

Agnes sighs before saying, "I'll stay Eve. For you."

"As will I," Crystal says.

The fourth figure shuffles and I recognise Clara who says "But I must ask what will you tell her? When the time comes?"

I look down at Mum as her movements halt, "I will tell her when she's ready."

"Can someone ever be ready for something like this?" Crystal asks, her tone apprehensive.

"She'll be my daughter," Mum says, pride and steely determination cloud her features, like grey clouds passing over a summer skyline. "She'll be ready."

I kneel and reach out a shaking hand to Mum, hoping she'll be solid. That she'll be here.

Just as my fingers are about to brush hers, the glittering dust dissipates and is caught on a breeze that's blown heavenward.

"No!" I cry out, watching the golden particles flutter outside. "Mum, no! Don't leave me!"

My head hangs as I let the tears roll down my cheeks. She'd been here.
She'd talked about me. She'd said she'd tell me something, something important, when I was ready. But then...

She died, the voice finishes my thought.

A sob bubbles from my chest and my tears land on the dusty floor, creating tiny puddles on the splinter ridden floorboards.

I look up and see a small light twinkle near a doorway. Shimmering. Like it's beckoning me.

I wipe my eyes with the back of my hands, wondering if they are playing tricks on me.

But it remains, shining bright like my own little personal North Star.

Follow it, the voice in my head says.

I walk towards the light as it begins winding up the ramshackle stairs and I have to be careful not to fall.

The stairwell is cylindrical and narrow. I dimly register that I'm climbing up one of the turrets. There's no handrail, so I have to place my hands on the walls to keep from falling.

The twinkling light waits patiently every time I need to stop to catch my breath or find my footing.

The stairs grow narrower, but once it stops I'm greeted by a small circular room, barely two metres in diameter. The walls are full of large gaps, which I assume was where the windows were meant to be.

The light hovers in the centre of the room.

"Mum?" I whisper as my body trembles. Mum's apparition would have been enough to push me over the edge normally, but after the last couple of weeks, it's just another thing to add to the pile.

I move closer to the glimmering light. It looks like a ball of sunshine. Just like she had been.

"Mum?"

The light answers by glowing a little brighter.

Happy tears run down my cheeks. "Mum, I miss you so much. I think about you every day. I wish you were here, I wish-"

I take another step and the light moves to the large north-facing window.

The wind from the Loch whooshes inside. It pushes all the air from my lungs and the gust whips across my face, making my hair swirl around me. I tuck the tendrils into my hoodie; the last thing I need is to fall out of a window because I can't see anything!

The light flickers, as if it's trying to tell me something. I walk toward it to peer out over the Loch and see something hovering on the horizon. A shape of something lingering just below the clouds and I have the strangest feeling that it's watching me. Just as I think this, it blinks.

"Wait," I squint, trying to focus, "is that an eye out th-?"

Before I get a chance to finish my question, a violent force shoves me out of the window.

The pink turret rushes past me. I look up at the sky, at the glowing light that chases after me as I fall.

Memories flash through my mind: dancing with Dahls, laughing with Finn, Mum cuddling me close at coven meetings, playing with Ink and whisky coloured eyes that seem to see into my very soul.

And then? Nothing but darkness.

Chapter Thirty ~ Seven

Nox

There's two images I wish I could erase from my mind. The first, is the image that Culum evoked as he described Sarah's torture. The second, is seeing Sugar crashing down from the sky like a fallen angel. Her arms spread wide like she accepts her fate.

The strange barrier that prevents me from crossing to the shoreline shatters suddenly. I race across the craggy landscape to the blur of pastel pink as it hurtles from the sky. I run fast. But not fast enough.

Her body hits the ground with a sickening crack. I'd sell every soul in Hell just to eradicate the sound from my mind.

She lies like a crumpled doll and both of her legs are bent at unnatural angles. I kneel beside her and place a hand to her neck; relief courses through me when I feel the faintest flutter of a pulse.

How she'd managed to survive a fall like that, fuck only knows.

Her breathing is shallow, and the faintest whimper escapes her lips.

I lunge into the Loch to dip my bloody arm into the water.

Calder appears as soon as it breaks the surface, which suggests he's been watching the scene for some time. An amused expression drapes across his arrogant, handsome face.

"Do you need something?" He sounds bored, but I don't miss the look of curiosity in his eyes.

"I need to get back to Edinburgh," I snap, hating the panic I hear in my voice. "Right now. I need to get her to the witches to make sure she's ok-"

Muir emerges from the Loch, and she wanders over to Esme.

Calder gives me the look a parent has when their toddler is

having a tantrum. "She looks like she'd be better placed at a hospital?"

Muir leans down and listens closely to Esme's chest, "That's a pity. She lives."

"Tactful as ever, Muir," I glare at Calder. "She disappeared into that invisible house, then fell from the fucking sky. If you had anything to do with this Calder, I swear I'll kill you," I snarl, my patience hangs by a thread. I look down at Sugar. She's covered in a strange glittery golden powder. She's always covered in glitter, but I swear there's more of it than usual. "She needs witches and fucking Magick to fix her."

"We have Magick," Muir says, her eyes wide as she feigns innocence.

"See, there's a problem with that," my jaw ticks, "I don't trust you."

Calder looks at me quizzically, "You care for her."

"What? No," I splutter. "I need her healed so that she can help me find the grimoire. I need to get her back to Edinburgh. She's a witch, she needs Witch Magick."

"You do," Muir's dreamlike voice is unnervingly close even though she hasn't moved from her crouching position. As quick as a blink, she's next to me and I have to fight the urge to swat her away like she's a fly. She leans in, her obsidian eyes as dark and wide as a starless sky. "You have feelings for the pink witch."

"Now really isn't the time to be having this discussion," I feel my cheeks heat and I try to ignore the smirk on Calder's very punchable face. "You owe me."

"He owes you nothing," Muir sighs wistfully. "Calder is indebted to nobody and nothing! Begone, demon! We shall wait until the witch dies and then we'll bring her to our home. I just made some freshly stewed frog spawn-"

"Sweet merciful Lucifer," I pinch the bridge of my nose. A gesture I seem to have picked up from somewhere. "Do you actually eat frog spawn?"

Muir opens her mouth to answer, and I hold a finger up, "Actually, don't answer that. Calder, see reason, you owe me."

"He does not," Muir whines petulantly.

"Actually, I do," Calder looks uncharacteristically awkward, at least as awkward as a Kelpie is capable of. Our bargain is as fresh in his memory as it is for me. "During the overthrow Nox actually did help-"

"Save the exposition for later, get us back to her flat," I put

322

more heat in my glare. "Right. Fucking. Now, Calder. Or I swear to Satan I'll waterboard you with scorching treacle and introduce you to what a real monster of the deep looks like-"

"Uh, I tire of this," Calder groans, feigning the demeanour of a petulant teenager, but I see the nervousness flash in his face. "After this, we're even, Nox."

"Sure. Fine. Whatever!" I snap. "Just get me the fuck out of here, there's only so much rural savagery I can take-"

Calder snaps his fingers and immediately I feel my stomach drop to the Earth's core and everything turns blindingly white.

Wonderful, now I'm blind! The cherry on top of this shit trifle of a day.

"Finn?"

I open my eyes and I'm now standing back in Esme's ramshackle living room whilst she lays crumpled next to me on a wine-stained rug.

I kneel back down, placing a hand on the witchling's clammy forehead, "No. The other one."

Dahlia lunges to grasp Esme's hand, "What's happened to Ez?! Where the fuck have you two been? And where the fuck did you come from?"

This witch swears more than I do. I almost like her.

"I will explain everything," I rip a bottle green throw from the sofa and gently place it over Esme's limp and shivering form. Her delicate hands are scrunched into tight fists and her nails dig deep into her palms. She may be unconscious, but it looks anything but peaceful. "Can you please get those two old crones over here now?"

"Do you mean Agnes and Crystal?" Dahlia's face creases into a frown, "Why?"

"Because whatever happened to her needs to be fixed by witches. Please just get their wrinkly asses over here," my jaw tightens, and I'm surprised at the volume of my voice. "I will then explain everything. Also, I need to borrow the cat."

Dahlia's eyebrows shoot up into her hairline, "The cat?"

"The small, furry feline that stalks this abode-"

"I know what a fucking cat is," she deadpans. "Why do you need Ink?" She looks hopeful, "Are you going to drown him?"

"Why would I drown him? I'm a demon, not a monster. I just need to borrow him," I answer. "Call the witches, and I'll call someone I know from work."

"From work? But you work in…" Dahlia's voice trails off. "You're calling someone from Hell?!"

323

I tuck a stray tendril of Sugar's hair behind her ear. A frown puckers on her face.

I stand and quickly catch sight of the furball slinking around the living room doorway.

The kitten looks up at me with wide, curious eyes and gives an unnervingly loud meow when I stand in front of him.

"Need a favour, friend," I kneel down and the kitten slinks up to my outstretched hand to nuzzle his velvet soft face into my palm. "Up for the challenge?"

He answers with a rumbling purr and offers another small meow.

I pick him up and he shoves his head into my jaw, "I'll take that as a yes," I sigh, heading to the bathroom and filling the tub. "Hopefully Culum will have a little more information than last time."

Ink balances on the edge of the bath as it slowly fills with water. Cats and crows have always been conduits to the Underworld. It's amazing how much the ancient Egyptians got right. Whilst water works for communication I need a stronger connection for a summoning.

"Nothing?" I slam my whisky glass down on the coffee table. "You mean to tell me that nobody is talking about why so many witches are being killed?"

"Look, I appreciate you've been trapped up here, boss," Culum leans back into the sofa, scrubbing a hand over his stubbled chin. "But shit's been going sideways in Hell. It's not a good place to be right now."

"Is Hell ever a good place?" Dahlia asks as she shuffles from the kitchen to the hallway, balancing a precarious number of charms and candles. She's been on gopher duty to the old crones for the last few hours.

Upon their arrival, Crystal and Agnes had promptly ordered I carry Sugar into her bedroom and to then get out, as demonic energy would hamper their abilities to figure out why she isn't waking up. They shoved a huge chunk of burning sage in my face and Crystal muttered the words "unclean" and "filthy demon".

Unclean? I wash this scrubby, miscreant mortal body every day and ensure his skin is doused in organic shower soaps and lotions twice a day. Better than the sweaty Birkenstock, sage smelling odour which follows that old crone around.

Culum watches Dahlia leave with absent curiosity before returning his focus to me, "I don't know what to tell you other than…

there's been a lot of rumours going around and there's some higher ups who are getting twitchy."

"About what?"

"Well, for one," Culum looks over at me with mischief in his eyes. "They are wondering where the hell you've been the last couple of months."

"It took this long to realise I wasn't there," I clutch my chest, feigning disappointment. "I'm almost hurt."

"What can I say?" he tilts the beer bottle to his lips. "The paperwork was beginning to pile up."

I look towards the door when I hear the creak of floorboards from Esme's bedroom and the mumbles of hushed voices.

"I know I shouldn't ask but," he sucks in a breath. "The witchling."

"Don't," I snarl, gripping the whisky glass tightly.

"Boss," he continues. "I know it's not my place to say but-"

"Then don't."

With that, he snaps his mouth shut.

I don't want to pull at that thread right now.

Agnes wanders in, her usually flamboyant demeanour dampened, no doubt by trying to patch up Sugar.

Both Culum and I stand, and I stamp down the memory of seeing Esme on that shoreline, bereft of her usual sparkle. It just felt wrong.

"She's resting," Agnes says wearily, pushing her clammy hair from her sweaty forehead. "We mended her broken bones and stopped the bleeding, but…"

"But?" my voice comes out strangled.

"She won't wake," Agnes looks at me sadly. "We tried everything. Spells, potions, candles and crystals… but still… she won't wake up."

I barge past Agnes making my way into the bedroom, where Crystal and Dahlia are both waving strange large twigs around Esme's still body.

"What the fuck are those meant to do?" I point at the branches.

"Cleanse the air of evil spirits," Dahlia balances on a chair above the bed, looking inches away from either falling on top of Sugar or toppling out the window. "Apparently."

Culum peers around behind me, regarding the strange scene, "Is it working?"

"Evidently not," Crystal narrows her eyes, her lips pursed tight in frustration. "You two are still able to enter."

"What's up your ass, witch?" Culum snorts.

Crystal bristles, "Esme has been returned to us in a state of unconsciousness. There's even more dead witches in the Highlands. It appears that wherever you go," she waves a bony hand in my direction. "Death follows."

"Huh," Culum steps around me into the room. "Damn sight catchier than that 'live, laugh, love' shit that gets tossed about all over the place."

"You shouldn't be able to cross the threshold!" Crystal points down at the line of salt along the doorway entrance.

"Wow, weird," I step over the salt as well. "It's almost like this is all bullshit. Maybe I should have taken Esme to a hospital? She'd be awake by now."

"The reason the salt isn't working is because she," Crystal points down at Sugar, "is blocking the Magick. Somehow her will is overpowering our spells."

"But she's unconscious?" Culum arches an eyebrow. "How would she be able to stop your Magick when she's comatosed?"

"I don't think she's really asleep," Crystal looks down at Sugar. "All of the spells we did should have woken her. It's more like her consciousness is bound."

"For fuck's sake this sounds like bollocks," I push past the old bat and march to the side of the bed. The summer sun shimmers down on her like she's a glitter-covered statue of an angel. "Why is she still covered in this golden shit?"

"We tried to rub it off," Dahlia sighs, her voice tired. "But every time we do, we're stopped."

"Stopped?" I arch an eyebrow, "Stopped by what?"

Neither of them answer me, but they exchange a nervous look.

I give her shoulder a small shake, "Rise and shine, Witchling! Those strawberry daiquiris won't drink themselves!"

I suddenly reel backwards, winded as if I've been punched in the stomach by an invisible fist. "The fuck was that?"

"That," Dahlia looks down at the pink haired sleeping beauty, "was Ez."

"How the hell did she do that?" I ask once I get air back into my lungs.

"The same way that she's not able to wake up," Crystal continues to waft the branch around the room.

I reach for the sleeping witch again and I'm shoved back. A

326

sensation I remember from the last time I was manhandled by an unseen force. To my surprise, it appears everyone is affected, and we are all dragged out and unceremoniously thrown into the hallway. The door snips shut with a haughty click, and I hear the key turn in the lock.

"Huh," Culum rubs at the back of his head which had smashed into the wall. "Didn't think witches usually had that much power."

Agnes peers at us from the living room regarding us with wariness, "No," she rings her hands. "Most witches don't."

"So, what do we do now?" I try to turn the doorknob to the bedroom and am met with an electric shock. "We can't just stand around here. She could be in danger!"

"Whatever power is in that room," Crystal looks at the closed door, "has made it abundantly clear we are not to meddle. It will let us enter once it is ready."

"What kind of apathetic bullshit is that?" I sneer at her. "I might as well sit and watch paint dry. We need to get in there and-"

Another punch to the gut and I drop to my knees. This body is by no means weak so to be left doubled over by an unseen force is more than a little disconcerting.

"Alright," I hold up a beseeching hand to whatever is beating the shit out of me like it's their favourite new hobby. "Alright! Fine, I'll go sit in the other room and wait like a good little demon."

"I'll whip up a batch of tea," Agnes calls from the kitchen.

"Fuck that," I rub at my bruised ribs. "I'm finishing that whisky."

It's 2am by the time Agnes and Crystal vacate the flat, claiming there's nothing more they can do, and they'll be back in the morning.

Dahlia had quickly followed suit by retiring to her bedroom after she'd thrown blankets at Culum and me.

Fortunately, I'm not tired. Demons rarely need sleep; we do on occasion, but it's more for entertainment or when we need to mimic human behaviour. The last time I did sleep was with Sugar in the cottage. Something twists in my chest, and I rub at it absently wondering if it's Finn's feelings for the witch or mine. I rub at the spot and feel the pain twist like my heart is in a vice.

"You ok, boss?" Culum asks from the other side of the sofa, a pile of discarded bottles surrounding him like fallen soldiers.

"Fine, just a weird pain in my chest," I rub at the spot again.

327

"Like heartburn?"

"Maybe," the twist tightens. "Fuck."

"Boss," Culum leans forward and picks at the label on the beer bottle. It's a habit he does when he's nervous. I've seen him do it countless times. "Do you think it might be because of-"

"Her?" I cut in. "No, I don't."

"No," he frowns. "The possession. You've been inhabiting that body for months, for longer and longer stretches of time. I know it's one of the perks of being a demon- stealing skin-suits for test drives but," he peels a long strip of paper from the bottle. "But that's what it's meant to be, a test drive. Not a permanent residence. I remember what you told me years back, you said things can go bad. And... and the amount of time you've been in this boy's body... do you think you might be starting to feel the effects?"

I stand and walk to the window to look up at the moonless night sky.

"What kind of effects?" I rub at the spot again, willing it to go away.

"You once told me," he says slowly, "that if a demon inhabits a human body for too long, the essences can merge."

"Merge?" I dimly recall the conversation we had all those years ago. A demon and human soul are made up of different components, like oil and water, the two could never mix but after prolonged exposure, they can kind of emulsify. The lines begin to blur.

"Do you think you and Finn might be," he clears his throat. "What I mean is, do you think there might be some crossover?"

I sit back down on the sofa, picking up my whisky and swill the amber liquid. It could be happening. I have been maintaining a tight leash on the body, squashing down any of the mortal's attempts at control but he has been getting stronger.

There is also this strange pervasive sentimentality. Sentimentality towards her. Could that all be because of Finn and his feelings? There is something... there... for the pink haired witchling. The blur of lines would make sense. And if so, this new development is unsettling. It would mean Culum is right, which is disconcerting, but it means the side effects of this possession are finally rearing their ugly head.

I stretch my memory back to the horror stories I was told centuries ago about possessions going bad, but I'm drawing a blank on the end result. I think it involved an ex-colleague of mine, Solemn Screams? I think that was his name. Ugh. Why did dear old Lucy think that alliteration in demon names would help inspire fear?

I swig down the remains of my scotch, "Do you remember what happened to Sol in the end?"

Culum slumps back in his seat, "Oh that poor bastard," he peels another strip of label from the bottle. "Wasn't he, erm, killed?"

I nod grimly. Culum shifts uncomfortably in his seat as he realises why I'm asking.

"Aye, killed," I tilt my head back to stare at the ceiling. "Possession. Him and his human host, they'd rotted alive."

Chapter Thirty - Eight

Esme

As I fall from the turret, a sense of peace wraps around me like a blanket. Wait, no, that's not metaphorical, there is actually a golden blanket encircling me. I feel warm, safe, loved and protected. Which is handy, because the ground rushing towards me doesn't look soft or pillowy.

Stop worrying, the voice says. *Sleep.*

Wait, what? I don't want to sleep, I would like to stay awake, please!

I manage to turn my head slightly and see the blur of a shape that looks like Nox moving, no, sprinting, towards me.

The golden blanket swaddles me tighter and my mind goes blissfully blank. I'm not asleep but I'm so calm, even as I realise, I can no longer move my arms or legs. Or open my eyes.

The strangely comforting blanket cradles me on the ground, at least, I think it's the ground? The falling feeling seems to have stopped.

There's the scent of sandalwood, autumn leaves and ambrette. Nox. He's beside me. I can feel his warmth as he searches my face.

Nox! I scream in my head, wishing I'd somehow developed telepathy. *Nox! I'm awake! I'm alright!*

"Fuck," he murmurs, barely above a whisper and I feel his presence move away.

I try to wriggle free of my blanket prison but it's hard to summon up the energy to fight against this overwhelming cosiness.

I hear gentle splashes from the Loch, like something is breaking the water's surface.

"Do you need something?" I recognise Calder's voice. He

sounds like he'd rather be anywhere else.

"I need to get back to Edinburgh," Nox sounds like he's panicking. Weird. "Right now. I need to get her to the witches to make sure she's ok-"

Scents of moss and citrus flood my nostrils and I feel the mildest touch of ice-cold fingers across my cheek which I wish I could squirm away from.

Calder's voice sounds closer, "She looks like she'd be better placed at a hospital?"

I feel a cold weight press against my chest. "That's a pity. She lives." Muir sounds disappointed.

I try to move again, but it just causes the blanket to tighten. I'm surprised that the squeezing hasn't cut off my breathing yet as drowsiness tries to take hold again.

Nox, I have to stay awake for Nox. He's worried about me, and I need him to know that I'm ok.

I'm dimly aware that he and Calder are still bickering. Apparently, there's no love lost between Kelpies and Demons. Or maybe it's just between these two? The atmosphere between them is so cold it could cause frostbite.

Wow, it's so weird not being able to feel my toes. Maybe all this swaddling is cutting off my circulation?

Silence falls and then Calder says, "You care for her."

"What? No," Nox sounds utterly appalled. "I need her healed so that she can help me find the grimoire..."

Something stings in my chest which feels like pain. I register his words, but the blanket seems to soothe the hurt. The grimoire? What grimoire?

"You do," Muir says. "You have feelings for the pink witch."

I hope to Goddess I am not blushing. Not that there's much I can do about it. I'm just stuck lying here, trapped in a giant magickal marshmallow.

Besides, what do I care if he does or doesn't have feelings for me? I don't even like him.

Now who's lying, the voice in my head teases.

Nox and Calder resume their bickering and after a few more minutes it seems like Calder acquiesces to Nox's demands. How is a Kelpie going to transport us back to Edinburgh? If we're expected to hold our breath, I'm screwed. I can't do anything other than just lie here in this weird fugue state.

Calder lets out a groan and sighs, "After this, we're even, Nox."

Wait, I try to telepathically shoot at Nox. *How are we meant to get back we-*

That strange weightless feeling returns. Like being in a lift that drops a little too quickly. I feel the smallest prick of panic in my chest that is quickly swallowed up as the sense of calm swells and urges me to sleep, only this time, I don't have the strength, or the inclination, to fight it.

I finally manage to wrestle free from sleep, which feels a lot like battling a slippery eel in a bouncy castle.

I hear raised voices around me, but when I try to open my eyes, they still feel like they're glued shut.

The shouts grow louder, and I recognise the voices of Nox and Dahlia, who are arguing near me. No, not near me. Around me.

"How the hell did she do that?" Nox demands, he sounds wheezy and pissed off.

"The same way that she's not able to wake up," a haughty voice answers, and I realise it's Crystal.

Why the hell is Crystal here? And why does everyone sound so pissy? They all need to spend some time wrapped up like a Magickal burrito.

They are too distracting, the voice says. *They need to leave.*

Speaking of things overstaying their welcome, I answer dryly. *You're still here.*

Time is running out and we need to speak plainly, the voice says. *They need to go and then we shall talk.*

Fat chance of that happening! I can't even open my eyes, let alone usher anyone anywhere!

I can, the voice says smugly.

There's clattering around me and I hear a door locking.

There, the voice proudly exclaims. *Now we're alone.*

Great, that's not creepy at all!

So now the voice in my head can Magickally manhandle people. Wow, I could so easily freak out.

Ok, so what now? I ask into the void of blackness.

The truth, the voice answers, as the void swallows me whole.

The blur of shapes and shadows begin to emerge from the darkness. Movement passes in front me, and there is the sound of multiple footsteps.

The blurs become clear, and I see Mum, Agnes and Crystal.

We're back in the pink house. Only now the ramshackle

building is no longer barren; it's full of life. Flowers, climbing vines and exotic plants grow around the room. I feel like I've stepped into a garden. They continue their conversation, oblivious to my presence.

"Can someone ever be ready for something like this?" Crystal asks.

"She'll be my daughter," Mum answers. "She'll be ready."

Agnes and Crystal kneel beside her, and I see what she's holding when I saw the vision earlier. A very large, and very sharp, rock. It glitters in the sunlight, a mixture of blush pinks and emerald greens that dance across the stone's surface. The edges are so jagged the rock looks like it could be a dagger. Crystal moves to tug the stone from Mum's grasp, but her attempt is unsuccessful.

"I have suffered too many losses," Mum says quietly, tears perch on her lower lashes as she looks down. "So many. The Goddess will understand."

"Eve," Crystal's face is pinched with tension. "No one can question the grief you've experienced, but I must ask, is this the path you truly want to take? It's not natural-"

"Natural?" Mum's head whips up viciously. "I should be able to do the most natural thing: to create life and I can't do that? I've had so much heartbreak; I can barely stand it. I deserve to be happy, to be complete and hold my child in my arms. To be a mother. It's all I've ever wanted."

She'd never told me about the miscarriages and hearing this breaks my heart. She looks at the shimmering rock in her hand, "I've tried everything. All the herbal teas, fertility spells, even entrusted my body to the hands of Mundane science," tears fall from her eyes. "This is my last chance to have a child of my own."

"But this is dark Magick, Eve," Crystal warns. "You're using the essence of something incredibly old and powerful."

"As I already said," Mum reaches behind her and produces a jewel encrusted dagger. "I am well aware of the risks."

Agnes and Crystal both shift uncomfortably as Mum places the stone on the ground and raises her hand. I take another step forward as she slices a large cut into her palm and holds the wound over the stone.

"This blood is my blood. This blood is your blood," Mum says quietly. "Sanguis meus, sanguis meus est. Hic sanguis tuus est sanguis."

"Sanguis meus, sanguis meus est," Agnes and Crystal repeat. "Hic sanguis tuus est sanguis."

More blood trickles onto the stone, creating a swirling mixture of crimson, jade and blush.

"Da mihi potestatem huius crystalli et novam vitam secum affer," Mum chants, her voice lower and steady as Crystal and Agnes repeat her words.

Give me the power of this crystal and bring new life with it.

"Vita nova," they chorus. "Vita nova."

New life.

The stone begins to glow, beneath the droplets of blood and golden rays begin to bloom from the rock.

"Profer vitam novam."

Bring forth new life.

"Deam precor omnium lucis et umbrae matrem," the rock grows brighter and begins to shake on the bed of flowers beneath it. "Profer vitam novam."

I pray to the Goddess, the mother of all those in light and shadow. Bring forth new life.

The rock explodes into a dust so fine it catches in the wind and permeates the air with golden glitter. The force of the little explosion creates a crater in the earth, transforming the leaves and flowers into a confetti of charred plants and smoke.

"Did it work?" Agnes asks, looking confused.

"Whatever had been trapped in the stone is now released," Crystal's voice is full of concern.

The scene dissolves in front of me and I'm thrown into a new space. A space I know so well.

The enchanted bookshelves bloom with midnight blue roses and the charms and crystals shimmer from the dim streetlight outside. It's so empty and quiet; the only noise is my pounding heartbeat.

I'm standing in the shop. My shop. I look down and realise two things: I'm gripping the necklace, and my feet are bare and bloody.

My knees buckle as a wave of nausea sweeps through me.

"How did I get here?" I whisper.

I led you here, the voice answers.

"Why?" My voice is sore and hoarse, like I've been screaming.

Because it's time you understood.

"Understand what?" I spin around, looking at the shelves I've traced my hands over countless times. "You've given me fragments. Snapshots. Nothing of any substance. You keep saying you'll show me the truth, but I still don't understand anything!"

334

Frustrated tears flood my vision, "I don't understand anything. You keep showing me visions of Mum. Doing… what… I don't know, a spell?"

She wanted you so much, the voice says. *She was willing to tamper with Magicks she didn't truly understand. That by releasing the power of the stone, it would allow her to have a child. But what it did was-*

"Esme?"

I whirl around to see a tall figure in the open doorway. His form cloaked in shadow.

I hiccup as a sob bubbles over. Whatever the voice had been about to say has been silenced.

I inhale and recognise the scent as demonic, but he doesn't smell like Nox. He smells like cardamom and aniseed.

Danger, the voice warns.

"Who are you?" I demand.

"A friend," the demon steps inside, his obsidian eyes stare at me.

"You're not my friend," I take a step back. Away. I need to get away from whoever, or whatever, the fuck this is.

The stranger chuckles and it makes my skin crawl.

He walks forward, mirroring my progress, "I never said I was *your* friend." He takes another step towards me in this strange backwards dance.

I accidentally bump into the table of candles, sending them tumbling across the chequerboard floor.

"I must say I'm surprised," the stranger lifts a shoulder in a half shrug. Dark clouds begin to encircle his feet, snaking around his legs like serpents. "Who knew little Esmerelda would grow up to be so…" his grin widens as he licks his lower lips lasciviously and I suppress a shudder. "Striking. I take it by the look on your face you were expecting someone else," he winks at me, "Noctis has been a busy boy up here."

A flush creeps across my skin, "I don't know what you mean."

"Oh, I think you do," his fingers trailing across the candles. "His scent is all over you."

I feel my back bump against the door, and I reach behind me for the handle.

"Tell Noctis, Eli says it's time to stop this foolishness and to come home," he offers me a congenial wave. I manage to get the door open and take a backwards step outside. "Oh, and Esmerelda, do be careful on the way home. I hear there's some terrible things

335

happening to witches. It would be a shame to see someone make a mess of your pretty face. Best hurry back, or there will be Hell to pay."

I step back onto the street and as the shop door closes Eli disappears into a cloud of smoke.

"Huh," I mutter. "I always thought seeing someone do that would be cheesy, but nope. It's just terrifying."

I shakily lock the shop and quickly turn to run up the hill.

Eli's warning hangs above me and I pick up my pace, hoping that his threat was just meant to scare me. But the nagging dread continues to expand, and I know I'm just trying to hide behind my optimism.

I push my body up the incline, passing by all the closed coffee shops and tourist traps. I have absolutely no fucking clue what time it is... but there's no one around, so it's either very early or very late.

Hurry, the voice in my head urges. *You need to go faster!*

I'm trying! I snap back. *I'm not really dressed for it!*

I look down at my Disney princess pyjamas and wonder who'd had the misfortune of having to dress me. Please for the love of Goddess not Nox!

My running is also hampered by my braless predicament. The absence of a trusty over-the-shoulder-boulder-holder means I'm in real danger of giving myself either two black eyes or causing some very interesting bruises!

I continue to sprint until I see my building up ahead, the moon shining brightly above it like a beacon. I catch sight of something moving in the shadows of one of the alleyways opposite. It's a cat...? Although it'd have to be a pretty big cat.

I shove the thought away; I push open my front gate and nearly tumble into the hydrangea when I see the front door is open.

I climb the stairs and find the door to my flat is ajar. I push it further, "Dahls?" I call out into the darkened hallway. "Nox?"

I tip toe inside, "Anyone here?"

More silence.

I walk into the living room to find it in complete disarray. Broken plates, pillows and blankets thrown around; the space in utter chaos.

"Ink?" I whisper. "Are you in here, baby?"

I walk towards my room, wondering if the kitten has taken refuge under my bed when pain explodes in the back of my head. Red spots burst in my vision.

Is this you? I ask the voice. *There are easier ways of*

disclosing information that don't involve knocking me unconscious you know-

I hear a sickening crack as another strike lands on my skull but I'm too concussed to feel the pain. The red spots in my eyes erupt like volcanos just as I crash to the floor.

Chapter Thirty ~ Nine

Nox

Something hits my foot and I flail a leg to get it to go away. I rarely sleep, so this is a novel experience.

Another thump, this one shoots pain up my leg.

"Cease your infernal tapping," I grumble, kicking out in retaliation, but my boot only meets thin air.

"For fucks sake..." a female voice grumbles. I hear footsteps move away and then return. A cold liquid is splashed into my face, and it jolts me awake. I sit up to the sight of Dahlia holding an empty glass of water.

"What was that for?" I snarl as I stomp over to the kitchen sink and grab a dishtowel. Which is pink and covered in red hearts. The colour was bad enough, but the hearts are overkill.

"You were asleep," she snaps.

"What's so wrong with me catching a little shut eye?" I dab at my shirt, fortunately it's salvageable. If it had been red wine she'd be on the wrath-end of a very soggy, pissed off demon.

"Ez is missing!" She puts the glass on the sink, her eyes wide with fear. "I went to the bathroom, her bedroom door was open and she was gone."

I throw the towel into the sink, "You should have led with that?!"

I barge past her and storm towards Esme's bedroom. Her pastel bed is abandoned. Only the faint scent of shortbread and sugar echo in the room.

I run a hand through my hair, "Shit!"

"Fucking aye, shit," Dahlia calls from the living room. "She's gone and I have no idea where she could be!"

I hear stirring from the living room and Culum staggers to us,

338

"What's happening?"

"Esme is missing!" Dahlia snaps at him and he has the sense to not come out with one of his usual smartass responses.

"Have you tried calling her?" I shout as I return to the living room.

"Fat lot of good that'll do when her phone is on charge in the bedroom," Dahlia snorts, pulling on a leather jacket. "You go to Crystal and Agnes'."

I furrow my brow, "Why?"

"Because," she pulls her hair out from under the collar of her jacket, "I'm shit at locator spells and those two, despite their age and stuffiness, are pretty handy in a crisis."

I open my mouth to argue, and she holds up a hand to stop me.

"Nox," she warns. "We need to find her, if you care about her. Help!"

Care. Do I care? However much my logic screams at me not to, yes, I do care. The four-letter word unlocks something in my mind. I didn't even realise I was still capable of feeling that emotion for anyone since Sarah. I want her... here with me. Safe. Protected. The thought of her alone in the night... vulnerable. It makes me want to rip the world apart to find her. Yes, I do care.

"Ok, fine," I make my way towards the front door as Dahlia trails behind me. "Where are you going to go?"

"The shop, the park," she grabs her bag from the coat rack, "see if she might have gone there..."

"Is that safe for you to do that alone?" I ask. "There's obviously someone out there murdering witches?"

"I'll go with her," Culum follows behind us as he rubs sleep from his eyes. "Problem solved."

Dahlia studies him before rolling her eyes, "Fine. But don't talk to me."

Culum chuckles softly and gives her a mocking salute.

Dahlia looks at me, "You go get Crystal and Agnes." She walks to the counter and begins scribbling. "Go to Crystal's first then to Agnes. Stay with Agnes and we'll meet you there-"

"What if she comes back here?" I ask as Dahlia hands me the paper.

"There's a spell that can alert me if Ez comes back."

"How long will that take to do?" I open the front door and step out into the stairwell. If Sugar is out there, alone in the dark... who knows what kind of trouble she'll run into.

A ghost of a smile traces her lips, "Already did it. As soon as I realised Ez was missing," she shoves Culum through the door and locks up the flat behind us. "If she comes back, I'll know."

I look down at the scrap of paper, "These streets are miles away from each other!"

She smirks at me before clambering for the stairs, "Good thing you're a demon, hopefully your stamina can hold up   !"

I grumble as we head out; the streets are as silent as a graveyard.

Crystal's flat is forty minutes from here, but I can make it in an even fifteen.

Dahlia and Culum begin jogging down the hill towards the shop.

I turn on my heel and sprint in the opposite direction.

Just as I pass by some crumbling old terrace, I feel myself being shoved into the passenger seat. I push back and take control again.

"You really do pick excellent times to try and grow a backbone," I growl. "Pipe down, Finnster. I'm trying to save our girl."

I mentally kick myself. His girl. Not our girl. And most definitely not, my girl.

Fuck only knows how long she's been on her own out here. Hopefully, she's at the shop, or fallen asleep on a park bench… or she could have been hurt or murdered?

I pick up my pace, passing by a blur of pastel houses, their colours are as inconsequential as dust against the inky blackness of the night.

Another mental push. Finn is one stubborn little bastard tonight.

"Look," I continue to sprint, "if you want to make sure she's safe, the best way to do that is sit back and keep me in control. We both know, if anyone's going to make sure she's alright it's going to be me."

Finn gives another petulant push before he relents and slinks back into the shadows of our mind.

I look between the scrap of paper and the number on the door, I shove open the gate and jam the buzzer to 4a.

After a couple more pushes of the button there is a click and a muffled, "Hello?"

"Crystal?"

"Who is this?" the bristly witch sounds more alert when I say her name.

340

"It's Nox."

"The demon?"

"How many other Nox's do you know?"

"What do you want?" The hostility from the little speaker is palpable.

"Sug- Esme," I correct. "Esme is missing."

"Missing? When we left, she was comatosed and barricaded in her bedroom-"

"Well, she decided to wake up and go for a wander."

"Hecate's sake," disappointment bristles through the speaker. "I need two minutes-"

I bite my tongue at her patronising tone. Now is not the time to lecture her that I am hundreds of years older than her. I need her on my side.

"We need to go to Agnes'," I interrupt her mid-sentence. "You don't by any chance have a car or anything like that do you?"

"Not a car as such," she answers ominously. "As I said, I need two minutes," she says just as she hangs up.

I pace up and down the path and keep a wary eye on the gaudy porch ornaments. There's another gnome here. However, the cheery painted grin doesn't waver, and his gaze doesn't spark with the same child-like wonder as the late Salacious had possessed.

The door opens and Crystal appears, dressed in a brown poncho over pyjamas covered in rubber ducks. Charming. She drags a huge burgundy holdall and a large contraption over the narrow threshold.

I move to help, but she quickly bats me away with an inpatient hand, "I may be old, dear boy, but I'm not an invalid."

I back up but keep my hand outstretched.

She arches an eyebrow.

"Please may I have the keys to your car?" I bite out.

She lets out a small chuckle, "My dear boy," she tugs again at the weird amalgamation of metal and rubber through the doorway. "I don't have a car! No, no, they are not economical and they're terrible for the environment."

I shove a hand through my hair, and fight the urge to scalp myself, "Maybe I can carry you and we can run up there?" Carrying the old crone, along with her massive bag, will make this take twice as long.

"So, there are some things that even Demon's don't know about?" She snorts self-righteously, "No need to carry me; this is a tandem bike!"

Riding a tandem bike uphill with someone who smells like boiled herbs and natural deodorant is going to be a new torture when I get back to work.

I'm not sure what the impact would be on women, but for men this will work a treat. My bollocks feel like I'm being molested by a power drill and for the last ten minutes I keep willing for numbness to take over, but so far, it's just fucking agony.

"How much longer to go?" I manage to grind out as the saddle makes me its bitch.

"Another fifteen minutes," Crystal puffs out as she pushes the pedals down.

For an old crone, she sure can cycle.

"Wonderful," I mutter sarcastically. "Hopefully I'll still be intact when we arrive."

Crystal chuckles in front of me, "Intact? Aren't you possessing that poor human boy's body?"

"It's a rental," I grumble.

She sniffs, "It's rotting."

"What is?" I manage to ask. I feel like a mallet is being smashed into my nether regions with the venom and vigour of a coked-up kangaroo on a bouncy castle.

"That poor Mundane body you're stealing," her tone is drenched in judgement.

"Borrowing," I correct.

I feel a twist in my mind as Finn shifts belligerently.

"Don't start that again," I warn him. "Unless you fancy taking over and having your balls pummelled. If so, be my guest."

Finn slinks back into the shadows.

I chuckle, "Coward."

Crystal turns and gives me a wary glance, "The lines are blurring, aren't they?"

I clear my throat, "Possibly."

She shakes her head at me before looking at the road, "Trust me, no good can come from this possession. The more intertwined you two become, the harder it will be to separate."

We navigate around a particularly precarious looking pothole, "I know. But it's rare for it to have any real side effects."

"The longer possession continues the more the demon and mortal will become tangled. If they are, then-"

"Let me guess," I interrupt, "terrible things will happen?"

She turns to look at me again, a grave expression on her

face, "Both souls will eventually rot and decay."

"I've heard all this before," I scoff and try to avoid thinking about Sol, "and it rarely happens."

But then again, how long do possessions usually last? There's not any guidelines for prolonged stays. Just ominous warnings.

"If it is so infrequent, dear boy," Crystal shoots me another wary glance, "how would witches know about it? Judging by the state and smell of you, it's already taking effect."

I lift an arm and inhale. I smell like my cologne, L'occitane Karité Corsé Eau de Parfum. No rot, whatsoever. I take another sniff. Maybe it is my imagination, but there is the faint hint of something... akin to spoiling fruit. I lower my arm.

"That's bullshit," I grumble, I continue to peddle and try to ignore the seeds of doubt that permeate my mind.

We cycle in silence and Crystal keeps her head forward for most of the ride, except for a couple of wary glances back at me.

Once I get off the testicle torture device, I surreptitiously check that I am still intact as Crystal places the bike up against the wall.

She checks her watch and presses the buzzer. After a couple of minutes there's a clatter through the speaker.

"It's four o'clock in the morning," Agnes grumbles.

"Well aware of that, Agnes," Crystal snips back. "We have a problem."

"What took you so long?" Agnes says. "I've been waiting for you to arrive."

Crystal glares at me, "We got here as fast as we could."

"At great risk to my nether-regions I may add," I bite out and Crystal and Agnes, both give me a collective shush.

"It might be easier to have this discussion inside," Crystal says to the speaker.

"That's a shame," I deadpan. "All the best meetings happen on a fucking pavement!"

The buzzer sounds and we're granted entry into the abode. We climb a narrow flight of circular stairs and Agnes is hovering at an open doorway, wearing a neon green dressing gown with huge rollers in her hair. She holds a finger to her mouth and beckons us forward.

"What do you mean 'waiting for us to arrive'?" I ask as soon as Agnes closes the door. Her hallway is just as chaotic and colourful as the woman herself. Blood red walls with mustard tiles along with a

343

sky-blue chandelier that I must duck to avoid hitting. This apartment is an assault on the eyes. And I thought Esme's flat was bad.

"I had a vision over an hour ago," Agnes shuffles around me and I realise she's wearing a floor length kimono that drags along behind her. "I saw poor Esme, on the floor. Wounded and surrounded by shadows and something… demonic," she stops to look cautiously at me. I'm getting tired of everyone looking at me like I'm about to drown a bag of puppies. "Where were you?"

"Asleep," I baulk. "Stop looking at me like that."

Agnes shakes her head, "It was demonic."

Crystal narrows her eyes at me.

"I was asleep," I pinch the bridge of my nose. "Stop looking at me like I did something. I'm not the only demon-" I halt my tirade. If it was a demon, then that can only mean one thing: they know I'm here.

Silence hangs between us all before Agnes huffs out an exasperated sigh, "Let's tackle one thing at a time, shall we?"

I kneel at the table and place my hand on the orb, but Crystal slaps my hand away.

I raise an eyebrow at her, "I thought I needed to do this as well?"

"You're a demon, dear," Agnes explains kindly. "Your essence isn't conducive to Magick. Crystal and I need to combine our power to try and find out where Esme is."

"So, what shall I do?" I lean back on my ankles. "Just sit here and look pretty?"

"You could make us a pot of tea," Crystal waves offhandedly, as if shooing away a fly. "Nettle and bergamot to help wake up our mental acuity."

"Great," I stand, "I nearly lost my manhood just so I can be a bloody tea maid!"

"If you could make the tea in silence," Crystal calls, as I make my way into what I assume is the kitchen, "that would be preferable."

"Patronising old windbags," I mutter quietly, hoping that super-hearing is not one of the powers Crystal possesses. Once I finish brewing up a pot of what smells like pond water, I return to find that they're still clutching the orb, muttering something hushed and incomprehensible.

"Is that thing meant to be doing something?" I place the pot and mugs down next to them, haphazardly shoving the crystals and cards out of the way.

"It should," Agnes frowns. Both she and Crystal are wearing the same frustrated expressions and sweat beads on their wrinkled foreheads.

"Buuuuut?" I pour the tea into the mugs.

"Something," Agnes mutters. "No, someone is blocking us."

"So," I sit down on the mustard armchair opposite the table, "unblock it?"

"It doesn't work like that, dear," Agnes says softly, but I hear the irritation in her voice. "It's strange, I could see Esme so clearly earlier… and now. Now it's like someone is hiding her."

"Maybe when Dahlia gets here, she can help?" I offer, after all three witches must be better than two.

Agnes shakes her head, "I can't find her either."

I stand, "Well this is fucking useless. I'm going to go to the shop and see if they are there and-"

"Wait," Crystal's voice is cold and detached. "The power that is cloaking them, it's akin to your aura. Something dark and ominous."

"I don't know whether to be flattered or insulted," I halt in the doorway. "Are you saying something is blocking your ability to see them?"

They both give me a small nod. Agnes gives me a look of apprehension, "Nox, I must warn you, the power that is cloaking them. It's the darkest energy I have ever felt-"

"Ok, now I'm definitely insulted!" I cross my arms, "I'm filled to the brim with evil energy! Ask any of my colleagues at work, I never refill the kettle and I was nominated runner up for BDE!"

They both look at me with puzzled expressions.

"Big Demonic Energy," I explain. "Look, don't worry. I'll go check the shop and then head straight back. You keep trying with your strange globe thing, drink your tea and I'll be back here in no time."

"Nox," Agnes clambers to her feet with difficulty, nearly tripping over her kimono. "Whatever it is, it's dangerous."

"Not as dangerous as me," I snarl as I open the door and head back into the night.

Chapter Forty

Esme

Wake up! The voice in my head screams for what has to be the tenth time.

In a minute, I grumble back.

No, now! Wake up!

My eyelids snap open, and I realise I'm lying on my front but something seems odd. I'm not in my squishy, comfortable bed; I'm laid on a hard cold plank and my hands and feet are tied. My head is still swimming from the blow. I manage to look around enough to discover I'm somewhere dark, dank and definitely not my flat.

I try to wriggle my arms, but the strange binds tighten like vices and I let out a hiss of pain.

"Oh good," a male voice next to me says. "You're awake."

I blow my hair out of my face and see the shape of a figure in front of me, dressed in black.

"Look, Mr," I try to sound loud and authoritative. Which is tricky when my head feels as loose and floppy as overcooked spaghetti. "I don't know who you are, or why I'm tied onto this... well, it feels like a table, but if you can untie me and let me go, I'd be more than willing to put all this business behind us!"

The figure chuckles darkly before moving out of my eyeline. I take the opportunity to look around. The exposed bricks and the echoing of my kidnapper's footsteps suggests I must be in some kind of cellar.

The sound of metal clangs and I can't stop my brain running through the unpleasant possibilities of what it is that he's fiddling with. The footsteps return.

"Why are you doing this?" Panic surges up inside me. "Just, let me go, we can talk and-"

346

Another laugh, ominous and foreboding, "Now why would I want to do that?"

Shadows move at my side, and I turn my head to look at him, but all I can see is his torso. I strain to look up, but the most I can see is a pair of very large, very strong shoulders.

When he kneels down, and I see his face all my insides turn to stone.

Mark's handsome features are contorted into disgust, "Believe me, Ez. Part of me had wished that the rumours hadn't been true."

"Wait, what?" I buck against the constraints. "What rumours?"

"That you followed in your mother's wicked footsteps," he tilts his head and looks at me with curiosity. "You're a witch."

I try to move again but the welt in my head screams at me to lie still.

"Did you kidnap me?" I ask, already aware of the answer.

Just keep him talking, the voice in my head says. *Until…*

Until Nox gets here, I answer.

Mark nods, a manic gleam in his eyes, "I had to break into your flat and make it look convincing."

"But-but," I struggle for breath, "I have protection wards. You shouldn't have been able to come inside."

"I had some help to sort that little predicament out," he answers darkly.

"But why?" I keep my eyes trained on his face, trying to stop my vision spinning from the concussion. "I thought we were friends?"

"Ez, we *are* friends," he answers softly. "That's why we are doing it this way. I could have killed you back at the flat, but I want to help you. To help you on your path to redemption." His eyes take on a dream-like quality as a manic smile spreads across his face. "For the longest time I just thought that you were misunderstood. A little strange, not able to fit in with the other kids in the village. But then you came back, and I saw it. I saw the evil coursing through you. And part of me had hoped that you'd heed the warnings."

"Warnings?"

"I killed that old crone," Mark tilts his head and watches me. "Then I set fire to your cottage. I mean," he laughs manically. "I even killed your fucking cat, but it doesn't change anything. I thought the warnings would make you stop. Make you change what you are. Who you are inside," he strokes the knife down my cheek. "You're wicked, Esme, and I have to help you purge the evil."

I choke on a sob. He did all these things. These horrible

347

things. He killed Snow, my one link to my mother. All for what? Some archaic belief that witches are evil? He's insane.

"I have to do it," he traces the knife over the curve of my mouth as he licks his lower lip. He's looking at me like I'm a prize, like he wishes it were his lips that brushed against mine instead. I have to suppress a shudder.

"Do what?" I manage to croak out, staring into the face of my childhood friend who now looks like a stranger to me. Those warm eyes, which had always consoled and comforted me are gone. Now what glares back at me is cold hatred.

"I have to cleanse your body before I can cleanse your spirit," he mutters as he holds up a very long dagger.

"Wh-what do you mean 'cleanse my body'?" my voice sounds strangely distant.

Mark turns the knife so that it catches the light overhead, "I have to peel away the layers of lies to uncover the truth."

I splutter, "Why don't I like the sound of that?"

"Believe me, Ez," he sounds almost regretful as he stands. "If there was any other way to do this I would but... but this method proves the most successful."

I try to lift my head to see where he's going, but then I feel the fabric of my pyjamas being sliced away, exposing my skin to the cold air.

"What method?" My tone is shrill as panic takes hold.

I feel the trail of the sharp blade against my naked back.

"Flaying," he says quietly. I feel the knife pierce near my spine. It isn't the intense pain of a stab wound, but a sharp and tentative slice. Just when I think it's over, he begins to carve deeper, turning the knife sideways and pushing it beneath my skin. My scream erupts as he peels away a layer of my delicate flesh in a long ribbon.

"Please! Stop!" I sob.

"I wish I could," Mark says, his tone cold and distant.

"Why are you doing this to me?" I tilt my head to see Mark's face inches away from my bloodied back.

"You're a witch, Ez," he answers with deathly calmness. "The devil's whore. You need to be punished for your wicked ways."

"But I've never done anything to you!" I cry out as tears stream from my eyes. "We played together as kids, we were friends. We are friends!"

"Hell sends its prettiest demons to tempt us," he stabs into my lower back with the dagger and begins the process again. It slices between skin and flesh as he drags the knife upward. "Don't you see, Ez? Once I have cleansed your body, I can then cleanse your soul. Then you can repent your wickedness and you can be free. You will be clean and pure-"

"Mark," I wheeze between pained gasps. This is agony. "I don't know what you think a witch is but... I don't worship the devil. I'm not evil. I love plants and flowers... My favourite movie is 'Enchanted'. I've never hurt anyone or anything. All my mum and I wanted was to make people happy-"

"Your mother," he halts, slamming the knife on the table. "She was Satan's whore, a harlot, a temptress, a practitioner of the Devil's art-"

"She made cookies for the Sunday bake sale in the village," I manage to say through gritted teeth. "She helped old people by buying them groceries! She bandaged your knee when you fell in a bramble hedge. She cared for you, looked after you-"

"All of these were acts to mask her true face," he sneers. "She was Lucifer's concubine. My father taught me the ways of the hunter, how to spot a witch and what to do when you find them. He taught me how to hunt them, how to make them confess and how to cleanse their wicked souls."

I lift my head, ignoring the blinding pain, "Mark, did you..." I suck in a breath. "Did you do something to my mother?"

He leans down and inserts the blade back into the open wound and begins slicing. "Her soul could not be saved."

"What the fuck does that mean?"

"It means," his gaze remains fixed on his bloody task, "that despite our best efforts, we couldn't cleanse her soul and rid her of the evil that inhabited her mortal flesh."

"Who did it?" I twist, ignoring the searing pain in my limbs and back. "Who?"

"My father," Mark answers proudly. "He knew for a long time and had to wait for the opportune moment. Part of being a successful hunter is the planning."

I remember Mark's dad; he was always distant and wary. No matter how much kindness and warmth Mum would try to bestow on the stuffy prick. I had never liked him; he had always been abrupt and rude.

"He's lucky he's dead," I sneer through my tears. "Because I promise you this, Mark, you'll pay for what you've done."

"I have done God's will," he snaps. His calm exterior cracks and the mounting hysteria beneath starts to slip through. "Witch

349

hunters are ordained by God to seek out and punish the wicked."

"You kill anything that you don't understand," I bite out as the knife peels off another sheet of my skin. "Being different doesn't make someone evil. You ignorant bastard. All your lot have ever done is hurt, punish and kill strong people who didn't fit into your little, tiny world view."

He laughs humourlessly, "Spoken like a true heretic!"

"If your God," I gasp through the pain, shutting my eyes to the torture, "condones treating people like this. Then your God is as much of an asshole as you are!"

I feel the knife shake in his hand and I take a second to revel in angering him.

Careful, the voice says. *Tread lightly and bide your time.*

Fuck being careful, I snarl back. *Fuck treading lightly, trying to buy time and wait to be rescued. This isn't some fairytale, and I'm not a frail, useless maiden. Fuck anyone who thinks they can overpower someone and claim they are doing it as a kindness.*

My anger rises and I feel my body begin to shake with righteous rage.

People deserve to be different. I deserve to be different. To take up space with my difference and to Hell with anyone who tries to stop me. And that includes you. I am as the Goddess made me. I am the daughter of wise-women, sister to all outcasts and the eccentrics. I am a witch.

Fire crackles beneath my skin. That same fire which I have tried to temper and squash down. But now I no longer fight against the heat and flames. It flows through my veins as naturally as the Magick in my blood.

I close my eyes, relishing the power as it washes through me, and I do nothing to dampen the inferno. Even if the flames take me with it, I don't care. It'll be worth it to get rid of this poisonous pitiful excuse of a man.

"Mark," I smile sweetly at him as I know it's the last thing he'll ever see. "Burn in Hell."

The flames in my body rush forward and wash over him like a tidal wave crashing against the shore.

He screams like a man who knows he's damned, who knows he won't make it out of this room alive.

His wails and cries die as his body tumbles to the floor, and when another wave of fire engulfs him, I can't stop the triumphant smile on my face, even as I see the flames catch hold of the scraps of rubbish and debris in the room.

The inferno quickly spreads, and I realise Mark isn't the only one not getting out of this room alive.

You're braver than I was, the voice says. *When I faced the flames, I begged for the Goddess to take my soul before I could feel my body burn.*

The smoke clouds and flames billow in the tiny room.

"It's weird," I splutter, gasping for air as I close my eyes against the sting of the smoke. "I never even gave you a name, I just kind of thought you were some kind of imaginary friend."

I already have a name, the voice says. *I'm Sarah.*

I cough as the smoke invades my lungs, "Guess that's not a coincidence?"

"No," the voice says. "It is not."

I tentatively open one eye and see a golden silhouette, a delicate female form looking down at me with wide eyes, a small sad smile on her face.

"So, you're Sarah," I choke out. "Nice to finally meet you. In person so to speak."

"An interesting turn of phrase," Sarah looks down at me. "We have known each other for a long time. Well," her lip quirks up. "I have known you for a long time."

"So, are you possessing me?" I try hopelessly to wriggle out of the ropes and again my escape attempts are unsuccessful. "Like Nox is with Finn?"

"No, I'm not possessing you," she moves towards the knots at my wrists. She pulls my bindings free, and I let out a relieved gasp. Sarah glides to my feet and repeats the process.

"Are you a ghost?" I sit up and the smoky room spins in my addled mind.

"Ghosts have to be from dead spirits," she floats in front of me again, her body a strange mix of shadow and solids. "I am very much alive."

I shake my head slowly, trying to clear the smoke and concussion. "What are you then?"

"You," she smiles warmly down at me. "I am you, and you are me."

My brow furrows, "You've lost me."

She lets out a small musical laugh, "We are the same essence," she holds out a hand to me which I hesitantly take.

Cool, my hallucinations are now corporeal, that's fun.

"The same soul," she continues.

I stand, the pain in my back screams at me, "I'm your

351

reincarnation?"

Something seems to flicker across her face, "It's a little more complicated than that."

A beam from the ceiling groans and collapses, bringing down a cloud of rubble and debris. Everything in the room which isn't stone, or metal is on fire. I can't see a door or window through the smoke.

"Can I suggest we continue this discussion when I get you to safety?" Sarah offers congenially. As if this is a perfectly normal conversation to be having.

"That'd be nice," my vision fogs as the oxygen from the room and my brain rapidly disappears. "But I don't know how the hell to get out of here!"

"Allow me," Sarah tugs on my hand, pulling me forward.

"I-I can't," I splutter. My brain is foggy, and my body grows heavy and slow. All I want to do is curl up and sleep, "I can't breathe."

"Perhaps I can remedy that," Sarah pulls me again. For an apparition she sure is strong.

"Wait, how?" I splutter.

Sarah disappears and my hand drops to my side like dead weight. Which is exactly what I'm going to be in two minutes, I think numbly.

Just let me take control, Sarah says in my head. *I'll get us out of here.*

My vision goes white just as I'm wrapped up in a strange mental golden blanket.

Did you just take control of my body? I ask in my head.

I've done it to save us, Sarah answers.

Maybe ask next time, I snap. *Kind of rude, you know.*

You'll thank me in a minute, she says smugly, and I realise her and Nox aren't that different.

Chapter Forty - One

Nox

I forego more bollock torture and sprint back down the hill. Fucking Edinburgh and the fucking hills.

Finn squirms restlessly.

"Look," I mutter aloud, passing by the quaint terraced houses. "I get that you have this desire to be her white knight, but here's the thing, Finnster: you're mortal, and I don't particularly fancy piecing our body together when your ass gets handed to you." My feet pound the pavement at a frenetic pace. "So, if you can just sit back, relax and let me do what I do best, that will make both our lives a hell of a lot easier."

Finn's frustration shoves petulantly at me again before slumping back in defeat.

"Good boy," I push my legs harder. My muscles scream at the strain as I run faster than any mortal body should. "Although, by the end of this, we may need to sort out getting you a new skin suit."

Finn grows alarmed at this. Maybe the warnings were true. Possessions usually come with an expiration date, and I may be pushing this frail human form to breaking point. I squash down my apprehension and push forward.

The nauseatingly pink shop front comes into view. As I reach the flower filled windowsill, I peer inside to see if there's anything or anyone. It looks dark and undisturbed but on trying the door handle I'm surprised to find it's unlocked.

As I walk inside, I'm greeted from above by the jingling bell. The shop is quiet, but there might be a chance Esme is sleeping in the back.

"Sugar?" I peer around the back of the till and look around the shelves. "Are you in here?"

I wander to the stockroom, flick on the light and I'm met by a cloud of slithering smoke in the corner of the room.

"Save the parlour tricks for the tourists, Eli," I sigh when my colleague appears. Just as smug and arrogant as he alway is. Onyx eyes twinkle in his deceptively youthful face. If you didn't know better, you'd think he was just an obnoxiously wholesome teenager.

"Good to see you too, Tenebris Noctis Daemonium," Eligos traces his hand across the bookshelf.

"Oh, I'm being full named," I lean against the opposite shelves. "I must be in trouble!"

"Trouble is putting it lightly," his black eyes regard me coolly. "He who leads us is not pleased."

"Is Lucy ever really pleased?" I drawl. "The last time I saw him happy was when we had the busload of Tories arrive and we got to try out the new fingernail extractor."

"I don't know how you managed to break the rules of your banishment," Eli waves a hand at me, "yet here you are, parading around in a decaying skin suit."

I lean to look at the mirror on the shelf opposite. Sure, I look a little pale, but I wouldn't think that's anything to be concerned about. I give my reflection a wink.

"Frankly, I don't know either," I smirk. "But as you put it, here I am."

"The Devil himself is pissed off with you, you're going to draw too much attention from upstairs-"

"When did we start caring what they thought?" I lean forward. "Besides, I quite like attention."

"Clearly," he tuts. "All this cavorting around with witches is-"

"Witch," I correct him. "One. Past tense. I'm up here for Sarah."

"Well, that's not strictly true now, is it?" Eli smiles knowingly at me. "Rumour has it you've been getting very close to the lovely Esmerelda, daughter of Eve," he winks. "She's mouth-watering."

Dread sinks in my stomach and Finn's anger riles in my head.

"Have you seen her?" I ask, trying to keep my tone casual.

"Oh, I've seen her," his smile grows wider.

I pounce on him, hauling him by the neck and shoving his body against the shelves. His legs hang uselessly beneath him, but he doesn't struggle, he just keeps smiling. I ignore the pain in my wounded arm which screams at me from the exertion.

"What did you do to her?" I snarl. White hot anger and jealousy scorches through me, burning away any notion that I'm only here for Sarah. The idea of Eli touching Sugar, someone so pure. It feels like blasphemy.

He continues to beam at me, "She's so... sweet."

I squeeze my hand around his neck, ignoring the icy chill of his skin biting at my fingers.

"What did you do to her?" I ask again as I tighten my grip.

"Nothing," Eli answers conversationally, ignoring that I hold his life in my hands. "But I must say the way your scent was all over her. I assumed you must have gotten over Sarah?"

Realisation hits me. Whilst Eli is just trying to provoke a reaction, he may not be entirely wrong.

My grip falters and he looks at me triumphantly, "What's the matter, Nox?"

I release my hold on Eli's neck and drop him to the ground. He quickly rights himself and straightens his tartan shirt.

"Don't be vulgar," I step back. "She's... good. She deserves to be with someone good."

Someone like Finn. I turn my back on Eli to face the bookshelves and ignore the twist in my chest. I try to ignore what my heart and mind have been screaming at me for weeks.

"Poor old Nox," Eli chuckles, "in love with a witch. I guess it's to be expected. You never did stop loving her."

I spin around to scowl at him, "What the fuck are you talking about Eli?"

He chuckles, "Do you not know?" His eyebrows shoot up in surprise. "Oh, this is priceless! I wish I had a camera!"

I stalk towards him again, "Tell me what you know Eli, or I swear to the Devil himself I'll find a way to kill you!"

"Alright fine," he rolls his eyes, "I knew that Sarah's soul had been hidden by the witches and when Culum started asking them questions in Hell I became interested. It's then that I noticed you were missing and more importantly who you were with."

My brow furrows in confusion.

He rolls his eyes before continuing, "I admit it took me a few days to put the pieces together, but once I did it became so obvious. Don't you see it, Nox?"

"Obviously not," I grind out.

"Do you know any other witches that can control plants and fire? Life and death; two diametrically opposed schools of Magick?"

My heart stops beating for a second and it's only when Finn's alarm rises, I remember to breathe.

I grab hold of his arm and twist, "What did you tell her?"

He wriggles free of my grasp and slinks back into the corner, "Nothing. I gave her a friendly message to pass on to you and sent her on her way."

"Message?" I growl. "What message?"

"Strange, I thought that was why you were here," he shrugs. "I told her to hurry back and tell you that it was time to stop being foolish and return home."

"She hasn't delivered any bloody message to me," my temper is seconds away from snapping. "When was this?"

Eli shrugs noncommittally, "A couple of hours ago... I think," he sighs. "It's so hard to tell. Time moves strangely up here."

I turn on my heel and sprint towards the shop's exit, the bell jingling above me.

"Oh, and Nox," the Duke of Hell calls after me. "I'm not the only one who's been sent to bring you back. If you don't heed these orders, there will be consequences."

I bite my tongue to prevent myself giving him a snarky response and instead bolt up the hill heading back towards the apartment.

The flat door is open, and it looks like it's been hit by a tornado. It's in even more disarray than usual.

"Sugar?" I call as I scour the living room before sprinting down the hallway. Vanilla, rose, sugar and Magick permeate the air. I track the scent and pick up the metallic tang of iron. Blood.

Soft dawn light comes from the open bedroom door, beckoning me forward.

When I reach the doorway to the pastel pink bedroom I am greeted by a macabre sight; she's laid on her stomach on her bed, her cartoon character pyjamas hanging off her in soggy, bloodied rags. The ivy spreads across the bed sheets, as if reaching for her.

I walk forward, my breath caught in my chest. Her ruined back is a mess of flesh and gore.

"Witchling," I rush forward, relieved to see the slight hitch of her shoulders. She's breathing. The sight horrifies me. With these wounds, it's amazing she's still alive. I place my hand on hers.

"Nox," her eyelids flutter and a soft breath escapes her chest.

"I'm here," I stroke a hand over her clammy forehead. She's burning up. "Who did this to you?"

Her eyes open, meeting mine immediately, "Remember Mark? The police officer, he was the hunter."

"The creep at the cottage?" I grind my molars. "I'm going to rip him to pieces."

"You'll have to get a dustpan and brush first," she smiles wanly. "I set him on fire." She tries to raise up onto her arms but lets out a small yelp as pain flashes in her emerald eyes.

"Stop moving," I gently pull her hand back down to rest and she acquiesces. Strange, a few weeks ago I'd have had to argue with her until she relented. "I need to get you to a hospital, or to Agnes and Crystal-"

She offers me another small smile, "There's no need, Nox."

"But," I look at her ruined flesh. "You're hurt. Your back is-"

"A damn sight better than it was half an hour ago," she grimaces. "Trust me."

"How?" The sheets are covered in blood, her blood. But as I look closer at the wounds, I see small flecks of gold dust shimmering across the surface.

"I'm healing," she says into the pillow. "I've figured out how to do it. I'm channelling power."

I look around her room at the vines and English roses which I could have sworn weren't this big earlier.

"From the plants?" I ask quietly as one of the fuchsia roses blooms before me.

"Partly," she hisses as she manages to lift herself to look at me. "But also, from myself..." her eyes cloud and darken like rain over a forest floor. "Ourself."

The clouds in her eyes clear, and her focus returns to me, "I'm starting to remember."

"What?" My voice comes out strangled, like my heart has stopped beating to hear her words. I won't believe what Eli said until they come from her lips.

"Everything," a solitary tear traces her cheek, catching in the early morning light. "It's still coming to me in bits and pieces but... Sarah and I... we share a soul." I search her face, no trace of sadness or anger at this realisation, just calm clarity. I don't know how to process this news, so Lucifer only knows how she is feeling.

"But, what does that mean?"

"I'm still trying to figure that out," she lifts herself to sit up and I watch as the wounds on her back continue to knit together. "For now, I have to make sure the wards are back up on the flat. Mark said he had help getting inside and the last thing I need is another hunter breaking in to finish what he started."

She tries to stand but shakes like a leaf in the breeze. The remains of her top hang off her shoulders and her back glistens as she moves.

"You're in no fit state to do that," I warn, "you can barely stand. Tell me what you need me to do, and I'll do it."

She looks up at me and she wrinkles her nose as she sniffs, "You stink, Demon- Boy!"

I chuckle, "Not your best insult, Sugar," I place my hands on her shoulders, and I see her relax at my touch. "But you're injured, so I'll give you a pass. I have been running all over the city so excuse me for perspiring!"

"No, it's not sweat," she leans forward, sniffing again before she shudders in disgust. "Something is rotten. Ew, Nox! How can you not smell that?!"

Before I have a chance to stop her, she grabs hold of my arm and peels the gauze off the wound. My arm is a putrid, puss-ridden angry gash.

"Nox!" She gasps and pinches her nose. "This is infected! Why didn't you say anything?!"

I grimace, "Been a little busy, Sugar. Had to hunt for a witch, deal with a demon-"

She grabs hold of my hand and parks me on the edge of the bed, I look up at her and smile as I say, "I thought you had a rule about no touching?"

"Aye, well," she plucks a petal from the fuchsia rose and rolls it in her fingers, disintegrating the petal into a paste. "Things change."

She sits down next to me and places the rose mulch onto my arm. I flinch and she giggles quietly, "Goddess, Nox," she strokes the mixture across the infected wound. "Quit being such a baby."

She holds my arm, keeping her palm pressed against the wound and I have a strange tingling feeling, "What are you doing?"

She smiles up at me from beneath her eyelashes, "I told you. I have new powers." The tingling begins to tickle and as I look down, I see her hands glowing. Actually glowing.

"Er, Sugar, I know people often say you're a little ball of sunshine," I shift warily. The last thing I need is to lose my arm when we're in danger and Sugar can barely stand. "But I'd prefer it if you didn't set me on fire."

"Relax, Nox." The tingling continues, and whilst it's not unpleasant there's something distinctly disconcerting about it. "Just let me fix your arm. I can't take that smell!"

"It's not that bad," I say, fighting the urge to gag.

"You're a terrible liar," she chuckles, and her hands seem to glow even brighter for a second before returning to their normal ivory

358

hue. "There!"

She moves her hands away and I look down at my arm, no sign of infection, barely any sign of a wound at all. She gives me a dazzling smile despite looking a little grey. "All better!"

"What about you?" I ask, tilting her head to look at her face.

"I'll be fine, Nox," her smile remains, but it's a little dimmer. "I'm a tough cookie. It's just taking a little while," she playfully nudges her shoulder with mine. "Give a girl a break, it's my first time growing new skin." She attempts to stand again, and I pull her back down gently.

"No," I point a finger at her. "You stay here, and you tell me what I need to do, ok?"

She gives me a small, pained nod, "Ok, ok. Can you bring me the amethyst, quartz and herb bundle at the door, and I will bless them and then they need to go back exactly where they were. You'll also need to sprinkle a few drops from the vial in my dresser onto the windowsills and doorways."

"Got it," I give her a bow, causing the smallest sparkle to appear in her eyes and it warms my chest. "Crystals, herbs and the sprinkle water. Easy peasy."

"Did you just say 'easy peasy'?" she chuckles. "Not very demonic of you."

"Hey," I stalk out the room in the direction of the hallway, "I'll have you know my demonic status remains unparalleled!"

"That and manly?" Sugar calls from the bedroom.

"Not a man," I call over my shoulder. I scour around the hallway seeing no trace of the objects I've been instructed to collect. "You sure the rocks and weeds are meant to be out here?" I call down the corridor.

"Crystals and herbs," Sugar chastises. "They should be by the door."

"There's nothing here," I head back down the hallway and just as I turn the corner something strikes me in the face before I have a chance to register what happened.

Another smack in my nose, causing my nostrils to gush with blood. Another and another come reigning down.

Culum stands above me, his hands brandishing iron knuckle dusters. He lands another punch turning my face into pulp.

I spit out a mouthful of blood and teeth across the tiled floor, "Is this a new way of saying hello? Because I have to say I'm not a fan."

He kneels over me and lands another series of blows to my

face and chest.

"Tie him up," a female voice says. "Quick, before he gets his strength back."

Chapter Forty - Two

Nox

"Hey Culum." I wheeze from my now broken ribs, "maybe next time you have a workplace complaint, you could take it up with HR?"

"Shut up," my soon to be fired colleague snaps at me. "For centuries all I've ever done is take your shit, mop up your messes and cow-tail to you. You pompous, self-righteous prick!"

"So, you are filing a workplace complaint?" I spit a tooth out of my dislocated jaw. "Because if not, I'm putting you on a disciplinary!"

"For fuck's sake will you just," he lands another blow with the giant knuckle dusters. "Shut the fuck up!"

"Why don't you both shut up?" A feminine voice behind Culum snaps. "I've still got to find Esme and you two having a work-place disagreement is distracting!"

"Sorry babe," Culum turns and grins at Dahlia as she heads to Sugar's bedroom.

"Babe?" I sneer between the two of them, "since when did you two decide to team up?"

Culum stamps down on my ankle. The sickening crack and pain that shoots up my leg tells me that it's broken. I try to stand and stop Dahlia, but Culum grabs hold of me, throwing me back onto the sofa.

Dahlia storms back in, her black hair swirling around her manic expression. She halts inches away from me, "Where the fuck is she?!" Spittle flies at my face.

I wipe a hand down my bloodied jaw and give her a look of disgust, "No idea."

Pride blossoms in my chest; Esme managed to transport herself to safety even in her weakened state. She really is

361

extraordinary. Hopefully she'll stay away until it's safe to come back when… when they've killed me. A knot forms in my stomach as I feel Finn's panic.

"Sorry about all of this, Finnster," I mutter quietly, hoping he knows my apology is genuine.

Dahlia screams at me like a deranged harpy before whirling on Culum, who has the sense to take a step back.

"Get him to tell you where the fuck she is," she snaps. "Now! We need to find her before those old bitches come snooping around here!"

She storms off again, heading towards Sugar's bedroom and I hear wardrobe doors being ripped off hinges and pillows being shredded. I look around the room trying to find something, anything, I can use as a weapon.

The room is a bombsite: broken plates, cutlery and smashed wine bottles strewn all over the place. Sadly, none of these are going to be of any use against a demon. I look closer at the strange knuckle duster accessory Culum is waving around on his tattooed hands.

"She's a delight. Although I sense trouble in paradise," I drawl before Culum lands another hit on my jaw. "If the spark is already going out of the romance, it might be time to pull the plug?"

"We've been together for ages, you ignorant fuck," Culum snarls. "Not that you ever noticed. You never pay any attention to me!"

"Save your daddy issues for someone who is related to you," I sneer. "I'm your boss, not your confidante."

"I was your friend," Culum lands another hit. "Your only friend."

"Some friend," I deadpan. "Shall we braid each other's hair, have a sleepover and talk about boys?"

"Where the fuck is she?!" Dahlia screams from the bedroom. I hear a yowling cry just as Dahlia screeches, "Fucking cat!"

Ink bolts from the bedroom, a small bundle of fur fleeing the scene, he quickly hides somewhere in the shadows of the living room, and I pray he stays there.

"So, I have to ask," I arch my split eyebrow, ignoring the screeches from the other room. "What are you getting out of this? Aside from fucking that crazy bitch?"

"That crazy bitch is one powerful witch," Culum takes a step back to roll his shoulders. He's tired from trying to turn my face into the consistency of mashed potato. "Do you remember all those warnings we got told in Hell? How the witches and demons teaming up was forbidden? That it always had to be transactional and never anything more than that?"

"Are you wanting me to answer, or are you just going to keep asking questions?" I groan as I try to pull myself up on the sofa.

"Dahlia and I have been together for a very, very long time. For a while it was just business, but we teamed up when she needed to get rid of someone," there's a glint in his eyes. "I needed her help, so we started working closer together. After a while, I finally saw why you became so pussy-whipped by Sarah. I never realised that the reason they stop demons and witches being together was to stop us from getting too strong. To keep us in our place. The Magick Dahlia gives me is…" his eyes take on a dreamlike quality, "it's unreal. And she gets more powerful from being with me. It's like, what's it called when remora fish eat the parasites off sharks?"

I can't believe the topic of my ex-colleague's exposition has devolved into a conversation about fish.

"A symbiotic relationship?" I say slowly, like I'm speaking to a monkey trying to use tools.

He ponders for a second, "Nah," he rolls his neck and I hear his muscles pop and crack. "It's when something is good for both the fish and the shark?"

"Lucifer's sake," I grumble under my breath. "I have a broken ankle, but this is more painful."

Culum leans in, "What did you say?"

"Nothing," I offer him an innocent, and semi toothless, grin. "You were saying?"

Dahlia lets out another scream which echoes through the apartment. It's amazing we've not had any of the neighbours banging on the door.

Something smashes in the other room.

"So, as I was saying, I can see why Hell doesn't let us partner up with witches long-term," Culum cracks his knuckles. "I always thought it was a bit weird that they made such a big song and dance about you and Sarah."

I narrow my eyes, "What song and dance?"

"I'm not supposed to say anything. But since you're not going to be able to tell anyone, I guess I can," he leans in, a mischievous glint in his eyes. "I was the one who pointed that hunter in Sarah's direction, a little whisper here, a rumour there. Human hysteria is the easiest thing to incite."

My blood turns to fire. "You did what?"

"It was so fucking easy," he roars with laughter. "After all

363

these years, it's a relief to finally say it out loud!"

"You killed Sarah," my voice comes out flat. Detached. A far cry from the rage that's seconds away from erupting. "You caused her to be arrested, tried, tortured and murdered."

He has the nerve to look proud. "Sure did, boss!" He claps a hand on my back, "At the time I convinced myself I was helping you by keeping you out of trouble, but now I'm with Dahlia, I can see I was just jealous. For centuries I've played the faithful and loyal best friend-"

"Not my best friend," I correct.

"-And I fooled you, for all these years," his smile widens. "I beat you. I mean, I've practically beaten you to a pulp, and I've barely broken a sweat!"

"You're well aware that you're cheating, right?" I point at the coldiron knuckle dusters. "Speaking of, how the fuck are you even able to hold them?"

He puffs out his chest proudly, "Dahlia enchanted them so that the wearer doesn't feel any of the nasty, unwanted side effects! Pretty cool, right?"

Silence has fallen from the bedroom, meaning either Dahlia has tired herself out or something bad has happened. Anxiety coils in my gut.

Culum seems to realise I'm distracted, "I'm sorry am I boring you, boss?"

"No more than usual."

There's a small squeak and a clatter from the direction of the bedroom, which distracts him, and he turns around.

I pounce and quickly grapple him to the ground. I may be trapped in this mortal skin-suit, but I have enough Hellish rage to tear Culum apart. I grab hold of the knuckle dusters and, to my surprise the traitor is right; I wrap them around my fist, and they don't burn me, instead they imbue me with their power. Before Culum realises what's happening I slam my fists into his face.

"Well since you class me as a friend," I snarl, as I land another punch on his cheekbone. "A little word of friendly advice." Another viscous hit to his jaw splits his lower lip. "Don't turn your back on torture victims who aren't tied up." Another punch. "I deliberately let you get a few licks in, so I could find out about you and Dahlia." Another hit. "Now that I have. It's. My. Fucking. Turn." Culum's head slams into the oak floorboards, which are now painted with his blood.

He lets out a low pained moan. "Please. Stop. Nox."

"Are you asking for mercy?" I look down at him with disgust.

"From a demon?" I stand and I kick him in the chest. "As your superior, I thought I'd taught you better."

"Get the fuck away from him," Dahlia storms into the room, madness burns in her kohl rimmed eyes.

"Or what?" I raise my foot to stamp down on Culum's face.

"Because if you don't stop," she holds the pink vial in her hand. "I'll make sure you never find your precious Sarah."

A humourless laugh escapes me, "You really have no fucking clue, do you?"

"About what?" sweat coats her upper lip and she looks like a rabid dog.

"About anything really," I chuckle. "I guess Culum was smart enough to keep a few things hidden from you in the end."

She lets out another screech as she launches herself at me, "I'm going to rip out your heart-"

"Dahls," Sugar appears in front of me, blocking Dahlia's attempted assault. "I think it's time you move out."

Dahlia stumbles back, her eyes wide as saucers, "Where the fuck did you just come from?"

"Ok, spoiler alert, but I've been here the whole time," she says. I look at her back which is now fully healed. A golden glow radiates from her skin. "You have been a really shitty roommate," Sugar holds up a finger, "One, you dismantled my wards and set a hunter on me. Two, you set your bonehead demon on my, erm," she flounders, and I hear her heart skip a beat. "Nox."

"Fine," Dahlia scoffs. "I thought a garrotting spell, pushing you from a tower or setting a hunter on you would be enough! Why are you so hard to kill? Honestly, I don't give a shit anymore. I just want you dead!"

It all makes horrible sense: the night at the cottage when Esme was strangled; the 'accident' at the Loch. Everything had been orchestrated by her.

"Why are you doing this Dahls?" Esme's shoulders shake and I can tell she's crying. "We were like sisters, what did I do?"

"Nothing," Dahlia snaps viciously. "Nothing matters. Except power," she looks beyond Sugar. At me. "Nox knows that. All he wants is to be able to manifest his demonic form. Culum told me," she says proudly. "He doesn't give a shit about who, or what he hurts!"

"She's wrong, Sugar," I say quietly, my tone pleading. "I do care. I won't lie, that's why I needed to find a way up here, but then you and I-"

Culum surges up from the ground holding a butter knife that

he drives into my chest. Into my heart.

I fall back onto the sofa, my mortal body desperately trying to keep me alive. To keep Finn alive.

Ink launches from the shadows at Culum, but Dahlia grabs him in midair. There's a sickening crack as Dahlia breaks his neck.

"No!" Sugar cries.

Culum towers over me, ready to finish the job.

My vision blackens but I see pure hatred on Sugar's face, "You try to take his heart," her voice sounds like it's echoing. "We'll take yours."

Sugar punches her arm through Culum's chest. He falls to the ground in front of me, a cavernous hole in his torso. I look up at Sugar, who grips a black and bloody heart.

"Th-that," Dahlia stumbles back, terror in her eyes. "That isn't possible. Demons can't be killed-"

Sugar holds out the heart to her like a macabre offering, "Weird. Because I just did it?"

I let out a wheezing laugh as my heart slows.

Sugar reaches down to me and cradles my head. She looks at the knife embedded in my chest; she reaches for it, but I grab her hand to stop her "Nox, I can take it out and see if-"

"Sugar, even if you take out the blade. This body, it's... it's dying." I offer up a small smile. "It's been decaying for a while, I just thought..." I look up into those jade eyes. "Maybe things might get better?"

She lets out a small chuckle even as tears form in her perfect face, "I thought I was the one with the rose-tinted glasses?"

There's a clatter as Dahlia runs out of the apartment to avoid meeting the same fate as Culum.

Sugar looks down at the blade in horror, tremors wracking through her shoulders.

"Maybe you're finally a good influence on me?" I offer as I cough up a gurgle of blood. I guess that the son of a bitch had managed to pierce my lung as well as my heart. Stupid mortal body.

"At least you finally realised," her lower lip trembles and I raise a hand to trace my thumb across that soft tilt at the corner of her mouth. Like a hidden secret at the edge of her smile. Except there's no smile now, only sadness.

Sure, this isn't how I had planned to go out. Truth be told, I'd never pondered my death. Few Demons ever need to. But as I lie in the witchling's arms and she cradles me with such care and kindness, I couldn't ask for a more perfect place to spend my final moments alive.

I feel Finn's growing apprehension in the back of my mind, and I hope he knows how sorry I am.

My eyelids grow heavier and as I let out one final shuddering breath, I hear four simple words above me.

"Don't leave me, Nox."

And then the rest is silence.

Chapter Forty - Three

Esme

"Please, Nox," I sob. "Please wake up!" Pain twists in my chest. He can't be gone. How can I lose him when I've only just found myself?

Bring him back, I scream at Sarah.

I don't have the power, she answers sadly.

Fine, then you tell me what I need to do, I snap. *And I'll bring him back-*

A golden form stands in front of me. I glance up to see Sarah looking down at us; conflict clouds her pretty features, but my eyes return to Nox, wishing his chest would move just slightly to let me know he's still here.

"It's Magick that I don't know," she warns. "No living being should, it goes against Nature-"

"He already goes beyond fucking Nature!" I snap, my voice shrill as my panic rises, every second he's gone the further away he'll go. "We all do! He's a demon possessing a human body and I'm some sort of reincarnation of a witch from the 1600's!"

I hold him tighter as my lip wobbles, "I thought you loved him? You should want to save him!"

"This isn't the way," Sarah answers, her tone regretful. "It's against the rules."

"Fuck your archaic rules. Fuck your fear," my temper snaps like a burst damn. I sound like Nox. "I thought you were some badass bitch witch, not a coward!"

"Who is swearing so much?" I hear clattering from the hallway and Agnes and Crystal tumble into the room.

"Help me!" I cry out, begging for someone, anyone, to heal

368

Nox. "Please?"

Crystal and Agnes look between us and the floating silhouette of Sarah.

"My Goddess," Agnes rushes forward and places her hand on Nox's throat, whilst Crystal stays in the doorway, her focus locked on Sarah, "What happened?"

"Culum," I manage to stutter. "He-he stabbed Nox."

"Where's Dahlia?" Agnes looks around the room as if expecting my treacherous ex-best friend to come rushing in.

"She and Culum were working together," I sob. "They're the ones who have been sending hunters after us. Culum stabbed Nox and now I can't heal him. He's dying!"

"No, dear," Agnes's tone is grave. "He's already dead."

"He can't die," I stutter. "He's a demon."

"He's a demon possessing a mortal body," Crystal says from the threshold, like she's afraid to step inside. "He already pushed the bounds of Nature by inhabiting a Mundane's form for longer than he should have. He rotted the body and corrupted the mortal boy's soul."

"Nox isn't evil," I interrupt. "Sure, he's a demon. But he's kind, he helped me, protected me and believed in me, even before I did." A tear from my eye lands on him, "I may not know who he was in Hell. But I know who he is when he's here," I brush my tears from his cheekbone. "When he's with me."

"And I'm sure Ted Bundy's mum would say he was a lovely boy when he was little," Crystal says curtly from the door like some kind of Birkenstock-wearing panto villain.

"Why is it so hard for you to be open-minded?" I frown at her, and before I can stop myself the words slip out. "Not everything can be divided into good or evil. You two both claim you'd never tamper with certain types of Magick, but you were both willing to help my Mum with that forbidden spell?"

Silence and stillness envelop the room and the only movement is the golden shimmer of Sarah walking over to the window.

"That was different, dear," Agnes finally says. "We helped your mother because she was in pain. She was our friend. She was a mother without her child."

"And I am a witch who loves a demon," as I say the words I see both their features twist in horror. "He's as much a part of me as she is," I signal towards Sarah, who is barely more than a shimmer.

Agnes squints towards the corner of the room, "There's nothing there, Esme dear."

"Sarah," I huff out a breath, brushing at my tears, "stop hiding, and show yourself."

Sarah appears again and Crystal turns green.

Sarah looks embarrassed, "I apologise for hiding."

"What is that?" Crystal squeaks from the doorway, her voice full of alarm.

"That's Sarah," I point towards the golden figure. "She is the spirit that you both used to help Mum have a child. Only the spell you did didn't so much create new life-"

"-but reincarnate it," Sarah finishes. Her voice is clear and rings with truth. "Esme and I share a soul."

"And that's not even to mention the cloaking spell Mum put on me to hide my powers," I look directly at Crystal. "Which you both knew about. You knew how powerful I could be, and you deliberately helped hide it. You lied, you tampered, and you meddled," I glare back at Crystal who is about to argue with me. "Don't tell me not to break the rules or go against Nature because that's all you two have ever done to me-"

"That is not true!" Crystal's wrinkled face is blotchy with rage. I don't think I have ever seen her look so angry.

Before I have a chance to reply, Agnes steps in, looking at her friend with sympathy.

"It is, Crystal," she sighs and it's then that I notice how tired Agnes looks. "She's right," she looks at me with a weird mixture of sadness and pride. "We were cowards. We didn't stand up to your mother, even when we knew what we were doing was wrong. I wasn't honest about the enchantment we put on you when you were a child and I'm sorry," she lets out another heavy breath. "And whilst I don't have the power to help you bring your demon back," she looks down at Nox. "I can do something else."

"Agnes, no," Crystal finally steps into the room, warning flashes in her features. "We cannot."

"We have to," she answers in a clipped authoritative tone.

"Do what?" Sarah and I both ask in unison.

"We can remove the last traces of the cloaking spell." Agnes busies herself by pulling out an old looking grimoire from her polka dot handbag. "It seems like most of it has worn away, but I can get rid of the last remnants."

"Eve wouldn't want us to do that," Crystal's voice is filled with wariness.

"Well, too bad for Eve. She's not here," Agnes retorts and begins flicking through the pages. "I'm sure one day she'll have some

370

strong words for me, but for now, there's not much she can do about it! Ah!" She stops and thumbs a page, "here we are, now Esme dear if you can stand in front of me. This shouldn't take too long!"

I carefully place Nox's limp body down to rest on the sofa and stand awkwardly in front of Agnes. She is swaying with her eyes closed and mumbling something very quietly.

"Should I move closer too?" Sarah asks nervously.

"Beats me," I mumble, arching an eyebrow at Agnes who is whispering Latin at breakneck pace.

"There, all done!" Agnes's eyes snap open, "the cloaking spell is now lifted."

"Huh," my eyebrows raise in surprise, "kind of thought there'd be more fan fair, like fireworks or a resounding sound of applause, or," I look over at Crystal's terrified expression, "fire and brimstone?"

"You shouldn't joke about such things, girl," Crystal's nostrils flare. "You have no idea what kind of power you are in possession of."

"I also wouldn't be calling her girl," Sarah steps forward, crossing her arms. "Considering that mine and Esme's combined age is three times older than you!"

Crystal backs out of the room, careful not to fall over her sandals. "What have you done, Agnes? This cannot… I will not…this can't happen…"

Sarah stares at the space where Crystal had been standing.

"What?" I ask.

A small frown furrows her brow. "There's just something about that woman I don't like."

"I don't think you're the only one who's ever said that about Crystal," I say as the front door opens and closes quietly and I give Sarah a gentle smile. "Thanks for having my back, well, our back."

"I decided it was time I stopped hiding and helped," Sarah offers me a small smile. "Be that big bad bitch witch you told me to be."

I give her a small nod, "Thank you."

"So, I may have a way of getting Nox and Finn back," Sarah looks back down at the sofa. If I didn't know better, I'd think Nox was asleep.

"How?"

"I'll go get him," she answers.

"Could you not have done that earlier?" I ask as I sit next to Nox's body.

"No, I didn't realise we were being suppressed, but now the cloaking spell is gone I can see a way," she answers. "But it'll be dangerous. Our soul, whilst we are made of the same essence, is still split. We're vulnerable and if I go down to the Afterlife without a strong enough link to the living-"

"You'll get stuck there?" I offer.

She gives a grave nod, "Exactly."

"So, what do we have to do?" I ask, I have no idea what's going on, but I know that every second that passes, it's going to make it harder to get Finn and Nox back into their body.

"We need to go into a trance," Sarah sits down in front of me, her face taut with anxiety. "Once we're in limbo, I'll be able to stretch out our tether and go and get them."

"How long will it take?"

Not long, Sarah's voice sounds in my head. *We're already in one.*

I look around, realising I'm no longer in my body, instead I'm standing beside it. Staring down at Sarah and I as we sit opposite each other.

There you go again, without asking, I quip.

Sarah chuckles beside me; she's more solid in the trance and I see her copper hair glitter with golden flecks. I even notice the light dusting of freckles across her cheeks.

I'll work on it, her voice is a teasing tone.

So now what do we do? I ask.

I start walking, and you make sure that the tether stays unbroken.

What tether?

Sarah laughs softly and points at my chest and then at hers, and sure enough there is a gold vine of ivy between the two of us.

So, I just stand here, make sure this vine thing doesn't snap? I look down at the shimmering rope.

Sarah shrugs, *pretty much.*

She begins walking out of the room towards the shadows, which I can only assume is the Astral plane.

Oh, and don't make any noise or move anything. Make sure nobody notices that you're here, Sarah warns.

Who's going to know we're here? I look around and my corporeal body is still beside Nox. Agnes is standing mid-step on the way to the kitchen.

One of the high demon lords has been missing for months, Hell is going to be on the hunt.

Hunting for what? I hate myself for asking.

Sarah flashes me one final smile before disappearing into the mist.

Us.

I feel the tether pull and have to counter my weight against it to make sure the vine remains taut but not too tight.

I wonder what the difference really is between tight and taut…

You shouldn't be here, a low growl comes from the smoke.

Hello?

I mentally chastise myself for answering. Sarah had just told me not to draw any attention and to stay quiet.

You shouldn't be here, the voice says louder, closer. *It is forbidden.*

Annoyance pricks at me and before my survival instinct can pump the brakes I mentally shout back, *I'm getting really tired of being told what I can and can't do.*

The tether seems to jiggle, and I have to take a step towards the mist when there's a sharp tug.

You're her, the voice sounds closer now. A smell of sulphur and iron permeates the air. *The Witch.*

I'm a witch, not sure I'm The Witch, I blather on. Hopefully it's just a nice benign ghost who got lost on his way to limbo-

I'll eat your soul and rip your puny human form to pieces, the voice snarls.

I suppose I was probably being optimistic.

Er, there's no need for any eating or ripping, I look down at the tether and see the vine tighten and loosen again. *I'll be on my way soon.*

You're here for that demon, aren't you? The bellowing voice echoes around the space. *You're his filthy whore. Why don't you come here, and I'll show you what a real demon is like.*

The tether goes completely slack and drops to the ground. I take a step back, heading towards my physical body.

Er, no thank you. Another step. *I'll be on my way soon so no need for, erm, any kind of show and tell, thanks though!*

The ivy suddenly hoists up and I'm dragged forward, towards the mist.

Sarah! I scream, *where are you? Hurry your non-corporeal ass back here!*

Another tug and as I near the door the tether snaps.

Fuck! Not good, not good! I look down at where the tether had been and see nothing. Just my chest.

"Sarah?" I open my eyes and I'm back sitting on the sofa,

nestled up next to Nox's body.

"Esme dear, are you alright?" Agnes kneels in front of me.

"Where's Sarah?" I ask. "She was with me a second ago. We were tethered and then she was gone. She's…"

I look around the room, searching for any sign of golden shimmer that might be her.

"Fuck me," a grumble sounds beside me. "I need a drink."

Nox opens an amber eye and looks up at me.

"Oh, my Goddess!" I squeak and launch myself at him, "You're back! She did it! She got you back!"

"Ow, dammit Sugar," he grumbles under my embrace. "Can you be a little gentler with the demon with the chest wound?"

"Oops, sorry!" I pull back and see him smirking at me.

"Kidding," he smiles wider, those golden eyes glowing up at me with affection.

I look down to see the stab wound is completely healed.

"You're all healed?" I press a hand to his chest, feeling the warmth of his body and the beating of his very alive heart. "You came back."

"Of course I did," he smiles at me, but concern clouds those whisky eyes. "You brought me back, remember?"

"I," I falter. "I didn't, but Sarah did, and now Sarah is…"

Images flash in my mind of grabbing hold of Nox. Crowds of greedy, taloned hands reach from the mist clawing at him, trying to drag him back into the shadows. I pull with all my might, guiding him through the fog towards the light…

The tether, it didn't break. I realise numbly. It was absorbed. Which means that…Sarah and I… we are… one.

I place a hand on my chest, feeling a warming glow in the centre. A feeling of completeness. Past, present and future versions of my soul are all melded into one.

"Nox?"

He arches an eyebrow at me, "Sugar?"

"Can I speak to Finn?"

He sighs and scrubs a hand over his jaw, "One second."

He leans back into the sofa and becomes completely still. For a second I think they've died again but then he opens his eyes and a sky-blue gaze looks up at me.

"Pupperfly," Finn leans forward and places a hand on mine.

"Hey, Finn," I give him a small smile. I realise Agnes has mumbled something and moved in the direction of my room.

"Ez," he fingers over my knuckles. "I know there's no right

time to say this but… but I think we'd be better off as friends."

I furrow my brow, "Sorry?"

"Look," he shuffles uncomfortably in his seat, "with everything that's been happening… and me not actually being able to use my body… I think I need time to figure some stuff out. I'll always love you; I don't think I ever can't love you. And I'll always be grateful to you for bringing me back to life. Twice. But I think it'd be best if I take some time to figure out some stuff. Besides," he nudges my knee with his. "I realised something."

"What?" I ask numbly.

"You're too old for me," he chuckles. "We worked so well together but we…"

"We're too different now," I finish his sentence.

He's right. I love him too, a part of me will always love him. But times have changed. I've changed too much. I can't be the woman he knew ten years ago, and he can't give me what I need now.

His blue eyes are full of fondness. "And the whole thing with Nox-"

"What?" I furrow my brow, but feel my cheeks heat. "What thing with Nox?"

"Ez," he rolls his eyes. "The guy-"

"Not a guy," I interject.

"He's in love with you," Finn finishes his sentence. "He's been in love with you for a long time. It's just that the idiot didn't realise. Also, Ez," he sighs, I hear the note of annoyance linger in his words. "If you can ask Nox if I can have a bit more time in my body, that'd be great. It is mine after all."

I chuckle, "Sure thing."

"Thanks, Pupperfly," with that Finn blinks and his eyes transform from sky blue to amber.

"Sugar," Nox pushes upright and wraps his arm protectively around me. "Are you alright?"

I let out a small laugh, a golden glow inside me feels like it's radiating from the inside out. "I remember," I place a hand on his jaw. "I remember it was raining outside the first night we met. I remember thinking how handsome you were-"

Nox's breathing hitches, "You're really… you, aren't you?"

"I am," I smile up at him. "And I really do mean it, even after all these years."

"Mean what?" he asks. His golden eyes. Those eyes I'd stared into all those centuries ago. The face isn't the same but there is a likeness, Finn's features have taken on so much of Nox's manifestation.

"That I love you, Nox," I plant a kiss on the tip of his nose just as he smiles, and his dimples return.

Chapter Forty ~ Four

Esme

Agnes leaves shortly afterwards, claiming she needs to go check on Crystal but I guess it's so she can give us some time alone.

I disentangle myself from Nox's embrace long enough to check that his wounds are fully healed, before he tugs me back onto him and insists on cradling me in his lap.

His eyes are full of wonder as he studies me, like I'm a precious diamond that he's just discovered. A sense of warmth lingers everywhere he looks, making my cheeks flush and my mouth blossom into a beaming grin.

But he doesn't kiss me, as though he's frightened that if he closes his eyes I'll disappear.

Finally, his control wavers and he lowers his head to trail the lightest shower of kisses over my bare shoulder, bestowing one to each of my freckles. His hands linger around the curve of my hips before he pulls me closer.

His mouth moves to my collarbone, and when he exhales it feels like his breath stokes the embers inside us both.

"I can't believe it," he murmurs into my neck between his kisses. I hear the smile in his voice as his lips brush my throat. "I can't believe you're really you. I found you."

"Technically," I lean back to see his dimples tease me, bewitching me to move closer to him again. It takes all my willpower to not fall under their spell. "I found you! You, Demon-Boy, just got yourself killed and had to get your ass saved," I stick my tongue out at him. "By me. Again."

Fiery heat flickers in his eyes but his grin widens. He pulls me closer to nestle me into his warmth.

"You really are the most infuriating witch," he gives my neck a

377

playful bite.

"I remember you referring to me as, what was it you said…" I shift in his lap to kneel over him and wrap my arms around his neck. I feign innocence when I see the molten desire in his expression. "The most brilliant witch you'd ever known?"

His hands tremble before he grabs hold of my waist and coaxes me lower onto his lap. We gasp in unison as I straddle him. Closer. We need to be closer.

"I don't remember that," his voice strained.

"Do you remember this?" I swirl my hips, causing him to let out a groan.

"Sugar…"

I bat my eyelashes feigning coyness. "Yes Nox?"

"Witchling," he growls when I grind again. He sucks in a shaky breath. "Please."

I lean in to savour the scent of sandalwood and cinnamon and whisper into the shell of his ear as his breathing hitches. "So, I'm infuriating, huh?"

I sit back to find his expression is a war of longing and restraint.

"No," he grips my hips tighter, guiding my movements. "I mean, yes. Yes, you are. You're willfully stubborn, you're frustrating, you're bossy, you have a crippling sugar addiction-"

"-Oh so this is a character assassination?" I circle my hips once more, but his expression turns serious, so I halt my teasing.

His hands move to cup my face with care and reverence. He looks at me with such longing that my heart skips a beat. He looks at me like I'm precious. "But you're also beautiful, clever, brave, powerful, fiercely kind, strong and…" his thumb moves to my bottom lip and his attention locks on my mouth as though it's the most extraordinary thing he's ever seen. His dimples return before he whispers, "You're so sweet."

His thumb continues to stroke my lip. Everywhere he touches desire and heat ignites a carnal desire deep in my core.

"Sugar," he inches closer, his focus still locked on my lower lip. "I told myself I wouldn't, that I shouldn't… not in this body, but I can't…" he sucks in another wavering breath. "I can't go another second…" His finger continues to stroke my lip.

"Another second before…?" my voice is no more than a whisper.

"I can't go another second without your lips on mine," that same pained expression flickers across his face, "but I know it's not

378

the right time, or place. I'm not even really me, but-"

Before he can say another word, I capture his mouth. I steal a kiss like I did the first time all those centuries before. The moment our lips touch, sparks of desire engulf me in an ocean of flames.

He groans as he presses his lips to mine. He pulls me closer, until there's nothing but need between us. His kisses are all consuming, but I'm the one in control. A dance he wants me to lead. He returns my kisses. He echoes my caresses. Every moan that escapes me harmonises with his. He relinquishes his power to me. He wants to show me what words can't say: that he's mine.

This isn't just a kiss; it's a supernova of passion, but it's also as delicate and precious as a snowflake in the breeze. This was meant to be. We were meant to be. Then, now and always.

A whimper escapes me as he clasps the small of my back and pulls me to him.

Embers become sparks, sparks become flames, flames become an inferno.

"Does this count as our first kiss?" I gasp as he nibbles and kisses my throat.

"Do you remember our actual first kiss?" His mouth returns to mine before allowing space for my answer.

I smile at the memory. My boots had been ruined from stepping into a puddle. I'd gotten a cold, but I had demanded that we stay outside. I'd wanted to see the lightning split the sky. I pepper his face with kisses. "You wouldn't stop nagging me to go back into the inn. But there was a thunderstorm and I wanted to watch. There was someone singing from the window above-"

"So, my concern for your well-being was a mood killer? Noted," he captures my mouth again.

Heat. So much heat. His kisses are like being burned alive and I welcome the flames. I thought I knew what Magick truly felt like but kissing Nox, that's what true Magick is. I twist to wrap myself around him. Closer, we need to be closer.

"Please Sugar," he lets out a pained groan again. "I'm begging you, please stop moving about so much, I don't want this to happen with someone else's body. Kissing is one thing, but-"

Someone else's body. Finn's body. All playful flirtation evaporates.

"Is Finn still in there?" I ask, peering into his golden eyes.

"He is," Nox leans back, but does not relax his hold around my waist. "And he's not too happy about it."

"I'll fix it," I peer into his gaze, as if trying to communicate to

Finn directly. "I'll find a way for Finn to have his body and for you to manifest."

Nox frowns, his grip on me relenting. He tilts his head looking puzzled.

"What's wrong?" I ask, sitting up straight.

"He's actually talking to me," Nox finally says. "Finn. He's never spoken to me."

"What's he saying?"

"He says," Nox's frown deepens. "He said he did what needed to be done."

"What does that mean?" Dread returns to my gut.

"What he means," a cold, crisp voice behind me says, "is that Nox should have listened to me when he had the chance."

Chapter Forty ~ Five

Nox

"Eligos," I stand, gently pushing Sugar protectively behind me. "Didn't we have enough of a tete-a-tete earlier? Or do you fancy trying out some more neck strengthening exercises?"

Eli looks down at his nails, a bored expression on his face. "Oh Nox. I did warn you earlier. You needed to return to Hell," he looks almost apologetic. "And you didn't heed the warnings, and now, well, it's out of my hands."

Sugar steps around me, "He doesn't need to do anything he doesn't want to."

Eli looks her up and down, "Ah Esmerelda…" he peers at her with curiosity, "or should I call you Sarah? Looks like someone finally got her big girl pants on."

"You do well to not talk to her, Eli." I snarl, wrapping an arm around Esme's waist.

"And you do well to remember that you're the one in hot water, Nox," Eli wags a finger at me. "Now both sides are involved."

"Both sides?" I frown, "I don't understand-"

"Well then allow me to enlighten you," a voice drawls from the hallway and in walks that elongated streak of piss.

"Sentiō," I give him a curt nod, trying to keep the disdain out of my voice. "Good to see you."

He looks just as arrogant and stuffy as he did the last I saw him all those centuries ago.

The angel chuckles, and dusts at the sofa before deigning to sit his ivory suit on the corner. "Oh Nox, just as charming and deceitful as ever."

"And I see you're as much of a clean freak as you ever were," I point towards his suit. Sugar gives me an incredulous look, "I'm neat

381

and tidy in a cool way, not like him." I inspect Sentiō's pristine outfit, "Bet that must be a bitch to keep clean. Though I suppose being management means you don't tend to get as involved in the dirty work, do you?"

"Ordinarily, no," Sentiō flicks at an imperceivable fleck of dust on his jacket. "But in this instance, I thought I'd make an exception."

"Look, Mr," Esme steps forward. "I don't know who you are, or what your problem is with Nox, but I'm sure we can sort it out. I was just talking to him about it. We just need to manifest his body and-"

Sentiō regards Sugar coldly, before holding up a hand to silence her, "What part of banishment, do you not understand, Nox? Your curse cannot be broken."

"I found a loophole," I sigh. "What's the big deal?"

"Curses cannot be broken," he says coldly.

"No," I give him a shit eating grin, "the rules on them are quite strict, the fact I am up here must mean I'm not breaking it."

"My question is how though?" Sentiō regards me coolly. "How after all this time did you manage to find this loophole?"

Everyone turns to Esme, and she stares back wide-eyed, "What?"

"Interesting," the angel tilts his head, regarding Sugar the way a cat would a mouse, "that he found a way to come back through your summoning," Sentiō narrows his eyes at her.

I move to block his view of Esme, "why are you here Sentiō?"

"I was informed of a demon tormenting a mortal soul. Corrupting his very essence? You've had your fun. Now it's time to go back."

"You can't make him," Sugar snaps. "You can't control him-"

"Oh, you poor, sweet child," Sentiō chuckles coldly. "Of course I can. He's in violation of the rules. And more than that, you, Witch, are in breach of several of them yourself. A soul that should have been in the Afterlife centuries ago. Mixing creation and destruction Magicks?" He looks her up and down, "You shouldn't even be able to do it. It would be for the greater good to tear that soul from your body and drag you to the afterlife for judgement."

Sugar clamps her mouth shut and I tuck her behind me.

"So, what do you want?" I ask, trying to keep my tone casual and congenial, despite wanting to rip the angel's head from his neck.

"I want you to go back to where you belong," Sentiō stands and straightens his already perfect bow tie. "In return, I'll let your witch live out her natural days and I'll even let that poor mortal boy you've been inhabiting stay up here, he's paid his penance having to share a body with you."

Sugar gulps beside me and Sentiō chuckles. His laugh doesn't meet his eyes.

"But-but," Sugar stammers. "Why? Why would you make sure Finn and I live?"

"All part of the service," Sentiō clucks his tongue. "Afterall, if it hadn't been for Finn alerting us to his plight, we may never have been able to track down Nox."

"Finn, did this?" Sugar says quietly. 'But he said…"

I feel Finn's energy shift in the back of my mind, there is a small fleck of pride, a smug satisfaction that he has beaten me.

How did you do it? I ask him.

Honestly, I don't know. He answers, *over the last week or so something has been making me more powerful.*

"Well played, Dahlia," I mutter so quietly that only Sugar can hear it.

"Finn was trying to save you," Sentiō's tone is patronising. "His love for you is so powerful he moved Heaven and Earth to ensure he would always be with you. It's really quite-"

"Sweet," Eli interjects as he swaggers forward and gives Esme a lascivious leer.

"And what happens if I say no?" I ask Sentiō. "What if I tell you to go fuck yourself or would you rather I beat the shit out of you again?"

"Well," Sentiō begins pacing. "If you were to say no, which I would strongly recommend you don't, I'll kill your little friend there and not only that, but I'll also personally ensure her soul is destroyed."

Terror swirls in my stomach. "You don't have the authority to do that."

"Oh, Nox," Sentiō's eyes glint with manic glee. "I'm an angel. If I believe it's for the betterment of Heaven and Earth; I can do whatever the fuck I want."

"Better yet," Eli moves in front of Sentiō, "I just take Esmerelda to Hell with me, and I show her what being a demon's whore really entails? Trust me, she'll wish her soul had been destroyed by the time me and my boys are done with her."

"You'll do no such thing," I snarl down at the Duke of Hell.

"Then see reason," Sentiō places a hand on my shoulder, those lizard-like eyes gauging into me. "You need to return to Hell, now. Or I'll destroy Esmerelda," he smiles again. "After I make you watch what Eli does to her."

"You're sick," I shrug out of his grasp, wanting to take a

scalding shower.

"I'm an angel of my word, Nox," Sentiō clicks his fingers and Eli pounces on Esme, dragging her back against him.

He licks up her neck like a rabid animal, twists her arms behind her back and I see the pain and fear cloud across her beautiful face.

I lunge for him, but the angel grabs me with all the might of the Heavens.

"Alright," I snap. "I'll do whatever you want. Just… just leave Esme alone."

Eli pouts and shoves Esme down to the ground; she quickly crawls towards me, her scent clouded with the citrus tang of fear.

"Nox, you can't," she pleads. "You can't leave."

I pull her up to me and hold her in a tender embrace. "I will do whatever it takes to keep you safe."

"But, I love you," tears streak her face. "You can't-"

"He has to," Sentiō says behind us in a bored tone. "It's surprisingly sweet. Who knew that demons could be such romantics?"

"Time to go, Nox," Eli snaps.

"I will find you," Esme promises, placing a soft kiss on my lips. "I will find a way to get you back."

"Oh, I'd love to see you try, Sweetness," Eli drawls.

"There's no way back for him to return to Earth," Sentiō interjects. "I know your name now demon, and I fully intend to ensure no other human soul is corrupted by you."

"You don't care about the soul of humans," I growl. "You just want to make sure everyone follows the divine and physical laws, but if they can be broken then they're not laws, they're just stupid rules you've made up."

"Nox, you've made multiple enemies in the Afterlife," Eli says with a sinister glint in his eye. "I'd be cautious about adding to that tally. There's a lot of demons in Hell and plenty of them are absolutely itching to get hold of *her*."

"Please, Sugar," trying to convince her with my words. "Please forget about me. I need you to stay safe."

She opens her mouth to argue, but halts when I place a kiss on her nose, "I'll love you forever, Witchling."

And with that, Sentiō clicks his fingers, and my world becomes darkness once more.

Chapter Forty ~ Six

Esme

When Nox is ordered back to Hell, I stand frozen in the living room in a catatonic state. Finn has disappeared along with everyone else. I'm alone.

After a couple of minutes, it hits me. All of Sarah's memories. My memories. Sarah's time as the head witch of her coven, her time with Nox. Her trials and her torture. And then the strange feeling of being present but also not, which I guessed was when my soul had been trapped inside the stone.

I collapse to the floor. My head is on the verge of exploding as more and more memories come crashing in.

"A little slower, please." I press my palms into my eyes as boundless images of a handsome stranger leaning down to smile, kiss and hold me flood into my brain. The panic stills when I recognise the stranger's eyes. Amber whisky eyes.

His features were so inhumanely beautiful I can understand why demons were fallen angels. He was stunning; a statue of pure perfection and power crackles from his manifested form whenever he appeared in front of me. Nox. So many memories with Nox. Him smiling, laughing, loving…

"Help," I whimper, staring down at the ground, speaking to no one and everyone. Anything. "There's no one I can trust… Dahlia's gone. Agnes has lied to me… I'm all alone."

I've got to find some way of getting Nox out of Hell and I have no idea how the fuck I'm going to do that. The only fleeting memories I have of the Afterlife are when Sarah pulled Nox out of it only a few hours ago. And it doesn't exactly help that I seem to be on the bad side of the two most powerful forces in existence.

I must find my vial of protection oil. I need to douse every single window and door frame. The last thing I need is creepy Sentiō and even creepier Eli popping by for another visit. I don't know if it would even work against beings that formidable, but it's better than nothing.

I make my way towards the bedroom and trip on something soft: Ink's lifeless body. Dahlia tried to kill me... but instead she just took everything. She left me alone, with not even my beautiful kitten for comfort. All thoughts of wards fall from my mind as I collapse into the floor, cradling Ink, absorbing what little warmth still remains in his broken body.

I don't know how long I was there, but when I'm suddenly jolted out of my grief by the sound of a loud bang on my front door the sun has set, and Ink's body has gone stiff.

I consider ignoring it, but I stand and wipe the tears from my face and make my way down the hall to investigate. I open the door and I'm greeted by large eyes that I immediately recognise, but for a moment I don't know why, then in a flash it becomes obvious.

"How?" I manage to gasp out.

"Well, I couldn't exactly leave you to deal with this on your own now, could I?" The man at the door ruffles his inky black hair. "Where's that bitch gone? If she thinks she can kill me and get away with it-"

My knees buckle and I stare up at the human form of my kitten.

"Wh-wh-why?" I manage to splutter.

He quickly swoops down and picks me back up, "I'm your familiar, Ez, I couldn't leave you to deal with this shit alone!"

My mouth hangs open as I stare up at him. He's a tall, handsome young guy with stylishly tousled hair and dressed head to toe in black clothes. I'd named him well.

"H-how?"

He shrugs and gives me a lop-sided smile, "I'm not sure, I just knew I needed to get back to you. I don't think we're supposed to be able to do that to be honest?"

"No, I mean how are you, Ink? What's a familiar?"

He rolls his eyes, "When the cloaking spell started to fade, I spotted you immediately, and I just knew I was meant to be with you. Us imps like power. We also like food. Have you got anything in? I'm starving!"

He saunters past me, and I have to rub at my eyes in case I'm hallucinating.

I find him hunched over in the fridge rifling through the

shelves, "Have you got any cheese? I've got a huge craving for cheese, I know, I know, it's just calories but... you only live once." He turns and gives me a wink, "Well most people do. You and I are the exception!"

I pinch the bridge of my nose, ok I'm in shock. My mind has finally broken under the stress. Too many memories and traumas, and now I'm hallucinating this drop-dead gorgeous guy. All I need to do is close my eyes, count to ten and then everything will be fine and-

There's a loud clicking sound near my face and when I open my eyes the guy is snapping his fingers in front of me.

"Look," he takes a sip from a milk bottle. "I get that this has been a bitch of a day, but we're on a deadline here."

I wander to the sofa and collapse face first into it, "I'm finally having a mental breakdown."

"Ok, so while you do that," Ink's voice gets quieter which makes me think he's walking away. Or maybe he's disappearing. Please Goddess, let him disappear, then I can get back to my breakdown in peace.

"I'm going to go look for something else to wear. The journey back here was... eventful, to say the least. Do you have anything that doesn't look like a fucking rainbow? I like clean, quality lines... preferably black."

"You sound like Nox," I say into the pillow. "He always preferred black."

There's the sound of hangers being shuffled and then feet padding back into the living room.

Guess my hallucination is here to stay: I turn my head to see Ink return, wearing low slung black trousers and a tight fitted t-shirt.

"Oh, I know," he sits down next to me. "That man sure can dress!"

"Not a man," I say automatically.

"So," he leans into me and looks at me with those eerily familiar eyes. "Like I said, we have a lot of work to do."

"Work?" I sit up straight, my head swimming. "What work?"

"Getting Nox out of Hell, Ez!" He taps a finger on my forehead. "Keep up!"

I bat his hand away. "I think my brain may be broken. I've had a very stressful few months and I think my mind has finally decided to give up the ghost, so if you wouldn't mind scampering off and leaving me in peace that'd be great!"

"Esme, sweetheart," he leans in, and it would almost seem threatening, if there wasn't a milk moustache coating his lips. "We've

387

got a short window of time where the veils between worlds are easier to slip between. Samhain isn't just all fun and games for witches and mortals. It's *the* party season when demons can kick back and come up and have a little fun, and that my dear, is the perfect time for us to slip in and rescue Foxy Noxy!"

"Please don't call him that," I grimace.

"Demon Daddy?" Ink falls back into the sofa giggling, "I think that one's the winner!"

"My Goddess, I've snapped, I've finally bloody snapped!" I begin rubbing my temples. "It was only a matter of time I suppose, there's only so much stress a mind can take before- Ow!"

I rub at the back of my arm where Ink just pinched.

"What the fuck was that for?" I edge away from him.

"You're being deliberately stupid, and I'm bored," he says. "Face it, Doll. I'm your familiar. I'm here to guide, support and in this case, inspire you to get your cute little peppy attitude into action!"

"Ok, fine," I grimace, rubbing at my arm. "Fine, I believe you! So, what am I meant to do? I don't know the first thing about Hell and what makes you such an expert on it?"

He bats his eyelashes at me, "Ez, that's where I'm from! I've already called in a favour from one of the imps I know in demon resources and pulled a few strings."

My eyebrows knit together, "No, no, no, if anyone finds out that I've been tampering with anything to do with Hell, they'll punish Nox for it!"

"Relax," Ink leans back on the sofa, looking every bit the lounge lizard. "I can be very discreet."

"Ok," I allow myself to relax a little. "So, what did you do?"

"Well, I have been able to get someone out."

"Out? As in out of Hell?"

He gives me a dazzling grin, "You're as clever as you are pretty!"

"Who?"

I hear shuffling from down the hallway and a pained groan, coming from Dahlia's bedroom. I look over as a figure emerges and I'm relieved that I'm sitting down.

Hazel, as beautiful as she ever was, a little groggy and confused, but that never dimmed her sparkle before. She's wearing the same outfit from that night all those years ago, although thankfully she's not covered in bloodstains.

"Hey roomie!" She chirps brightly, "has Inky filled you in on Operation Demon Daddy yet?"

I bury my face in my hands and can't figure out if my new roommates are going to be a blessing or a curse. But one thing's for sure, Hell is not prepared for what's about to come barging through its door.

Epilogue

A woman stands by the shoreline, her black hair swirling around her.

She'd been foolish to think it would be easy. Culum had underestimated just how powerful Esme is. But her fire burns too bright and viciously, she can't control it… her power can easily be taken.

She clutches the red grimoire to her chest and smiles at the crashing waves.

"Good things are never easy," Dahlia says as she watches the sea slam onto the rocks as thunder rumbles in the distance.

She turns and walks away, the sky above her darkens and lightning cracks across the sky.

Dahlia's attention is so focused on the pages of the grimoire that she doesn't notice the shape in the sky that watches her every move.

To be continued…

THAT
DAMNED
WITCH

Book two
Flames & Flowers

<u>Coming 2025</u>

Acknowledgments

First, I must thank you. You - the person who picked up this book and read my story. It means so much that you've taken the time to read this, and I hope you fell in love with Esme and Nox just as much as I did.

This is my second book, but in many ways, it feels like it's my first.

The Damned Witch Duet's journey to paper has all been done because of the amazing support I have around me. Cheering me on at every milestone.

The support I've had from my friends and family has been incredible and I'm truly blessed to have such wonderful people around me.

To my wonderful husband and best friend, Rich. You have supported me on every step of this journey. On countless read-throughs, outlines and rewrites. You mean the world to me, and I'll never be able to tell you how thankful I am to have you in my life.

Thank you to my family and all your support and encouragement.

Mum- you inspire me every day with your optimism, kindness and strength. You sparked my love of stories and I hope I've done you proud.

To my amazing sister, Nik - whilst you may be the younger sister I always feel like I'm learning from you.

Dad - your support of me following my dream has meant so much to me and I'm so proud to have you as my father.

To my beta-readers and editors. Rose, Joe and Tanya - your feedback has been invaluable and hearing your words of encouragement has kept me going on many long nights of rewrites.

Next up, I must give a special thank you to my wonderful friend Cazzy for helping design the book cover - it's truly a thing of beauty! Also shout out to Josh who gave the very wise advice of opting for green with the cover (you were right!)

I also need to thank some wonderful people who have supported me on this journey - Brit, Schu, Jack, Josh (check you out with the double mention!) Ethan, Steven, Kelli and Renee... Oh and Renee, this one's for you, because I promised I'd get it into my second book, "Twat Waffle!"

Thank you all.

Love and Sparkles,
CJ Rose

Printed in Great Britain
by Amazon

21171019-9a32-4109-a840-f93f6435b204R01